WINDS

"Bennett R. Coles ranks among my go-to list in SF. Entertaining and intelligent storytelling and terrific characters. In *Winds of Marque*, Coles may well have invented a whole new subgenre that has me scrambling for a description— Steam Space? Whatever you call it, [it's] a blast to read. Here's hoping that many more adventures are in the offing for Blackwood and company."

—Steven Erikson,
New York Times bestselling author

"Science fiction fans of the Hornblower or Aubrey-Maturin sailing sagas will likely thrill as the cannons are run out for battles in space." —*Publishers Weekly*

"The kind of authentic-feeling space navy action that you'd expect from a master like Jack Campbell. Outstanding action that will keep you turning the pages with enough twists to keep you guessing until the end. Looking forward to the next book in the series."

—Michael Mammay, author of *Planetside*

"*Winds of Marque* maintains a brisk pace from the get-go. . . . Coles cleverly preserves many of the naval traditions that have become synonymous with historical seafaring adventure stories. The leadership structure aboard *Daring,* the divisions between the sailors and the officers, and even the commands shouted out in the middle of a battle feel ripped from the pages of a Patrick O'Brian novel." —*BookPage*

ALSO BY BENNETT R. COLES

Blackwood & Virtue Series
Winds of Marque

BENNETT R. COLES

DARK
STAR
RISING

BLACKWOOD & VIRTUE

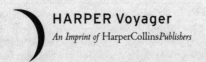
HARPER Voyager
An Imprint of HarperCollins*Publishers*

DARK STAR RISING. Copyright © 2020 by Bennett R. Coles. All rights reserved. Printed in the United States of America. No part of this book may be used or reproduced in any manner whatsoever without written permission except in the case of brief quotations embodied in critical articles and reviews. For information, address HarperCollins Publishers, 195 Broadway, New York, NY 10007.

First Harper Voyager mass market printing: October 2020

Print Edition ISBN: 978-0-06-302269-0
Digital Edition ISBN: 978-0-06-282038-9

Cover design and illustration © Damonza.com
Cover images © Shutterstock
Author photograph by Janis Jean Photography

Harper Voyager and the Harper Voyager logo are trademarks of Harper-Collins Publishers in the United States of America and other countries.

HarperCollins is a registered trademark of HarperCollins Publishers in the United States of America and other countries.

FIRST EDITION

20 21 22 23 24   QGM   10 9 8 7 6 5 4 3 2 1

To Steven Erikson.
Amazing what a coffee meet-up can lead to.

DARK

STAR

RISING

CHAPTER 1

IF THERE WAS ONE THING WORTH COMPLAINING about, it was the lack of rum.

Petty Officer Amelia Virtue scanned the ornate liquor cabinet one more time, hoping that among all the crystal decanters and curving bottles there might be hiding a flask of good old Navy rum. It seemed such a libation was beneath her host, however, and she sighed in gentle defeat.

"Champagne it is," she muttered.

"What was that, darling?" came a deep, familiar voice behind her.

Amelia turned, feeling the weight of her dress spin and the layers of silk brush past her legs. It would have been roasting, if not for her bare neck and shoulders. And a fair bit of bare cleavage, she was reminded, as the eyes of the gentleman before her flashed down before returning to meet her gaze. She grinned.

"I was just looking for a drink to calm my nerves," she said. "This is my first grand ball."

Subcommander Lord Liam Blackwood rose from his seat. He'd only arrived in her chambers a few minutes ago and she was still admiring his appearance. She'd seen him in uniform countless times, but never before in his formal dress uniform. The deep blue jacket was cut short at the waist, narrowing with his lean figure over a white shirt with, she was relieved to see, a minimum of poufy ruffles. The jacket was accented with his gold rank insignia on the broad shoulders and a pair of starburst medals on his left chest. As he turned to face her he tucked a thumb into the gold sash around his waist, its ends hanging loosely down the left side of his white trousers. Black riding boots thumped on the wooden floor as he stepped closer.

"You'll do absolutely brilliantly," he said with a smile, taking her hand in his and kissing it. "I can't wait to see every head turn when you enter the room."

She glanced at the long mirror and her own reflection in the exquisite gown, deep green with gold highlights. Her dark hair, thankfully long enough to style into something she hoped would befit this crowd, was swept up. Her bare neck only accentuated the smooth skin of her shoulders, the eye naturally drawing down . . .

"Stars, Liam, even I can't help but look at my cleavage!"

He laughed, coming up behind her and planting a kiss on her neck. It was smooth and sensual, and a sigh escaped her lips. Followed by a gasp as he smacked her playfully on the behind.

"Outfits for the grand ball are intended to showcase the male and female forms," he said with a grin. "Revel in it—just try not to stare too much."

She craned back and kissed him, enjoying the feel of his firm lips. She tasted a certain, familiar sweetness.

"Do you have rum?" she blurted, turning to face him.

With a conspiratorial smile, he reached into his inside pocket and produced a thin silver flask.

She took it and popped back a swig of the fiery liquid. It warmed her throat, and she enjoyed the sudden rush of something familiar amid all this exotic finery.

"Lady Riverton has exquisite tastes," Liam commented, nodding toward the liquor cabinet, "but perhaps she still lacks the common touch."

"I've got plenty of that," Amelia said, handing him the flask. "Now I guess we should go? I'm sure her ladyship is waiting."

Liam offered his hand. She took it and walked at his side out of her chambers—she still couldn't believe she had a sitting room, a dressing room, *and* a separate bedroom—and down the arched hallway of the residence. They started to descend the main staircase, and Amelia grabbed the front of her dress to avoid tripping.

"No, darling," Liam said quietly. "Let it hang naturally."

"But I'm fighting about fifteen layers of silk under here—my feet are in close combat with every step."

He laughed. "Don't fight it, then. Just take tiny steps and let the dress cascade down the stairs."

"Easy for you to say."

She forced herself to slow, slipping each foot blindly down to the next stair and gripping Liam's hand for balance. Her eyes dropped to gauge distance, and she kept the descent slow but steady. Liam was right there with her the entire time, his movements small and smooth. About three-quarters of the way down, she finally decided that she had the hang of it, and she lifted her eyes.

Three figures had appeared in the foyer ahead of her and stood watching with various flavors of interest. She recognized the commander and two of the officers from *Daring*—no pressure, she thought to herself with gritted teeth.

She felt her heel slip on the step, but she planted it and braced herself against Liam's steadying hand. Swallowing a curse, she made her way down to the floor at last.

Commander Lady Sophia Riverton stepped forward, her dark, luminous eyes as unreadable as ever. She was robed in a stunning outfit, the likes of which Amelia had never seen before. It was a ball gown, in the general sense of her own, but it had the same colors as Liam's formal uniform, deep blue at the top fading at her narrow waist to white and then black as it rustled down to her feet. She wore the same gold sash around her waist, and gold rank insignia curved into half-moons at the edge of her shoulders. Miniature versions of her starburst medals hung along the edge of her left neckline. Her gaze moved quickly over Amelia in assessment and she offered the faintest of smiles.

"Your first stairway descent, Ms. Virtue—well-executed. Far better than my own."

Amelia's instinct was to knuckle her forehead to her commanding officer, but she resisted and instead lowered in a curtsey, her free hand gripping at her dress in a token show of lifting the fabric.

Riverton nodded, then turned her eyes to Liam.

He gestured down the flowing lines of her dress. "Your Imperial gown is truly stunning, my lady."

"Thank you," she said simply. A most uncharacteristic smile threatened her severe expression, and Amelia saw a sparkle in her eyes. Riverton glanced down at her own gown once, then turned and strode toward the front doors of the house. "The carriage will be here momentarily."

Before Amelia could take another step, the other woman in the foyer moved in to embrace her. Sublieutenant Lady Ava Templegrey was beautiful in her own version of the "Imperial gown," although hers lacked any medals and the rank insignia was much more subtle than Riverton's. Amelia guessed that the gowns were a kind of uniform, and she wondered if she could get one or if it was just for officers. Not that she was complaining about her own dress, which was by far the most gorgeous thing she'd ever worn.

Templegrey's fingers closed around Amelia's bare arms, and Amelia breathed in an exquisite perfume as she received kisses on the cheek.

"Oh, Amelia," Templegrey gushed, "you're going to be the most beautiful woman at the ball."

Facing the graceful, noble medical officer, Amelia had her doubts, but she couldn't help but smile.

"Thanks. You look amazing, too."

Templegrey's eyes lit up and she stepped back to do an elegant twirl, the skirts of her dress rising just enough for a flourish. It was such a natural movement, Amelia could see, done with barely a thought but executed to perfection. If the other ladies at this grand ball had the same sort of style and training as Templegrey, Amelia knew she didn't stand a chance. She gripped Liam's hand tightly. He squeezed back and glanced down at her with a smile.

"Shall we board the carriage?" Liam suggested.

"Yes, my lord," Templegrey answered, reaching out her hand to the man who stood quietly to the side, dressed in a formal uniform like Liam's. "Lieutenant Swift, attend."

Lieutenant Mason Swift scoffed openly as he stepped forward to take Templegrey's hand. With his shaved head and intelligent eyes he had a certain rugged charisma, and as the only other commoner in this crowd Amelia intended to follow his lead.

"You're loving this, aren't you, my lady," he growled.

"To be attended by such a handsome officer," Templegrey replied with a sweet smile, "what lady wouldn't?"

"You know I only agree to come to these things for the food," he said, guiding her toward the doors.

"And the drinks," Liam added.

"And those, my lord."

Amelia snuggled against Liam as they stepped out into the warm, evening air. The sun had long since set but this far in toward the Hub the sky was awash with stars and the street before them was as bright as a foggy day back home on Passagia. Colors were muted and shadows were deeper, but her eyes adjusted in moments. She even descended the four stone steps without incident, casting a triumphant look up at Liam.

"You're a natural," he offered.

The carriage was large and comfortable. Amelia settled herself into a plush seat, remembering to keep her feet planted, knees together, and hands in her lap. The fancy dress and uniforms were still a novelty, but as the carriage rolled into motion she found herself feeling surprisingly comfortable. These people were her shipmates and she'd spent almost every day with them, often in close quarters and sometimes in extreme danger, for many months. She'd been nervous in the lead up to this grand ball, but as she looked around the carriage she felt a reassuring calm. This was just another day in the lives of the officers of HMSS *Daring*.

The ship herself was anchored in orbit, most of the crew on liberty to explore this beautiful world known on Imperial charts as Cornucopia III. And unlike most port visits, the ship was actually docked under her real identity, with no disguises or false pretenses. For a few days, at least, *Daring* and her crew were off duty.

And Liam was finally making good on his promise and taking her to a grand ball.

"Lord Blackwood," Riverton said, "you know our hosts quite well, don't you?"

"Yes," Liam replied, "although it's been a few years since my last visit."

Amelia didn't look up, but she sensed the slightest edge to his easy response. "I don't know Lord and Lady Brightlake myself," Riverton said. "But I went to school with . . . their daughter."

"Such a tragedy," Templegrey suddenly added.

"Yes," Liam added stonily. "Not the sort of news any noble house wishes to be known for."

No one seemed willing to expound on what the tragedy was, Amelia noticed, feeling not for the first time like she was being left out of some secret noble conversation.

"Are the Brightlakes one of the great houses?" she asked.

"No . . ." Liam considered for a moment. "They're notable, but not part of the inner Imperial circle. I think Lady Riverton would have a higher title?"

Riverton's lips pursed in thought, and she offered a slight shrug. "On the Imperial Homeworld, perhaps. But this is their world, and I'm merely a guest this evening."

"But how does that work?" Amelia persisted, genuinely curious about how nobles jockeyed for position. "Does Lord Brightlake bow to you, or do you curtsey to him?"

"The host of a grand ball is always in the position of honor," Riverton said. "If Lieutenant Swift decided to hold a ball in his new country home, even a lord from Homeworld would bow to him."

"I like the sound of that," Swift muttered.

"How is your new country home, Mason?" Liam asked.

"Big enough to house the entire family," Swift replied, his expression lightening. "Although my sisters are still arguing over who gets which wing. Their husbands are wisely keeping quiet and spending most of their time fishing."

The prize money from their first mission had been a life-changing windfall, and Amelia smiled as she thought of the town houses she'd bought for her parents and each of her own three siblings. She'd splurged a bit on herself, of course—she rubbed the fine fabric of her ball gown—but for now the rest was tucked away safely. It was enough for her family to live comfortably, and for her to choose freedom whenever she wanted.

A few of *Daring*'s crew had chosen exactly that, retiring from Navy service with their new wealth, but most of them had done what sailors always do whenever money was burning a hole in their pocket. From what Amelia heard, the upscale taverns and brothels on Passagia had struggled to meet demand for the first few weeks after the payout. Word had spread across *Daring*'s home port that this little frigate was spewing forth riches, and no end of hopefuls had requested to join the crew. Too bad, Amelia remembered, that almost none of them were qualified to even set foot on a star sailing ship. Commander Riverton had been forced to cut short their shore leave, just to get *Daring* out of the limelight.

"I assume you're comfortable enough in this formal setting, Mr. Swift?" Riverton asked.

"Yes, ma'am. The XO was kind enough to drag—that is, invite me to several balls on Passagia."

Riverton's gaze shifted to Amelia.

"And you, Ms. Virtue? This is your first ball, isn't it?"

"It is, ma'am," Amelia replied, suddenly hot under her voluminous fabrics. Liam hadn't said anything, but she sensed that it had taken considerable effort to convince Riverton to let another commoner attend this evening. "But everyone has been coaching me on how to act."

"No doubt. But do remember that nobles spend their entire lives practicing for events like these. You'll do best if you don't stand out in any way."

"Yes, ma'am . . . milady."

"Just remember," the captain said, taking in all of them, "we're here for a reason. The pirates won't wait while we dance the night away. I'll meet with my contact as quickly as courtesy allows, and the rest of you will ensure I'm not disturbed." She glanced at Liam. "I may need you to use your connection to our hosts this evening. Because I'm one of the ranking nobles they'll likely want to keep me close, but I need to be free to meet with my contact."

Liam's face was locked in a neutral mask, most unlike what Amelia had seen so far this evening, but he nodded. "Yes, ma'am."

Amelia reached out and took his hand. He glanced at her in mild surprise but squeezed her fingers affectionately. She felt his warmth beside her and noticed Templegrey smiling as she tried not to watch. Riverton had turned her gaze out the carriage window, but in such a small space Amelia knew her action was lost on no one. It was nice to be able to display their relationship openly, at least in front of the officers. Discretion was all the captain seemed to require.

The carriage rolled to a smooth stop, and the door was opened from the outside by a liveried servant. Liam exited first, followed by Swift, and they both extended their hands up to guide Lady Riverton down the steps. Lady Templegrey followed, and finally Amelia rose to her feet and stepped to the door's edge. She took Liam's hand to her left and Swift's to her right, and with tiny movements placed her feet on the wooden steps. She heard the hard click of her heels striking the stone walkway and she let Swift's hand go. Staying close to Liam, they slipped into place behind Swift and Templegrey, who followed Riverton through the beautiful open doorway of the Brightlake castle. Amelia knew that it wasn't really a castle—just an ornate, stone-fronted manor house—but it was the closest she'd ever been to a real castle, and it was plenty good enough for her.

Through the doors was a great hall, with a towering, vaulted ceiling that drew her eyes up to the arched windows through which starlight streamed. From each pillar projected a colorful banner, the meanings of each Amelia could only guess, and at the far end of the hall was a massive fresco depicting heroic figures battling mythical monsters. It was all Amelia could do not to stare.

"And you say the Brightlakes are *not* a great house?" she whispered to Liam.

He shook his head and smiled, but his expression lacked its usual, easy charm. His eyes were already returning to the obvious focus of his attention ahead. She peered past Templegrey and spotted a collection of nobles standing in the broad doorway beneath the fresco.

"Is that the receiving line?" she asked, remembering the briefing he'd given her.

"Yes," he responded. "I'll do the talking, if you like."

"Yes, please."

The hosts consisted of two couples, the first about Amelia's age and the second a generation older. She watched as Riverton curtsied then received a kiss to her hand, speaking to the first couple before moving on to the second. Swift and Templegrey were next, repeating the procedure without incident. Then it was her turn.

Amelia composed her expression into one of polite interest, lowering herself in a quick curtsey as Liam gave a half bow. The young couple before them nodded in return.

"Lord Blackwood," the gentleman greeted with a smile, reaching out to grasp Liam's forearm, "how nice to see you again after so many years."

He was shorter than Liam, with a thick, powerful build. The light gray of his civilian tunic contrasted his olive skin and black hair, and a bright red sash dominated the outfit.

"Lord Brightlake," Liam responded with his usual ease, "it's been too long. But no doubt affairs of the estate and married life have kept you busy."

Brightlake made a quip about boating that he and Liam both apparently found funny, even if its meaning went right over Amelia's head. He then introduced his wife, mentioning that she was from another noble house Amelia had never heard of. Liam then took Amelia's hand in both of his.

"Allow me to introduce my dear friend, Ms. Amelia Virtue."

Her real rank of petty officer wouldn't serve her well in this snooty crowd, Liam had warned her earlier. Since she had no title they'd agreed it best just to keep her background mysterious.

Brightlake swept up her free hand and kissed it, barely meeting her eye.

"Welcome, Ms. Virtue."

And with that, the encounter was over. Amelia felt Liam guiding her forward to the older couple. The family resemblance to Lord Brightlake was obvious, and she guessed that she was about to meet the real lord and lady of this household. Before Liam could speak, though, the woman reached out to take his hands.

"Liam, what a pleasure. Welcome back, my child."

"My lady," he responded quickly, dropping Amelia's hand in surprise. "Your hospitality has always been a fond memory for me."

The woman was smiling, but Amelia could see a glistening in her dark green eyes. She stared at Liam with a strange fondness that stretched into a long moment as she held his hands. Her skin was surprisingly pale, suggesting a heritage far out in the Halo, but

Amelia was most fascinated by her hair—a waterfall of deep red curls, swept up at the sides but cascading back down around her shoulders.

Amelia broke her stare and glanced at the gentleman she assumed was the lord of the manor, watching as his expression darkened.

"Lord Blackwood," he said suddenly, "welcome back to Brightlake."

Liam gently extricated himself from the lady and bowed. After a moment Amelia remembered to curtsey.

"My Lord Brightlake," Liam said, "it's a pleasure to return to your beautiful home."

"And is this Lady Blackwood?" Lord Brightlake asked—rather bluntly, Amelia thought.

"This is my dear friend," Liam said, his hand pressing protectively against her back. "Ms. Amelia Virtue."

Both lord and lady regarded Amelia for a moment before Lady Brightlake brushed back a stray curl of her fiery hair and grasped Amelia's hands.

"Please enjoy your evening here, Ms. Virtue."

"Thank you, my lady," Amelia said automatically.

Then Liam guided her forward again and they passed through a hallway toward another open space.

"Are receiving lines always like that?" she whispered.

"They can be a roll of the dice," he admitted. "Depending on how much the hosts have had to drink."

"I gather they know you well . . ."

"I knew their son, whom we met first, and their daughter, when I was younger." Liam grinned down at her. "Perhaps the lord and lady are remembering my youthful exuberance."

"Yeah . . . what's the tragedy surrounding their daughter?"

"Well," Liam paused, still leading her forward down the hallway. "It's a sad story, certainly."

Amelia was about to query further, but all thoughts of past intrigues were forgotten as they stepped into the ballroom. Her jaw dropped, and she actually stopped in midstride.

The ballroom was the largest enclosed space she'd ever seen. Delicate stone pillars towered up to a fan-vaulted ceiling, and between the pillars magnificent glass windows created a transparent wall through which she suddenly saw the reason for this estate's name. Manicured green lawns stretched down to the shore of a lake so smooth that only the faintest of ripples made the reflected stars dance and sparkle. The lake was small enough that she could see to the far shore, and jagged, rocky peaks ringed the water like a bowl of stardust.

Amelia tried to speak, but nothing more than a faint gasp escaped her lips as she stared outward. Finally, she felt a finger press against her chin, and she looked up in wonder at Liam.

"I didn't know such a beautiful place existed in the whole galaxy."

He nodded, his eyes strangely distant. Then he focused anew on her, the affection in his eyes warming her heart. He leaned in and kissed her, swiftly but firmly, then took her hand and led her forward to the curving stone steps that led down to the main floor of the ballroom.

"What is it with these blasted steps," she said with a grin, forcing her eyes down from the beauty around her to ensure she didn't embarrass herself.

Long tables were set up along the opposite wall from the view, coverings hiding what she assumed was food. A servant approached them with a tray of glasses, and she gladly accepted one, recognizing the golden color and bubbles of champagne.

"I'm going to need a few of these," she said, toasting Liam, "if you want to get me out dancing."

"Then I'll keep them coming," he replied.

Swift and Templegrey were nearby, she noticed, in polite conversation with another couple. Riverton was engaged in a discussion with a civilian gentleman near the food tables. Dozens of other guests moved about, clusters of conversations ebbing and flowing. Most people favored the edges of the ballroom, leaving the central dance floor mostly empty.

"So what now?" she asked. "Do we . . . mingle?"

"First we drink a bit more, and let the other guests get settled in. We stay close to the captain and ensure she doesn't get bogged down. The servants will keep the drinks coming—making small talk with strangers is much easier when everyone is tipsy."

"Ava doesn't seem to have a problem." Amelia admired Templegrey's ability to engage with anyone, from any background, with a smooth sincerity that could win over even the most jaded sailor. It served her well as the ship's doctor—sailors were actually more inclined to follow her advice—but no doubt it was a skill she'd honed at events just like this one. Already a cluster was forming around her and Swift, and the propulsion officer was doing little more than sip at his drink.

"I think she's drawing extra attention with her new Imperial gown," Liam opined.

"It's gorgeous," Amelia agreed.

"But it's more than that. She and the captain each spent a fortune to have those gowns made. See how the colors blend into each other so subtly, and how they mirror the colors of Swift's uniform? The Imperial gown was first created for a princess who insisted on serving in the Navy but hated having to wear our standard dress uniform to balls. So she created her own version."

"As princesses do, I suppose."

"Yes. But they're optional for female officers—the first time I met the captain she was wearing a uniform almost identical to mine—and only the wealthiest of noble officers take on the expense." He glanced down at her in emphasis. "Both Lady Riverton and Lady Templegrey are making a statement here by wearing Imperial gowns, that they are not to be dismissed lightly."

"They make a statement simply by the outfit they wear?"

"Of course. Nobles rarely communicate with words— we have an entire language embedded in our expressions, in where we choose to show up, in whom we choose to speak to, and yes, in our outfits."

Amelia thought back to her years in the taverns and the nightly insults and arguments hurled between tables.

"So if you don't like someone you don't say it with words?"

"Never. Or at least not unless you want to offer the gravest insult imaginable."

"How about me getting drunk and punching someone in the face? That's not using words."

"It would send a very strong statement, darling."

She burst out laughing and drained her glass. "Get me another one of these, would you?"

Liam gestured for a servant to approach. He downed his own glass and traded for two more.

"It's one of the things I adore about you, Amelia," he said. "You always speak your mind. It's refreshing after so many years of courtly scheming and doublespeak. I could quite honestly leave all this nonsense behind."

"Is that why the captain's so tight-lipped and unreadable? Because she's trained in your noble ways?"

"Yes. And she's trained as a diplomat."

"But why is Ava so sincere? Is she breaking protocol?"

"She isn't sincere," Liam said flatly. "It's her chosen persona. As an unmarried noblewoman, she only has a few choices. Most noblewomen like her affect an aloof, icy persona that makes them mysterious and keeps most suitors at a distance. Ava, thankfully, has chosen the opposite persona and charms everyone she meets. It makes her much more pleasant to have aboard ship."

Amelia turned her attention to her shipmate in the gorgeous Imperial gown, practically surrounded by men and women who seemed to hang on her every word. She loved having Ava in the wardroom, loved her bubbly personality. Was it all just a well-practiced noble pretense?

"I have a lot to learn," she decided.

"No you don't," Liam said as he slipped an arm around her waist. "They have a lot to learn from you."

As more guests filtered into the ballroom and empty space became rarer, Amelia and Liam moved closer to Riverton, watching as she casually edged herself closer to her contact, an elderly noblewoman who sat serenely at the edge of the room.

"Why doesn't the captain just walk up and talk to her?" Amelia whispered.

"It would be too obvious," Liam replied. "Lady Riverton has to give the appearance of moving through the room without intent or priority."

As more guests closed in, Amelia wrapped her hand around Liam's arm as they glided through spontaneous conversation clusters that came and went. Liam slipped into his own persona, charming everyone with a quick wit and ready compliments. Amelia noticed that as soon as she was introduced as "Ms. Virtue" she was mostly ignored, and listening to the mindless conversations she soon began to appreciate that. How Liam was able to maintain such a vapid level of engagement was beyond her. As long as the drinks kept coming, though, she was fine.

The younger Lord Brightlake was also moving through the crowd, Amelia noticed, and after a few minutes she realized that he was vectoring for Riverton. The captain was only a single cluster away from her contact.

"Liam," she whispered, pulling him down, "the captain needs cover."

Liam glanced up, his gaze assessing what Amelia could only think of as the "tactical" situation, then he leaned in.

"Whisper to me again," he muttered, "but more forcefully."

"We have to move," she practically hissed.

His face melted into the most patronizing smile she'd ever seen, and he raised his eyes to glance apologetically at the lords around them. He patted her arm indulgently, then pulled her gently forward.

"Excuse us, my lords," he offered, even tossing an eye-roll that she saw the lords around her reflect back.

It would have been humiliating, if it wasn't all a complete act.

"Stars," she muttered to him as they cleared to a few paces of open space, hugging his arm, "you can be a dandy when you try."

"Thank you, darling."

The younger Brightlake was just extricating himself from a cluster of guests, eyes on Riverton, when Liam and Amelia stepped into his way.

"My lord," Liam announced, "it's so good to be in your beautiful home again. Thank you so much for having us."

Brightlake couldn't ignore such a public compliment, Amelia supposed, and he stopped in his tracks to stare at Liam. But the hostly smile was quick to appear and he again clasped Liam's forearm as he had in the receiving line.

"It really has been too long, Liam," he said. "If only we could get the boats out on the lake this evening, eh?"

Liam patted Brightlake's arm. "Do you still have the strength for a race? I'm not sure the years have been as kind to me."

Amelia joined the round of laughter, watching as Riverton took the final steps and curtseyed before the elderly lady. The seated noblewoman dismissed her entourage as Riverton leaned in.

"I'd offer a tour through the gardens," Brightlake said, "but the chill is still in the air."

Amelia didn't recall it being cold outside, but Liam nodded in apparent understanding. "I do fondly remember the maze in our youth—shame it was taken away."

"Quite," Brightlake said, voice suddenly husky. He and Liam looked at each other in silence for a long moment, then his expression lit up. "But if we can't escape to the boathouse like in the old days, perhaps we could arrange for a hunting trip?"

Liam responded with a joke about someone Amelia had never heard of. The two men droned on, the chatter about this season and that region going completely over her head. Then Lord Brightlake made a comment about not being able to secure the latest rifles, and Amelia sensed Liam stiffen beside her. The conversation continued in an easy back and forth, but she noticed that both men were suddenly serious. The topic never wavered from hunting, including fond reminiscences of hunting trips they'd done in their youth, but Lord Brightlake's expression hardened. He eventually stepped back, his face melting into a perfect smile. He wished them a good evening and departed.

Liam sipped thoughtfully at his drink.

"What just happened?" she demanded.

"Hmm?"

"Don't play dumb with me, Lord Blackwood. I didn't understand a word of that, but even I can tell you had an entire conversation underneath what was said."

"Well . . ." he said thoughtfully, "the first part of the conversation was about Lord Brightlake's late sister. I expressed my sympathy again at the family's loss, and he suggested that I not mention it to his father."

"His sister died?" Even in her own ears, the bluntness of her words was like a wrecking ball smashing through the doublespeak.

Liam's lips pursed in sudden emotion, his gaze at her almost a glare.

"Yes, Lady Zara perished in a solar storm. It was many years ago, but I fear it still weighs heavily on her family."

There was something more that he wasn't saying, she could tell, and part of her knew just to drop it. But the words flew from her lips anyway.

"And all that talk of hunting? Are you and Lord Brightlake planning to hunt down that solar storm?"

"Not at all." He smiled sadly. "The rest of the conversation was on a different topic. Lord Brightlake asked me for money. I declined."

"For money?" She looked around at their stunning environment. "This isn't enough?"

"This isn't money, Amelia." His eyes cast around the cavernous room, at the line of food and drink, at the lake outside. "This is expense."

She frowned at that. Obviously this all cost money to maintain, but surely that was just part of being a noble. They swam in money, didn't they?

"You said no," she commented.

"I did. For starters there's no way I, or my entire family, have the sort of cash they no doubt need, and . . ." He frowned, considering his next words carefully. "Even if I did, I'm not so inclined to help them."

"Why not? I thought you were old friends."

"Things are rarely as they seem in this world, darling."

"Do tell."

He stared at her, considering. Then, finally, he sighed.

"There was once talk that Lady Zara and I might be wed. Obviously it didn't happen, but my relationship to the Brightlake family is . . . complex."

"Why didn't you marry her?"

He didn't meet her eye, obviously composing himself.

Shut up, Amelia, she told herself firmly.

He glanced over to where Riverton was still sitting with her contact, then tilted his head as music swelled in the room. "A discussion for another time, please. I promised you a dance, and the dancing is about to begin."

She looked toward the center of the ballroom and saw men and women lining up across from each other.

Suddenly wishing she'd had a few more drinks, she took his hand.

"Can we watch the first one?" she asked.

"Certainly. This is a group dance, anyway. Let's wait until they announce one for couples."

A distinct edge was forming between the crowd of onlookers and the open dance floor. Amelia spotted Templegrey in the line and noticed Swift, carrying a plate crowded with bite-sized delicacies and ambling over to join them in the crowd.

"Not dancing with your date?" she asked him.

"Like I said, I'm just here for the food." He offered the plate to Amelia.

She glanced around, noting that no one else nearby was eating. But the smells were making her stomach growl, and she grabbed a thick cracker covered in some dark paste. She took a tiny bite, savoring the exquisite taste of the mystery topping.

"Good, isn't it?" Swift said, helping himself to another selection. "You should try these ones."

Amelia popped the rest of the cracker into her mouth and took one of the recommended tidbits from Swift's side of the plate. It might have been some kind of fish?

"What is it?" she asked as she chewed.

"I don't know. But it's tasty, and I haven't thrown up yet."

"Good enough for me," she laughed, slipping the whole thing into her mouth. It had a rich, silky texture, and was definitely fishy.

Out on the dance floor, the overture ended and the dance officially began. Amelia focused on Templegrey, watching how she moved through the steps, from partner to partner in a smooth choreography.

"Stars, Ava's elegant," she muttered to Swift. "I'm sure she's the most popular woman here."

"She does her best," Swift agreed, "but that yellow hair doesn't help."

Amelia thought Ava had beautiful hair but glancing around she suddenly realized that she couldn't spot another blonde anywhere in the room.

"Do they not have blondes in Cornucopia?"

"Probably," he answered, "but any noblewoman would dye it dark. Ava likely doesn't because she's aboard ship most of the time. None of us care, but in this crowd it marks her as Halo even more than her pale skin."

"Is being from the Halo bad?"

Swift shrugged. "It's farther from Homeworld, and that apparently means something to these folks. At least Lady Brightlake's red hair adds a different color to the room—I'm sure that makes it acceptable."

Amelia shook her head, suddenly noticing how pale her own skin was compared to that of most of the people around her. The blazing suns of the Hub certainly darkened complexions, but it wasn't her fault where she'd been born.

The dance ended to a round of applause, and Templegrey strode over, beaming. Another overture sounded, and Amelia felt Liam's hand at her back.

"It's a couples dance, darling. Care to join me?"

She meant to step forward, but a nervous pit in her gut held her fast. Did she really want to step out in front of all these fake people and possibly make a fool of herself? All the smiles and laughter around her suddenly seemed so false, and every eye that passed over her seemed to carry judgment. Were there already whispers circulating about this "Ms. Virtue" with her pale skin and common accent?

Liam had turned and was looking down at her. "Amelia? Would you like to dance?"

This was supposed to be a wonderful moment, full of fun with her beloved. But she felt only heaviness. He was looking at her with new concern, she noticed, and she didn't want to make a scene.

"Let me watch one more time," she said, "just to go over the steps in my head."

"I'll guide you," he said with a smile.

"Dance with Ava," she blurted. "Show me how it's done."

Liam straightened in surprise but didn't press the issue any further. He turned to Ava beside him.

"Lady Templegrey, may I have this dance?"

A brilliant smile lit up her face, but she glanced questioningly at Amelia.

"Go ahead, Ava," she said. "Get him warmed up for me."

Liam took Ava's hand and together they walked out onto the dance floor. Final moments passed as the last of the couples found a place, and then the music started. As one, the dance partners swung into motion, the lilt of the music slowly building to a merry cadence. Amelia watched as Liam glided through the motions, his powerful form graceful and smooth. He smiled contentedly as he led Ava through a series of twirls that Amelia recognized from her hours of practicing on her own. She felt herself shifting on the spot, anticipating the dance's next move, recognizing the beats of the music even if she didn't know the tune. She watched Liam's hands, noting how he led with one and supported with the other, and she suddenly longed to have him so close to her. When the dance finally concluded, she knew she was ready.

Liam and Ava returned amid the applause, and Amelia pushed Swift out of the way as she reached out to Liam.

"Lord Blackwood," she declared, "I care to dance."

He laughed and took her hand, but paused as the music faded to silence. Glancing toward the entranceway, he cast her an apologetic look.

"I think our host is about to greet us," he said. "Have patience for a few minutes, darling."

Amelia looked through the crowd and caught a glimpse of the elder Lord Brightlake standing at the top of the steps. Silence descended over the assembled guests.

"My lords and ladies," Brightlake said, his voice amplified around the vast room, "thank you all for coming, and welcome to my humble home."

Polite applause spilled forth, and Amelia tugged at Liam's sleeve.

"How long do these speeches last?"

"Anywhere from five minutes to an hour—I hope you can hold it."

She smacked him playfully.

Lord Brightlake had begun to speak again, but Amelia couldn't quite understand him. There was another sound, a sort of rhythmic metal banging, in the background. Was it pots from the kitchen? The banging grew louder and mixed with a rising murmur from the guests. The cadence of the banging was familiar, and Amelia suddenly realized what it was: marching soldiers. She glanced up at Liam, who was staring toward the entrance with a grim expression. Rising up on her toes, Amelia strained to see.

Lord Brightlake turned as a troop of soldiers spread out to occupy the raised platform. Their swords were sheathed, but their breastplates and helmets were dull and well-used. Amelia had seen enough tavern brawls broken up to know that these were no ceremonial guard—these soldiers meant business.

As the last of the soldiers halted, forming a wide half-moon around Lord Brightlake, another figure emerged through the entrance. He was very tall, with sandy-blond hair over a handsome face that was locked in a sneer. He wore a Navy uniform with the rank of captain.

"Oh, blessed stars . . . ," Amelia whispered, taking Liam's hand.

"What's he doing here?" he muttered back, before sharing glances with Swift.

"I'm surprised he's still allowed to wear that uniform," Swift growled.

Brightlake stepped back in shock as the Navy captain strode to the edge of the steps and spoke, his voice carrying to the far walls of the ballroom.

"Lords and ladies, my name is Captain Lord Silverhawk, and I am here tonight on grave business." He paused as astonishment rippled through the crowd. "It is my sad duty to declare that the Brightlake estate is bankrupt, and that their assets are to be seized in order to pay their debts."

Amelia heard open gasps around her, noting true horror on the formerly composed faces around her. The guests stood in absolute silence.

Lord Brightlake, red in the face, finally managed to find his voice.

"How dare you, sir! You have no right—"

Silverhawk's sword was out and thrust through Brightlake's heart in a single, swift motion. The blade protruded from his back for a terrifying moment, then sliced out. The old lord stood frozen in shock, then collapsed. The only sound in the vast room was the thud of his body against the stone floor and a crack as his head struck down. The silence was broken by the anguished sob of Lady Brightlake. She ran forward, stumbling up the steps to collapse over her husband. The younger Brightlake pushed forward but was forcibly restrained by the guards.

Silverhawk pulled out a cloth to wipe his blade, then sheathed it and faced the crowd.

"I am here," he announced to the room, "with the authority of the Imperial laws of bursary."

"The what?" Liam whispered.

"Oh no," Templegrey breathed on Amelia's other side. "Suns and stars protect them."

"I am assuming ownership of this property," Silverhawk continued, "effective immediately, and you are therefore now my guests."

His face split into the most horrible smile Amelia had ever seen. He gestured broadly across the entire room.

"You are welcome to stay and enjoy the music and refreshments that have already been paid for. But I kindly ask that you not bother the new Lord Brightlake, as he will be quite busy for the next few hours."

He strode over to where the younger Brightlake was still held by the guards. With a curt gesture toward the entrance, Silverhawk bid Brightlake to follow. They departed, surrounded by soldiers.

Liam turned to Amelia, his gaze taking in Swift and Templegrey. "We should leave. Now."

"I can't believe," Templegrey said slowly, looking ashen, "that he just did that."

"It's never done that way, ever," Liam agreed, obviously shaken as well.

"All the more reason," said a new voice, fast approaching, "for us to take our leave immediately."

All eyes turned as Lady Riverton strode up. Her eyes were hard, but Amelia could only guess at the strategies she was no doubt already calculating behind their dark depths.

"I have the information I sought," she continued, "so the mission is complete."

"To the carriage, then," Liam prompted, squeezing Amelia's hand before releasing it and turning to go. She stepped in beside him and heard the others follow.

"What's he even doing in uniform?" Swift repeated. "I know for a fact his ship was a wreck when we pulled her alongside."

"Removed from command," Riverton clipped, "but still commissioned on half pay. I suspect Lord Silverhawk has been causing nothing but trouble since his only useful distraction was taken away from him."

"I hate to think we, and our entire ship, were just a 'useful distraction' for a lord," Swift spat.

"I never would have guessed the Brightlakes were in such hard times," Templegrey said. "I might have reconsidered when the young lord asked me for a loan."

"He did?" Liam asked, turning slightly even as he kept up the pace. "He asked me the same."

"And me," Riverton added.

"Well," Amelia couldn't stop herself, "maybe if he'd just explained the situation for real, instead of yabbering on about hunting trips, you might have understood."

"That's not the way it's done," Liam replied, with little conviction.

"More importantly," Riverton snapped, "estates are not seized of an evening. Nor are lords executed summarily in their own homes. There's something more going on here, and we want no part of it."

Amelia needed no further encouragement, ignoring etiquette and hiking up her hem as they hurried up the steps. They passed through the arched corridor and back into the great hall. Soldiers loitered in front of every doorway, and four of them stood guard at the main entrance to the house. Their eyes scanned Amelia and her colleagues, and one of them stepped forward, politely raising his hand.

"Forgive me, my lords and ladies," he growled, "but I must ask you to identify yourselves."

Liam was in the lead, so he responded, calmly listing everyone, including noble titles and military ranks. The soldier seemed indifferent, until Liam identified the captain. All the guards stiffened slightly in their stances, and any idle expressions vanished.

Liam caught the shift. "Is there a concern?"

The guard nodded to one of the others, who hurried off down a side corridor.

"No concern, my lord. But there may be a slight delay."

Riverton stepped forward, interposing herself directly between Liam and the guard. Amelia couldn't help but smile. The captain was not one to hide behind any man.

"Any delay," she said with a tongue of ice, "is a concern to me. My officers and I need to return to our ship."

"I'm sure it will be but a moment, my lady," the guard said, holding his ground. "But I have my orders."

"From whom?" she demanded.

"From me, Sophia," boomed the voice Amelia had once upon a time grown to despise and now suddenly feared.

She didn't turn, but she heard Captain Silverhawk stride past her. He took a stance directly in front of Riverton, glaring down at her from his great height. His hand rested casually on his sword.

"When I saw the guest list I noticed your name," he sneered, "and I remembered that we have unfinished business."

"I did exactly as ordered, sir," Riverton countered, chin jutting out. "I took your cousin as a member of my crew."

"And then insulted him."

"If you consider locking up a man for attempted mutiny an 'insult' then yes, I suppose I did."

Silverhawk glared at her, but Amelia saw more cunning than true anger in his eyes.

"I should have you stripped of your command," he said.

"I'd like to see you try," Riverton countered.

Silverhawk's gaze ran down and up Riverton's form, then shifted to take in Templegrey. Amelia didn't see the usual gleam of lust from a man sizing up a woman, though; there was something else in his gaze.

"You've apparently done well for yourself, Ava," he said suddenly. "An Imperial gown for a young sub-lieutenant is a rare sight indeed."

"Thank you, my lord," Templegrey said quietly, dropping in a quick curtsey as her face reddened.

"And the loyal executive officer . . ." Silverhawk's eyes narrowed as he focused on Liam. "Still pulling strings in the background, Mr. Blackwood?"

"I serve my captain to the best of my ability," Liam replied, "as I always have."

Silverhawk's fist lashed out, striking Liam in the jaw. He stumbled backward, steadied by Swift.

"That's for my cousin," Silverhawk stated, rubbing his knuckles. "Learn your place, you insolent cur."

"Yes, sir," Liam said, straightening but keeping his eyes down.

Amelia kept her clenched fists at her side, just waiting for the order from Riverton to take this idiot down. But the captain stood impassively.

Silverhawk took a deep, satisfied breath, his eyes passing blankly over Amelia as he surveyed the group. Finally, he turned to Riverton again.

"This isn't over, Sophia. I suggest you board your old tub of a ship and start running, as fast as you can."

Riverton met his gaze, then lazily examined the soldiers blocking the door. "May I go now, sir?"

Silverhawk waved for the guards to stand aside, then strode away without a backward glance.

Amelia followed the others out into the warm air, forcing her fists to unclench as the adrenaline surged through her.

"Why didn't you just punch him back?" she hissed, reaching up to inspect the shallow cut on his cheek. Before anyone could answer she voiced her own frustrations. "Because that's not 'what's done'?"

"No," Liam said, stopping short and pulling her to a halt. The others followed Riverton toward the carriage. "Because I would have been arrested without question and tried in the Imperial court. You think all this," he waved at the magnificent Brightlake manor and grounds, "is impressive? This is a cottage to someone like Silverhawk. This is the estate of a midlevel lord. Silverhawk is a *high* lord, meaning he's one step removed from royalty. He exists in a world you can't even conceive of. There is no law that can contain him, but he is very capable of using the law against anyone who crosses him."

"That isn't right," she said. "Sounds like someone needs to take the law into their own hands to deal with him."

"We may deal with pirates and criminals all the time, Amelia," Liam said, his face darkening, "but we shall *not* become like them."

She frowned. "It seems Lord Silverhawk has no qualms becoming like them."

"And do you want to become like *him*?"

She spat on the steps in disgust, grabbed her dress, and strode off to catch up to the others.

The carriage was just pulling up as she arrived. Riverton and Templegrey boarded efficiently, and Amelia ignored the offered hands as she pulled herself up and in. Liam was close behind her and Swift brought up the rear. They took their seats, staring at each other with an intensity Amelia had come to know well, and to welcome.

"XO," Riverton said, "send out the recall for our crew. We sail on the next large tide."

"Yes, ma'am," Liam replied.

"Propulsion," she said to Swift, "cancel any maintenance, and go to one hour's notice to sail."

"Yes, ma'am."

"Doctor," to Templegrey, "ensure you have an adequate supply to counter the headaches and sickness we'll have from a drunken crew. There will be no layabouts."

"Yes, ma'am."

"Quartermaster"—the captain's gaze burned into Amelia—"ensure we're fully stocked for at least forty-five days."

"Yes, ma'am," she said automatically, even as her mind started to run through the provisions she'd already ordered, and what space she had in the holds.

"I confirmed the location of the pirate ship *Black Hand,* barely two days' sail from here, and there may be truth to the rumor that Dark Star is personally on board," Riverton announced after a moment. "I intend to strike with all haste."

Amelia sat back in her seat as the carriage jostled through the town. The voluminous folds of her dress smothered her legs and she suddenly couldn't wait to get back into real clothes. Looking around the carriage, at her officers in their finery, she could tell by their expressions that they felt the same. It was time to get back to where they all belonged.

CHAPTER 2

LIAM BLACKWOOD STAGGERED AS HE LEFT HIS cabin, caught off guard by a sudden pitch of the ship's deck. The armor plate of his knee clanged against the bulkhead, and he fought to steady himself as the ship rolled. *Daring* was sailing hard athwart a stiff solar breeze. She was making good time, but the ride was less than comfortable.

Pulling his cabin door shut he eased himself forward, adjusting to the added weight of his armor, and the saber and pistols on his belt. The gauntlets made grabbing for handholds challenging, and he had to adjust to the restricted movement under the polished black breastplate. It had been many weeks since he'd last donned his fighting gear, but the extra bulk was like an old friend and as he shuffled toward the bridge door ahead he settled himself. He clung to the door as *Daring* pitched violently again, then swung it open.

The swirling light of the squall outside cast dancing shadows over the deck as he stumbled forward to grab the nearest console. It was currently unmanned, but several paces ahead he could see the regular bridge crew closed up. Commander Riverton was seated in her port-side chair, the officer of the watch stood at her central console, and the clutch of sailors hunkered at their sailing helm, lookout and weapons controls forward, the coxn keeping firm watch over them all.

It was unseemly for the executive officer to appear unable to handle a storm, and Liam barely paused before staggering forward again to grip the corner of the central officer of the watch console.

Sublieutenant Charlotte Brown was at her usual station, feet planted firmly on the deck and hands gripping her console. Her dark hair was tied up in an efficient bun and her young face scanned her displays with keen intelligence before turning to face him. Her complexion was decidedly pale, with even a touch of green, but her voice was as confident as ever.

"Ship is at battle stations, XO, five minutes to estimated intercept."

Liam looked up through the clear canopy of the bridge, at the dazzling view of the Hub off to port and the wisps of nebula gas streaking past the ship. The squall was playing havoc with this corner of the nebula's tendril, he could see.

"Do you still have visual on the pirate?" he asked.

"No, but we spotted her two minutes ago, four points off the starboard bow."

Liam instinctively glanced upward, searching the puffs of gas for the telltale silhouette of a ship. Movement and shadows masked the entire vista, though. The brilliant glow of the thousands of stars in the Hub cast plenty of light, but the nebula was thick with the remains of an ancient, exploded sun. The solar winds had been tearing at the expanding gas cloud for millennia, and here at the border the scape was chaotic and ever-changing.

"I believe you," he said, giving up his search. "Keep a sharp eye for any trickery."

"Yes, sir."

Rounding her console he took half a dozen shaky steps to grip the raised command chair. Riverton was strapped into her seat, screens spread out around her.

"Looks like our long hunt is at an end, XO," she said. "It's definitely *Black Hand*. The last sighting confirmed her distinctive raised quarterdeck"—she glanced at him for emphasis—"and additional mounted beam weapons."

"They're really not even trying to be subtle anymore," he mused. "Where's the fun in hunting pirates when they make it so obvious? I've rather enjoyed the last two months of cat and mouse . . ."

As usual, she didn't share his easy humor.

"It means I'm not launching you in the boats," she stated. "You'd be picked off before you could cover half the distance."

"Maybe we could approach through one of the clouds."

"It's too uncertain." Her tone indicated the end of the discussion.

"Grapple boarding, then?"

She nodded. "Port side. Our starboard hull is still a bit tender and I'd like to keep it out of the direct fire."

"Yes, ma'am. But I recommend both cannon sides be armed and manned—in this environment we'll want maximum flexibility."

Riverton glanced up at the swirling clouds and gripped her armrests as the ship bucked again. She nodded.

"We're going straight in, hopefully catching them by surprise. There may only be time for a single broadside before we grapple."

"My team will be ready."

She surveyed the scene outside again, then gave him an approving look.

"Fair winds, XO," she said, with the hint of a smile.

"Following rays, Captain."

He retreated from her chair, grabbing the hatch cover in the deck astern of Brown's station. His armor was like a second skin now and he clambered down the ladder with ease, pulling the hatch closed behind him.

One deck down Liam paused, surveying the final preparations of the gunnery crews. The gun deck had a single, wide corridor down the center of the ship, with twelve reinforced doors on either bulkhead leading to the individual cannon compartments. The forward doors were already closed, and the last bags of gunpowder were being passed through the aft doors by blackened, grim-faced sailors.

One sailor noticed him and straightened slightly to knuckle her forehead. "Who did we find, sir?"

"*Black Hand,*" he said, noting with satisfaction the instant recognition alighting on her face. This crew took their mission much more personally than any he'd sailed with in the past.

"Will we engage soon?"

"Everything's ready," he replied. "We're starting our final approach."

"Another bold advance, straight in?"

"Of course," he grinned. "We have to be daring."

She returned the grin, and one of the other sailors laughed.

It had become the ship's catchphrase, and her name had become her crew's philosophy. Liam gave the sailors a final nod then grabbed the ladder for the next descent.

Another deck down, Liam weaved carefully along the ship's main passageway, the deck rolling steadily beneath him. A sudden crash of crockery followed by a curse through the bulkhead to his right told him the cooks were having trouble securing the galley. Usually the crew had hours to prepare for battle as *Daring* slowly closed a fleeing foe, but here at the fringes of the nebula sightlines were almost zero, and this battle had caught everyone unexpected. But Liam had no concerns—in the time it had taken him to don his armor, the entire ship had been brought to battle stations. He reached the midships ladder and thankfully grabbed the handrail, descending the steep steps as *Daring* bucked and creaked around him.

The boarding party was assembled in the passage-way, all eyes turning to him as he stepped down onto the deck. His eyes immediately sought Amelia, who met his gaze with an excited grin as she flexed her shoulders under her new armor. Many of the sailors still wore the standard, padded protection issued by His Majesty, but Amelia had invested some of her prize money in personal protection. She was encased in a smooth breast-plate, shoulder guards, and leg guards, the steel dull and without ornamentation. Her only special addition was on the gauntlets, where wicked spikes protruded from each knuckle.

"I'm more used to punching thugs at close range than stabbing them," she'd explained sweetly when she'd first showed him. "This will help."

Liam forced his gaze to break from her and survey the rest of the team. Fourteen sailors in total, seasoned veterans all, and he saw nothing but quiet determina-tion on their faces. Finally, his eyes came to rest on *Daring*'s assaulter, Chief Petty Officer Harper Sky.

"Boarding team ready, sir," Sky said, lifting her helmet in one hand to slip it down over her short brown hair.

The deep green of her armor hinted at its quality, as did the lack of dents and scratches across its surface. It was possible the assaulter spent all her spare time buffing out damage, but Liam suspected that she was just very talented at not getting hit in the first place. Liam glanced down at his own black armor. The polish and gold filigree were forever marred by the scars of

Sectoid acid damage, and he hadn't yet gotten around to having the last of the dents banged out.

"We're closing to grapple," he said without pre-amble, motioning for the team to separate fore and aft into their two groups. "My team will board aft and Chief Sky's will board midships. We'll take the bridge and you take the cannons."

Murmurs rose around him as glances were exchanged, but he sensed no objection. Just the usual mutterings of sailors facing sudden change.

"Priorities, sir?" Sky asked.

"This is *Black Hand,*" Liam said, again noting the recognition in the faces before him, followed by a new determination. "She's one of Dark Star's flagships, and no doubt she carries information vital to the pirate efforts. We've also heard"—he paused for emphasis—"that Dark Star may personally be on board."

A few excited expletives punctuated the rumbled reaction.

"Capture whoever you can," he concluded, "and save what loot you can. And by the Abyss don't let them wipe any memory cores."

Another round of muttering rippled through the team. It was an ongoing shell game with the pirates—everyone in *Daring* knew that there was a larger organization behind what looked like common brigands, and each pirate crew fought unusually hard to destroy any evidence before capture. Tossing treasure out the airlock was their favorite distraction, and a painful one to ignore.

All voices were cut off by the sudden roar of cannons above them. *Daring*'s first broadside heralded the opening of battle.

"To your airlocks," Liam ordered, turning and heading aft. Amelia plus their team of six followed, weapons clinking as they fumbled to stay on their feet. A constant pressure to port indicated the ship heeling into a sharp turn, and another roar of cannon loosed above them.

Liam let his sailors lead the way into the airlock, grabbing a handset from the bulkhead as he peered forward to ensure that Sky's team was in position. Activating the comms, he heard Riverton's voice crackling in his ear.

"*Captain.*"

"Captain, ma'am, XO. Both teams in position for grapple boarding."

"*Very good. We're in range and firing hooks with the next salvo. Board when ready.*"

"Yes, ma'am."

Liam hung up, stepped into the cramped airlock, and shut the heavy door behind him. His armor pressed into Amelia and she shuffled forward, but there was little room. The rest of the team was eyes forward, watching as best they could through the small porthole in the outer door.

He slipped on his helmet, feeling the calming silence that came with it. Amelia noticed the motion and donned her own headgear, a simple covering of smooth metal that curved from her eyebrows back to her neck.

She smiled, her restless gaze lingering on him. He gave her a wink, then turned his attention to the vista through the porthole.

The massive form of Master Rating Atticus Flatrock, his body tensed for the assault, blocked most of the view, though. Beside him was Able Rating Mia Hedge, her sword already drawn as she prepared to be first through.

Liam saw the dazzling starlight through the porthole fade as the shadow of *Black Hand* fell across them, but he barely had time to look before he heard another blast of cannon. Seconds later, the entire ship lurched around him as the massive grappling hooks dug into the pirate ship and took hold. The mottled hull of *Black Hand* was visible outside, steadily drawing closer as the cannon crews reeled in their catch.

"Extend the skirt," he ordered. "Get ready."

Flatrock manipulated the controls to extend the flexible tube on the outer hull, even as the airlock door on *Black Hand* swung into view and closed in. Liam glanced upward to his unseen bridge, marveling again at the ship-handling skills of Riverton and Brown. There was a crash as the two vessels gently collided. Under the grinding of metal Liam heard the hiss of air as the skirt was flooded, and then the outer airlock door slid open.

Hedge was through in a flash, floating across the zero-gravity space and slamming her override tool into the manual airlock control on *Black Hand*'s hull. Seconds later the pirate door slipped open and Hedge disappeared into the darkness beyond. Flatrock was across the gulf a moment later, followed by the rest of the assault team. Amelia stepped forward, and Liam followed. The sailors who usually manned their boat, Faith and Hunter, hung back as rear guard to protect the airlock.

Liam watched as Amelia sailed across the space between ships, landed on the far deck, and drew her sword. Liam grabbed the frigid rim of *Daring*'s open airlock and pushed himself off, his cheeks barely feeling the chill in the air before he reached the opening at the end of the skirt. Amelia pulled him through and he felt gravity kick in as his feet slammed down on the deck.

The team had fanned out in a defensive circle, holding until everyone was aboard. The storm was pounding *Black Hand* as much as *Daring,* and everyone lurched as the deck shuddered. Liam drew his saber and hefted a pistol.

"Three decks straight up," he ordered. "Move!"

As always, surprise was their ally and speed their greatest weapon in these first few moments of a boarding. Hedge was up the nearest ladder in the blink of an eye, her quickness in stark contrast to the lumbering power of Flatrock behind her. Liam heard shouts above him and the clash of blades, but by the time he ascended the ladder the quick melee was already over. Two pirates—one Human, one Theropod—lay sprawled on the deck in growing pools of blood. Hedge was already up the next ladder.

Liam followed Amelia's armored form up another two decks, then quickly surveyed the scene. His team was gathered in a low space, a short passageway leading aft and a heavy door forward. The pirate ship bridge lay beyond that door. Hedge was manipulating her lock override, but the door remained closed.

"They've got a local fail-safe," she snapped, glaring back in frustration. "I can't override the lock."

Liam sheathed his sword and drew his second pistol. "Flatrock, plant charges. Blow that thing open." He glanced at his gathered team. "I'm through first. Fan out to the sides and shoot to wound. We want prisoners."

Each sailor drew their pistol as Flatrock pulled a pair of shaped charges from his satchel and pressed them against the hinges of the bridge door. Liam tensed, watching Flatrock step back and depress the trigger.

The blasts tore through the bulkhead—the door flew off its hinges and careened forward through the dense smoke. Liam charged through the opening. He ran blind through the smoke for the first few steps, then his vision cleared enough to see a reptilian figure dead ahead, raising a gun. Liam fired twice. The Theropod collapsed backward. Liam staggered forward on the heaving deck, firing suddenly at movement to his left. A Human pirate peeked up from behind the command chair and fired twice, the bullets pinging off Liam's breastplate. He responded in kind, but his shots punched into the chair as he tried to suppress the target for capture.

Shots and shouts erupted behind him as his team stormed the bridge, but Liam didn't hesitate in his charge forward. Taking cover would only make him look like a pirate to his own sailors, he knew, so he kept moving forward, back to his own troops, and trusted his armor to take the hits. A bullet cracked off his helmet, stunning him, but he instinctively swung and fired at the nearest movement. A pirate staggered, clutching his shattered arm. Liam slammed the empty pistol into its holster and drew his saber. The smoke had billowed through most of the room and visibility was barely arm's length.

His attention snapped to sudden movement to his side, where a huge pirate slashed down with a sword. Liam's own blade rose in sheer reflex, but the power of the strike sent him staggering. He retreated, raising his second pistol to fire. The pirate blade swept upward, smacking flat against Liam's hand and knocking the pistol clear. Liam jabbed inward but the pirate dodged, cutting down with a vicious backswing. Liam ducked under the strike and stabbed forward in a counter, but again the pirate evaded. Their blades clashed, steel scraping as they fought the heaving deck as much as each other. The pirate drew forward, his expression hard as he glared at Liam across their locked swords. His young, rugged face was clean-shaven and his pale eyes were cold, with none of the panic Liam saw so often in common pirates. This man moved with a calm, murderous intent. He suddenly withdrew a step, giving them both some room. Then he unsheathed a short sword and pressed the attack, forcing Liam back as he blocked the heavy strike and tried to dodge the quick stabs against his armor.

Out of the smoke a short, armored form rushed into the fray. Liam pivoted in defense but immediately recognized Amelia's smooth steel helmet. She swung her cutlass at the pirate, forcing him to retreat a step before he batted her blade aside. Liam saw the opening and lunged, but the pirate sword was like quicksilver as it slashed back and parried Liam's strike. Liam staggered off-balance, grunting as the pirate slammed his sword down against Liam's torso. He dropped to one knee and swung ferociously at air.

Forcing himself up he attacked again, but the pirate deflected his blows with the ease of an Imperial bodyguard. Amelia pressed the attack on the other side, their foe deftly giving ground and parried their strikes, always keeping his distance. His longsword was almost too fast to follow, and Liam could feel himself tiring as he defended against the barrage.

The pirate suddenly shifted, his sword slashing down with such force that Liam felt his legs buckle as he blocked. His own saber was pushed against his helmet, barely holding back the blow, and he dimly saw the pirate's short sword batting Amelia's cutlass clear out of her hand.

Liam kept his saber up, bracing for impact as the pirate reared back for a single, devastating strike. He readied his weary legs—whether that blade struck toward him or Amelia, he would be there to parry it.

Amelia, empty-handed, wrapped one forearm around the pirate's short sword, pinning it to her own breast-plate. He tried to wrench it free but she hung on, lifting clear off her feet as she swung in close to him. Her fist smashed upward into the pirate's chin and the big man staggered. She struck again and he crumpled, his swords clattering down from limp fingers as he collapsed in a heap. Liam righted himself, ready to run the blaggard through, but Amelia's hand reached out to stop him. Blood dripped from the spikes on her gauntlet.

"He's done," she gasped, grabbing her sword and bringing it to bear. "And we might have just taken down Dark Star himself."

Liam gulped air, surveying the bridge.

Through the smoke he saw the precise, guarded movements of his own team as they searched the space. Unmoving pirate bodies lay sprawled at their feet.

"Sound off," he ordered.

His sailors each responded, still alive and well. He gave orders to gather the pirate casualties, bind and search them, secure the bridge, and start copying data.

"You okay?" Amelia asked him.

He nodded, scanning for his lost pistol even as he warily watched the unconscious pirate at their feet.

"You're right," he said, kicking the pirate blades well clear. "This gentleman is worth talking to. He clearly has formal training in swordsmanship."

"Just no experience with brawling," Amelia replied, holding up her spiked gauntlet. "Told you it would help."

"You prove your worth yet again," he said, then added quietly, "darling."

The forward end of the bridge was clear of smoke, and Liam stole a look through its canopy toward the bulk of *Daring* grappled alongside. His ship was almost as large as this one, but with her dust-caked hull and strap-on cargo containers she lacked the elegant, aggressive lines of this pirate ship. No doubt any observer would have bet fully on *Black Hand* before this battle began. Spotting his stray pistol, Liam took a deep breath and holstered the weapon, his eyes moving between *Daring*'s bulk and the unconscious pirate dueler on the deck before him.

As with so many things in his life and mission these days, first impressions were rarely accurate and little was as it seemed.

A CLUTCH OF PRISONERS WAS HERDED OVER TO THE brig in *Daring* without incident, but the transfer of supplies from one ship to the other took several hours. Liam had a standing rule that search teams moved in groups of four, always with an officer or senior sailor present, to try to minimize the personal looting that inevitably went with the seizure of a pirate ship. In theory all the cargo was logged by the quartermaster and stored for distribution among everyone when the mission was over. No doubt a few trinkets went missing here and there, and Liam honestly didn't begrudge a sailor's occasional petty acquisition, but the official line was zero tolerance. It always made for grumpy sailors during the search process, but it maintained a sense of fair play that was ultimately far more valuable for crew cohesion.

Once everything of value had been taken, Lieutenant Swift and his team scuttled the pirate ship. They pulled out as much of the air as they could, then they forced open all the airtight openings and blew the airlocks. The vacuum rushed through the dead ship, freezing everything. Reduced to a dead hulk, *Black Hand* was set adrift, to be lost amid the vastness of space.

Liam was seated at his usual table in the senior mess, poring over the pirate logs with Amelia and Temple-grey, when Swift strode through the door.

"One less pirate ship," the sailing officer declared, "and I need a drink."

Liam gestured him over to the table, where a decanter of rum was already open. Swift flopped down next to Amelia and wrapped a friendly arm around her shoulder as he reached for a glass.

"Oh," she said with a shiver, "you're freezing!"

"Just finished sending another ship to its grave," he said, pouring himself a generous portion. "It's chilling business."

"I don't know why we don't keep them," Amelia said. "I'm sure those ships would be worth something if we sold them."

"We could," Liam replied, "but we don't want any pirate spies recognizing their former vessels. Best we scuttle them and let them disappear into the Abyss."

"I know, I know," Amelia sighed. "It just seems a shame to waste perfectly good ships."

The rum flowed freely enough as they discussed their latest findings, comparing information from *Black Hand* with intelligence already gathered. They were joined in time by the coxn, Chief Oliver Butcher, and the assaulter, Chief Sky. Spirits were always high after a successful battle, as the fear and adrenaline worked through everyone and was replaced by relief, and a mix of other emotions. Liam himself luxuriated in the sense of triumph, and he recognized in Amelia her usual delight at a mission well-accomplished. Glancing around the table he saw the grim satisfaction in Swift, Sky, and Butcher—hardened professionals just doing their job.

And on his right, her regal façade firmly in place, Templegrey sat quietly. As the ship's doctor, she knew better than anyone the cost these battles sometimes brought, and her bright, relieved eyes spoke more of the boarding party's success than any report. She was often a keen participant in the discussion of the intelligence, but today she seemed withdrawn, focusing her attention on helping Amelia check the lists of seized stores and valuables.

On an impulse, he reached out and squeezed her hand.

"You all right, doctor?"

She lifted her gaze to him, a perfect smile forming. "Yes, fine. Why?"

"You seem a bit subdued. You don't normally bury yourself in stores reports."

"There's just so much," she said, gesturing at the lists shared between her and Amelia. "I wonder if, at this rate, we'll have room for it all."

"Did we seize any good food?" Chief Butcher interjected on her other side.

"Food, yes," Amelia answered, "but I don't know yet if it's any good."

"How will we ever know," Butcher continued, leaning forward, "if we can't eat any of it?"

"We'll eat when it's time, Chief," she retorted.

The coxn continued to stare at her expectantly, and Amelia's brow furrowed. She glanced up at the wall clock, and her eyes went wide.

"What the—" She burst up from her chair, a colorful string of curses peppering the air as she stormed for the door.

Liam glanced back at the clock, suddenly realizing that it was ten minutes past the usual start time for dinner. Yet no stewards had appeared to lay out settings, and most certainly no food had appeared. His stomach suddenly growled, and he caught a smirk from the coxn.

"Let's clear this paperwork, everyone," he said. "I suspect the quartermaster will be back shortly with some apologetic stewards."

By the time the table was cleared and the chairs were rearranged for dinner, the door burst open and harried sailors rushed in, Amelia close behind them. With a cacophony of cutlery the table was laid, and plates piled high with stew were placed down in front of everyone. Amelia shooed the steward and cooks out and took a seat at the far end of the table.

"Having trouble with your department, Quarter-master?" Sky mused.

"Trouble comes when we're down to half strength," she said with a heavy sigh. "Three of my four stewards retired with their riches after the last payout."

"With all those hopefuls begging to join the ship, couldn't you find any good stewards?"

"If you wanted to be served by clumsy, cussing hooligans as likely to spit in your food as serve it, sure." She sighed. "Good stewards are surprisingly hard to find. So we've got one, and he's often needed in the galley just to help the cooks."

"They need all the help they can get," Swift winced, tasting the stew. "What happened to that amazing chief cook we used to have?"

"She retired." Amelia shrugged. "I think she opened her own restaurant on Passagia."

"Does she cater to deployed ships?"

Liam joined in the laughter around the table. "At least they've figured out the coffee. I don't think my stomach has recovered yet from the Templegrey blend."

More laughter and catcalls saw Templegrey lift her hands in defense.

"I was just trying to help," she said. "I don't know how any of you can drink that ghastly stuff."

"When you make it," Sky offered, "trust me, we can't."

The lone steward did return eventually and cleared the plates away, and as everyone sat back with full bellies Liam poured himself a portion of rum and ceremoniously passed it to Swift on his left. The sailing officer filled his own glass and passed it to Sky, then to Amelia, then Butcher, and finally Templegrey. Everyone held their glass expectantly and silence descended over the table.

"Mr. Swift," Liam said, "if you please?"

Swift rose from his seat and lifted his glass in salute.

"On this, our second day in space, I offer a toast to our mighty vessel, His Majesty's Sailing Ship *Daring*— long may she serve and protect us."

"To *Daring*," Liam called, the others echoing his words around the table.

Liam drained his glass, then pushed back his chair and stood.

"Thank you, everyone. I'm going to brief the captain. I'll update her on our latest intel."

With a rumble of chairs and contented chatter, dinner broke up. Liam gathered his papers from the afternoon's discussion, noting that Amelia herself was collecting the empty glasses. He smiled to himself. She still struggled with the idea that she had any sort of privilege over the crew and was happiest when she was getting her hands dirty.

"Sir, a moment?"

Templegrey's hand rested on his sleeve, and he looked over at her questioningly. "Yes, doctor?"

"I've been thinking about the crew, and the way we distribute the prize money."

"We're not changing the traditional split," he said immediately. "Everyone gets their portion as tradition allows."

"No, no," she said, brushing her hand along his arm, "I'd never suggest changing that. I was just thinking about the timing."

"How so?"

"Well, the captain pays out very rarely, and only when there's a large bounty to share. I worry that this infrequent and large method of payment is encouraging bad habits in the crew. Please remember, sir, that these sailors have never seen this kind of money before, and too many of them are wasting their fortunes in the occasional orgy of frivolous spending."

"I see your point. But payout is also when we lose sailors, as they take their earnings and flee." He gestured to the empty, disheveled mess and the petty officer currently tidying it. "If we divide the prize money more often, might we not lose sailors more often?"

"I don't think so," she said. "If prize payment was smaller but more regular, it would seem to the crew more like a stable income than a huge windfall, and they would be more inclined to spend it wisely. Right now, I fear they think their big payout might be their last chance to enjoy life. There is uncertainty, and risk." She stepped closer, eyes sparkling up at him. Her hand slipped off his arm and onto his waist. "If we paid out more frequently, there would be stability, and certainty."

She was really pouring it on, he couldn't help but notice. He'd been to enough gala balls and courtly settings to recognize a determined—and, admittedly, effective—charm offensive underway. Templegrey was clearly motivated if she felt the need to bring her courtly powers to bear. Six months ago he would have been irritated at a commissioned officer attempting such tactics, but he respected Templegrey enough to let it slide. Her argument, as usual, made sense, and she clearly held strong feelings on the matter.

"I'll bring your suggestion to the captain."

"Thank you, sir."

Her hand dropped away and she walked for the door, offering Amelia a dazzling smile and a quick compliment. As the door shut behind her, Liam stepped toward Amelia.

"That was—"

His words died as she wrapped her arms around him and kissed him passionately. The sudden intensity surprised him, but he regained his balance and gripped her close. He leaned into her warm body, savoring the taste of her soft, rum-sweetened lips.

Finally, she pulled back, eyes shining with emotion.

"Hi," he said. "How was your day, darling?"

"Long, violent, and frustrating," she said kissing him again quickly. "But I hope it ends well."

"I hope I can help with that. Just let me report to the captain, first."

"She better not get too close to you." Amelia stepped back slightly, running her hand down Liam's arm to his waist. "Ooh, sir," she said in her best imitation of Templegrey's noble accent, "can you do something for me? If I bat my eyelashes enough will you do whatever I want?"

He scoffed, turning curiously toward the closed door. "That *was* weird. She definitely has an agenda there."

"That agenda better not include you," Amelia said, fist rising. "Honestly, if I didn't like that little blonde tart so much I'd smash her pretty face right in."

Liam gently pressed her fist down, recognizing just how drunk Amelia was. She was cute when she was drunk. But knowing Templegrey as well as he did, the idea that she was actually coming on to him was rather absurd.

"No, darling, it's nothing like that. Ava believes in what she's saying, and she doesn't want to risk the chance that her idea will be ignored. So she was trying extra hard to convince me."

"I'm surprised you even remember what she said, with her hands all over you."

"It's standard. You've said it yourself—we nobles live and die on our charm. This idea is important to her, but instead of just acting like a regular officer, she fell back, probably unconsciously, on ingrained habits. Likely because they work."

"Are they working now?"

"Her idea has merit, but if I bring it up with the captain it will be for that reason, not because of the doctor's charms." He gave her an earnest look. "What do you think of her idea?"

Amelia stared up defiantly for a moment, then punched him lightly in the stomach.

"Yes," she admitted, "it's actually pretty smart. Sailors have no idea how to handle sudden riches, and for most of them the only outlet they can think of is taverns and the like. Listening to the scuttlebutt, a lot of our crew are already broke—they've drunk and played away everything they've earned. Our last visit home to Passagia saw Flatrock dubbed 'King Atticus, Lord of the Golden Tower.'"

He didn't get the reference.

"It's the most expensive brothel in town," she explained, before slumping her shoulders in a sigh. "You don't have to worry about most of them retiring—they know this is the only way they'll ever make this kind of money. If they got paid more regularly, though, they might learn how to spend it better."

"Okay," he said thoughtfully. "That means a lot, coming from you."

"It was awfully insightful of Ava to recognize that about the crew." Amelia tried to frown but it curled into a smile. "Stupid cow."

Liam laughed out loud and kissed Amelia anew.

THE CAPTAIN'S CABIN WAS DIM, LIT BY STARLIGHT streaming in through the porthole and a single lamp on the table. Commander Riverton was seated in that pool of lamplight, notes spread out around her. Her uniform coat was draped over a chair behind her and her white shirt seemed to glow in the darkness. She looked up with a cool expression as Liam sat down across from her.

"A bit of revelry in the senior mess this evening, XO?"

Honestly, he thought to himself, how did she do it? He'd even paced his own drinking through the afternoon because he knew he had to report to her.

"Nothing excessive, ma'am," he admitted. "Just a bit of stress release after today's excitement."

"Who has the mid watch?"

"Templegrey. Beyond the toast of the day I believe she drank only water or tea."

"Very well." Riverton sat back, folding her arms. "Do you think we have Dark Star himself in custody?"

"I don't know," he said, exhaling. "One pirate we subdued obviously has training from the Imperial Academy, and we confirmed he isn't actually the captain of *Black Hand,* suggesting he might be an important visitor. As much as we could tell, the rest of the pirate prisoners seemed to defer to him."

"You'll be speaking with him soon?"

"I'll give him a few days in the brig to soften up. But yes, soon."

"Any new insights on Dark Star's operations, based on our captured information?"

"Yes, actually." Liam leaned forward, spreading out a star chart between them. "The *Black Hand* logs revealed two attacks on merchant ships"—he pointed out the locations—"here and here. *Black Hand* has met with two other pirate ships in recent months, indicating a tighter control by Dark Star over assets than what we used to see. We also found messages that reported other pirate attacks, and this corroborates what we suspected for the missing merchants on the border of the Silica and Iron Swarm sectors."

"But does it still look like reduced pirate activity overall?"

"Yes, ma'am. Over the past six months there has been a clear drop in attacks on shipping. No doubt our destruction of the pirate base hurt them, and they're taking time to rebuild. But what's interesting is that they don't seem to be rebuilding in the same way. *Black Hand* was in good shape and well-stocked, but her attacks were less frequent recently than, say, a year ago. This agrees with the overall pattern we've observed in the region. I'd propose that Dark Star is changing tactics after the blow we dealt."

"Clear signs of close coordination across multiple star systems," Riverton mused, "which is worrying. Random thugs the Empire can deal with, but this is something much more dangerous."

"We recovered code words and key phrases," Liam added, "secret signals that can be dropped into a conversation between pirates to confirm identities. They're date-linked and valid only for a few more weeks. This suggests a very high level of coordination."

"Agreed," Riverton said, her eyes alight with new respect. "Do you think we can use them?"

"I'd like to have my usual team—Swift, Sky, and Virtue—study them. If nothing else we can train ourselves to listen for them when we're ashore."

Riverton nodded, her fingers tapping thoughtfully against the table.

"We haven't been able to recover any specific orders from Dark Star that indicate a strategy," Liam admitted. "Have your connections suggested anything?"

"Dark Star's influence is limited to the Halo, but it is expansive. As for motive, nothing beyond robbery and greed has suggested itself."

"There has to be more to it, ma'am."

"I agree, XO. But how do we uncover it?"

"I think it's time for *Sophia's Fancy* to make another stop at Windfall Station. I can check in with my usual contacts, but I'd suggest we use those coded pirate phrases while they're still valid and take a closer look around."

"Very good." Riverton suddenly leaned forward, her eyes hardening. "Something bigger is going on here, XO. Bigger than any of us can see. We need to move swiftly before Dark Star surprises us all."

CHAPTER 3

AMELIA STEPPED THROUGH THE AIRLOCK TUNNEL, her nose wrinkling as she left *Daring* behind and caught her first breaths of air from Windfall Station. The stale air was heavy with the lingering residue of close-in bodies and old machinery—it was never pleasant, but she realized it had a certain homey familiarity that she'd come to appreciate. As she stepped onto the station proper, her eyes automatically drifted upward to take in the soaring heights of the main promenade.

Daring—or, in her merchant disguise, *Sophia's Fancy*—had tied up at what was becoming her usual berth at the station, down the line of docks and out of the way of most curious eyes. Amelia strode out across the rough surface of the loading area, glancing back once at her ship's mottled bulk visible through the clear station hull before scanning the line of commercial establishments stretching away along the central street.

Their façades looked like those of regular planetary buildings, even though she knew their interiors were built into the airtight compartments of the space station. High above, the dark bulkheads gave way to glass windows that revealed the dull brown surface of the planet Farmer's Paradise. The gnarled trees beneath the windows were sprouting new leaves, and Amelia hoped a season of growth might improve the air quality.

"Amelia," she heard Liam call behind her, "a moment, if you please."

She paused, noting that Liam was giving quiet instructions to the sailor standing as brow's mate. They were all dressed in civilian clothes typical of a merchant crew, but she smiled as she saw Liam turn. The motion let his coat fly open for a moment and she noticed that he was indeed wearing the blue sash around his waist that she'd picked up for him on their last port visit. He walked up to her with a smile and motioned them forward.

"Nice sash," she commented. "Someone pick that out for you?"

"It's exactly the sort of thing a person with no taste would think rather elegant," he replied, one eyebrow raised.

"I thought Captain Stonebridge would love it."

"He does."

Captain Julian Stonebridge was Liam's alter ego as he played his ongoing role of faded nobleman turned merchant captain. He was becoming quite well-known in this sector as a man who reliably delivered his cargos through pirate-infested space and was sometimes even sought out by merchants desperate to move goods. Any observer would expect Captain Stonebridge to be making a fair bit of money, and little extravagances like the silly blue sash sent a clear—if gaudy—message that *Sophia's Fancy* was doing well.

Amelia was quite content to play the role of loyal cargo master, mostly staying in the shadows while Liam drew attention. Sure enough, as they strolled down the promenade he was greeted with enticing calls from the local brothel, and the owner of the only tavern open this early waved his welcome. Liam studiously ignored them all, even lifting his nose slightly, and Amelia suppressed her smile at his ability to play the fop.

The central stalls of the promenade were busy with foot traffic, and Amelia cast her eyes across the assortment of wares on offer. Windfall Station was the biggest transit point in the sector and saw a huge variety of cargo. Supply was never consistent, though, and she'd learned that if she saw something good she had to grab it right away, because tomorrow that stall and its contents might be gone.

There were the usual foodstuffs and basic household necessities, no doubt precious to the hardscrabble locals but nothing she couldn't requisition from Navy stores. But one stall caught her attention. It had more open space than usual, and her eyes rested on what was clearly a family, all standing together in a pose and staring in the same direction. There was a flash, and then a second one. Intrigued, she touched Liam's arm and slowed.

The family—two parents and four children—were dressed in their finest, and they crowded around the merchant who had emerged from under his hooded device and was carefully manipulating a machine.

"It's a picture-maker," Liam said. "I've seen them farther into the Hub."

Amelia frowned, peering toward where the merchant still hunched over his machine.

"Does it have little brushes and paints inside?" she asked.

"No, it's not a painting. It captures the light onto a special sheet and preserves it." He leaned in very close and whispered into her ear. "I've heard that our most modern ships have it fitted, to make copies of what our telescopes are seeing."

The merchant triumphantly held up a thick, shiny sheet of paper and the gathered family gasped as one. On the sheet was a perfect black-and-white image of them in the pose they'd held just moments before.

Amelia was astonished at the clarity of the image and delighted that this family could have such a record to carry home with them. She grabbed Liam's arm.

"I want one of you."

"Of me?" His lips curled into a puzzled smile.

"So that when I'm all alone in my cabin, trying to block my ears against Chief Sky's snoring, I can have a picture of you to fall asleep gazing at."

He laughed, glancing at the stall. "You know I'll have to be in character of a noble Stonebridge . . ."

"Just don't sneer."

The family had paid for their precious image and were departing excitedly down the promenade. The merchant wasted no time in sizing up his next potential customer, gesturing grandly at Liam.

"Ah, my lord, you would be an outstanding subject for my next image. A piece of history and a work of art combined into one."

"Yes," Liam said, adopting his most foppish accent, "I quite agree, good man. What do I do?"

The merchant helped Liam take position in front of the backdrop and made a few suggestions of pose. Liam stood tall, one hand resting on his short sword as he stared off into the distance. It took only seconds to capture the image, and another minute to produce it. At Liam's request the final image was made small enough for him to put into his inner pocket.

"What do you think, Cargo Master?" he said, handing Amelia the sheet.

It was actually a very handsome picture, Amelia realized, fighting down her giddy grin and merely nodding politely. "A true and noble likeness, milord."

"Excellent." He slipped the image into a protective case and then into his pocket. A startling number of coins exchanged hands—Amelia hadn't actually thought to consider how much it would cost—and then Liam indicated haughtily for her to follow. When they were well clear he leaned in with a wink. "The things I do for you, darling."

Realizing they were in public she restrained from hugging his arm, but she did add a skip to her step. "Thank you."

Their destination loomed ahead, a brick-fronted façade from which a sign hung declaring this café to be the Cup of Plenty. A patio full of tables hosted the regular crowd of patrons, a few of whom glanced up without interest as Liam and Amelia walked to the door. The air inside the café carried the soothing aroma of coffee, laced with the sweetness of pastries. It was Amelia's favorite moment whenever they came to Windfall.

The café was arranged in neat rows of long tables, each able to seat three a side in comfort, on a dark, tiled floor under a vaulted roof. Wealthier clients were scattered around the room, enjoying the fresher air and richer fare, and Amelia immediately spotted a familiar face. Propped with his back to the wall on the left side sat their usual merchant contact, Matthew Long. His broad form hunkered over his cup, a pot of coffee, and additional cups resting before him. His dark eyes rose and did their usual pass over Amelia's form before settling on Liam. He struggled heavily to his feet.

"My lord," he greeted, his deep voice wet with phlegm, "welcome back to Windfall."

"Thank you," Liam responded, taking the nearest seat. "It's been a while. I hope you're keeping well, Mr. Long?"

"Well as always." He gestured for them both to sit, and his eyes roamed up and down Amelia again. She always felt the need for a wash after an encounter with this odious fellow, and the obviousness of his lechery was a shock after her recent visits to more sophisticated worlds Hubward. Liam would inevitably need her, but maybe she could skip the small talk.

"Milord," she said suddenly, "perhaps I'll inquire into some pastries for us. It would be a pleasant treat after our long voyage."

Liam had already taken his seat and looked up in surprise. But he followed her lead and adopted an amused expression, which he tossed toward Long.

"My cargo master has a weakness for the sweet treats here at the Cup of Plenty." He waved dismissively at her. "Go on, then, Amelia. None for me, thank you, but please indulge yourself."

She nodded her thanks and turned, feeling Long's eyes on her as she strode down the tables toward the delicious-looking pastries. Her boots thudded softly against the tiled floor, matched suddenly by a second series of thuds approaching her. She looked up and saw one of the owners of the Cup of Plenty.

This was the female Theropod, based on the lack of ornamentation on her small, triangular head. Her long neck was curved into an S-shape and her body was horizontal in the walking stance, her long tail stretching out behind her. Her powerful legs propelled her effortlessly toward Amelia, triangular boots hiding her three-toed feet and their vicious claws. She was dressed in her usual black outfit, faint smudges of coffee grounds visible on her white apron.

She paused at a polite distance from Amelia, her head lifting up so that her reptilian eyes were level with those of her guest. Her scaly lips parted and she growled in her own language.

"Welcome, lady," said the translator around her neck. "It is good to see you again."

"Thank you," Amelia replied, remembering to speak slowly and simply. She wanted to smile, as she genuinely liked the Theropod couple who ran this upscale joint, but she knew that the baring of teeth was a sign of aggression to them. Her lips curled up but remained firmly closed.

The Theropod stared at her in patient silence.

"My name is Amelia," she said on an impulse. "What is your name?"

The brute barked suddenly, which Amelia recognized as laughter.

"You could not pronounce it, lady."

"But you can. I'd like to hear it."

A clawed hand reached up and switched off the translator. The lips parted to reveal daggerlike teeth and a pair of syllables growled out. Amelia listened carefully and tried to repeat them back.

"*Behhh-larrr . . .*"

Another bark. Amelia laughed in return. The Theropod reactivated her translator.

"We have a Human name," Amelia said, "which sounds like yours: Bella. May I call you that?"

The brute's head cocked slightly. "I have not heard my name in the Human language. It does not sound painful on your tongue."

"Does it sound painful to your ears?"

"No." She barked again. "You may call me that . . . *Arr-meh-ley-arr.*"

Amelia suppressed a grin down to tightly pursed lips and nodded in delight.

"May I get you anything?" Bella asked.

Amelia looked over at Liam and Long, who were deep in discussion over a sheaf of cargo manifests between them. She probably had time to enjoy something, and she gazed along the table of sweet treats.

"Do you have anything with fruit centers?" she asked.

Bella pointed with her small arms at a cluster of icing-covered baked goods. "We were able to acquire a selection of fruit preserves, but there are not many left."

"It's good to see that the trade lanes have opened again," Amelia said, selecting one of the pastries, "now that the pirates have disappeared."

"There was a period of calm." Bella pulled tongs from her apron and deftly placed the treat onto a small plate. She handed it to Amelia. "But trouble is returning."

"Oh? I hadn't heard of new pirate attacks."

The Theropod's eyes flicked left and right.

"Not attacks on ships. Trouble here at the station."

"Local thugs?" Amelia couldn't help but glance at Long.

"Newcomers," Bella said. "Pressuring all of us merchants to pay them, with money and information."

"What kind of information?"

Bella's head cocked again.

"Information about you."

THE LIST OF CARGOS WAS IMPRESSIVE, LIAM THOUGHT, as he leafed through page after page. Destroying the local pirate scourge had definitely brought positive growth to this sector, and he was quietly proud of his ship's service to the people. But Julian Stonebridge would have no such thoughts, and he kept his face neutral as he reviewed another manifest.

"I see you've been able to reconnect with the Iron Swarm," he commented. "There are several shipments from that blasted place here."

"Your bold delivery helped reassure the Swarm's merchants that trade was once again possible," Long replied. "Are you heading back that way, my lord?"

"I don't know," Liam said with a sniff, wanting to keep his options open. "It's a ghastly place."

Long waited in silence as Liam reviewed the rest of the options. Many were local deliveries within the Silica sector, with a few to the chaotic jumble of the Iron Swarm and even a few bound for worlds closer to the Hub. One local shipment caught his eye, having come from his home system of Passagia. And he almost skipped past a nondescript cargo of ore, until he saw that it had originated in Labyrinthia. Intel from their capture of *Black Hand* suggested that Dark Star's tendrils were wrapped tight around that mysterious patch of space.

"I say, is this really from Labyrinthia?"

Long examined the manifest for a moment. "So they claim."

"Silica seems a long way to come to deliver ore." Especially since Silica was well-known as a mining system.

"I don't usually ask questions," Long said with a heavy shrug. "I have a buyer for this ore here in Silica and I'm happy to facilitate the transfer. It would be a quick run for you, my lord—Silica 7 and back in no time."

Amelia sat down next to Liam, her pastry on a plate before her. She gave him a grin before taking a tiny bite. He showed her the manifest.

"Is there anything unusual about this ore, Amelia? It comes all the way from Labyrinthia."

She examined the sheet, taking another bite and chewing thoughtfully. "It's pretty low-grade, from what I can see, but if it's from Labyrinthia . . . who knows?"

"Who brought this shipment to you, Mr. Long? Do they often bring ore to Silica?"

"They're a new crew," he admitted. "But like I said, my lord, I don't usually ask questions."

Liam made a show of surveying the stack of cargo lists again. Most of it was routine stuff, the clearest message simply that overall trade was picking up. Matthew Long certainly seemed less dour than usual, and as Liam glanced around the room he sensed an overall optimism in the patrons. Out here in the Halo life could be hard, so any boon was welcome. Perhaps if Windfall Station could make enough extra money they might even get their air filters replaced.

Amelia was still enjoying her pastry so Liam sipped slowly at his coffee. But he could tell Long's patience was starting to wane.

"This is an impressive collection, Mr. Long, and I suspect we'll want several of them. But I'll need some time to plan a route and assess costs."

"Of course, my lord." Long drained his cup and sat back heavily. "Perhaps my man can call upon you at your ship this evening?"

"Splendid idea." Liam collected the manifests up into their leather folder and tied the strings. "Good day, Mr. Long."

The merchant eased himself up and, with a nod to Liam and a smile to Amelia, shuffled away.

Amelia watched him go, then leaned in.

"Bella says that there are troublemakers on the station, asking questions about us."

"Oh? What kind of troublemakers?"

"Sounds like gangsters to me. Demanding protection money, wanting local intel. But why would they be asking about us?"

"We're still new in these parts," Liam suggested, considering. "Most local merchants—as few as they are—would be known quantities to folks like Long. We're a bit of a mystery."

"But it looks like new ships are coming to Silica," she said, tapping on the manifests. "We're just one of many new outsiders."

"Maybe the thugs are asking questions about all of us?" A sudden thought struck him as he reviewed her words in his mind. "I'm sorry, who's Bella?"

A grin burst across her face. "The Theropod who runs this place! She and I got talking and we finally exchanged names."

"Her name is Bella?" Liam glanced doubtfully toward the brute as she cleared one of the tables.

"Well, sort of. It's as good as I can pronounce it."

He nodded, his eyes moving slowly across the room again. The optimism he'd sensed earlier was still there, and he supposed that in a place like Windfall petty organized crime was just a fact of life. With new prosperity came new interest from criminal elements.

But it was through exactly this sort of petty thuggery that the influence of Dark Star was spreading across the Cluster.

"Dark Star's pirates were well-established here in Silica when we first arrived," he said. "It wouldn't take much to go into hiding and reemerge as gangsters."

Amelia wiped her fingers and lips with a cloth napkin, raising an eyebrow. "Are you suggesting we go looking for trouble?"

"No . . ." Liam opened the folder and flipped through the sheets until he found the Labyrinthian ore. "But I think it might be worthwhile inspecting some of these cargos—or at least, the people currently holding them."

"Looking like this?" she asked, plucking at his sash and then at his fine coat.

"I hate to say it, but I'm not the one for this mission. Too many people on this station know what I look like."

"I could probably move about unnoticed," she offered.

"Agreed. But you're going to have help."

AMELIA HAD BEEN SHARING A CABIN WITH CHIEF Petty Officer Harper Sky for months, but still didn't feel like she really knew the ship's assaulter. She knew Sky snored softly, and that she was fastidiously tidy, and that she preferred to read romance books in her leisure time. She knew that Sky was fully aware of her relationship with Liam, but never a word about it had been spoken in their cabin. Amelia had a delightful suspicion that Sky had a crush on *Daring*'s coxn, Chief Oliver Butcher, but if anything had happened on that front she was utterly unaware. Aside from sleeping she and Sky were rarely in the cabin together, so it was surprisingly crowded as they both prepared for the next mission ashore.

Amelia had managed to source a few sets of utilitarian worker's clothing several port visits back, and these were invaluable in letting them go ashore without looking like sailors. She and Sky each kept a set in their footlockers and had pulled them out for a quick change.

Sky pulled off her uniform shirt, her elbow just missing Amelia in the close confines. Amelia was slipping into her worker's shirt, figuring that the wrinkles would help her look that much more disheveled. Sky reached down to grab her own worker's garb, powerful arm like a corded rope wrapped in scarred sandpaper. Her torso was like a shaped pillar of iron, any lack of curves made up for in sheer strength. Not for the first time, Amelia felt like a waifish girl next to her powerful shipmate and she hurried to tug her own shirt down and try to look bulkier.

Sky's movements were quick and precise, and before Amelia had even started lacing her boots the assaulter was fully dressed and slipping past her toward the door.

"See you at the brow, PO," was all Amelia heard before the door shut.

On an impulse, Amelia grabbed her own bicep and flexed it under the rough material of the shirt. There was strength there, she reminded herself. And she'd proven herself in combat enough times that she knew Sky respected her. Maybe it was just that look Sky had given her, the night they'd left the Brightlake ball and headed straight back to the ship—the assaulter had seemed less than impressed when Amelia had swirled in with a ball gown big enough to fill the entire cabin. Amelia had been forced to grab her uniform and head down to the stores office to change, so voluminous had the dress been, and in the stores office the gown still hung. She couldn't help but laugh at the absurdity. Maybe next time Sky could attend the ball—perhaps on Chief Butcher's arm.

Amelia's guffaw filled the cabin as she laced her second boot, strapped on her shoulder holster with pistol contained, and threw on her worker's jacket. Stepping out into the passageway she began tying her long hair up into a bun as she made her way toward the brow where Sky and Swift were waiting for her.

The sailing officer was dressed in the same charcoal-gray clothes as she and Sky, and a cap hid his bald head. A rugged leather bag was draped over one shoulder, the pouch hanging in front of him. He shoved his hands into his trouser pockets and hunched his shoulders. The effect was subtle, but it somehow entirely changed his appearance.

Sky was learning how to slouch, but it was still hard to believe that she was anything other than a bodyguard when they went ashore. Not that this threatened their cover, as places like Windfall were filled with toughs for hire, but it was always best to keep the assaulter in the back of their little crowd.

Amelia frankly worried most about her own ability to blend in. Putting her hair in a bun and wearing baggy clothes certainly changed her appearance, and from a distance she knew she might even be mistaken for a young man. But pretty women got noticed in places like this, and she was only too aware of the glances her way whenever she accompanied Liam ashore as cargo master. She fixed a scowl on her face, like she did when she left a tavern back home and wanted no company. Hopefully it would be enough of a disguise from her usual smile.

Liam arrived moments later, still dressed as Stone-bridge. He gave them all a quick once-over, nodding in approval. He held up the folder of cargo manifests, opening it to show the ore shipment from Labyrinthia.

"Your mission today is to find the warehouse where a few of the shipments are being stored, particularly this one. I'm not so worried about the cargos themselves, but about the people guarding them. We need to get a sense of who we're dealing with."

"Do you suspect Dark Star agents?" Sky asked.

"Possibly. Are you all familiar with their code words?"

Amelia had been studying the files seized from *Black Hand,* including a series of passwords and responses shared throughout the pirate organization. With that capture so recent, it was doubtful anyone knew that *Black Hand* had been compromised.

"Yes, sir," she answered. Sky and Swift both nodded.

Liam handed the sheaf of cargo orders to Swift, who slipped it into his bag.

There was a long moment of silence. Amelia was eager to get going and she sensed the same from her teammates. But Liam was clearly hesitating.

"You can't come on every mission, sir," Swift said finally. "And on this one you'd just be in the way."

"You'd be a liability, frankly, sir," added Sky.

"I know," he sighed. "Good luck to you all."

He wanted to say more, Amelia could tell, but he held his tongue and retreated into the ship.

"You got an idea of where to start?" Sky asked Amelia.

"I have a plan on how to get a conversation started," she said, suppressing her instinctive grin, "and I think it might help our coffee problem in the senior mess."

"Sounds good to me," Swift muttered.

They departed across the brow one at a time to minimize activity on their berth. Sky went first and Swift followed a minute later. Amelia counted down in her head, then stepped through the airlock tunnel and back onto the station. She nodded to Flatrock, who stood, in shabby merchant sailor attire, as brow's mate and then strode across the open space of their berth toward the low fence that acted as a useless security feature between the ships and the promenade.

Down here at the end of the line of berths traffic was light, but within moments she was slipping through the increasing pedestrian crowd as locals went about their daily business in Windfall. Many others wore working clothes similar to hers and no one spared her more than a glance as she weaved past shoulders and arms toward the nearest tavern. Swift and Sky loitered near its front door, looking bored and tired, but they both fell into step behind her as she walked past. She ignored them, making her way along the central street until she reached the Cup of Plenty.

The patio was half-full and Amelia strolled through the patrons, selecting a table close to the door. She allowed herself a single, wistful glance inside, but knew that common workers like her could never afford to enter. She sat down, Sky and Swift pulling up chairs opposite her. With her back to the wall she could survey the entire patio and the merchant stalls beyond. No one gave them a glance as the bustle of the promenade continued around them.

Within a few minutes, Bella emerged with an empty

tray in hand, clearing up a vacant table. Her body almost seemed to slither between the tables as she moved, her small head snapping left and right as she surveyed her customers. Her raised tail moved with flowing grace behind her, tracing a perfect path between the tables. Amelia caught a few glances from patrons at the tail, in the typical distaste for aliens she saw everywhere.

Bella weaved around the patio, finally spotting Amelia and her shipmates. The reptilian head jerked back slightly, but she continued her graceful approach.

"Welcome back, *Arr-meh-lay-arr*," she said. "May I bring you and your friends something?"

"We unfortunately don't have a lot of time," Amelia said, motioning Bella closer. "But I was wondering if I might purchase a bag of your coffee to take back to our ship."

Bella bobbed her head up and down. "Of course. What size of bag?"

Amelia shrugged, opening her hands to suggest a standard sack. "Enough to last us for the next voyage."

The Theropod flicked her nose toward the alley beside the patio. "Come to our kitchen door and we can help you."

"Thank you."

Bella moved off and Amelia rose. Swift and Sky followed her out of the patio, around the fence and down the alley. The light from the promenade spilled down the narrow path between buildings, and a single lamp illuminated a door set into the brickwork. Amelia weaved past the garbage bins and ignored the rats scurrying in the shadows.

The door opened and Bella peered out. No, Amelia suddenly realized, noticing the ridged crests on the Theropod's head running from the nostrils to above the eyes, this was the male.

"You are here for coffee?" he asked through his translator.

"Yes, Bella said to come here."

The Theropod's head cocked, then he shifted back, motioning Amelia to follow. She stepped through the door, reveling in the sudden wash of glorious cooking smells. The kitchen was surprisingly large, with expansive floorspace between the low counters. To her left she saw a pair of ovens with trays of raw pastries waiting to be baked, ahead she saw a cleaning station and to her right were stacks of shelves, perhaps half-full of supplies.

The door on the far wall knocked open as Bella glided through, her head rising up as she spotted Amelia and the other Humans.

The male switched off his translator for a moment, and the kitchen echoed with a series of growls and hisses, ending in a distinctly forced *Beh-lahhh*. Bella barked in laughter, her head bobbing playfully with his for a moment. She padded over to Amelia.

"My husband thinks your name for me is very funny. He wants a Human name, too."

Amelia looked the male Theropod up and down, noting the utilitarian gray coveralls that draped his powerful, reptilian form. "What is your name, sir?"

Bella repeated the question in their language.

Translator still off, he opened his mouth and rumbled a single syllable.

"*Saaarhm*," Amelia repeated. She thought for a second. "How about Sam? That is a popular Human name."

Bella translated, and then flicked at him to turn his device back on.

He tried out the new sound a few times, and both Theropods barked. He reactivated his translator.

"It is a funny name—I like it."

"I am glad to offer amusement," she said. "And to be able to address you without burning my own throat."

Sam bobbed his head, then motioned with clawed hands for Amelia to follow him to the shelves. He pointed up at several sacks of coffee, marked with colored tags of various hues.

"These two varieties are what we serve on the patio—full-bodied and strong. They are very nice, but from what *Beh-lahhh* tells me your captain is a man of refined tastes." He shifted forward and pointed at the next sacks. "These two varieties are our finest imports, very difficult to obtain, but well worth the price."

"My captain is indeed a man of taste," she replied, "but we humble crewmembers can get by with one of your delicious patio blends. Plus, I wouldn't want to take your last bag of the good stuff."

Sam glanced between the sacks. There were four bags each of the lesser blends, but the single bags of the premiums were both clearly half-empty already.

"We will always get more eventually," he said.

A hiss from Bella didn't translate, but Amelia guessed it was a caution.

"Perhaps I will buy just a small pouch of your finest blend for my captain," she offered, before pointing at one of the patio varieties, "and a sack of this for the crew."

"Yes," Sam said. "We do have certain clients who are also regular patrons of our finer blends. It would be a shame to run out before the next shipment."

"Especially if they steal another sack." Bella's voice was soft, but the translator relayed her words at regular volume.

"Are you having problems with thieves?" Amelia asked.

"Nothing to worry about," Bella said, gathering up her tray and heading for the café door. "Just one time. I need to see to our customers."

She swatted aside the door and disappeared.

Sam had moved to a counter where a ledger rested. He took up a pen and began scratching out an invoice.

"Do not worry about her," he said. "We are used to dealing with chaos."

He showed Amelia the price for the coffee and she nodded her agreement.

"She mentioned earlier that there are new people on the station, possibly making trouble."

"No more trouble than anywhere else. You should visit a Theropod world some time. A Human gang is no trouble for us." Sam stood up in his stance to look her in the eye. "But I sense they may be trouble for you. They have asked many questions about your ship."

"So I hear. I don't know why—we're simple merchants."

"It is your captain they ask about. They seem very interested in Human lords."

"Why?"

"I don't know. We have no such thing within our people." He cocked his head. "Why do you have lords?"

Amelia's lips twisted in a smile. It was a good question.

"I don't know," she answered.

"Do you want to take your coffee now?"

"No," she said, digging into her pocket to pull up enough coins to pay. "Can you please deliver it to our ship by the end of the day? *Sophia's Fancy*—berth twelve. We have some other things to do right now."

Sam bobbed his head. "I will bring them by this evening after we close."

"Thank you." She made to go, but then pretended to have a sudden thought. She motioned Swift closer and pulled out the cargo manifests. She showed Sam the warehouse listed on the top of the sheet. "Can you tell me where this is?"

His third eyelids flicked as he leaned in to examine the writing. His nose moved between Amelia and Swift.

"Yes, it is on this level. But it is controlled by the people who ask about you."

"Oh!" Amelia feigned surprise. "Then we will go somewhere else. Can you tell me where this is, though, so that we can stay clear?"

Sam considered for a second, then gave her the directions.

"They are dangerous people," he warned, "and we like you. Stay clear of them."

"We like you, too," she said, stepping back and bowing slightly. Sam lowered his stance in a reciprocal gesture. "And we look forward to enjoying many more cups of your delicious coffee."

With a final farewell she led her team back out through the alley.

"I'm never going ashore without you again," Swift said. "You could charm a Sectoid."

Memories of strapping herself to a Sectoid thorax as it skittered up to the ceiling to check hanging water bulbs flashed through Amelia's mind. What a ride that had been.

"Way ahead of you, Mason. Let's go find these pirates."

Windfall was a big enough and busy enough place that three common workers were barely noticed, and Amelia sensed no unusual attention directed their way as they moved along with the crowds. The promenade began to narrow, the ceiling closing in, until the space station's true form became clear. The starlight faded as the high windows were left behind, replaced by a dull, yellow glow from periodic wall lamps. Amelia brushed past another pedestrian as she stepped over an airlock lip, her eyes straining to read the letters and numbers over the wide cargo doors on either side of the passageway. Dark, narrow alleys periodically stretched away left and right. Foot traffic dwindled, until the three of them were the only visible travelers in the corridor.

Finally, Amelia spotted their destination. Rolling double doors were open enough for a single person to walk through, with no guards or anything to draw attention. Just under the address she saw a scrap of paper attached to the wall. On it was a simple black cross. She traced her finger along it.

"A dark star," Sky muttered.

Amelia nodded. They were clearly in the right place. She peeked through the opening and stepped into an open, square space wide enough for half a dozen people to form a circle with outstretched hands. On three sides a chain-link fence stretched to the ceiling and beyond were shelves and pallets with sacks and crates scattered under the dim amber lamps.

A middle-aged woman sat behind a shabby desk, flanked by a large, younger man. Both stared at Amelia with what she could only feel was aggressive indifference. She felt a touch of relief as she heard Swift and Sky step in behind her. Adopting her own scowl, Amelia reached back and into Swift's bag, pulling out the cargo manifest.

"Hey," she said to the woman at the desk, "we're here to check out some cargos for a ship."

The woman cast dubious eyes over them, then held out her hand for the manifest. Amelia handed it over.

"What ship are you with?" the woman asked.

"I don't know," Amelia replied. "We were hired to come and confirm these cargos. Some out-system ship I haven't heard of. You guys catch the name?"

She glanced back over her shoulder. Swift shrugged, eyes down at his feet as he breathed through his mouth. Sky shook her head, absently scratching her ear. Amelia turned and leaned on the desk, offering a resigned expression.

"You got these cargos, or are we in the wrong place?"

The woman's hard eyes were clearly assessing, but she handed the sheet to her companion. "Show 'em, Luke."

Luke took the paper and unlocked the chain-link door leading into the warehouse. He motioned for Amelia to follow.

"You two go," she said to Swift and Sky. "And actually use your measuring tapes this time."

She cast a weary look at the woman and got the glimmer of a smile in return.

Swift and Sky passed through the door but paused as Luke called back.

"Hey, Mary—is this the refined ore, or raw?"

"Raw. It's over on the left."

Mary gave Amelia an eye roll of her own. "Hard to get good help, isn't it? I lost my best loader last month—took off as crew on a fancy new cutter headed to Passagia."

The phrase was delivered so casually Amelia almost missed it. But there it was: mention of a cutter to Passagia. The opening phrase of the pirate identity exchange.

"Shame," she replied nonchalantly. "But if it had been going to Cornucopia I'd have been on it myself. You seen the planets in that system?"

Mary's expression shifted in acknowledgment, but her eyes narrowed. She leaned back in her chair, arms folded.

"I don't know you," she said simply.

"I don't know you, either," Amelia replied, hardening her expression. Silence hung heavily between them for a long moment.

Finally, Mary shrugged. Her posture relaxed visibly and she glanced toward the shadowy forms of Luke and the others deep in the warehouse.

"What ship are you really with?"

"*Black Hand*. She's still in space, though—I just came in on a boat to check in. Gotta report how we took down a Navy ship that was tailing us."

A single eyebrow raised on Mary's otherwise bland expression, but it was enough to indicate her sudden interest.

"The Navy put up a fight?"

"Sure, but with ol' Double Swords on our side we hacked our way through."

"Never heard him called that," she said with a breath of a laugh. "What's he think of your nickname for him?"

"You think I say it to his face?"

Mary's laugh was fuller this time, but Amelia didn't relax under the woman's calculating stare.

The pirate stretched lazily in her chair. "He must have loved taking down the noble officers."

"None of us even got a swipe." Amelia remembered previous pirate attacks, where regular crew had been killed quickly but nobility had been tortured first. "But he made it long and painful, especially for the captain."

Mary's lips curled in a knowing sneer, but she offered no further comment.

"You got anything for us?" Amelia asked.

"Not much. There's a civilian trader in port right now, headed by some noble idiot, and we're trying to figure out where he comes from."

"What's the name?"

"*Sophia's Fancy* is the ship. Captain's name is Stone-bridge."

Amelia made a show of thinking before shaking her head. "Don't know the family name—but that ship's been in the sector for a few months, hasn't it?"

"Has it? I didn't know."

Mary's face was blank, putting Amelia on edge. She grabbed the initiative in the conversation.

"You didn't? How long have you been here?"

"About two months," Mary replied, defensiveness sneaking into her expression. "I was leading an enforcement team in Pacifica until . . ." She pushed back her chair and pointed down. Amelia peered over the desk and saw only one leg stretched out. The other had been sliced off above the knee. A wooden stump was fastened with straps to her thigh.

"Sorry," Amelia offered coolly.

"Brute tailsword," Mary said, eyes afire. "But I got the bastard before I fell. You can live with a leg chopped off, but not a head."

"Nice job."

"I got a compliment from the Piper, even." Mary sat back smugly, and Amelia guessed that she was supposed to be impressed by that.

"From the Piper," she said cautiously. "Really?"

"From her own lips," Mary replied, her eyes daring Amelia to question the claim.

"I just . . ." Amelia thought quickly. "Don't hear of her giving out too many compliments. I'm impressed."

"Yeah." Mary was trying to play it down, but real pride shined in her eyes. "Not too much impresses her or Dark Star. But I guess when you're born in chaos, you have high standards."

"Too bad you had to lose a leg for it, though."

"It's nothing compared to what Dark Star has given up," she countered, sudden passion melting the defensiveness on her face. "When the new society is set up, and we're on top, I'll get me a solid gold leg to strut around on."

New society? Amelia's mind raced. This was unusual, even coming from one of Dark Star's pirates. But Mary's eyes burned with the most honest intensity she'd displayed in this entire conversation.

"Made from the Emperor's own crown?" Amelia said quickly.

"You said it, sister."

Here it was, more hostility toward the nobility and the royals, Amelia noted. This was a common refrain from the more intelligent prisoners *Daring* had captured, but it wasn't just random anger toward authority—during interrogations it was specifically directed at noble officers like Liam or Ava Templegrey. Amelia herself had never felt personally targeted by the anger of their prisoners; if anything they seemed to think she was just a puppet in the bigger game. What Mary was talking about was more than just anger at those in power, though. She was talking revolution—a remaking of society. It was absurd, but a part of her actually felt some sympathy for the idea.

Mary suddenly grabbed a cane and pushed herself out of her seat. She was quite tall, Amelia realized, and was imposing even with half a leg missing.

"What's taking those idiots so long?" she muttered, shuffling out from behind her desk.

"Let's go, I haven't got all day!" Amelia shouted into the dim shadows of the warehouse, as an alert to her shipmates that time was up. She touched Mary's arm to pause her advance. "Sorry, those two really are local hirelings. I picked the dumbest I could find to ensure they didn't notice what I'm up to while I do my rounds."

"Yeah," Mary said absently, freeing her arm and hobbling through the chain-link gate.

There was a sudden crash and a shout, followed by frantic scuffling. Mary quickened her pace, nearly tripping on her peg leg, and Amelia pushed past her to run forward. She rounded a pair of stacked crates and saw

Luke unconscious on the floor, a heavy sack spilling chunks of ore by his head. The angry red bump on his forehead might have been caused by a falling sack, but she guessed it was the quick work of one of Sky's limbs. The assaulter was making a show of collecting the spilled ore and stuffing it back into the sack. Swift was just pocketing a data stick and he kept his hands in his pockets as Amelia heard Mary limp up behind her.

"What happened?" Amelia demanded before Mary could speak.

"We was reaching for some of those bags," Sky said, pointing at the shelf, "and one of them fell off."

"Hit him right on the head," Swift added dully.

"Pick him up," Amelia snapped. "Get him back to a chair."

Swift and Sky complied, carrying the unconscious Luke back to the cleared foyer, where they plunked him heavily into Mary's seat. The sound of Mary's wooden leg was still several paces away and Amelia exchanged confirming nods with her teammates. By the time Mary returned, Swift and Sky had stepped clear and adopted suitably shamefaced expressions. Under her glare, both of them dug out a few coppers and dropped them on the desk, mumbling apologies.

"I think we're done here," Amelia sighed to Mary. "Hopefully his headache isn't too bad when he wakes up."

Mary shook her head but said nothing.

"Next time," Amelia scolded, motioning for the others to precede her out the entrance, "check one of the lower bags for weight."

She followed Swift and Sky out into the corridor, keeping up a mild tirade as they retreated toward the promenade. When finally the corridor widened out again and they found themselves blending into the crowds, Swift slowed and turned.

"I hope you had enough time to make friends," he said. "Our buddy Luke went down in seconds and we were able to scan all the cargos on the list."

"Did you get anything useful?" Amelia asked.

"I kept one of the ore chunks," Sky said, revealing the bulge in her jacket pocket.

"Encrypted signatures for all the cargos," Swift added, patting his pocket with the data stick. "We should be able to figure out exactly who put these cargos together, and where."

"And then we take them down?" Sky suggested.

"For the glory of the Empire," he said with a scoff.

Amelia smiled automatically, but Swift's words rang particularly hollow to her. She was never one to question her mission, but a knot was forming deep in her gut. A knot of doubt, and she didn't like it.

CHAPTER 4

THE BRIG IN *DARING* HAD BECOME QUITE THE PER-
manent structure, Liam thought, considering it was
actually nothing more than a converted cargo container
bolted onto the ship's hull. From the outside it looked
like just one of a dozen bulbous additions masking
Daring's smooth lines, but inside it was a full eco-
system. Heavily guarded and permanently locked away
from the rest of the ship's interior, it was like a separate
vessel hitched along for the ride.

And it was currently full.

Liam followed Amelia through the airlock, past the
two sailors standing guard in *Daring*'s passageway, and
greeted the next pair of guards standing inside the brig.
The harsh, white light of the space was a stark contrast
to the dim interior of the ship and Liam shielded his eyes
as he took in the cell doors on either side of him. There
were five doors on each side, with ladders and catwalks

leading to a second story of cells above. When *Daring* had first set sail with her letter of marque Liam had thought space for twenty prisoners was excessive, but the recent capture of *Black Hand* had filled every one of them. Five of the cells were even doubled up, each with a Human and a Theropod prisoner who were denied a translator device to minimize potential scheming.

Liam and Amelia had been alternating with Butcher and Sky, slowly working their way through the prisoners using intel uncovered by Brown and the others to prompt specific questions. To date most of the Human prisoners had been less than helpful, either through stubbornness or sheer ignorance. The Theropods had been more willing to say what they knew—group loyalty was clearly not a dominant Theropod trait—but this willingness had been offset by a genuine lack of detailed knowledge. It seemed the Human pirates held little love for or trust in their reptilian counterparts.

But today it was finally time to speak to their major prize, the mysterious Double Swords. Amelia led the way to the last cell door on the right, then looked up questioningly at Liam.

"Same routine as usual?" she asked.

"You're always the more believable nice guy," he replied, "although you did smash his face in."

"That just means he'll take me seriously," she said with a sweet smile.

The guard unlocked the cell and swung the door open. Liam ducked through first, his feet kicking aside empty food bowls as he warily eyed the prisoner. The big man was sitting on his cot, and his head barely lifted as his gaze flickered over. Both his hands were manacled to heavy chains that were secured to the deck near the back of the cell. He'd been given enough freedom of movement to lie on his cot or use the toilet, but little more.

As Amelia stepped in beside Liam, he took a moment to study the man. He was young, perhaps a few years younger than Amelia, and taller than Liam with a broad, powerful build. Even through his baggy clothes his shoulders and arms bulged with muscles, and his legs were like tree trunks. Liam might have taken him for an elite soldier, if not for his shaggy blond hair, matched now by the recent growth of a beard.

"You have a fine crew, sir," Liam said. "They've been very cooperative."

The man glanced up wearily, disdain etched across his features. "Torture people long enough and they'll tell you whatever you want to hear."

"But that's just the thing," Liam replied. "They didn't know what we wanted to hear. We just let them talk. I hope our discussion today can be as productive. It would be unfortunate if we did actually have to resort to torture."

"I have nothing to say."

Amelia crouched down, still safely out of the prisoner's reach but able to meet his gaze.

"But why not?" she asked. "Your battle is over, and there's nothing to gain from making our job difficult."

"When *Black Hand* fails to appear as scheduled, my brothers and sisters will know something went wrong, and they'll come looking for us. I just need to be patient."

His accent was common, Liam noted, but educated—much like that of Sublieutenant Brown's.

"Unfortunately," Amelia replied, "we pulled into Windfall Station and used your code phrases to report that *Black Hand* is still sailing free. As far as your brothers and sisters are concerned, all is well."

"Don't waste your time lying to me."

"I spoke with Mary. I'm aware that you know her. Noted by the Piper herself for her bravery on Pacifica. Tough lady"—she tapped her knee—"missing a leg."

His eyes widened in recognition, then he dropped his gaze in frustration.

"No one's coming for you," Liam stated. "No one even knows you're missing."

"They will," he muttered.

"Why would they care? You think you're someone important?"

He didn't take the bait but merely stared down at his manacled hands.

"What do they call you?" Amelia asked.

"I think 'whelp' would suffice," Liam sniffed.

Powerful fists tightened, then relaxed. The man didn't raise his head, but his eyes flicked to Amelia. "You can call me Blade, I suppose."

"I'll grant that you're a great swordsman," Amelia offered, "so that makes sense. We don't see many pirates who can swing blades like you can. I'd even guess you went to the Imperial Academy."

"The Academy would never accept such a ruffian," Liam scoffed, letting his accent drip with contempt.

"Only youth of good breeding are allowed into such a hallowed place."

"Or those who prove their worth," Blade snapped.

"True, I do recall us having a few commoners around to serve us when necessary. I suppose some would have found you delightful and perhaps given you some pity lessons."

Liam had never even been to the Academy, but he'd heard stories. And based on the sudden darkening of Blade's expression, he guessed they were true.

"You're going to burn one day," the young man muttered. "You and your entire hierarchy."

"What, by you? A chained prisoner from a brigand ship no one even knows is missing? Your brothers and sisters have already forgotten you, my friend. But if you cooperate we might be able to lessen your sentence before the Imperial court."

He let those final two words hang in the cell for a long moment. It was widely known that justice at the Imperial court was related directly to one's noble rank. As a minor noble Liam might expect a fair hearing for himself, but for a commoner it was a certain sentence to a painful death.

"This ship will never make it to Homeworld," Blade said finally.

"And why is that?"

Blade sneered at Liam but otherwise didn't reply.

Amelia straightened, casting a quick look at Liam. He gave a tiny nod.

"My lord," she said, "may I have a minute to speak to this man alone?"

He made a show of huffing in frustration. "There's no point."

"Indulge me, my lord."

"Very well." He stooped toward the cell door. "But don't fall for any trickery!"

"Of course, my lord."

Liam stepped out of the cell and cleared to the side. The door was open and the guards were present, but with the constant hum of ship systems in the background he knew Amelia would have all the privacy she needed.

AMELIA MOVED FORWARD, CROUCHING DOWN AND making a show of glancing over her shoulder.

"Blade," she said quietly, "I only have a few moments until that lordling starts to suspect something."

He glanced up, surprise clouding his youthful face. The bruising was almost gone, but his nose was askew and his cheek carried the scars from her spiked gauntlet.

"This ship isn't headed for Homeworld—we're going back to Windfall. I can get a message to the Piper through Mary. What do you want me to say?"

"What?" he said, his expression twisting in doubt.

"They don't know who Mary really is," Amelia hissed, jerking her thumb back toward the cell door, "or the Piper. But it's only a matter of time before the Navy figures out what they're on to. I've been planted here for months and I'm out of the loop. Do we have a ship nearby that can mount a rescue?"

He studied her closely, but she could tell the fatigue and stress were taking a toll on his ability to think clearly.

"You're with us?" he asked skeptically.

"Yes," she said quickly, glancing over her shoulder again. "The vision, the new society, the nobles torn down, and the Dark Star rising. I can't wait for it to happen, but we need you and all our leaders to remain free."

She was groping in the dark, she knew, and just hoped that her words were imbued with enough sincerity to convince this young revolutionary.

"We're so close," she added. "We can't let this little setback slow us down."

"Why don't I know you?" He wanted to believe, she could tell, but was too smart to just give in to that desire.

"It's a big galaxy, I guess. I was part of Mary's enforcement team on Pacifica. I remember when that brute took her leg. I was moving to help when Mary lopped the thing's head right off. I helped get her out of there but we had to scatter before the authorities closed in. This ship was in port, looking for volunteers, so I hid out right under the Navy's nose, and I've been feeding what I can back to the Piper."

A sudden hostility flared in his eyes. "Then why did you fight me on *Black Hand*?"

"Because I knew who you were," she said, her thoughts scrambling, "and I had to keep you alive. The rest of the bridge was taken and that lordling's crew were going to shoot you from behind. Sorry about the face"—she offered a shrug—"but it's better than bullets in the back."

He frowned, staring at her.

She glanced back toward the door, letting a touch of panic light her face. "I'm not going to have another chance to talk to you, and with the Navy holding all of *Black Hand*'s logs and codes, they're going to piece it together soon enough. What ship can I contact to get us out of here?"

He exhaled slowly, still staring at her. She held his gaze in silent pleading. Her heart was actually thumping, and she honestly wasn't sure why.

"*Storm Wind,*" he said finally. "She's not far and she's got a good captain."

"Good," she said, letting out the breath she'd been holding. She nodded to herself, then gave him a smile. "Good. Stay strong—help is coming."

LIAM WATCHED AS AMELIA EMERGED FROM THE cell.

"There's no point in questioning this prisoner further, my lord," she declared.

"No surprise," he scoffed loudly. "Guards, seal that cell."

He followed Amelia out of the brig and back into the soft illumination of *Daring*'s lower deck. She strode with purpose and seemed agitated. They were already up two ladders and approaching the senior mess before he finally tugged at her sleeve.

"How did it go?"

She slowed, turning to regard him with a fiery expression.

"Patience, Lord Blackwood," she said, placing a finger to his lips. "I'd like to report my findings only once, and our team awaits."

He knew her well enough not to argue and instead opened the door to the senior mess for her. He followed her in and saw the table scattered with charts and papers, the surrounding chairs occupied by Brown, Templegrey, Butcher, and Sky.

"So," Chief Butcher asked, "do we have Dark Star himself on board?"

"I don't think so," Amelia answered immediately, before Liam could open his mouth. "He's someone important, but he's not the heart of this whole operation."

Gazes turned to Liam as he took his seat at the head of the table.

"I see no reason to disagree with the quartermaster," he said. "And she had a conversation with him to which I wasn't privy."

Amelia breathlessly relayed the full conversation with Blade, and Liam was impressed with her quick thinking to pose as a pirate mole. Getting him to name another pirate ship was gold.

"There's definitely some sort of political agenda to all this," she concluded. "We've seen it all along from senior pirates we talk to. At first I thought it was just the odd radical who'd fallen in with criminals, but it comes up too often. Blade might be a disaffected intellectual, but Mary on Windfall is a grounded realist if ever I met one. And they both share this vision of taking down the Empire."

"It seems to be a common purpose that motivates them," Templegrey said. "No doubt something invented by their leaders to build loyalty beyond just petty thuggery."

"Or it might be real," Amelia snapped.

Templegrey's eyebrow arched, but she offered no further comment. Liam watched Amelia, curious at the fire still burning in her eyes.

"It's definitely a common thread across all our interrogations," he said. "And something we need to take seriously. I'm glad Amelia was able to make that connection with the prisoner."

"Nice work," Sky agreed, nodding her appreciation. "And now we know the name of another nearby pirate ship."

"Our next target?" Brown asked.

"Well, slow down," Liam said, gesturing at all the documents in front of them. "What else are we looking at here?"

Brown and Sky had been leading the investigation of the *Black Hand* intel, and over the next few minutes they summarized their latest findings. The destruction of the base in Silica by *Daring* and the Sectoids had clearly disrupted the pirate agenda, and it appeared that a new base, or at least a concentration of forces, was emerging in the frontier system of Morassia.

"Lot of brutes on Morassia," Butcher commented. "It's the only planet where the two races freely mix."

"Plenty of freedom for criminals to move about," Sky added.

"But there were also quite a lot of instructions regarding Honoria," Brown continued. "The pirates always speak vaguely in their messages, but I'm pretty sure that something is being planned for Honoria in the future."

"What's on Honoria?" Amelia asked.

"One of the Imperial treasuries," Templegrey replied immediately. "Enough gold to buy the entire Halo."

"Or an entire army," Sky muttered.

"*Black Hand* was at Honoria," Brown said, "and she was met by a ship, a fast cutter, if the records of the rendezvous are accurate, both before her visit to the planet and afterward. I wonder if the cutter was Dark Star's personal ship, because *Black Hand*'s logs do mention, during the visit to Honoria, how the captain moved out of his cabin. I think he was making room for a special guest."

"So Dark Star was in *Black Hand* at Honoria," Liam concluded. "We just didn't get there in time."

"I believe so, sir."

"Okay." He cast his eyes around the table. "What else do we have?"

"I examined that piece of ore I lifted from Windfall," Sky said, reaching down into a bag by her feet, "and I discovered why the pirates would care about it."

She pulled out a chunk of dull, rocky metal, then turned it to reveal where she'd smashed it open. The interior glittered as jagged edges caught the light.

"Gold," she said simply. "Carefully hidden inside fragments of regular ore that, to a quick survey, would look like any regular hunk of rock."

"So the pirates are moving gold between the systems," Liam concluded, "using regular merchants as mules."

"I suggest we start tracking shipments of unrefined ore out of Labyrinthia," Sky said.

"Yes, good."

"Here's something else," Templegrey said suddenly, tapping her finger thoughtfully on the pages of a thick book. "There's an entry here, one of the last ones recorded on *Black Hand* before we caught her. It's a comment by the captain in his log, saying that he's ignoring an order to head for Cornucopia to collect some seized goods—because he knew he was being pursued and needed to hide out in the nebula."

"So he had advance knowledge of our pursuit?" Liam said with a shrug.

"Yes, but what struck me was the order he was ignoring. Do you think he's talking about the Brightlake estate? What other 'seized goods' would there be on Cornucopia at exactly that time? And why would a pirate ship be given an order to go and collect it?"

Liam's eyes locked with Templegrey's, and he knew she was thinking the same terrible thing that he was.

"If a bunch of crooks on the surface robbed somebody," he heard Butcher say, "they might need a quick transport off the planet with their loot."

"But it wasn't a bunch of crooks who seized the Brightlake estate," Templegrey said quietly. "It was Lord Silverhawk."

Liam broke her gaze and offered a half shrug. "Maybe it's a coincidence. Maybe there was a criminal raid on another location around the same time. Cornucopia's a big planet."

"Still, I'd like to find out where the Brightlake treasure has gone."

It was quite a leap she was taking, he knew, and would probably result in a lot of wasted time chasing down a false lead. But it was just unsettling enough to make him not want to dismiss it as coincidence.

"Okay, inquire into what you can."

"Yes, sir."

"Shall we start searching for *Storm Wind*?" Brown asked. "It'll probably take weeks."

"No," Liam replied, smiling as an idea formed in his mind. "I'd like to play this game of pirate informant a bit longer. Amelia, send a brief message to your friend Mary on Windfall and tell her that *Black Hand* was lost in a storm as it evaded a Navy attack. You and a few survivors—including Double Swords—were picked up by a fat merchant ship called *Sophia's Fancy,* laden with gold. Can Mary get word to *Storm Wind* to rescue you? Be sure to give her *Daring*'s basic description and course."

He sat back, appreciating the admiring looks from Butcher and Sky.

"We don't need to find *Storm Wind,* Charlotte. She'll find us."

CHAPTER 5

"ARE YOU SURE THIS IS THE SMARTEST IDEA?"
Templegrey asked.

Amelia finished adjusting her belt, grimacing at the
lack of weapons hanging from it. A part of her shared
Templegrey's doubt. Pirates were closing *Daring,* and
they were not coming for tea. She looked up at her
colleague.

The doctor stood in the ship's corridor, her arms
crossed as she gave Liam a stern, questioning gaze. She
was wearing an elegant off-the-shoulder gown, with her
hair tied up in a fashionable style. Large diamonds hung
from her ears, matching the necklace that followed her
plunging neckline. In the drawing room of a country
home it would have looked beautiful, but here in space
the outfit struck Amelia as fairly ridiculous.

"You have to catch their eye," Liam said from behind Amelia, "and draw them this way."

Hunkered in the open doorway to the crew cafeteria, he was in full armor and weapons, with a pack of sailors behind him.

"Once we get their main boarding party tangled up in here, Chief Sky and her assault team will board their ship and take them while understrength."

"Don't you think," Amelia added, "that the pirates will think it strange for someone to be dressed like that in deep space?"

"In the heat of battle they won't be thinking that clearly," Liam replied. "All they'll see is a target."

"Oh, splendid," Templegrey sighed.

"Trust me," Liam said with a reassuring smile.

"*Stand by for boarding,*" Brown's voice suddenly called down on the speakers, "*starboard side, Two Deck.*"

Amelia had known Liam long enough to recognize one of his classic traps, but it was the first time she'd been part of the bait. The pirate ship *Storm Wind* had found them in remarkable time and was closing even now. She took Templegrey's arm to lead her a few steps down the corridor. She was dressed in common sailor clothing and was at least thankful to be in trousers rather than a dress. The gentle sway of the solar winds was interrupted by a sudden bump, and Templegrey's hand reached out to grip Amelia's shirt.

"Remember," Amelia said, "we just have to look scared. As soon as they see us, we hightail it to cover."

Templegrey steadied herself, surveying her outfit with an arched eyebrow. "I'm just glad the XO didn't insist I wear high heels, or you might have seen my tail going very high as I tripped over myself."

Thumps against the hull caught them short. Amelia's eyes scanned upward to the emergency hatch in the deckhead above them. Metal creaked, and she heard the distant hiss of a skirt pressurizing.

"Here we go."

Templegrey moved to stand in front of her.

"Let them see me first," she said, "but then I'll lead the running."

"A noble lady abandoning her commoner friend?"

"It's in character," she admitted, "but more to the point your butt looks better in those trousers than mine in this silly dress. Give them something to chase."

Amelia's laughter broke the tension in the silent corridor.

The circular handle on the hatch above them squeaked as it began to turn. Amelia took a couple of steps back, but no longer felt afraid. The familiar rush of adrenaline coursed through her, and she stepped to the side to allow Templegrey a clear path to flee.

The hatch swung upward, and a pirate jumped down heavily. His cutlass was up and he looked around quickly.

Templegrey's scream was loud enough to shatter glass. She froze in place, her hands up dramatically against her cheeks.

Another pirate dropped down, predatory eyes already focusing on the noblewoman before him.

"My lady," Amelia shouted, tugging at her, "run!"

Templegrey turned and fled, screaming again. Amelia paused for a moment, watching as a third pirate jumped down. As one, the attackers started to move. She turned and bolted, following Templegrey through the open door to the main cafeteria. The large space was flooded with shadow, only a single lamp casting a dull yellow glow from the far wall. Another scream directed her to the right to follow Templegrey, and then she felt strong hands pulling her behind the line of defenders. She crouched down, struggling to hear the rumble of the approaching pirates over Templegrey's dramatic sobbing.

The pirates burst into the room, their swords up as they peered into the darkness.

"I can't see anything," one of them shouted back as they slowed to advance cautiously.

"But you can hear well enough," came another, educated voice from the corridor, "capture that noblewoman!"

There were now fully six pirates in the room, all Humans, spreading out to search. One more stepped through the door, dressed in more expensive armor and with an elegant longsword instead of a brutish cutlass. Experience told Amelia that this was probably the entire pirate boarding party, with barely enough crew still on board to man the guns and sails.

"Fire!" Liam roared from the darkness, obviously sharing her assessment.

The flashes of pistols blinded her, but she heard the cries of alarm and awful thuds as bullets ripped through padded armor and flesh. The deafening barrage continued, then was replaced by the heavy shuffle of sailors advancing. A few clangs of blade on blade indicated some resistance, but within seconds her crewmates were pouring out into the corridor.

LIAM SURGED AHEAD, SHOULDERING THE COLLAPS-ing pirates out of his way. Up ahead, the pirate leader was running for the escape hatch. Liam raised his pistol, taking careful aim.

The shot tore into the pirate's unprotected leg, and he stumbled to the deck. Gripping the wound he crawled beneath the hatch, but couldn't pull himself up. Another pirate jumped down to help, but Liam put his last two bullets into the newcomer.

Sky and her team burst out from the senior mess, where they'd been hiding, and charged for the airlock.

"Ambush!" the wounded pirate leader screamed up through the hatch. "Cast off!"

Without hesitation the hatch slammed shut. Liam grabbed for the circular handle seconds later, but already he could see the mists of freezing air from an emergency withdrawal.

"Secure that prisoner," he barked, directing his sailors to the pirate leader, who gripped the wound in his leg.

Chief Sky knocked the pirate's longsword away and threw him roughly down on his stomach. She grabbed his hands and manacled them behind his back, resting a knee on him before motioning Able Rating Song forward. The medic ripped open his pack and started tending the wound.

So much for the second part of his plan, Liam thought, frowning at the closed airlock. But at least they had a prisoner, and *Storm Wind* now only had a skeleton crew. She'd be easy to capture once Liam got his boats manned.

"Chief Sky," he said, "get the boats ready for boarding."

Without waiting for a reply, he jogged back down to the cafeteria and looked through the door. More lamps were being lit, and the pirate bodies were being expertly searched by Flatrock and Hedge.

Amelia stood nearby, a pistol out and covering in case any of the pirates were not quite as dead as they appeared.

"Everyone all right?" Liam asked the entire room.

"Cafeteria secure, sir," Amelia responded. "No friendly casualties."

"Well done, everyone," he said. "Secure this space and get the team ready for our own boarding of the pirate ship."

His words were punctuated by the sudden roar of *Daring*'s cannon.

It was answered moments later by distant clangs that echoed down the masts. He knew what that meant, and it wasn't good news.

"I'm heading to the bridge," he said.

He hurried back up the corridor, staying clear of the pinned prisoner. The man lay in stoic silence, glaring at Liam with that same zeal seen in too many of these pirates. But there would be time later for interrogation; right now there was a battle underway.

The clang of chain shot smacking against *Daring*'s masts echoed again as Liam hauled himself up the ladder to the gun deck, and then to the bridge. He emerged through the hatch to hear the quick but quiet voices of Riverton and Brown as they maneuvered the ship. The deck started to heel as *Daring* moved into a turn, but Liam could already tell that the movement was sluggish.

Riverton turned at his approach.

"They're shredding our sails," she stated.

He glanced up through the canopy, noting the wild flapping of torn sheets. *Storm Wind* was trying to escape, and slowing her pursuer was now top priority.

"I'm turning to follow," Brown added, "but I'm having trouble catching the bow wind with so much tearage."

"Have we switched to chain shot," Liam asked, "to slow them down?"

"They're already out of range," Riverton replied. "We can pepper them with round shot, but we can't slow them down."

Liam watched as the starscape continued to shift in *Daring*'s broad turn. *Storm Wind* came into view as a silhouette against the glow of the Hub, her shape indicating that she was already turned away.

"Sailing control," Riverton ordered through her comms, "enemy fire has ceased. Get those sails replaced."

"*Yes, ma'am,*" came Swift's reply from below.

"She's a fast ship," Riverton commented. "It's going to be hard to catch her even when we're at full sheet again."

"We captured their leader," Liam offered. "He'll survive for interrogation."

Riverton nodded, her eyes still on the fleeing ship. Liam waited, absently listening to Brown as she coordinated the crew.

"So your little ruse worked?" Riverton asked finally.

"Yes, ma'am. I heard the pirate leader specifically order his men to 'capture that noblewoman.' There's no question they're specifically targeting the aristocracy."

"Is Sublieutenant Templegrey unharmed?"

"Completely. As is Petty Officer Virtue."

"Any other prisoners?"

"No, ma'am. The ambush was overwhelming. No casualties on our side."

"Good." Riverton sat back in her chair. "Get the prisoner secured. Then stand down your team for now. It's going to take a while to catch our prey."

"Yes, ma'am."

Liam cast another glance toward the distant silhouette of the pirate ship, her four masts at full sail as she tacked against the steady wind pushing out from the Hub. It was a slower course than simply turning Halo-bound and putting the wind behind you, but Liam could see from the lie of the sheets that *Storm Wind* was cutting across the headwind efficiently. *Daring*'s sails were larger but not as nimble, and it would no doubt take all of Brown's skill to close the distance.

But Liam had faith that they would hunt their quarry down.

AMELIA READ THROUGH THE LAST LINES OF THE stores report on her screen, satisfied that all was well. The ship's sudden departure from Cornucopia III had made it impossible for her to meet the captain's order for forty-five days' worth of rations, but their quick port visit to Windfall had allowed her to make up the shortfall. If there was anything she hated about her job as quartermaster, it was being unable to comply with the captain's orders. Otherwise, she thought as she stood up and stretched, she pretty much loved her job. This office was her own private kingdom, the cargo bays her dominions. She did a twirl in the middle of the room, much as Templegrey had done when she danced with Liam.

Amelia's eyes came to rest on the ball gown that still hung on the bulkhead behind the door. She smiled when she thought of the first part of that night, at how beautiful she'd felt and how handsome Liam had looked. And that ballroom looking out across the shimmering lake . . . what a magical setting.

Her smile faded, though, as the later images of the evening flooded her mind. The host of the party executed in front of them all; Silverhawk's sinister smile and his threats toward Commander Riverton. She tried to block them out with images of the dancing, regretting not accepting Liam's invitation to that first dance. Humming a tune to herself she moved through the steps again, remembering how Templegrey had added style and flourish to each step and gesture. Amelia imagined herself in Liam's arms, gliding through the dance together.

But her mind kept going back to memory, and to Ava Templegrey in his arms. They'd been the picture of elegance after Amelia had failed to step up. Liam had also danced in that ballroom before, she reckoned, with the young Lady Brightlake. If the daughter had possessed any of the good looks of her mother, with that fiery red hair . . . Amelia abruptly stopped her practice, her arms falling flat against her sides.

It was one thing to recognize a rival for her man, but how was Amelia supposed to compete with a ghost? She sighed, wondering once again how much longer Liam would spend with a crass commoner like her. He certainly hadn't stopped Ava from flirting with him that evening in the senior mess. Had she met with him on other occasions to convince him of her suggestion?

Amelia was being silly, she knew, and staying cooped up by herself in here wasn't helping. She needed to get back to her crowd.

The ship was technically still in battle, she realized as she stepped out into the main passageway and spotted the closed airlock doors in either direction. The chase of *Storm Wind* was now in its twentieth hour, but while progress was being made it was still at least another watch until things got interesting again. She'd managed to get a few hours' sleep once the adrenaline of battle had given way to exhaustion but sleep never came easily when the enemy was near. Checking stores always made her feel better, and with her little kingdom sorted she moved with easy purpose up the decks to the senior mess.

As she pushed open the door she heard Charlotte Brown's familiar voice.

"Are you kidding? We heard it all the way up on the bridge!"

Laughter washed over Amelia as she stepped into the space, and she noticed all eyes were on a smug-looking Templegrey seated with the others at the table.

"Classical training in song is essential for any lady," she replied, eyes sparkling as she spotted Amelia. She offered a friendly smile, then turned back to Brown, Sky, and, next to her at the head of the table, Liam.

"So you were trained in singing Theropod songs?" Liam said. "That's about what those screams sounded like."

Templegrey folded her arms in a big show of pouting.

Liam rubbed her back, Amelia noticed.

"I'm sure my partner in the trap would agree my performance was most convincing?" Templegrey offered to Amelia.

"Truly impressive," Amelia replied, reaching for the coffee. "It nearly made my ears bleed."

She appreciated the laughter as she turned away and poured herself a drink. All just good, friendly banter after a stressful situation. Usually now someone would take a shot at her, or Brown, but Amelia felt a sudden urge to maintain the current target.

"You didn't make this, did you?" she said to Temple-grey, hefting her coffee.

More laughter filled the room as Templegrey shook her head.

"I've been banned from ever undertaking that task again," she said with a sigh.

The sudden warble of the comms system caught everyone's attention. Liam reached for the handset.

"Senior mess, XO . . . I'll be right there." He rose from his seat, glancing at everyone. "We're still hours from intercept, but the bridge reports that another ship is closing the pirates fast."

He strode for the door, the others rising to follow. Amelia put down her mug and slipped in close behind him. They ascended the two decks to the bridge, and as soon as her vision adjusted to the glare through the canopy Amelia made her way forward. Swift had the watch, and Riverton was in her command chair.

Liam exchanged quick words with Swift, tactical information that was too brief and specialized for Amelia to follow. He grabbed a telescope from the officer of the watch console and scanned ahead. Within moments Brown and Templegrey also had telescopes up, and Amelia felt like she was missing the party. Glancing around, she found a spare viewing device.

The telescopes always surprised her by how heavy they were. The outer casing was solid brass and the lenses were no doubt thick, but she suspected that it was the microcomputer innards that really added to the heft. She extended the device out and lifted it to her eye.

It took a moment to adjust to the narrow view filled with stars, but Amelia remembered what Liam had taught her. There were almost always stars in view— they lived in a galactic cluster, after all—but the trick was to look for the shadows among the stars. Ships often appeared as holes in the starscape where their bulk occulted the distant light. Peeking around the bridge she noticed that everyone was looking dead ahead, and maybe slightly to port. She moved her telescope slowly across the sky.

There! The unmistakable cross-shape of a sailing ship came into view. It was big, suggesting it was close. She could see all four masts clearly, meaning the vessel was pointed either directly toward her or directly away. She guessed that this was *Storm Wind,* its sails straining to starboard as it ran abeam of the wind. Amelia looked up through the bridge canopy and saw *Daring*'s own top-mast and the sails billowing in a similar manner.

"Stars, she's fast," Liam muttered.

Amelia lowered her telescope, noting that his own instrument was pointed more to port.

"She's riding a stern wind," Riverton replied, "full sheet."

"I can actually see her moving across the starscape," Liam commented.

That last sentence obviously meant something important, but Amelia didn't follow until she stepped close to Liam, pointed her telescope down the same bearing as his, and realized how easily she was able to lock onto the new vessel.

"Usually at these distances," he added for her benefit, "we can't see movement. That ship is flying."

"She's a cutter," Brown interjected, telescope still up, "built for speed. I can make out her raked bow, and she has extra sheets extended from her bowsprit."

The ship was wedge-shaped, long and narrow, and from this side view Amelia could see the huge sails straining forward from her masts, and the extra sails ballooning out in front like Brown had described.

"Didn't Dark Star sail in a fast cutter?" she asked. "Maybe this is a rescue ship—they'll abandon the other tub and escape in that little stallion?"

"Possibly," Riverton mused. "What's our time to intercept?"

"Eight hours," Swift replied, "at present speeds."

Amelia stepped aside as Brown eased past her, moving to a large, flat table on the other side of the captain's chair. The table was marked with a series of concentric circles and a starburst of straight lines out from the center. The young sublieutenant placed a ship marker on the table, then a second, to the left. She made a few quick calculations on a wheeled device, then measured the distance between the two ship markers.

"Estimate the cutter will intercept *Storm Wind* in ten minutes," she announced.

Swift muttered something under his breath, but otherwise the officers replied in grim silence.

"Can we go any faster?" Amelia asked.

"No," Swift replied. "We're straining the masts as it is just to maintain pursuit."

"Keep track on the cutter," Liam ordered. "A ship that small can't stay in space for long—it must have a base nearby. If we can—"

"The cutter is opening fire," Riverton interjected.

Telescopes snapped up all around Amelia, with the trained precision of a drill movement. She fumbled to lift her own instrument.

Sure enough, the tell-tale flashes of cannon fire were erupting from the cutter's bow, and even as Amelia watched the sails began to shorten. Then the masts started to retract, lowering to rest snug against the hull. She'd been in enough battles now to recognize the openly aggressive posture being taken, and the continuous flashing of cannon meant that these were no warning shots. *Storm Wind* still looked intact, but even from this distance Amelia could see the flailing of torn sails and the awkward bend of the top mast.

"The pirate's being crippled," she said.

"I don't think this is a rescue," Liam agreed.

"Bad blood between criminals?" Templegrey suggested.

As *Daring* rode the winds there was nothing to do but watch as the cutter slammed into the pirate ship and locked on. All outward violence ceased, but Amelia could well guess that a boarding was underway, and a vicious battle was playing out within those two dark hulls. But because of the great gulf still separating them, there was nothing to do but watch and wait.

"Both ships have slowed," Swift reported. "Our estimated intercept is now four hours."

Eventually the watch turned and new sailors started taking their stations, but it was obvious none of the senior staff were leaving. Swift had a brief conversation with Templegrey to hand over duties of officer of the watch, but other than handing over the belt with pistol and saber, neither of them moved or eased up their monitoring of the situation. The series of standard reports from the new watch to Templegrey were a familiar buzz of routine and Amelia barely listened.

Finally, after nearly three hours, and with the locked ships large enough to see with the naked eye, the lookout reported new flashes from the cutter. They were quickly identified as thrusters, and the smaller ship pulled away from its prey. It drifted clear and began extending its masts.

"Are we within weapons range?" Liam asked.

"Missiles, yes," Templegrey replied, "but not cannon."

Missiles were a last resort, Amelia knew. *Daring* only carried eight of the long-range weapons, and the destructive power of a single shot could easily tear a civilian ship to shreds. They were for self-defense, and only in extremis.

"Keep track on the cutter," he ordered. "Let's see if we can catch her before she can build up speed."

"Yes, sir."

Amelia felt the deck sway as *Daring* strained against the stiffening wind, heard the masts creak as she leaned into her pursuit.

"Captain," Templegrey said suddenly. "Incoming signal from the cutter."

"To us?"

"To you personally, ma'am."

All eyes turned to the captain. If there was any surprise in her heart it was hidden beneath layers of aristocratic training as she turned an icy gaze toward the cutter ahead.

"Let's hear it."

Templegrey spoke over the channel, then activated the speaker.

A crackly voice filled the bridge. "*Commander Riverton, I assume you can hear me?*"

The voice was familiar, even through the static, and Amelia cast Liam a questioning glance. He frowned thoughtfully.

"This is Commander Riverton," the captain replied. "With whom do I speak?"

"*Sophia,*" the voice replied, and even across the vacuum Amelia could sense the sneer, "*you really need to try harder. Perhaps get yourself a faster ship than that miserable old tub. This prize is mine, and mine alone.*"

A blinding flash erupted from the cutter. Before anyone could react a missile smashed into *Storm Wind*. Its hull tore open and the masts spun away into space.

Amelia gasped. No civilian ship should have access to that kind of weaponry. She dimly heard Templegrey sounding the drums to bring the ship to battle stations. Swift and Brown both burst into action, and seconds later Amelia heard the distant whine of the energy weapons spinning up.

"Who is this?" Riverton demanded, her cool voice an eye in the storm around her. "As the captain of His

Majesty's Sailing Ship *Daring* I command you to surrender and prepare to be boarded."

"*No, Commander,*" the voice continued with a sigh, "*you're not giving the orders here. This is Captain Silverhawk of His Majesty's Sailing Ship* Arrow, *and I'm ordering you to stand down and keep clear.*"

Riverton's lips parted slightly, and she blinked several times. Then her eyes narrowed.

"Authentication flags flying on the cutter," Liam reported, telescope to his eye. "They match the code of the day and designate the rank of captain on board."

Riverton sat like a statue for a long moment, staring out at the cutter as it began to unfurl sails.

"Officer of the watch," she ordered, her voice cutting through the din of battle preparations, "come hard right, clear to outside of missile range."

"Yes, ma'am."

Riverton activated the circuit again. "Yes, sir. I am keeping clear."

"*Good girl, Sophia. I look forward to seeing you at the next grand ball. Perhaps I'll have a new outfit made special for it.*"

"Shall we stand down from battle stations, ma'am?" Templegrey asked.

"Not a chance," Riverton snapped. She climbed down from her chair, and Amelia stepped clear as she saw the fury blazing in the captain's eyes.

"Maintain defensive posture," she said, calm returning to her voice, "and hold station on the pirate wreckage outside of missile range. Inform me when *Arrow* has cleared the area."

Riverton's boots thumped loudly on the deck in the sudden quiet. She retreated through the aft door, shutting it gently behind her. In the silence of the bridge Amelia just heard the distant, violent slam of the captain's cabin door.

"Sublieutenant Brown," she heard Liam say behind her, "Sublieutenant Templegrey—we have a shift in our research priorities. Find out what happened to the money of the Brightlake estate."

CHAPTER 6

IF EVER THEY WANTED TO FOLLOW THE FLOW OF money, Liam thought to himself as he stepped through the airlock, a space station like this was a good place to start.

"Wow," he heard beside him, "I think the interior decorators in Windfall Station could use some pointers."

He smiled at Amelia as her large eyes continued to roam upward. Then he followed her gaze to take in the main concourse of the Emperor's Reach space station. Or, at least, the concourse he could see. The broad gallery extended away in both directions, eventually disappearing around the curve of the station's hull. It rose to the height of thirty men, the far wall carved into pointed arches and the clear glass wall behind him revealing the line of ships floating just beyond. The concourse was divided by the dark ribbon of a road, with dockyard workers moving efficiently on this side while townsfolk ambled among the shops on the other. Carriages whisked past as the bustle of the largest station in this corner of the Empire continued at a regular, pulsing pace.

"It helps to be the only safe port within a week's sailing," Liam said, jerking a thumb back toward the ships in the vacuum. "The taxes are high but are preferable to the alternative. The station was a massive investment in its day but the Imperial coffers are overflowing because of it."

"I guess they should really call this one Windfall, then," she offered.

"I think 'Cash Cow' would be more appropriate."

"Speaking of which," she said, nodding toward the shops across the road, "I think I might go amuse myself this evening parting with some of my cash."

"I'd rather you were with me," he said, glancing down at his own dress uniform, then at her casual outfit.

"Me, too," she said. "But you're right—for tonight you need a companion with poise and polish. I'll drown my sorrows in a mountain of new clothes."

"You'd fit right in among the noble circles," he chuckled.

"I see that the captain agreed with your recommendation. The division of prize money was a welcome surprise, but not so much that sailors will lose their minds."

"I hope you're right." Liam looked out at the vast concourse, then back toward the ship. "But it wasn't my idea, if you recall."

A flourish of movement caught his eye and he saw Ava Templegrey stepping across the brow and onto the station. She was wearing a ball gown of deep blue, with golden highlights and accessories that matched her hair. As she approached her legs were hidden beneath the voluminous skirts, so that she seemed to float rather than walk.

"Oh," Amelia said as Templegrey glided up to them, "you look absolutely beautiful."

"Thank you, darling," she said with her habitual smile, reaching out to brush her fingers over Amelia's cheek. "And you look adorable as ever."

Liam couldn't help but agree. It really didn't matter what Amelia was wearing or doing—his heart leaped whenever he saw her. On an impulse he took her hand and kissed it.

"Have fun with your shopping. Don't stay out too late."

"I was going to say the same to you!" She laughed. "Fancy, swanky, gala ball and everything."

Liam shrugged, knowing that this was a working evening. It would have been a lot more fun to have Amelia along, but they had all agreed that tonight was about staying low-key. Having a vivacious commoner would only draw eyes and set tongues wagging. He gestured grandly to his companion.

"Our carriage awaits, Lady Templegrey."

As the doctor rustled past in her gown, Liam gave Amelia's hand another squeeze. He turned to go, but her grip was suddenly fierce, holding him in place. He glanced at her.

"One request," she whispered suddenly.

"Of course."

"No dancing. The next one is for me."

He grinned instinctively, but the sudden earnestness of her gaze sobered his reaction. He nodded. "The next dance is yours, darling."

She blinked, then her usual smirk emerged again. She smacked him on the butt. "On your way then, Lord Blackwood."

He hurried to catch Templegrey, reaching the carriage first and offering his hand to help her in. He climbed up, taking the seat facing her in the small compartment. He looked out the window to where Amelia watched, and beyond through the glass to the dusty, bulky hull of *Daring*. The ship had berthed under her own name this time and the crew were free to take shore leave. It was a relief to not have to play the role of Captain Julian Stonebridge for this visit, but as he turned his mind to the mission this evening, Liam knew it was no time to relax.

Templegrey gazed out the window toward the shops as the carriage started to roll forward.

"I do envy Amelia," she mused suddenly. "I'd rather go shopping than endure another ball."

Bejeweled and bedecked, she looked the very image of a noble lady. But her expression was severe and her eyes were hard. Liam recognized the significance of this moment: alone in the carriage, away from all prying eyes, she was dropping her noble façade. It was something she rarely did even in the ship, and it spoke volumes to the trust she had in him.

"Why don't you two make a date of it tomorrow?" he suggested.

"Don't tempt me, Liam," she said, her eyebrow arching. "And I think she'd rather have the date with you."

"Yes, but then I'd have to go shopping."

She laughed appreciatively.

"Why the new dress?" he asked. "I thought you'd want to show off your Imperial gown again."

"We said this was all about blending in," she replied, her gaze drifting down. "I love that gown, but it would draw too much attention. With this"—she plucked at the folds of fabric—"I'm just another lady at the ball."

"Shall we separate to cover more ground? I wouldn't want to get in the way of your charms."

"I'd prefer," she said, with a sudden sharp look, "if you stay close, actually. Whenever I work a room alone it sends a message that I'm looking for a husband."

"Hmm. But if we're together, might it start a rumor of an impending union of the Blackwood and Templegrey families?"

"You could do worse," she quipped. "But honestly, rumors will start based on anything, even the color of my dress—those vapid fops die without gossip. If they want to whisper about you and me, it will keep them busy and buy me more time."

"Time for what?"

"Time for not being married." She sighed, staring out the window again as the bright interior of the station rolled by. "Studying medicine gave me an excuse, and serving in the Navy will give me a few more years. But eventually I'll be married off, and then what fun will that be?"

Arranged marriages were perhaps Liam's least favorite topic of conversation and he pushed down the sudden rush of old anger. The reaction surprised him. Templegrey's expression shifted and she stared at him curiously.

"No fun at all," he said finally. "I remember well being paraded around as a youth to grand balls, like a stallion in the market—but my older brother had it far worse. Are you the eldest?"

"Eldest daughter. And therefore the key to securing future wealth for the house Templegrey. If only our prize money was as life-changing for us as it is for the common sailors." She sighed and stared out the window again. "Eventually I'll have to do what every fine lady does for her family, and marry money."

Liam really did not like where this conversation was leading, and he tried to blank his mind.

"We'll have to find Lord Grandview early," he said, switching topics, "before too many other people start demanding his time."

"And let's hope Silverhawk isn't on the guest list. His ship is still in port."

Daring had shadowed *Arrow* all the way back from the attack on *Storm Wind,* the frigate's sails better suited to sailing into the wind than the cutter's. Riverton had berthed her ship on the opposite side of the vast station from Silverhawk's, and hopefully the vain lord would be too concerned with himself to pay them attention.

"You think he'll even notice us?"

"One must be prepared," she said with a tiny shrug. She lifted her eyes to meet his, a startling, vivid blue, and her lips parted in a perfect smile.

The moment of candor was over, he realized, watching her noble persona emerge once again. Her expression settled into one of regal contentment. She was right, he knew, and he had to get himself into the proper mindset. He pushed out all thoughts of arranged marriages and pirate missions, and began to think tactically like a courtier.

The carriage ride was surprisingly long, the docks on the outward side of the concourse giving way first to exclusive shops, then clubs, and finally residences. The carriage pulled to a stop in front of a façade elegantly crafted to look like a large manor house, complete with upper floor windows and real wooden trim. Liam climbed out and helped Templegrey down, offering his arm to her as they approached the grand double doors. There were the usual announcements, the receiving line with the hosts—a lord and lady from deep within the Hub, enjoying a leisurely tour of the inner Halo—and finally they stepped through into the ballroom.

The outer wall was mostly transparent, the station's hull cut into an undulating, wavelike form that gave stunning views of the Hub. No artificial lights were needed in the vast room as starlight flooded across the intricate patterns wrought into the floor and illuminated the banners of the Empire hung proudly. The guests moved among the brilliant rays, long shadows casting an ephemeral, dancing spell over the chamber.

"How lovely," Templegrey commented as she strolled on Liam's arm toward the outer windows. "But I confess I preferred the view from the Brightlake home. It was warmer, more welcoming."

She didn't know it, but Templegrey was slipping knife after knife into Liam.

"Yes," he said stiffly, "it was a beautiful home."

"And now seized by that wretched Silverhawk," she said, her grip suddenly tightening on his arm. "It's quite the scandal, and many noble houses are worried."

"Are there lots of debts?"

"Oh, yes. There always are, but until now it's always just been another form of influence and favors. No lender ever demanded repayment of the coin—the debt just became leverage in the never-ending game of scheming and one-upmanship that is the Imperial court. To have one of the major houses so humiliated and bankrupted . . ."

"So, this might happen again, to another house?" Out on distant Passagia, the Blackwood family rarely if ever had financial dealings with the inner houses.

She nodded. "The extravagances of court get more expensive every year. For any house wishing to maintain a presence there, it can be crippling."

"But houses do it to protect their reputation," he mused, understanding if not agreeing.

"I feel sorry for the poor Brightlakes. It's one thing to be in financial trouble, but to have your family name so disgraced . . ."

A turmoil of emotion churned through Liam.

Memories of so many happy days at the Brightlake estate overwhelmed his mental defenses and flooded into his mind's eye. He let himself embrace it all for a moment, then pushed it aside.

"They were a loyal family," he said finally, "steeped in tradition. They did not deserve this fate."

"How did you know them?"

"For a time," he said, "as a young man, I was a frequent visitor to their house. I . . . knew Lady Zara best."

"Oh." Templegrey rested her free hand on his. "I see."

"But soon enough she married one Lord Fairfield," he said, giving her a sympathetic smile. "Another arranged marriage for the good of the dynasty."

"I have my own personal connection to that, Liam," she said, her expression sad.

"How so?"

"Fairfield was my father's cousin," she continued. "I don't remember him—he and Lady Fairfield died when I was just a girl."

"You're related to Fairfield?" he asked tonelessly, managing to not spit the name.

"Well, yes, but they're all gone now, aren't they? Such a terrible loss, that storm."

Liam knew that the proper reaction to this was polite interest—an interesting connection but old news. But after so long, it still hurt too much.

Templegrey watched him for a moment but said nothing more. Instead she snapped her fingers at a nearby servant, who brought them drinks.

"To success in our mission, Lord Blackwood," she said, lifting her glass, "and to much wealth, happiness, and peace for us all."

"To success," he echoed. He drained the glass, then looked anew across the ballroom.

"SO DID THEY HAVE ANY GOOD BEER AT THAT swanky ball you went to?"

Amelia laughed at the question, putting down the shoes she'd been admiring. Able Rating Hedge—or just her old buddy Mia Hedge, this afternoon—stood across from her, holding up a pair of gaudy slippers as she waited for an answer. She made the slippers dance in the air.

"Did you have to spin and twirl until everyone puked?"

"No, they didn't have any good beer," Amelia replied with a grin, "and there was twirling on offer but I didn't indulge. I didn't want to puke on my dress."

"What fun is that?" Hedge scoffed, tossing down the shoes.

They'd been roaming the high street for several hours, just happy to get off the ship. Hedge had a full pouch of coins she was determined to part with this evening, but whether it was on clothes or booze she wasn't too fussed. So far they'd sampled a bit of both.

"I think I'm going to get something like these," Amelia mused, holding up a pair of dark brown boots that felt comfy but were strong enough to take the abuse of shipboard life. She glanced over to the rear part of the store, where the cobbler was hard at work. "Let me see if he's got some to fit me."

"You do that, and I'll check out the dress shop next door."

Hedge took her cloth sacks filled with shopping treasures and strolled out the door. Amelia showed her boots to the cobbler, who told her that he could make her a custom pair and deliver it to her ship in the morning. He expertly measured her, confirmed her choice from a selection of materials, and wrote up a receipt noting her down payment, all the while maintaining a pleasant hum of conversation. As she left the store, Amelia felt like she was the most important person in the world.

Yes, she admitted to herself as she entered the dress shop, she could get used to a life of privilege. She scanned the vibrant colors all around her: bolts of fabric, sketches of finished gowns, and, of course, a beautiful selection of dresses to admire.

Hedge was at the rear of the shop, already trying on a dress. She shifted and turned in front of a long mirror, examining herself from every angle. Her pretty face was screwed up in thought and she glanced at Amelia.

"What do you think?"

It wasn't her style at all, Amelia could see. But then again, all the fashions in a place like Emperor's Reach were like nothing they had back home on Passagia. Still . . .

"Hedgie, you're beautiful enough to make anything work, but you might be a bit too buxom for that dress."

Hedge cackled. "Isn't that what I'm going for?"

"Yes, but . . ." Amelia looked closely, trying to figure out exactly why it didn't work. The dress was simply cut for a woman of slimmer build—a waif who'd never even sniffed at real work let alone done any. Hedge's broad shoulders, powerful arms, and thick legs just wanted to burst through that thin fabric. "I'm worried that you'll tear it the first evening out."

"Better for a fancy ball than a night at the pub, eh?"

"I think so."

"Yeah. Let me try another."

As Hedge went behind the privacy screen, Amelia let her eyes drift across the gorgeous fabrics displayed along the wall. One side of the store offered completed outfits, but clearly this tailor did custom jobs as well. The woman herself was seated behind a broad work-table, humming to herself as she wove a delicate thread.

"You still got that gown in the stores office?" Hedge called from behind the screen.

"Yes, and I'm sure it will see plenty more action."

"I thought you needed a new dress for every event?"

"That's why I go to different planets for each one— same dress, different crowd."

Hedge poked her head around the screen, pointing. "Hey, Virts, get me that blue one."

She pulled the indicated dress off its hanger and handed it over. Not content to listen to Hedge's soft curses as she fought with the unfamiliar garb, Amelia wandered over to the bolts of fabric. She saw a deep, almost starry black at one end, and it made her think of Riverton's and Templegrey's stunning gowns at the Brightlake ball.

"Excuse me," she asked the tailor, "but have you ever made an Imperial gown?"

The woman looked up in mild surprise.

"I have," she replied, her eyes clearly assessing Amelia's likely worth. "But they're very rare."

"Could you use that black for the lower part?"

She studied the fabric for a moment. "Hmm. Normally, an Imperial gown requires a deeper black . . . but I see what you're thinking. It would be unorthodox, but beautiful."

"How do you get the colors to blend so smoothly in such a gown? I just can't figure it out."

"A trade secret, my dear," she said with a smile. "But I appreciate you noticing."

Hedge burst forth to show off her latest consideration.

"What do you think?" she asked as she sized herself up in the mirror.

The dress was more full-bodied and definitely more discreet in hemlines than the previous one.

"Not bad at all," Amelia said.

"You're so lovely," the tailor offered. "And that dress could be adjusted to match your figure perfectly."

"Yeah?" Hedge grinned at her own reflection.

"May I?" The tailor rose from her chair and approached Hedge, wrapping a measuring tape over her shoulders and holding a box of pins.

Amelia looked through the other dresses on display while the tailor made adjustments on Hedge. There were some beautiful outfits, but she really couldn't justify spending the money on another fancy gown when she had one hanging up on the ship. Maybe Ava could afford to have a new frock for every ball, but Amelia preferred to make good use of her existing supplies.

"Did you see Lady Templegrey as she left the ship today?" she asked suddenly.

"Yeah," Hedge replied. "I'd be happy to take her cast-offs. Like that amazing dress she had when you guys were on Cornucopia."

"Oh, that's her Imperial gown. I'm surprised she didn't wear it again tonight."

"She never wears anything twice, I'm sure."

"But I thought an Imperial gown was a uniform, so it could be worn again."

"Oh, yes," the tailor replied, adjusting the hem at Hedge's ankle. "An Imperial gown is the investment of a lifetime. It's a dress intended to be worn many times. I'd hope so, for the cost."

"How much do they cost?"

The tailor glanced up at Amelia, a sparkle in her eyes. "Do you really want to know?"

"I kinda do."

"About twenty thousand."

Amelia couldn't stop the gasp as her jaw dropped open. She'd been ready for a big number, but that was the equivalent of a full load of supplies for *Daring*. It was more money than most people would see in a lifetime.

"It appears," she managed to say, "that Lady Templegrey has a different perspective on money from us."

"You just figuring that out now, sister?" Hedge scoffed.

"Well, I . . ."

"You've been hanging out in that senior mess too long. I know we don't really see their wealth when we're in space, but come alongside, and . . . we might be on the same planet, but we're in different worlds."

Amelia thought back to the Brightlake estate, the most beautiful setting she'd ever seen. And that apparently belonged to a midlevel noble. Riverton and Templegrey both came from even wealthier families, and the Blackwoods couldn't be that far behind.

"Don't sweat it, Virts," Hedge said, not unkindly. "I know they're your posse on the ship, but just remember that this is the real world we're in now. I'm sure Templegrey and the XO are being fed champagne from the hands of scantily dressed servants right now."

Amelia doubted that, but she felt herself reddening as she imagined Liam and Ava gliding their way through another grand ball.

"Well, they're working this evening," she said, as much to herself as Hedge. "They won't have time for scantily dressed servants."

"Ha! You remember that pretty boy noble we had on the ship months back? You gave me the best advice when you told me to keep clear of him. You were right—he was nothing but bad news."

"Yeah, he was."

"So take your own advice," Hedge continued, smiling warmly. "Keep clear of the noblemen. They all eventually get married off to noblewomen, anyway."

"What?"

"It's that arranged marriage thing they do," she scoffed. "Do you think any of them actually marry the people they like? Trust me, the only real freedom we commoners have is the freedom to marry whatever idiot we want."

It was, Amelia suddenly realized, a topic Liam had never brought up. Not that she was expecting a marriage proposal or anything, but . . . what were his intentions?

"I know you still have a crush on the XO," Hedge blathered on, "and I think honestly he might be a little sweet on you—I notice these things. But don't chase the dream, honey. His family will have already decided who he's marrying."

She reminded herself firmly that Hedge knew nothing about how the nobility really worked. She turned away, focusing on the sketches of gowns mounted on the wall.

One in particular caught her attention, bold for its stark quality. The sketch showed the front of a pure white dress with a vertical black line bisecting it and a horizontal black line around the waist. It was almost like a black cross . . . or, she suddenly realized, a dark star. She stared at it, finally noticing the trim line of gold mixed with a deep red. Was this a message, or just a popular design? Amelia wasn't sure which idea frightened her more.

"Come on," she said suddenly, "buy that dress and let's get out of here. There's more shopping to be done."

THE BALLROOM WAS ENORMOUS BUT AS THE HUN-dreds of guests made their way in it began to fill up.

It was the usual extravagance of dandies with the odd uniform mixed in, and Liam scanned the military personnel. Sure enough, over by the largest punch bowl, he spotted a familiar figure moving through the crowd. Moving toward him, he realized without surprise. Rear Admiral Lord William Grandview's eyes met his and he guided Templegrey toward the edge of the broad windows, into one of the deeper shadows near the wall.

Lord Grandview moved with his usual purpose, his long legs propelling a broad form bristling with honors and awards from a lifetime of service to the Emperor. His craggy face was fixed in a magnanimous expression as he offered greetings to everyone he passed, even as his pace barely slowed. A member of the highest noble house on Passagia and the senior officer for this entire region of space, he was a man worth knowing.

Liam bowed as Grandview strode up to them, sensing Templegrey curtsey beside him. The admiral turned his body to face the windows, as if he was enjoying the view, but his eyes locked onto Liam's.

"Splendid to see you," he said quietly. "You have news of your search?"

As the senior officer in charge of *Daring*'s mission, Grandview was the only person outside the Emperor's inner circle who knew its true purpose. He had staked his own reputation on Riverton and Liam, and while their successes to date had made everyone wealthier, the threat to the Empire was still real. If further success wasn't realized soon, pressure from the court might jeopardize them all.

"We do, sir," Liam replied, giving a quick summary of the most recent intelligence in their hunt for Dark Star. The criminal organization was far-reaching, but was definitely centered in the Halo, with Silica still a main concentration, Morassia a potential hotbed, and Honoria a possible target. Their recent maneuvers had confirmed that Dark Star's people were specifically hunting the aristocracy, but their exact political agenda was still unclear.

"I've also heard about increased pirate activity in Morassia," Grandview said. "That might be worth investigating further."

"Yes, sir. The captain is supervising the transfer of our prisoners from *Black Hand* and *Storm Wind* into Imperial custody today," Liam replied, "and I'm sure her friends in intelligence will uncover more secrets than we were able to. Our own efforts continue."

"Well," the admiral said, turning to face him fully, "they're going to have to continue faster. The Emperor is much more concerned about this Dark Star than perhaps he once was. When we started this mission, Dark Star was simply a criminal kingpin undercutting His Majesty's legitimate revenues. Now, it seems, there is something much more seditious happening."

"Sir?"

"Over the past two months no less than four Imperial treasure forts have been attacked. The attacks were repelled, but my people have noticed a pattern. Each time, the raiders got one step closer to success. They weren't actually defeated or captured, but rather they withdrew."

"Almost like they were testing each stage of the defenses."

"Yes. Common brigands do not operate with this level of coordination. Dark Star is clearly planning something, and your intelligence now confirms the treasury on Honoria seems to be the target."

"What would an attack on that treasury mean for the Empire?"

"Chaos. For starters, there would be no money to pay for the Navy. That could be dealt with by credit notes, but a larger problem would result. The entire noble class would be scrambling to protect their assets—which would mean loans being called, investments canceled, jobs lost. Entire worlds could be left destitute as the high lords defended their fortunes. There is, frankly, no better way to cripple the Empire than by distracting and disrupting our peers. I don't know how long this plan has been in motion, but it speaks to a long game."

"Agreed, sir. Now that we know which ships are regularly involved in the smuggling, we were able to search back through Imperial records and track their movements. It's hard to pinpoint exactly, but the first indications of coordination between at least three of these vessels date back over twelve years."

Grandview's eyes widened slightly.

"So Dark Star is entrenched," he said, "and spreading across the Halo."

"Well, sir," Liam added, "we think that Windfall Station in Silica is still a major hub for Dark Star's organization and we intend to return with haste to continue our masquerade."

"Be careful. There have been whispers through the alleyways of the Halo about *Sophia's Fancy*. Your disguise may not last much longer."

"Yes, sir. We have a few solid connections at Windfall that I'd like to exploit at least once more. After that, we'll drop our current identity and begin with a new one—perhaps at Morassia."

"Good. I'll be deploying with a squadron of corvettes to the area," Grandview added. "Not much armament in a pitched battle, but fast. If you need help, you send word to me and we'll come."

"Much appreciated, sir. I suspect Dark Star will have more forces than *Daring* can handle on our own."

"The enemy forces are too widespread to counter everywhere. We need to chop off the head of this threat."

"Sir," Templegrey interjected, "we have a new problem: Captain Silverhawk."

Grandview shook his head in disgust. "That idiot is in disgrace with the Navy after wrecking his last ship. I made sure that he was kept clear of any space-going command."

"Sublieutenant Templegrey is correct, sir," Liam said, surprised at her outburst. He'd intended to brief Grandview on that next. "He now commands a fast cutter and he disrupted our last pursuit, killing the pirate crew and destroying evidence."

The admiral stood in silence for a moment, processing this news.

"Why would he do that?" Liam asked.

"And how did he get a ship?" Grandview echoed, his face darkening.

"It's not a class I recognized," Liam admitted. "Not a standard Navy hull. Very fast and not many cannon but armed with missiles."

"What the deuce is that idiot up to?" Grandview muttered.

Liam felt Templegrey's hand tighten on his arm again.

"I guess we can ask him ourselves," she said quickly.

Liam looked up in time to see a tall, uniformed officer walking toward them. It took him a moment to recognize Silverhawk, his shock of sandy-blond hair now short and black. He carried a drink in his hand and there was a slight wobble to his stride, but his eyes were fixed in a predatory gleam.

Grandview turned, offering Silverhawk a stony glare.

"Captain Silverhawk," he boomed, "I'm surprised to see you here."

"I was in the area, Lord Grandview," he said breezily, his gaze passing from the admiral, to Liam, and resting on Templegrey. "Not showing off your opulent wealth, Ava, with that gorgeous Imperial gown I saw you in at . . . oh, where was it? The Brightlakes'?"

"I chose restraint this evening, Lord Silverhawk," she said, curtseying.

"Wise," he said, taking another drink, "but too late. I already looked into your sudden source of wealth."

"I understand you interfered with a priority Navy mission, Captain," Grandview said, stepping forward.

"Not at all," Silverhawk replied lightly. "In fact, I was merely following my own orders."

"What orders?" Grandview scoffed. "HMSS *Daring* is undertaking a mission of extreme importance to His Majesty, and you are well-advised to leave her to it."

"A mission of extreme importance, yes." Silverhawk finished his drink with a flourish and handed the glass to Templegrey. "So important that His Imperial Majesty has decided that *Daring* isn't up to the task."

"What are you talking about?"

Liam stiffened as Silverhawk undid a button in his tunic and reached within. The captain pulled out a folded parchment with great ceremony and offered it to the admiral.

"I truly wish Sophia was here for this moment," Silverhawk mused as Grandview scanned the document. "I'd love to see even a hint of expression on her face."

Grandview handed Liam the parchment. The Imperial seal was large and clear at the bottom, and as Liam read the script he sensed an awful familiarity. The words were virtually identical to *Daring*'s own letter of marque.

"So you're not the only ones free to make a fortune while you serve the Emperor," Silverhawk said in triumph, snatching the parchment back and replacing it in his tunic. "And as you've clearly been ineffective to date, I'll be picking up the slack."

"You report to me, Captain Silverhawk," Grandview said, his face tightening, "and I never authorized this."

"Your quaint, Halo notions of authority amuse me, William. I served under your command at my own noble whim." He tapped his chest. "This comes directly from the Imperial court, where true power lies."

"As does our letter of marque," Liam stated firmly, "so we stand on the same authority, Captain."

"For now."

"And you carry the same risks as we do. If you fail, there will be no court, no rank, nor title that will protect you."

Silverhawk paused, his eyes narrowing. Then he stepped forward, his own face closing right in to Liam's.

"Then I shall not fail." Stepping back, he flicked a finger under Templegrey's chin in a mockery of an affectionate gesture. "Enjoy the evening, everyone."

He turned and strolled off.

Liam clenched his fists at his sides and held his tongue. Silverhawk was his superior, in both rank and title, and there was nothing more he could say that would matter. It was maddening, but it was the system they lived under.

"I'm going to investigate this," Grandview muttered. "Send Commander Riverton to see me before you depart."

"Yes, sir," Liam said as Grandview marched away.

"What are we going to do now?" Templegrey asked.

"We're going to double our efforts," Liam said, channeling his anger into action. "We're going to work this room, find out if any other ships have been attacked recently, where, and to whom they belonged. I want to figure out if Dark Star is targeting certain families, or just a certain region."

"No one will admit to that," she warned.

"No," he replied, taking her arm and guiding her back into the bright starlight, "but rumors abound, and there will be plenty of people willing to share gossip about someone else's misfortune."

"Quite right, darling," she said with a forced smile. "But this is going to be a long night."

CHAPTER 7

AMELIA HAD DECIDED THAT SHE HAD A NEW FAVOR-
ite port to visit. Emperor's Reach was clean, safe, friendly,
full of fun, and stuffed with the most amazing things to
buy, brought in from all across the Empire. Her shopping
expedition yesterday had revealed gifts for her entire
family, a collection of new clothes for her, and even
a special surprise for Liam. As she stood on the jetty
looking back at the boulevard, snug in her new boots just
delivered by the cobbler, she let out a satisfied smile. Yes,
if this was what awaited her farther into the Hub, she had
a new appreciation for the Empire.

"Nice boots, PO," she heard a deep voice call behind her.

Turning, she raised one foot up and admired the
soft, leather finish. Atticus Flatrock was on brow duty,
looking none the worse for wear after his late night
ashore.

"Thanks," she said. "I've been looking for something to wear just around the ship, sturdy but comfortable."

"Sounds like the kind of woman I hope to meet each night ashore."

She smacked him in good humor, rolling her eyes. Up close she could see the redness in his own eyes and the bags beneath them.

"Looks like you found some fun last night. What time did you roll back in?"

"I don't know, end of the mid watch. You should have stayed with us—Hedge even made it to last call without fighting." He suppressed a yawn. "But we weren't the last ones back. The XO and the doctor were just pouring out of their carriage as we crossed the brow."

"Oh?" she said, clamping down her expression. Liam and Ava had been out that late? So much for the gala ball being just about intelligence gathering. Flatrock was watching her, so she forced a wry grin to her face. "Were they still dancing and prancing as they came up the jetty?"

"The XO was practically carrying our young doctor," he laughed. "Probably tucked her right into bed as soon as they were aboard."

Amelia flushed, and she turned away from Flatrock, barking a laugh as she strode through the airlock tube that served as the brow.

Inside the ship, all was quiet. The second day of a port visit was always a rest day, with only essential duty watch personnel required to be out of their bunks. As XO, Liam was always sympathetic to the realities of crew life—an attitude that had made him popular—but as she stormed up through the decks, Amelia suddenly wondered how much of this generosity was fueled by his own selfish desires. Did Liam simply want the freedom to indulge in his own private pleasures? Her legs burned as she flew up another ladder. He certainly hadn't called on her last night. She reached the quarter-deck and marched aft for his cabin door. Her heart suddenly churned as she wondered who she was going to find on the other side of that wooden barrier.

Protocol—and basic courtesy—demanded that she knock and wait. Amelia grabbed the latch and flung the door open, striding in.

Liam was seated in the center of the small space, his white uniform shirt hanging untucked. His long legs were crossed, his booted feet resting on his desk and a tiny wooden box open in his lap. He looked up in surprise at the sudden entrance, but his face melted into a grin.

"Good morning, darling," he said, eyes flicking down to her feet. "New boots?"

Amelia stopped dead, her gaze darting past him to his empty bunk, then behind her as she shut the door. There was no one else here. She looked back at him again and saw his smile fading.

"Is something wrong, Amelia?"

"What time did you get back to the ship?" she barked, hating the harshness of her own words.

"About six bells of the mid watch. Much later than we'd planned but drawing out useful intelligence at a ball requires a lot of patience."

"And a lot of booze, no doubt." Her anger had a full head of steam, but he wasn't giving her an obvious direction for it.

"Not too bad," he said, considering. "Ava and I kept drinks in our hands to be sociable, but we let the fops lose their wits as the night dragged on, while we gathered information from loose tongues."

"Flatrock tells me you and Ava staggered back on board. Perhaps you drank more than you thought."

"We were exhausted," he countered, his face turning to a frown, "but I'd hardly say we were staggering. Flatrock, Hedge, and their mates certainly were, so I think I'm the more reliable witness."

Amelia scanned the cabin again, searching for any ribbons or other signs of Templegrey's presence. Finally her eyes came to rest on the box in his lap that he'd been so engrossed with at her arrival.

"I ask you again, Amelia," he said mildly. "Is something wrong?"

"What's that?" she asked, stabbing a finger.

He lifted the box for her to see. It was no larger than his hand, delicate carvings on each side. The top was fastened by brass hinges and was flipped open to reveal what looked like a diamond broach nestled against red silk padding inside. The central cluster was augmented by four points of a star.

"This is a gift I just received," he said thoughtfully.

"From Ava?" she snapped.

He brought his feet down to the deck with a thump, rising up and stepping back to offer her the chair. He sat down on his bunk and, when she didn't move, gestured for her to sit.

"No, Amelia," he said in a measured tone that couldn't hide his frustration, "not from Ava. Why in all the stars would I get a gift from her?"

Emotions were a difficult business, Amelia knew, and as she finally sat down she felt her anger morph into something else. But she wasn't going to be cowed. She took a deep breath, collecting her thoughts.

"You two have been spending a lot of time together lately," she said. "And I don't like it. I don't like the way she touches you, and how she flirts with you, and how she calls you darling and . . ." She wiped away a sudden, irritating tear. "And how *noble* she is."

Liam's face twisted in genuine surprise.

"Next to her," Amelia said, sagging in the chair, "I'm just a plump, ordinary, uncouth commoner."

"For starters," Liam said, reaching out to take her hand, "you are neither plump nor ordinary—you're stunning and extraordinary. I'll concede that you're uncouth"—his sudden smile robbed the words of any malice—"but there is nothing common about you."

"But I'm hardly a good match for a lord," she countered. "I'm sure you and Lady Templegrey were the talk of the ball as the new power couple. An ideal match for the next arranged marriage."

Liam's grip slipped away, and she could see him tense at her words.

"And now, suddenly," he muttered, "you're an expert in arranging marriages?"

"I think the whole thing is stupid! But I know that you all have to do it eventually."

"You don't know anything," he said, his eyes burning.

She knew she'd crossed a line, knew she should back off. But she had enough anger still in her to push forward.

"Why do you never talk about marriage?" she demanded. "Why do you never tell me what your family intentions are? You're not yet married, and you're getting old. It's bound to happen soon."

"How dare you . . ."

"So is this why Ava's here, on this ship? To test for suitability?"

"Enough!"

His voice was deafening in the cabin. He sat ramrod straight, one hand gripping the edge of the bunk as the other looked ready to crush the wooden box.

Finally, he stood, barely even looking at her.

"Get out of my cabin," he said simply.

Amelia closed her eyes to stop the tears. She blinked them away as she rose from the chair and headed for the door, her heart pounding. Her stomach churned as she stepped out into the passageway, and she fought the urge to vomit right there on the deck. She managed to get to the ladder and descend toward her own cabin.

Why did she say that? How had this entire situation gotten so quickly out of control? What was wrong with her?

"Darling," a familiar female voice said behind her, "is everything all right?"

She spun around and saw Templegrey just emerging from sickbay. She was wearing her duty uniform, her hair tucked neatly up in an efficient style that no doubt made her job easier. But also somehow looked fabulous as it showed off her elegant neck.

"No," Amelia said, stepping forward. "Everything is not all right, *darling*."

An arched eyebrow was Templegrey's only visible reaction to the spat salutation, but she stepped back into sickbay and motioned for Amelia to follow.

"Let's talk about it, then, Petty Officer Virtue."

Amelia followed her through, shutting the door behind her. Sickbay was deserted, the six bunks empty of patients and none of the medical assistants around. Templegrey moved to the center of the room, casting an assessing eye over Amelia.

"You look very upset," she said carefully. "Do you want to tell me why?"

They were just all so polite, these nobles, Amelia thought, trying to keep her anger going but unable to find the strength. They were all trained from birth to deal with people like her, and she didn't stand a chance in their world.

"I guess," she said finally, "that I just want to be heard. Maybe I can't stop the process of arranged noble marriages from rolling forward, but I don't like it at all."

Templegrey's expression furrowed. "I don't like it, either. But why is this so vexing to you?"

"If you and Liam are going to be married off, just tell me now. And I'll be on my way."

"What?" Templegrey's shocked voice rang through sickbay. She stared at Amelia for a long moment. "I'm not marrying Liam. Where did you get that idea?"

"I don't know how your rituals work, but I see how you can't keep your hands off him, and how you flirt with him. I could see it in how you danced together at the Brightlakes', and who knows what happened last night?"

Templegrey folded her arms, her expression revealing neither the defensiveness nor the aggression Amelia expected. Instead, she looked truly perplexed.

"I danced with him," she said eventually, "because you wouldn't. I looked like I was enjoying it because that's how one dances. As for last night, we both spent our entire time talking to drunken toffs and floozies to gain information about Dark Star's activities. Quite frankly, I would have enjoyed some dancing, and I asked Liam several times, but he refused."

"He refused to dance?"

"Yes, told me he was spoken for. So we kept up our dreary work of chitchat. It was exhausting and I was glad to get to my bunk." She pointed toward her workstation. "I've been writing my report this morning, if you want to review it."

Liam hadn't danced with Ava, Amelia realized, entirely because she'd asked him not to. Her heart at once soared at the thought and sank as she realized just how much trouble she'd caused.

"I'm a fool," she said, tears welling up anew as she stepped forward and grasped Templegrey in a hug. "I'm so sorry."

The doctor's arms wrapped around her, holding her close for a long moment. "What did you think happened?"

Amelia stepped back, wiping her eyes. "I thought you two were becoming an item. And then I thought that maybe you were being arranged to marry each other."

"I see," Templegrey said, allowing a small smile. "I can assure you that the Blackwood family is neither wealthy enough nor prestigious enough for my family to bother with. And I personally have no interest in Subcommander Blackwood romantically."

"Really? But all the flirting . . ."

"A game we nobles play as part of the courtly dance," Templegrey said, folding her arms and looking directly at Amelia. "Let me offer you another assurance. If ever I was intent on breaking up your relationship with Liam, he'd be the one left out in the cold."

Amelia didn't quite catch the meaning for a second. Until she recognized the way Templegrey was looking at her—it was the way men looked at her.

"Oh . . . I didn't know."

"I guess I enjoy flirting with you, too," she said with an elegant shrug. "But I mean nothing by it and if you knew my preferences you might have felt awkward. Trust me, you and Liam can both rest easy in your relationship."

"But you'll marry a man someday, won't you?" Amelia cursed herself inwardly as soon as the words blurted forth.

"Yes," Templegrey sighed, "for dynastic reasons. With luck my family will choose a nice gentleman who prefers the company of gentlemen."

Amelia just wanted to melt away in a puddle of shame. In the space of twenty minutes she'd managed to insult two of the finest people she'd ever met and make a fool of herself.

"I'm so sorry," she said. Then added, "I suck."

Templegrey laughed, but she didn't move in with her typical hand to Amelia's arm. She stayed back, her arms crossed.

"Most of us would say something more pompous like, 'Oh, what poor judgment I have displayed.' . . . You have a much better way with words."

A laugh escaped Amelia's lips, a release of emotion that was quickly replaced by a new feeling of nausea. Because Lady Templegrey was hardly the most injured party this morning.

"I have to head up top," she said, turning toward the door. "And perhaps display some better judgment this time."

She flew up the ladders once again, but whereas her heart had burned on her last ascent, now it constricted in a vise. She reached the quarterdeck, padding aft to the cabin door on the port side. She paused for a moment, catching her breath, then knocked. At the sound of Liam's voice, she turned the latch and opened the door slowly.

He looked up from his chair, his expression descending into a neutral mask.

"I'm sorry," she said. "May I please come in?"

He'd resumed his seated position with his feet up on the desk, and the wooden box was once again in his lap. He set it aside and rose to his feet.

"Of course." He shifted the chair for her and sat back on his bunk.

She sat immediately, leaning forward and clasping her hands together.

"Liam," she began, not even giving him a chance to speak, "I'm so sorry for what I said. For everything I said. I've been unfair, and I know that everything I accused you of was unfounded. Can you please forgive me?"

He looked back at her in silence for a long moment but feeling returned to his expression.

"You are a tempest, Amelia," he said, "and I don't always know how to react."

"That makes two of us," she said. "I want to be with you . . . but your world of nobility still confuses me. I thought it would be wonderful to go to a grand ball, but I feel like we've had nothing but trouble since."

"Why is that?"

"I guess because I worry that I don't speak the right way, and I can't dance the right way, and I can't do doublespeak the right way . . ."

"Those are your best qualities. Please don't ever lose them."

She looked up from her hands and saw the affection in his eyes once again.

"And I say careless, thoughtless things sometimes."

"I forgive you," he said, reaching out both hands to take hers. "I can see how Lady Templegrey might be intimidating, but I swear to you there is nothing going on between us and there never will be. She's a valuable member of my crew, but nothing more."

"I know."

He released her and reached for the wooden box. "But you asked me a fair question about arranged marriages."

"You don't need to explain anything," she said quickly.

"No, I think I do. It makes sense that you would be worried about us, and the possibility of me being stolen away for dynastic reasons."

Sudden fear at the thought clutched her heart. "Is that diamond star a betrothal gift?"

He held it between them, the broach sparkling warmly in the lamplight. When he didn't answer her question right away, she looked up sharply. His expression was clouded with sadness.

"No," he answered. "But it might have been."

"What do you mean?"

"This gift just arrived from Lady Brightlake, the older woman you met, whose husband was killed in front of us. She is now the dowager, watching helplessly as her son oversees the dismantling of their estate to Silverhawk."

"She seemed to think very highly of you when we met."

"She didn't always, but I think I remind her of happier times. Which is why she sent me this."

"It looks like a star reflecting off their lake."

"Yes, and it belonged to their daughter, Lady Zara."

"Oh." Amelia's heart sank. The ghost from Liam's past was here for good, apparently.

"Were you and Zara arranged to be married?"

"No," he said flatly, still staring down.

She started in surprise.

Then he slowly straightened and looked up at her. "Zara and I were in love, and we wanted to marry . . . but dynasty was considered more important than the feelings of a pair of silly youths, and the Brightlakes arranged for her to marry into one of the inner houses, to one Lord Fairfield. The Brightlakes built a powerful alliance, increased their wealth, and gained new status. And doomed their daughter to a life of noble servitude to a wretch of a man—a man who would make Silverhawk look like the paragon of honor."

"I can see why you all talked about her as a tragic figure. I guess arranged marriages are usually less wretched?"

"No, wretched marriages are all too common. But this one's tragic for what happened later, when she and her husband were sailing back from a visit to Cornucopia and their ship was destroyed in a storm. All lives were lost." He sighed. "In his letter to me, telling me of the news, her brother admitted that Zara had begged her father to release her from the marriage, to save her from her husband's depredations. But he refused and sent her back. He killed her—had the storm not taken her life, the arranged marriage would have taken her soul."

Liam looked down at the star again.

"This was her broach, given to her as a child by her parents. It was left behind by accident before that final voyage. I get the feeling Zara's mother has kept it close ever since. In her letter"—he flicked at a parchment on his desk—"she said that since it can't stay with her family I was the best person to have it."

"A noble gesture," Amelia whispered.

"Just fifteen years too late," Liam snapped.

He closed his eyes, his expression softening, and when he opened them again his eyes were filled with affection.

"I tell you all this, just to try and explain why I have no time for arranged marriages. I've told my own family that if they ever try to force me into one, I'll exile myself. And if they were to hunt me down, I'd kill myself. I will marry whenever—and whomever—I choose."

Amelia took the box gently from his hands and placed it on the desk. Perhaps it was time to exorcise this ghost.

"I understand now why you never told me about this." She sighed. "I hope that fifteen years is enough for your heart to mend."

"My heart had turned to stone," he admitted, before taking her hands anew. "Until a certain young quartermaster came into my life. A fearless, vivacious, beautiful, and kind woman who taught me how to fall in love again."

"You forgot jealous and tempestuous," she said with a sheepish grin, moving closer to him.

"They match my obtuseness and smug superiority," he countered. "Nobody's perfect."

Before she could reply his lips pressed against hers, and any further discussion was forgotten.

CHAPTER 8

SOMETIMES IT WAS HARD TO PLAY THE LOYAL cargo master to Liam's foppish merchant captain, Amelia thought as she walked at his side down the promenade of Windfall Station. All she wanted to do was hold his hand, but even such a simple gesture would betray their long-cultivated personas as civilian merchants.

"Do you think," she said suddenly, "that when we develop our next set of secret identities, we could do something that lets me kiss you in public?"

"Oh," he said with a raised eyebrow. "That suggests some interesting possibilities . . . a sly seductress, perhaps?"

She scoffed and gave him a long look up and down.

"I was thinking I could be an outlander chieftain, with you looming at my side . . . in a loincloth."

"What?"

She couldn't contain her laughter, both at the image in her mind and the genuinely shocked expression on his face. She tried to fight it down to a giggle.

"Please be serious," he said with a sigh. "I need to grill Mr. Long pretty hard today."

"Yes, milord."

His face melted into a noble sneer and he nodded to her.

It was all part of the game they played, and as the familiar façade of the Cup of Plenty came into view she suppressed a new smile. All this cloak and dagger was rather fun.

"Do you want me to order some more coffee for the ship, milord?" she asked him.

"Morale definitely improved when you brought back the previous batch," he mused. "Maybe double the portion this time, if they can spare it."

"I'll be their favorite Human, for sure."

"I think you'll always be Matthew Long's favorite Human," he said.

She cast him a withering glance. "Jealous, milord?"

"Terribly." His humor faded into sincerity. "But thank you for putting up with him—he's useful to us."

"I know. Just treat me to a private dinner at our next port visit to make it up to me."

"Let's hope he has some more odd cargos for you to track down. Just a few more and I think we'll be able to triangulate our target."

"I'll stop in on my new friend Mary again. Tell her about the failed *Storm Wind* rescue, and that I'm still hiding out in *Sophia's Fancy*. Then try to get some real info out of her."

"Agreed." Liam paused, casting a casual glance around the busy street. "Let her know that *Sophia's Fancy* is loading up something valuable and recommend another pirate strike. It's probably time to retire this identity, so we'll be free to fight any pirates openly. We need to speed things up: pressure's on now that Silverhawk has entered the game."

"Yes, milord."

The patio had a scattering of patrons, perhaps a few less than normal considering the bustling street just beyond the café's gates. Amelia didn't spot any familiar faces, but the population of Windfall was big enough and transient enough that she wasn't surprised. Anonymity was their greatest ally in this game, and hardly a glance shifted among the patio patrons as she and Liam strode through. Everyone was just going about their business.

The sweet calm of the café interior was like an old friend and Amelia savored a deep breath as she scanned the long tables and arranged pastries at the far end. But she sensed Liam slow beside her, and she took another look around. Their contact, Matthew Long, was seated in his regular spot to the left. But otherwise there were no patrons.

"Quiet today," she commented quietly. "I mean, even more than usual."

"Maybe they upped the prices," Liam replied.

Long struggled from his chair as they approached.

"Good day, Mr. Long," Liam said. "I hope the day sees you well."

"Well enough." Long stared at Amelia with unusual intensity as she went to sit down next to Liam. "Forgive me, my lord, but our discussion today would be best kept between just the two of us."

Amelia paused, glancing at Liam. He considered for a moment, then gave an elaborate shrug.

"Give us a few moments, would you, Amelia?" His tone was light, but the sharp look in his eyes told her that his tension level had just risen.

"Of course, milord," she said casually, moving to stand clear.

Habit steered her toward the table of pastries, and out of the corner of her eye she spotted the unmistakable form of Bella emerging from the kitchen. The Theropod strode over in her lowered walking stance, then lifted her head as she reached Amelia.

"Welcome back, Amelia," her translator said over her growls, "it is nice to see you again."

"Hi, Bella." It took a moment for her to register exactly what she'd heard. "Your translator has learned my name!"

"I had to train it a bit," she said with a soft bark. "It still struggles with your version of my name. It needs to hear it a few more times."

Amelia leaned in toward the device hanging from the S-curved neck. "Bella, Bella, Bella, Bella, Bella . . ."

A tiny clawed hand shooed her away amid another bark. Amelia straightened and saw Bella's nose pointed right at her, both of the Theropod's vertically slit eyes focused on her.

"You are a very nice person," she said, adjusting her translator so the volume dropped. "You have been kind to us."

"I'm happy to do so."

"And so I wish to be kind to you." Bella's head moved forward as her neck straightened. "There are bad people looking for your captain. It is not safe here for you."

"Do you know why?"

"I don't know, other than I hear talk. Humans sit at my tables and talk, forgetting that I'm there and can understand them." She tapped her translator. "I know that they mean to hurt him."

Amelia glanced around the room. It was empty, so no threat in here. But it was a busy street outside, and gangs of thugs moved with impunity on this station.

"Has something changed since our last visit, Bella?"

"Just in the last few days, I've heard people say that your captain is not who he says he is." Bella glanced over to Liam, and a half-standing Long. "Are you sure you know who he really is?"

"I think so," Amelia said carefully. Was Bella trying to get information out of her?

"Then I tell you to get out of here," Bella hissed. "While you still can."

Even through the translator, the sudden urgency was clear.

"GIVE US A FEW MOMENTS, WOULD YOU AMELIA?" As he sat down across from Long, Liam ensured that his tone was nonchalant, but he gave Amelia a pointed look.

"Of course, milord," she replied, before retreating toward the pastry table. The Theropod host was already emerging from the back and Liam figured Amelia would be occupied for a few minutes. He turned his attention back to Matthew Long.

"How was your last voyage, my lord?" the merchant asked.

"Lengthy and tedious, but successful."

"I suppose tedious is preferable to exciting, in our business." The heavy cheeks wrinkled in a faint smile.

"Quite so," Liam agreed. "Those pirates were certainly a concern for a while—I was surprised to see them disappear so suddenly."

"I don't question such surprises, my lord—I simply accept them gratefully."

"And business is booming again for you?"

"It has picked up again, yes. Trade is always difficult out here in the Halo, but we manage."

There was something different in Long's usual small talk. It was cautious and polite, as always, but Liam sensed an edge to the words. Almost an impatience.

"Usually my cargo master is essential to our discussions. Do you have something other than new shipments to discuss?"

Long poured coffee into Liam's cup, then took a sip from his own. He exhaled a long, rattling breath and leaned forward.

"I have some shipments for you, as always, and you are welcome to review them at my office. But I wanted to speak to you without other ears nearby."

Long never revealed much in his grim face, but Liam's hackles were rising. The absence of other patrons in the Cup of Plenty, the merchant's lack of cargo paperwork to review, and an instinct for trouble were all setting him on edge. He shifted his feet under his chair.

"You are my trusted associate," he lied. "I rely on you to keep me informed. I will even offer payment for good information that will help my business."

Long's expression froze, just for a moment, and Liam guessed that his words were being weighed.

"I may have an unusual shipment for you," Long said finally. "Very valuable, but it needs to be delivered quickly." He glanced to where Amelia was chatting with the Theropod. "But it would be best if you alone are aware of its contents, my lord."

"Why is that?" Liam's mind was racing, but he knew he had to play the foppish lord. "I'm not interested in skullduggery or unsavory activities."

"No, no," Long said quickly, "nothing like that. But the seller of this cargo wishes to keep a low profile, both for themselves and their goods."

"I don't understand, Mr. Long."

"Why don't you come with me to the warehouse and see the shipment? Everything will be clear then."

Beads of sweat were forming on Long's brow, and the intensity of his eyes was different from his usual avarice. Liam didn't sense any aggression . . . was it fear?

Liam sat back, holding his coffee up to breathe in the aroma but not sipping. He cast a long look around the café, his eyes moving high and low. It was truly empty of people, except for Amelia and the Theropod, who seemed to be sharing a laugh.

"Is the cargo bulky?" he asked, buying time. "I'd need to check our available space."

Long paused, the question catching him off guard.

"Not bulky, no," Long answered finally. "And my team would of course transport it to your ship."

"Is it perishable? Would I need to allow for special storage?"

"It will be easier for me to just show you," Long said, rising heavily from his chair.

"Sit down, Mr. Long."

The merchant froze, half-risen.

Liam leaned across the table, smiling as he raised his untouched cup of coffee.

"We haven't finished this expensive repast you ordered."

"My lord . . ."

"Sit."

Long obeyed, easing himself down again.

"Now," Liam continued, still smiling as he leaned close and lowered his voice, "why don't you tell me what's really going on."

Long stared at him, glanced over at Amelia and back. He drained his cup.

"I apologize for the secrecy, my lord, but I promise that everything will be clear once you see the cargo."

"I never assess cargo without Amelia. Can she come as well?"

"She can . . . but I would prefer not."

Every port visit saw Long practically drooling over Amelia, and he frequently manufactured reasons to see her.

"Why?" Liam asked simply.

Long dropped his eyes in defeat.

"I didn't want to trouble her. But if you insist, she may accompany us."

Every instinct was telling Liam to run, but instead he leaned back and folded his arms.

"My apologies, Mr. Long, for being such a boor. It's very kind of you to think of me for your special cargo, and I confess the strangeness of all this simply caught me off guard. There's no reason for Amelia to come with us. Please give me a few minutes to walk her back to the ship—I'll then return here and we two can inspect this mystery shipment."

Long's shoulders visibly relaxed and he nodded.

"An excellent plan, my lord. I will await you here."

"Won't be but a few minutes."

Liam rose from his chair and gestured for Amelia to join him. She offered parting words to the Theropod and made her way quickly to his side. He took her elbow in a friendly grip and guided her toward the door.

"People on the station are looking for you," she whispered. "Bella thinks they intend you harm."

"Mr. Long is planning to take me into a trap," he replied.

She didn't alter her casual pace, but he sensed her muscles tighten.

"What are you going to do?" she asked.

"Get back to the ship and set sail. We're not ready for this."

He led the way onto the patio, weaving through the tables toward the gate. A pair of patrons suddenly rose from the chairs in front of them, blocking the path. Liam felt an iron grip on his sleeve from the side, yanking him to a halt.

"Don't make any trouble, milord," growled a voice in his ear.

All the café patrons—eight of them, Liam assessed—were closing in from both sides.

"Amelia, run!"

He slammed his foot down on the man holding him, feeling the bones crush as the man cried out in pain, his grip falling away. Liam's hand grasped his ceremonial dagger and the blade flew out in a smooth motion, slashing across the man's chest. One target down, Liam carried through his swing. The next thug jerked back from the blade, but Liam stepped forward and stabbed, driving his blade into hard flesh. He pulled it free and slammed his fist into the sagging form, his blade striking out at the next target as he spun.

Amelia had thrown down a table to make a path and she was leaping over the patio fence when an attacker grabbed her. She was pulled down into a bear hug, but she snapped her head back. The attacker staggered away, stumbling as blood poured from his shattered nose. Liam swung left and right to keep his own attackers at bay. Amelia ran for the fence again, but another thug seized her hair and wrenched her down. Her head slammed against a table and she slumped forward.

"No!"

Liam drove his blade into the neck of another attacker, fighting his way forward to Amelia. She was moving, he saw, struggling to pull herself up. A huge man lumbered over and grabbed her in a bear hug. She tried to head butt him but her blows impacted harmlessly on his massive chest. His arms started to squeeze and she gasped in pain. Liam parried a knife strike and stepped closer, eyeing up a killing blow on the giant man.

Something huge and hard hit him on the head. All the sounds of battle faded into a muffled ringing, and Amelia seemed to ripple in front of him. He fought to stay on his feet and put all his strength into gripping his dagger tight. A flash of steel revealed a blade coming toward him. He leaned back and forced his hand up, but a sudden burning pain proved his failure to defend.

No, he heard someone shout, *he's not to be harmed.*

Something pulled at him, dragging him away from Amelia. He slashed behind him, heard the grunt of pain and felt the pulling stop. He staggered forward, lifting his blade again. Sounds were returning and he sensed movement on his right. A tall woman was approaching him, shuffling strangely, but her powerful arm was raised. In her hand was a club, and it smashed down onto his wrist. Pain shot up his arm, his dagger dropping from numb fingers.

Amelia was pinned in the giant's arms, and the attacker with the bloodied nose approached her.

"Stupid wench," he growled, raising his fist.

"No," the tall woman said, grabbing the man's arm, "she's one of ours."

Unable to fight the arms that grabbed him, Liam finally saw the woman's peg leg, and realized this was the pirate Mary. As he was dragged back through the entrance to the Cup of Plenty, he saw Amelia being released.

Finally, Mary limped through the doorway and sized him up.

"So, Captain Stonebridge," she said with a dangerous gleam in her eye, "you better prove valuable. The Piper wants to talk to you."

AMELIA GASPED AS THE VISE GRIP WAS RELEASED, collapsing forward onto the patio table and sucking in great gulps of air. The man with the smashed nose still glared at her, but the giant behind her was already moving to enter the Cup of Plenty. Two attackers were down amid the scattered chairs and the ground was sticky with blood. One thug was looking over the two casualties, and another sat heavily in a chair, breathing with difficulty as he tried to stop the blood flowing freely across his chest.

Amelia allowed herself a vicious smile. These goons had picked the wrong nobleman to cross.

"Get out of here," Broken Nose growled at her, "before I forget that you're one of ours."

With two dead, two badly injured, and one trying to

sew them up, that meant there were only two thugs inside with Liam, plus Mary and the giant. Amelia forced herself to straighten, backing away from the men and climbing over the low patio fence. To her right was the alley and what she knew was a back door.

Liam had told her to run, and she had the chance to sprint for the ship and come back with reinforcements. But that would take minutes, and she doubted Liam had that much time. Already forgotten by the thugs patching themselves up, she slipped down the alley.

The door to the café kitchen was unlocked and she cracked it open.

Then jumped back as a pan full of hot grease flew at her. The boiling liquid hissed down the door frame, and Amelia peeked around again, spotting Sam and Bella in low defensive stances. Spotting her, they raised up slightly, their heads snapping back and forth in wordless communication. Then Bella motioned Amelia inside.

"They've captured my captain," she whispered to them. "I need to rescue him."

Her pulse was racing, her every muscle tensed. Sam padded over to the door to the main café and peeked through. Bella moved closer, so that Amelia could feel her hot breath as she spoke.

"Why do you not run?" the Theropod asked. "You can still get free."

"Because . . ." She bit down the words she really wanted to say, her heart screaming as she pictured Liam in trouble, just beyond the wall. She blinked away furious tears.

Bella watched her closely, sniffing the air.

"Your fight or flight instincts are raging," Bella said. "And I can smell that you are ready to kill. Why?"

"Because those thugs are attacking an innocent man," she offered, feeling the press of the pistol under her coat. Sam returned, watching her with the same intensity.

"They attack the innocent often," he said. "Why is this different? Why don't you just run?"

Amelia had no time for these questions. She started to move toward the café door, reaching up for her pistol. Bella's sudden question halted her.

"Is the captain your mate?"

Through the translator it was such a bland question, but Amelia could see the earnest concern in Bella's reptilian eyes. Amelia looked back. Both Theropods were watching her, and she could see the muscles in their legs beginning to tense. The ridges on Sam's nose pulsated red.

"Yes," she whispered. "And I have to save him."

"Then let us save him," Bella hissed. She moved forward, nudging the door open a crack so that she and Amelia could see through.

Liam was slumped at a table, conscious but clearly dazed. Mary loomed over him, with the giant behind her. Another thug stood at the doorway to the street with sword drawn, and the last one had a blade pointed lazily at Matthew Long. The merchant sat miserably at his table, hooded eyes watching the scene.

Another figure then entered the café. All the pirates turned, and even Mary straightened slightly. The newcomer's features were shrouded behind a cloak, but Amelia spotted ringlets of black hair spilling out. The hand that reached out to stroke gently across Liam's lolling face was thin and feminine.

"Well done, Mary," the woman said in an educated accent. "It's exactly as Dark Star predicted."

"So you want him alive, Piper?"

"Yes, bring him to my ship."

Amelia drew her pistol. Bella's powerful form was beside her, Sam just a few paces behind. It was now or never.

"If I provide covering fire," she said, "can you two grab Liam—the captain—and bring him back in here?"

"I will get him," Bella said, her head going low as her lips pulled back to reveal a vicious smile. "My mate will be ready for the counterattack."

Sam's head bobbed from side to side, his powerful tail twitching.

"Ready?" Amelia asked.

"Ready."

Bella exploded into action, bashing aside the door and leaping the entire distance to Liam's table. Amelia swung through the door, raising her pistol. Three shots rang out, one of them embedding in the forehead of the giant. His dull face froze in shock as he toppled backward. Piper staggered, clutching her shoulder. Amelia fired at Mary. The pirate stumbled and fell. Bella's tiny arms grabbed Liam and pulled him up. He struggled to his feet and followed. The two thugs raised their swords and charged, but shots from Amelia sent them both diving for cover. Her pistol clicked empty. Bella and Liam were past her, and Amelia retreated to the kitchen.

Inside, Sam frantically waved at her to clear the doorway. She ran the few steps to grab Liam as he leaned against the storage shelves, his eyes struggling to focus on her. She kissed him quickly and saw the glimmer of a grateful smile before his face hardened and his vision cleared.

The café door burst open as the first thug careened through, sword held high. His charge was stopped dead as Sam's tail swung upward, the massive slab of meat and bone crushing the Human ribcage. The thug toppled and fell. But through the door Amelia saw the second attacker only steps behind. She grabbed the first heavy thing she could see—a sack of coffee—and rushed forward. As the thug burst through the door, Amelia heaved the sack upward into his face. The bag exploded on impact, knocking the thug clear off his feet. He crashed down on the floor, beans spilling all around him. Beyond the door, she heard shouts of alarm and the remainder of the gang running into the café.

"Retreat," she said, pointing for the alley door.

Liam led the way, his pistol out. Amelia grabbed another sack of coffee and followed. Bella clutched a metal box in each hand and Sam tore open the final sack, spilling coffee beans across the floor. As she fled into the alley, Amelia heard the café door burst open, followed by the skittering of feet and shouts of surprise as their pursuers went down.

Liam's pistol rang out once, followed by screams up

and down the promenade. He dodged to the left as a blade lashed out from the patio and fired again. The patio came into Amelia's view and she saw one thug hunched over, his blade dropped and his hands gripping his wounded midsection. The flash of metal caught her eye and she saw that he was reaching for a gun. Her sack of coffee swung down and bashed the thug into unconsciousness.

People were scattering to keep clear, giving Liam and Amelia a clear run for the ship. She heard the steady, loping gait of the Theropods behind her. Her own heart was pounding and as the last of the promenade buildings fell astern she felt the burning in her legs, but she kept running. Up ahead she saw their lone brow's mate, Able Rating Song, stiffen upon sighting them, pulling out his pistol and aiming. Aiming at the Theropods, she suddenly realized.

"Hold fire!" she screamed. "Hold fire!"

Liam burst through the broken gate onto the jetty and finally slowed as they reached the brow. He spun around, his pistol sweeping across their retreat, and Amelia paused next to him, gasping.

"Is there anyone else ashore?" Liam asked Song.

"No, sir."

"The captain isn't on a walkabout?" he demanded. "No secret departures by anyone?"

"No, sir. You and the quartermaster are the only two not on board."

Bella and Sam paused at Amelia's side, neither looking put out by the long sprint. Their heads moved back and forth between her and the promenade.

"Thank you," she said, reaching out to touch Bella's shoulder. "I couldn't have done it without you."

"We must go with you," Bella said. "We will be killed if we stay."

Amelia shot a glance up at Liam, who stared intently at the Theropods.

"We're not returning to Windfall," he said quickly. "We could never get you back here."

"We have all we need," Bella replied, holding up the two metal strongboxes in her hands.

"We can always start again somewhere else," Sam added.

Shouts down the jetty indicated that their pursuers were regrouping, and that there were more of them.

"You know she's right," Amelia said to Liam. "They're dead if they stay."

"But we"—Liam pursed his lips—"have *secrets* on board."

"And this is a big galaxy!" Amelia retorted. "They can be kept."

Liam glanced toward the growing ruckus, then at the two Theropods standing in front of him. Finally, his lips curled into a smile.

"Lady Sophia is going to hate me." He grabbed Song's arm and practically threw him toward the brow. "Get on board, emergency sailing!"

Song ran up the tunnel toward *Daring*'s hull.

"Once we're aboard, you stay at the brow," Liam said to Bella and Sam. "You don't go any further into the ship, for now."

"Yes," Sam agreed.

Liam gestured for Amelia to lead them on board. Amelia ran into the tunnel, hearing a couple of shots ring out before the pressure of the airlock shifted behind Liam closing the station door. Seconds later she was on board, Bella and Sam close behind her. Able Rating Song was in the middle of announcing an emergency sailing over the ship's broadcast, but his eyes went wide as the space was filled with reptilian forms.

Liam appeared, slamming the hatch shut and decoupling the ship from the station. As Song's emergency orders faded, Liam grabbed the intercom.

"This is the executive officer, sitrep: our landing party was attacked on the station, and further attacks are likely. *Daring* will retreat with all speed from Windfall and disappear into the blackness. We are now signal silent. Rig masts and sails for a full-speed run. Arm all gun positions, but do not fire unless fired upon."

He paused, taking in the sight of Theropods on his ship.

"We have two unexpected guests on board, who will remain at the brow under Petty Officer Virtue's supervision. Chief Sky, report to the brow, fully armed."

He paused again, and Amelia could see his mind swirling. A smile was again playing at his lips.

"Captain," he said finally, his voice still echoing on all decks, "I'll brief you on the bridge."

CHAPTER 9

THE SOUND OF HIS OWN BREATHING WAS A STEADY, calming rhythm. Liam didn't particularly enjoy venturing out into zero gravity, but he wasn't about to hesitate in front of his crew. The field of vision through his faceplate was wide enough to see his close surroundings, but the sides of his helmet thankfully masked the endless depths of the Abyss all around him. Two weeks out from their sudden withdrawal at Windfall Station, Liam didn't want to think about just how far away the nearest hospitable planet was. Pulling himself along the splintered remains of the pirate ship's after framework, he focused on what he could see at arm's reach, and on his breathing.

"Nothing salvageable from midships," Chief Sky reported over the suit comms. *"Just dust and shrapnel."*

At least he had something to grab onto, Liam thought, shifting from one broken stem of the pirate ship frame and reaching out for the next. Sky was free-floating in the dissipating cloud behind him, with nothing but a tether stretching back to *Daring* to anchor her. The debris cloud was all that remained of the central section of this wreck once known as the pirate ship *Red Sun,* and it was proving as worthless as the last two vessels destroyed by Silverhawk's missiles.

"*Understood,*" he replied. "*Come to the after section; start checking starboard side.*"

"*Yes, sir.*"

Liam came across a door, hidden in the shadows but still intact. Frost hinted at the air that had once filled the cabin beyond that door. The bulkhead around it looked solid—there might actually be a complete cabin beyond. He checked his own tether, turning in his suit just enough to look back over his shoulder. The line was thick, corded rope and it weaved back through the vacuum to the dusty bulk of *Daring*'s hull. The ship was close enough that a few quick tugs on the line would get him safely back, and she was holding her position perfectly. Reassured, he turned back to the wreckage and reached for the door handle.

The iron latch was stiff, but with a tug it came loose. Liam braced himself to pull against the frozen hinges and slowly the door opened. Activating his headlamp, he floated through into the cabin. His cone of light scanned carefully left to right, at first seeing an unmade bunk, an open chest, a desk . . .

And a man, flash-frozen in place.

Liam gasped, his gloved hand reaching for a sword that wasn't there. His light danced crazily around the room for a moment, then settled again as he calmed his breathing. He continued his scan and revealed the rest of the otherwise unremarkable cabin. Then he turned back to the frozen figure.

The man was standing behind the desk, seemingly in the motion of grabbing papers. His body, the desk, and the papers upon it were covered in a thin sheen of crystallized ice, a frantic moment in time forever captured by the sudden decompression and chill when Silverhawk's missiles had destroyed the ship.

"So," Liam said quietly, "what were you so desperate to collect?"

He floated over, looking down at the jumble of parchments. Pushing over to the chest he peered in, noting a couple of strongboxes but also some data storage units. Frozen to the deck were an emergency space suit and a sack of rations. This man wasn't expecting to fight—he was trying to escape. And if he was willing to abandon his crew to protect whatever he was gathering up here . . .

Liam smiled.

"Chief Sky," he called over the circuit, "bring the recovery team to this cabin I found, port side aft."

THE WARMTH OF THE SHIP WAS A WELCOME RELIEF. Liam knew his spacesuit was fully powered and designed to maintain a comfortable environment, but this far out in the Halo the cold of the Abyss was never far away. He shivered as he rose from his chair in the senior mess, eager to get another coffee. Habit made him approach the decanter, but movement in his vision suddenly reminded him of the new reality.

The female Theropod, Bella, swung her head around at his approach. She was wearing the same black outfit that had been her serving uniform at the Cup of Plenty, and it looked to be recently washed. A faint waft of perfume hung around her, and Liam was sure he recognized the scent as Amelia's favorite.

"Can I get you something, my lord?" Bella asked through her translator.

Liam paused, strangely comfortable with this particular brute serving food and drinks, even as his instincts recoiled at the idea of an alien moving so freely in one of His Majesty's sailing ships.

"I was just going to get a coffee, Bella," he responded.

Small, clawed hands moved with practiced efficiency to produce a cup of the hot, steaming liquid. No milk or sugar, just as Liam preferred. She rose to her resting stance and handed the cup to him, her nose lowered slightly. The brutes moving "freely" might not be the best description, he thought, watching as she kept her powerful tail tucked in close to her body. Human physique was essentially vertical, and the tight confines of this Human ship were no doubt a challenge to the horizontal body form of a Theropod. But Bella moved with a quick grace and nary a growl of complaint.

"Thank you," he said.

"You're welcome, my lord."

He returned to his seat, suddenly noticing that all eyes were on him. Brown, Butcher, and Templegrey didn't even try to hide their interest as he sat down.

"Can we keep them?" Brown whispered, her face alight.

"The food's never been so good," Butcher echoed, hefting his own mug. "And the coffee . . ."

Liam took a sip. It *was* divine. Even though they'd been drinking Cup of Plenty beans since their previous visit to Windfall, no Human apparently had the skill to mix it just so.

"And the desserts," Templegrey added, popping the last bite of her pastry into her mouth with a contented sigh. "I'm going to have to get all my gowns let out."

Liam allowed himself a chuckle. The crew seemed to have accepted their two passengers with remarkable indifference initially, which over the past two weeks had grown into enthusiastic support once Sam and Bella had asked to be useful and had started working in the galley. Sam was training the ship's cooks on the perfect blends of spices, and Bella had filled the gap in senior mess stewards with quiet efficiency.

"The thing is," Butcher added, "I've eaten brute food before. It's usually raw. And disgusting."

"Benefits of running a café that serves exclusively Humans," Liam observed. "They figured out what our tastes are like, and with those fantastic noses of theirs they can refine it down to a science."

"What are we feeding them?" Brown asked.

"Prisoners," Butcher quipped almost under his breath, to a ripple of nervous laughter and glances at Bella.

"Meat, eggs, and root vegetables," Liam said firmly. "Usually raw."

"Wonderful," Templegrey said. "Just wonderful."

"What did you recover from the wrecked pirate ship, sir?" Brown asked.

"The captain and I are reviewing it now," he replied, giving Brown a stern look as he nodded toward Bella. "I'll be asking for your input shortly, in a more discrete setting."

"Yes, sir. I'm looking forward to putting some more pieces together."

"Perhaps after dinner, then," he said, draining his cup and rising.

"Yes, dinner," Butcher said in anticipation, rubbing his belly. "We won't want to rush that, sir."

Liam stepped out into the main passageway, almost bumping into Amelia and the other Theropod, Sam, as they carried a tea serving and a meal for one, respectively.

"Hello, sir," she said, eyes dancing. "Back from your adventures?"

"Wreckage picked clean," he said, falling in beside them as they continued aft. "And I'm just starting to get warm again. Where are you two headed?"

"The captain requested an early dinner," she said with a smile. "I think she approves of our new head chef."

"I merely assist," Sam offered, in a soft collection of growls. "Your real chefs work very hard."

"I doubt they could prepare meals that would be so loved by a Theropod crew."

"Perhaps not, but no Theropod crew would ever be this big. I've never understood how Humans can stay together in cohesive groups like this. Or how you can feed them so efficiently."

Amelia led the way up the ladders, Sam balancing his long form carefully as he ascended the narrow steps. Liam followed at a respectful distance, wary of that tail. He'd seen too many similar tails, usually with swords strapped to them, to want to stay within reach.

Two decks up, Amelia knocked on the captain's door and, after a moment, entered. Sam followed in silence, but as he waited in the passageway Liam heard Riverton's voice and the brute's reply. Moments later, Sam padded back out through the door, bobbing his head politely to Liam. In the rush of air, Liam thought he detected something, and as Amelia emerged he turned questioning eyes to her.

"Is that my cologne?"

"I borrowed some," she said sheepishly.

"I noticed your perfume on Bella, too. Do our guests not bathe as often as us?"

"Oh, they do," Amelia said quickly. "But the simple fact is, they're aliens, and they smell different from us. When we're all this close together, it starts to get noticeable."

"So you prettied them up for the sake of our noses?"

"Actually," she replied with a smirk, "it's more to hide our smells from them. Bella admitted to me that it was getting a bit revolting for them."

Liam couldn't suppress his laughter. "Your kindness knows no bounds."

"Thank you, sir."

With a quick squeeze of his arm she hurried to catch up with Sam, who was slowly backing himself down the awkward Human ladder.

Liam knocked at the open door and peered in.

"Good afternoon, ma'am," he greeted, noting Riverton at her dining table. She was just starting to eat, but her tray was surrounded by the papers Liam had recovered from the wreckage of *Red Sun*. "I was going to discuss our latest, but I can come back."

"Now is fine," she said, gesturing for him to enter. "As long as you don't mind me eating while you talk."

"Not at all, ma'am. But the smell is certainly enticing."

She placed a couple of biscuits on a side plate and handed it to him, pouring a second cup of tea as he sat down.

"Apparently the Emperor himself employs Theropods in his kitchens," she said, before taking a delicate bite.

"Really?"

"If properly trained, they are unmatched in culinary skill."

"I'm glad we found some trained ones, then."

"I wouldn't say 'found' is quite the right word, Mr. Blackwood."

"No. 'Were rescued by' might be more appropriate, ma'am."

"True."

She fell silent for a few moments as she enjoyed her dinner, then gestured subtly at the papers between them.

"It's going to take a while to assimilate everything, ma'am, but I'm sure you see as well as I do that this is high-level communications."

"On parchment, no less," Riverton agreed, "with no electronic version to easily copy or transmit."

"And," he said, holding up one paper with a black, stylized cross at the bottom, "we have a personal mark from Dark Star."

"An elegant hand," she noted. "Clearly educated."

"Too bad the order was so brutish."

"I found another order with Dark Star's mark," Riverton said, reaching to a pile on her right. "It's curious, because it looks like a routine broadcast to all pirate captains—and was even stored with other administrative letters—yet it carries Dark Star's personal signature . . . and it's about you."

"Me?" Liam took the letter and scanned it. It was an open message to all captains, telling them to be on the lookout for Julian Stonebridge and providing a known area of his operations. But then, at the bottom, a new handwriting had added a specific instruction that Stonebridge was not to be harmed but was to be captured and brought to somewhere called "the boathouse."

"This ties in with the attack at Windfall," he said. Despite his many years of subterfuge and of laying traps for his enemies, Liam was shaken at the direct, personal attention he had earned from Dark Star.

"I think," Riverton stated, "that *Sophia's Fancy* will be lying low for a while."

"Agreed, ma'am. That last encounter was too close, and clearly our fake identity is compromised."

"But with this amount of intelligence," she said, indicating the covered table, "we should be able to zero in on our target. Hopefully the next time we face the pirates it will be Dark Star in person, and we will be flying our true colors."

"Yes, ma'am."

"What did you make of that woman who was in charge—the Piper?"

"Hard to say. I was still dazed at that point. I remember her speaking to me, and that she had very dark eyes." Liam shook his head, frowning. "There was something familiar about her."

"From a previous pirate battle? Perhaps at the comet base, where some of them may have escaped?"

"Perhaps." He dared to smile. "With her eyes and her educated accent, maybe she just reminded me of you, ma'am."

"Her accent was like mine?"

"No, she was a commoner . . . but there was something."

"Think on it further, XO. It could lead us somewhere important."

"So long as Silverhawk stays out of our way."

She continued to eat in silence. Liam took a bite of his biscuit and washed it down with tea.

"Yes," she said finally. "There is something not right about all that."

"Silverhawk is aggressive and cunning," Liam said, "but he really is rather stupid."

Riverton sipped at her tea for a long moment, and Liam suspected she was hiding her smile. When she set down the cup her face was set in its usual stoic mask.

"I think Lord Silverhawk has grasped the idea of prize money rather well," she concurred, "but his intelligence gathering skills are somewhat primitive."

"His team didn't even check the wreckage," Liam added, shaking his head as he recalled the drama from the day before.

Daring had been trailing *Red Sun* out toward the Iron Swarm, the latest target identified from Liam and his senior team sifting through mountains of data. Still nearly a day out from intercept, *Daring* had spotted *Arrow,* once again approaching with the winds at her back at speeds the old frigate could never hope to achieve. In a lightning strike, Silverhawk had closed to within missile range, lobbed a volley of destruction into the lumbering pirate ship, then turned to retreat with barely a passing taunt to Riverton. No attempt to board or capture the vessel, just simple destruction.

"Something is very wrong here," Riverton said, with sudden insistence.

"Is there anything about Silverhawk that isn't wrong?"

"But even more. About this incident in particular."

Liam frowned, not quite following.

"What was different about *Red Sun*?" Riverton asked, sitting back and folding her arms thoughtfully. "Why would Silverhawk make no effort to capture her?"

He thought back over what they knew about this ship.

"She's three weeks out from Windfall, where she dropped off a shipment of Labyrinthian gold hidden among unrefined ore. We know that this is a standard method of pirate smuggling, so not particularly special. She was headed for the Iron Swarm."

"What was she carrying on this leg of her voyage?"

"Linen and pottery." He shrugged. "Nothing special."

"And nothing valuable."

"No, not really."

"So nothing Silverhawk would want to claim as prize money."

Liam considered. "The cargo would have had some value, but it would be bulky and would need to be sailed all the way to the Iron Swarm to connect with the buyer. Certainly not worth the trouble to steal."

"I have sources who tell me that Captain Silverhawk is in financial trouble. Apparently his gambling habits have begun to strain even his family's reserves."

Liam remembered well his former captain's enjoyment of games of chance—preferably for high stakes and against other wealthy lords.

"It might explain why he foreclosed on the Bright-lakes," he suggested. "That's messy, unpopular business, but under the Imperial laws of bursary a sizeable percentage of the assets seized is paid to the person who does it—an executioner's fee, if you will."

"I've just never heard of one noble house doing it to another. That doesn't sit right, either, and I'm looking into it. All I know so far is that the Imperial court did *not* sanction it."

"Do you think the Silverhawk family is suffering under debt?"

"No, from what I understand quite the opposite— they've issued loans to many smaller houses. I think Captain Silverhawk has placed himself in financial difficulties all on his own."

"So he's looking for easy prize money, and *Red Sun* didn't offer it."

"But how did he *know* that?" Riverton leaned forward, her eyes burning into Liam's. "He didn't even board the vessel. And he hasn't been to Windfall to search through shipping manifests, and any network of informants he might possibly have access to wouldn't know this sort of mundane detail, nor would he have asked."

Liam began to understand her line of thinking. "Why would he go to all the trouble of hunting this ship down, if it had nothing of value to him?"

"Or did he hunt it down because the ship, or her crew, were a liability to him?"

"How could it be a liability? He wasn't involved with the smuggling operations."

"Are you sure?"

Liam was about to respond, but something in Riverton's gaze made him swallow down his scoff. What was she suggesting?

"Ma'am, Silverhawk may be a buffoon, but he's a lord of the realm and a senior officer in the Navy."

"Yes, for twelve years," she said quietly. "Twelve years of travel all around the Halo, often disappearing for days at a time when in port."

"Casinos and harlots," Liam said dismissively, remembering too many times he'd had to send an escort party to collect their captain before sailing.

"That's the official story. And didn't young Brown report that the first signs of Dark Star's tentacles appeared about twelve years ago? Very localized at first, but then spreading."

Liam knew that they had to entertain all possibilities, but the idea of Silverhawk as a criminal mastermind . . .

"Ma'am, with respect, he's a complete toff."

"And so is Julian Stonebridge," she retorted. "I believe it was my own XO who once explained to me that the simpering noble façade was an excellent way to hide in plain sight."

"Yes, but . . ." He grasped at the idea. "If Silverhawk is involved in this, why would he destroy his own ships?"

"To spite me?" Riverton snapped in a sudden rush of anger. She waved her hand at the wealth of new intelligence spread out between them on the table. "Although if that was his intention he did a very poor job of it."

Silence descended in the cabin.

"But that doesn't answer my question," Riverton said after a moment. "How did he know that *Red Sun* carried nothing of value, and even that we were chasing her? Have you sent a report of our findings to Admiral Grandview?"

"No, ma'am. I only deliver that kind of information in person."

"Have you shared this with anyone outside the hull of this ship?"

"No, ma'am."

"Has it been discussed when our two new guests are within earshot?"

"Absolutely not, ma'am. And they're both forbidden to send any kind of message from the ship. We'd know if they did."

"Who knew what cargo *Red Sun* was carrying?"

Liam thought for a moment.

"Anyone in the senior staff would have access to the info, but I don't know specifically what each officer or senior sailor knows personally."

"But they all knew that *Red Sun* was our current target?"

"Yes, ma'am. Our mission was clear to all of them."

"And any one of them is authorized to send signals, when required?"

"Yes, ma'am." This deep in space, *Daring* was free to transmit signals to specific planets without risking her identity. "There's usually one every day or two, for professional reasons."

"Silverhawk knew something very specific, which would only be known to the senior staff in *Daring*. I want you to examine those signals that have been sent since we departed Windfall." Riverton's expression darkened. "We have a spy on board, feeding information to Silverhawk."

Liam sat back in his chair, processing his captain's words. The idea was almost too awful to contemplate, but he couldn't argue with her logic. His eyes swept over the new intel that only he and Riverton had so far discussed, and the kernel of an idea formed in his mind.

"Yes, ma'am. And if the spy is covering their tracks very carefully, there's another way to flush them out. If you can help me."

DARING TURNED HUBWARD, THE STRONG HEAD-winds slowing her progress toward the massive heart of the star cluster. Liam briefed the senior staff on the basics of what had been recovered from *Red Sun,* but purposefully left any conclusions vague. As the ship struggled against the countering breezes, Liam set his trap. He let it be known to the senior mess that Morassia was their next planet of interest, and then looked for opportunities to speak to each officer and senior hand privately.

Being dishonest to Amelia was the hardest part. The steady trundle of shipboard life in deep space continued much as it always did, but one evening, sitting in the stores office with her, he saw his opening.

"Any idea when we'll make planetfall?" she asked, pushing back from her console and stretching. The long stretch turned into her arms wrapping around him.

"You know the captain's holding her cards close to her chest," he said, smiling down at her as he pulled her close.

"As always." Amelia jerked her chin back toward her console. "But it's hard for me to plan our stores consumption if I don't know where we're going."

"Well," he said, making a subtle show of thinking hard, "we're not going anywhere fast, because word is our quarry is still a long way from their destination. But . . ." He glanced at the closed stores door and leaned in.

"A ship called *Black Swan* is headed to Morassia, and we intend to intercept her. She's slow, though, and it will probably be a couple of weeks before she arrives." He gave her a firm look. "But that's just between us—don't tell anyone."

"Not a word," she said with a smile.

Over the next few days, Liam managed to find opportunities to drop in different tidbits with the rest of the officers and chiefs.

"Charlotte," he said quietly to Brown next to the officer of the watch station, "keep this to yourself, but can you search navigation records for a ship named *Golden Swan*? It's our next target."

"Stop whining," he chided Swift as they sat alone at the wardroom table. "Don't tell anyone, but we're headed to intercept a pirate ship called *White Swan*— you can replenish sails after that."

"Get the boarding team fitted for hot weather gear," he muttered to Sky outside the bosun's locker. "Not a word to anyone but looks like we're heading planetside on Morassia to intercept the crew of a pirate ship called *Silver Swan*."

"Coxn," he stopped Butcher as he came out of the brig, "look into the feasibility of upgrading our cell security." He glanced around. "This is between you and me, but we're looking to catch a pirate ship named *Mother Swan*."

"Doctor," he said to Templegrey, leaning against her desk in a quiet sickbay, "please check what vaccines we have in stores. Keep it quiet, but a pirate ship named *Soaring Swan* is headed for Morassia, and we intend to catch her crew on the surface."

News from the Empire trickled in as the days drifted by. Sailors gossiped about the skirmish reported between the Navy and Sectoid forces, although both sides had pulled back. Official word was that a confrontation had erupted out of a misunderstanding, and no further action was planned. But all ships were to remain vigilant for Sectoid incursions into Human space.

"What exactly is Human space?" Bella asked Liam one day in the wardroom as she cleared away the dishes after lunch.

He glanced at Amelia seated near him, who leaned her chin on her fist and gave him an inquiring look.

"It's the area of the galaxy that the Emperor claims sovereignty over."

"What does that mean?" Bella cocked her head. "My translator struggled with those last few words."

"The Emperor is the ruler of certain planets and star systems," Liam tried again, "and the space around those planets and star systems is called Human space. Because it belongs to the Human emperor."

"He rules the people on the planets, I understand," Bella said. "But he doesn't own the planets. Or the stars."

"Who does, then?"

"No one. How can any person think to possess a star? And how can anyone own empty space?"

She wasn't picking a fight with him, he realized. She was genuinely trying to understand. He considered how Theropod society was structured. It was based on clan groups, he knew.

"With your clan," he said, "you own the land which you occupy, right?"

"No. We exist there, but others existed there before we did, and still others will exist there after us. We are simply the occupants."

"What about your home world? The other races couldn't claim it."

"Of course not. It is where we come from."

"So your race owns that world."

"No . . ." Bella paused. "We live there."

Amelia, Liam noticed, was failing in her effort not to smirk.

"Well," he said, "I guess Human space is where we as a species live. And we include the empty space around the stars and planets because of all our ships and stations. And then we claim a bit more just to keep distance between other races who we think might threaten us."

"You don't think Theropods are a threat, then?"

"Not really," he admitted. "Your society is dispersed, and never unites to become a threat to us."

"As you do to us."

"Our unity comes from defense, Bella, not for attack. It's the Sectoids who we really worry about. Our unity as a species is nothing compared to theirs."

"Yes, they are very strange. But not as aggressive as my people."

"Good thing your people aren't united, then," he said with a closed smile.

She barked. "That would never happen."

"I suspect your people would be too busy fighting among themselves."

"Much as yours are." Bella moved away.

Amelia sat back, folding her arms triumphantly.

"What's with you?" he asked her.

"Sometimes we need to hear things from a new perspective, my lord."

"We're not perfect," he admitted readily. "But our system works."

"More or less," she conceded. But there was a dangerous gleam in her eye and he let the matter drop.

THE SLOW TRANSIT HUBWARD CONTINUED. SHIPS passed periodically in the distance, *Daring* adjusting course to leave a wide berth. It came as a surprise, then, when the officer of the watch reported a distant vessel transmitting an unknown type of beacon, and Riverton ordered *Daring* to close.

It took more than a day to cross the vast gulf between ships, but Liam made his way up to the bridge during the afternoon watch of the second day of the approach. Swift had the bridge, and Riverton was seated in her command chair. Up ahead, through the canopy, the mystery ship was clearly visible. Liam stepped forward, staring.

It was a perfect sphere, with four short masts extending in the cardinal directions, much like *Daring*'s, plus a fifth, much larger mast thrusting out in one direction. At first Liam guessed that the fifth mast was a forward spar like on Silverhawk's *Arrow,* but as he watched he realized that this large mast extended from what passed as the stern of this vessel. The sails on the four smaller masts were triangular in shape, and to Liam's eye looked too small to really catch the winds. But they were offset by the massive sheets that billowed from the stern mast.

"I've never seen anything like it," he marveled to Swift. "Is it a Sectoid ship?"

"No," Swift replied, his own expression lit up in wonder. "It's an Aquan ship."

"An Aquan ship?" Liam stepped forward, staring in shock.

"Do lift your jaw off the deck, XO," Riverton chided. She turned in her chair. "I don't want you gawking when we greet our guests."

"We're meeting the Aquans?"

"My diplomatic contacts arranged it. They have information for us."

He turned to her. "Have you dealt with Aquans before?"

"No," she admitted after a moment. "But I know that the hookup between ships will be using their airlock system, not ours."

"Shall I clear a path to the bridge for them?"

"No, they can't handle our ladders. You and I will meet them in the cargo loading area." She glanced down at him. "It will be a quick meeting."

"Can I be part of the security detail?" Swift asked suddenly. "I'd love to get a look at their environment suits."

"No," Riverton said firmly. "There will be no gawkers and no audience. Have the coxn positioned at the bulkhead aft of our position, and the assaulter at the bulkhead forward, both armed, with the doors closed behind them. Only the XO and I will interact with our guests."

"Yes, ma'am," Swift grumbled.

It took another hour for the two ships to maneuver alongside each other, with masts retracting and thrusters countering the very different sailing characteristics of the vessels. But eventually Liam stood with Riverton in full dress uniform down in the large space of the cargo loading area. A pair of heavy chests lay at his feet. Butcher and Sky were both in armor, each standing by the closed doors leading fore and aft. They both wore a pistol on each hip, heavy cutlasses slung at their thighs.

"How often does this happen?" Liam asked Riverton, adjusting his own saber.

"Officially, almost never. The environmental demands are just too much. But out in the Halo it happens sometimes between merchants."

"I guess even fish like to make money."

"*Captain,*" Swift reported over the speaker, "*the connection is holding and I'm reading stable air outside the hull. Permission to open the cargo door?*"

"Yes, please," she called. "Open the cargo door."

The bulkhead they were facing was almost completely taken up by a single large door used often to transfer stores to and from *Daring*. As Julian Stonebridge, Liam had conducted many a business deal with this door open, but he knew this next encounter would be anything but routine.

The door creaked as it started to rise. A rush of water poured through the crack, spilling across the deck. Liam tensed, but then saw clear air beyond as the door continued to climb. Beyond *Daring*'s hull there was now a low, wide tunnel becoming brighter as the cargo bay's light cast its rays within. Four dark shapes became visible, clustered together in the center of the tunnel. They jerked together to the left, then glided slowly forward. They were long and low, almost like coffins resting on six spindly legs. As they crossed the airlock threshold Liam realized that the legs rode on wheels, and that the leading ends of the coffins were bulbous and transparent. Forcing himself to remain still, he strained to catch his first glimpse of this mysterious alien species.

The four Aquans advanced together, clustered tightly in a diamond formation. Then they suddenly split, two of the coffins coming alongside each other as the other two veered off several paces distant. The central two rolled up to Liam and Riverton, and all four halted as one.

Looking through the transparent surface, he could

see an Aquan in each coffin. They were deep green, their scales shining in the cargo bay light refracting through the water. From what he could see their bodies were long and thin, with fins fluttering as they hovered in their tiny bubbles of natural environment. Huge eyes stared up at him, and their massive mouths opened and shut almost absently, revealing lines of wicked teeth. Those teeth were replicated in a heavy set of metal jaws slung beneath the coffin, he noticed immediately. The Aquan equivalent of a sword.

The only known water-based species to achieve space flight, the Aquans were a complete enigma to the Humans. Neither race could exist in the other's environment, but that somehow hadn't stopped wars being fought over resources on a variety of worlds. Trade was rare, but extremely lucrative for those few willing to offer the exotic wares of two species so different from each other.

"Welcome," Riverton said. "I am the captain of this vessel. This is my second."

There was a low-frequency rumble within the coffins, followed by another. Then the speaker on the coffin to the right sounded in smooth, translated words.

"Greetings. I am the headmaster, and this is my deputy."

"Thank you for making this effort to speak to us. I hope that together we can eliminate this mutual threat."

The headmaster shifted in his watery environment, his eyes resting on the chests at Liam's feet.

Riverton noticed his gaze as well.

"Please accept this gift from us. Pure salt."

The second Aquan rolled up to the nearest chest. He clamped his mouth around a control stick and a mechanical appendage extended from the outside of the coffin. It moved with care to unlatch the chest and flip open the top. As promised, it was full of white crystals. The appendage extended a tiny suction tube, and a moment later the fish rippled its lips. A deep rumble passed between the two Aquans and the chest lid was closed.

"There are many among us who do not differentiate between Humans," the headmaster said. "Yet the Sectoids assure us that you are fighting different schools among yourselves."

"In this case, yes. I serve the Emperor, and it is his wish to stop Dark Star."

"Dark Star is taking control of all Human trade with us in several systems." A small hatch popped open on the top of his deputy's coffin and a fist-sized lump of metal appeared. "This data block gives exact dates and locations of instances where our people were injured or killed."

At Riverton's nod, Liam reached out and took the data block. It was heavy, and still wet, but after a quick examination he saw how it would connect to *Daring*'s systems.

"We know that Dark Star's school intends to strike against your school very soon. We can tell by the shipments they command from us that they want to load a great many ships, and we see more Humans and Theropods gathering with weapons."

"Have you heard a location for this strike?"

"The name Honoria is whispered. Why would they strike a planet with so little water?"

"I don't know," Riverton said smoothly. "But you think it will happen soon?"

"The deadlines Dark Star has given our merchants suggest mass departure in three weeks."

"Then we will act immediately."

"You will bring Dark Star to justice?" the headmaster asked.

"As quickly as possible," Riverton replied. "It is our sole mission."

"And then you will take over the commerce in these systems?"

She paused. Liam glanced at her, noting the furrow of her brow.

"The commerce will fall under the power of the Emperor again," she said carefully. "But it will be open to any law-abiding merchant."

A series of low rumbles passed between the two coffins.

"Speaker Two-Seven-One spoke very highly of you," the headmaster finally said. "We had hoped you would control the Humans."

A Sectoid speaker praising Riverton to the Aquans? Liam couldn't think of a stranger compliment.

"I will ensure that the Emperor's laws are obeyed," she said. "As will my fellow officers. The threat will pass and trade can continue as before."

"I understand. Fare well in your hunt, Captain."

"Thank you, Headmaster. I wish you clear and swift seas."

The two Aquans turned sharply away, their guards forming up with them as they grasped the salt chests with side-mounted hooks and rolled through the open cargo door into the dim light of the airlock tunnel. Or waterlock tunnel, Liam supposed it was to them.

He glanced at the data block in his hand as the cargo door started to close.

"I'll begin examining this information immediately, ma'am."

"Keep your findings between you and me," she said. "If anyone asks, just tell them that this info supports what we already thought, and that the plan is unchanged."

He glanced at Sky and Butcher, still loitering out of earshot at opposite ends of the cargo bay.

"I'll do nothing to discourage the spy, ma'am."

The cargo door banged to a close. Moments later it creaked as water started to press against it on the outside.

"We need to sort this out," Riverton muttered, "and fast. If what the Aquans are saying is true, the clock is already ticking. And we have three weeks until Dark Star is ready to strike at the Empire's heart."

CHAPTER 10

THE QUIET, STEADY ROUTINE OF A SHIP AT SEA continued. Passing ships were noted and tracked, but *Daring* kept her distance. The watch rotations turned over like clockwork, the crew working industriously but comfortably to keep the ship clean, trim, and in fighting shape. Evening dinners in the senior mess were pleasant affairs, and the quality of the food remained surprisingly high, even as the fresh food disappeared and rations were brought out, thanks to the culinary expertise of Bella and Sam.

Then, on the evening before their landfall at Morassia, as he entered the captain's cabin for his regular report, Liam sensed the mood change.

Riverton was pacing in the tiny space, not even trying to hide her agitation from him as he shut the door and stepped forward.

"I've received word," she said simply, pointing to a message on the screen of her workstation.

Liam read the signal, sent via a secure, diplomatic channel that would be impossible for *Daring*'s bridge to decode. It was terse, with only three items of information, but clear. His stomach churned.

"They're certain?" he asked cautiously. "There's no possibility this is an error?"

"One hundred percent. The choice of words indicates that this is a firsthand account." She thrust a printed report at him. "And I discovered this, sent from our ship a day after you planted the seed."

He scanned it. "Then we know who the spy is."

"The traitor, you mean?"

His first instinct was to offer a defense, but the words died in his throat. One of his own crew, secretly feeding information to Silverhawk.

"Why?" Riverton asked.

"Let's arm ourselves, ma'am," he said, "and go find out."

Liam had descended the ladders to Two Deck countless times, but never with such a heavy heart. His saber clicked against his hip as he stepped down to the deck and his hand instinctively reached to check the holstered pistol. Riverton climbed down behind him, her expression dark.

"I suggest you do the talking, XO," she said. "I'm not sure I can remain ladylike."

Liam looked down the deserted passageway. The door

to the senior mess was closed and if the usual nightly routine had been followed their target would have left right after Liam. Less than ten minutes had passed since he'd concluded dinner, so the target would still be awake. He stepped aft, eyeing the names on the cabin doors.

He knocked. The unconcerned reply to enter sounded through the wood. Gripping his pistol, he opened the door and stepped through, Riverton close behind.

Ava Templegrey was dressed in her white uniform shirt and trousers, her hair hanging loose as she put down the last of her fasteners on a small vanity. Her eyes scanned between her two visitors, all expression dropping from her face. Her gaze went down to the weapons, then back up. Her lips moved slightly, eyes blinking rapidly as she tried to compose herself.

"To what," she said finally, "do I owe the honor of a personal visit from my commander and executive officer?"

"Put your hands where I can see them, please," Liam ordered. "And sit down."

Templegrey placed her hands flat on her knees as she lowered into the chair. Her cabinmate, Brown, had the watch, so Liam knew there would be no one disturbing them.

"We received word," he said, "that Captain Silverhawk has reached Morassia, and is inquiring into the whereabouts of a ship named *Soaring Swan*."

"Damn his eyes," she said quietly, her expression one of perfect neutrality. "How does he keep getting ahead of us?"

"Because someone aboard *Daring* is telling him our plans."

"That's absurd, sir," she said. "Why would anyone do that?"

"You tell me, Ava."

The color drained from her face, but otherwise her mask of calm remained unperturbed.

"Surely, sir," she said with a tiny smile, "you're not suggesting I contacted Silverhawk."

"I'm not suggesting anything. I'm declaring it as fact."

"But he could have gained this information from anywhere." Her poise was remarkable, but cracks were starting to show. "With his wealth he could buy a hundred informants who might feed him this information."

"No, just one. How much did he pay you?"

"Not a penny!" Outrage clouded her porcelain façade, and Liam sensed it wasn't for show. "Check all my accounts—all my holdings! I have never received anything from that man."

"Then what?"

"Captain"—Templegrey switched her gaze—"this is ridiculous. Silverhawk could have gained this information anywhere. Why would you accuse me?"

"Because there is no *Soaring Swan*," Riverton replied icily. "The XO made it up and fed you that information. It was a false lead given only to you, and you dutifully passed it along to your real master." She pulled out the printed report and slammed it down on the cabin desk. "Your 'scurvy report' to the Imperial College of Medicine—sent to an office that doesn't exist, to an inbox that is watched by an orderly in the employ of the Silverhawk family. Highlighting Morassia and a ship called *Soaring Swan* most prominently."

Templegrey dropped her eyes, slumping in defeat. She sat unmoving for a long moment.

"I ask you again," Liam said, "because I'm genuinely curious. What did he give you to make you betray us?"

"He gave me reprieve," she said, raising tear-filled eyes. "He spared my family the humiliation that he brought upon the Brightlakes. But that sword still hangs over us and is stayed only so long as I keep giving him information."

"The Templegreys are in financial trouble?" Riverton asked.

"Yes, ma'am. I give all my prize money to my parents to manage their debts, but the costs of maintaining our estates has recently become overwhelming."

"Why recently? What's changed?"

"We've struggled for years, frankly, ever since my father inherited the Fairfield estate."

"Wait—what?" Liam cursed inwardly at his sudden loss of calm, but the name Fairfield just salted the old wound.

"Lord and Lady Fairfield died in that storm with no children, and Lord Fairfield was an only child. My father, his cousin, was the closest relative. And so we took on all his holdings, and all his debts. It was manageable, but just recently our loan from the Silverhawk family came due. Captain Silverhawk renewed it, but at a much higher rate of interest. It has, frankly, brought us to the brink of ruin." She arched an eyebrow at Liam. "Why do you think I've been so keen to get prize money paid out more regularly? My family depends on it."

Liam frowned in thought.

She let out a soft laugh, shaking her head. "I was allowed one indulgence—that beautiful Imperial gown—which my father knew would help me secure a high noble husband. But I'm afraid that one luxury has now cost us all dearly."

"You couldn't afford it?" Liam asked.

"I certainly could, but Silverhawk took note of it at the Brightlake ball. He knew my family was in a desperate situation, and my gown caught his eye. I guess he made inquiries about where my sudden wealth had come from."

"And learned of our letter of marque," Liam finished.

"His family has more than enough influence in court to acquire a second, once they knew about it." She sighed. "And now he enriches himself in this new game, using our intelligence work and his fast cutter to steal the prizes."

"Or just scupper our efforts," Riverton added.

"Yes, ma'am. I guess so."

There was a long moment of silence in the cabin. Liam struggled to process everything, but Riverton's expression remained icy.

"Are you aware of the punishment for treason?" she asked finally.

"I'm sorry, ma'am," Templegrey replied. "I was trapped."

"Or just choosing other priorities. Family before fleet, eh, Lady Templegrey?"

Riverton's eyes were narrow, and Liam could see her whitening knuckles as she gripped her sword hilt.

"Ava," Liam said, taking a step forward to subtly interpose himself, "after all we've done together, why didn't you tell us?"

"One doesn't speak of such things to fellow nobles," she said with an attempt at a shrug. "I suspect this will all end with my being given to him in marriage. The ultimate bribe to save our family."

Liam could think of few worse fates. Especially for a woman like Ava, and especially to a wretch like Silverhawk. His mind flashed back to the diamond broach in his cabin, and another wonderful young woman whose life had been snuffed out by dynastic politics.

"I'm sympathetic," he admitted. "But you should have come to us for help."

Her gaze lifted with new intensity. "I tried to feed him false information—when we were last headed to Windfall I told him we were hunting near Passagia— but he figured out that I was lying. And he foreclosed on my family's summer home."

It was all scandalous, but with Silverhawk somewhat believable. But still . . .

"You know I'm going to check that, right?"

"It's a matter of public record," she said sadly. "But he kept it quiet—it was a message just for me. And he promised that the next time I crossed him, he'll call in all our debts and murder my father in front of a ball-room of guests." She suddenly stiffened. "Great stars! My message about *Soaring Swan* is false?"

Liam glanced at Riverton. The captain was watching the doctor with cool, assessing eyes.

"No," Templegrey gasped, fighting back a sob. "My family is ruined!"

"Perhaps not," Riverton stated. "We're still a day from Morassia, are we not?"

"Yes, ma'am," Liam answered.

"Then send a message to the Morassian port authority. Tell them we are the *Soaring Swan* and we are inbound."

Templegrey looked up, desperate hope in her eyes. Liam couldn't hide his own surprise as he turned to his captain.

"Your conduct is disgraceful," Riverton continued, her gaze boring into Templegrey, "and I'm not finished dealing with you. But you've proven your worth enough in the past to motivate me now. I won't let your entire family be destroyed because of our internal issues."

Templegrey reached out with both hands to grasp Riverton's. "Thank you, my lady."

Riverton snapped her hands clear, her expression dangerously close to a snarl.

"Don't touch me," she hissed. "Don't speak to me. And certainly don't thank me yet." She looked at Liam. "Remove this officer's security clearances. After you've sent the message as *Soaring Swan,* put *Daring* into silent sailing—no message leaves this ship."

"Yes, ma'am." He glanced at Templegrey. "Shall I confine her to quarters? It will cause the fewest questions among the crew."

Riverton considered for a moment.

"Yes, say that she's ill. Put Brown in Swift's cabin and move Swift in with the coxn. No one is to enter this cabin except to bring meals—and make it one of the Theropods, with no translator and with Virtue waiting outside."

Solitary confinement for Templegrey, and serious disruption for the other officers. Liam didn't look forward to explaining the sudden shift in bunks, but one look at Riverton was all the encouragement he needed. And as he shut the door on the silent, defeated Templegrey, he realized he had bigger things to worry about than Chief Butcher's glare or Lieutenant Swift's acid tongue.

Daring had confirmed disloyalty on board. And Captain Silverhawk was waiting for them on Morassia.

THE LIGHT SHIFTED IN LIAM'S CABIN AS THE LAMP overhead swung gently in the swells. The ship was fighting stronger winds as the Hub drew closer, and a steady breeze against the beam rocked the hull. Starlight shining through his porthole was enough to cast a glow across his desk, but the swinging lamp added a continuous shift.

He didn't know how long he'd been holding the Brightlake broach, mesmerized by the sparkling dance of the diamond facets. Too many memories were surfacing, he knew. Too many fond days with Zara Brightlake that he thought he'd banished from his mind forever. Long walks in the garden maze, quiet evenings rowing on the lake, stolen moments out of sight of her parents. She'd been a shining star just like this broach, her flame snuffed out by the aristocracy. It had been years since he'd even allowed himself to think of her.

"Zara . . ." he whispered. "I'm so sorry."

He put the broach down on his desk, next to the small box of old letters. It was pathetic, perhaps, that he'd kept Zara's letters all these years, and having re-read them this evening he could tell just how young and foolish they'd both been. How many times had he read these letters in years past? He knew every word, every flourish of her educated hand, as their tragic tale had played out.

His heart ached at the memory of the news of her betrothal, at the anguish they shared as the dynastic system tore them apart. Liam closed his eyes, fighting down old anger at his own helplessness. He'd watched impotently as she was cloistered away, and he was summarily dismissed from the Brightlake estate. She'd become a prisoner in her own home, her entire life reduced to preparing to be someone's wife. He'd dreamed of rescuing her, of carrying her away to . . . what? To live with him on Passagia? His own father would have been honor bound to return a wayward daughter of another lord. Zara had offered truly crazy ideas, too, of running away together and disappearing.

He smiled sadly. As a pair of young fools in love they'd never really thought it through. And in a way he was glad they'd never tried anything truly stupid—it just would have meant trouble for them both and their families, and ultimately changed nothing. But his own escape to the Navy had been exactly that, he knew—an escape. One that promised the freedom to act, and the authority to uphold justice. He might be a terrible lord, but he understood the system well enough to know that he could never truly escape.

He sealed the broach in its case and closed the box with the old letters. It was probably time, he knew, to just get rid of them all. It was time to focus on the present.

But as *Daring* continued on her mission, Swift and Brown now standing one-in-two watches through the night, Liam couldn't help but think of the other young noblewoman currently imprisoned in her own home. Ava Templegrey was no traitor, he knew. She was a strong and intelligent person trapped in a system too big and powerful to counter. She'd betrayed the ship, yes, but only to protect her own family.

Liam sat back, staring at the swinging lamp. Was there some lovely young lady out there pining for Ava's return, even knowing that they could never be together? It was a sickening irony that the death of Zara and her odious husband had led to Ava's family facing financial ruin.

If the Templegrey fortunes weren't restored, Ava's marriage to Silverhawk was only too likely. The foppish lord loved to surround himself with beautiful things, and he'd treat Ava as just another part of his collection, until he grew bored of her and looked for amusement elsewhere.

Liam's fingers closed around the broach, squeezing tightly. He may not have had the power to save Zara, but maybe he had the power to save Ava. She didn't deserve the noose that he knew Riverton was actively considering. The Empire didn't have to suffer another brilliant noblewoman becoming a casualty of its own rules.

He put the boxes away in a drawer. Confronting Riverton directly was pointless. But they were still twelve hours from Morassia, and perhaps he could create an opportunity to influence the captain's decision.

It was a fool's errand, he admitted. But he had to try.

CHAPTER 11

THE HEAT CLUNG TO HER LIKE A WET BLANKET, AND she felt her whole body sag as she stopped to rest in the shade of one of the tall buildings, dropping her bag to the ground. Amelia was used to the wet, but on Passagia it was a cold damp that seeped into the bones. Here on Morassia it was a thick soup that sapped the energy.

"Are you unwell?" Bella asked, her head lifting up from her walking stance.

She and Sam paused in the street, setting down their packs. The sunlight gleamed off their scaly skin and new clothes. The trip ashore had finally given them a chance to acquire clothing beyond what they'd fled Windfall in. Amelia had hoped to see what kind of flamboyant fashions her Theropod friends might enjoy, but they'd both chosen drab, practical garb.

"Not unwell," she replied, "just so *hot*. How can you stand there in the sunshine?"

Sam took a deep breath, his nostrils flaring as he lifted his head toward the sky.

"This planet is much more like one of our own," he said. "A good temperature and not bone-dry. It no longer hurts to breathe."

"Why do you think there are so many of us here?" Bella added.

Amelia scanned the broad square. Bordered by permanent building three or four stories tall, the open space was packed with cafés and market stalls, with a heavily laden mule train even now plodding through from the main street toward one of the warehouses. It was bustling with activity, but with a quick survey Amelia noticed that the number of tall, dark heads of Humans was almost matched by the number of shifting, bobbing reptilian heads of Theropods. In their two hours ashore so far she'd certainly seen plenty of them, but she hadn't realized just how many there were. And how actively they moved compared to the sluggish, irritable Humans.

"I've never seen so many Theropods before," she mused.

"We rarely cluster," Sam replied. "Territorialism is a difficult instinct to overcome."

"But I think this planet is the only one we've ever really fought Humans for," Bella added.

Most of the stories Amelia had heard about brutes were from the Morassian War, she realized. Her knowledge of history was patchy, but she couldn't think of any other major organized conflicts between the two races. Mostly it seemed to be local skirmishes over homesteads or extraction rights.

"Well," she said, plucking her shirt off her neck, "if it had been up to me, I'd have given you this place. Besides, we seem to be sharing just fine."

"I think 'tolerating' would be a better word," Sam said. "Which is the most we can expect even from our own people."

"You don't get along with each other?"

"Beyond our immediately family," he said, "everyone else is competition."

"But family is everything," Bella added, stepping closer and rubbing her head along his neck. "And worth risking everything to protect."

Amelia smiled. "Bonded for life."

"For life," Sam agreed. "You understand, Amelia. You are not like some other Humans."

"They seem to put vaguer things before family," Bella continued. "These strange concepts like 'empire' and such."

"It's because we have to," Amelia said, hefting her bag wearily. "If we don't obey the laws, no one will protect us from the pirates and other criminals who always want to steal and destroy. We're stronger together . . . although many of us wish we could live another way."

"How would you live? In family groups like us?"

"No, bigger than that." She shrugged. "Just sharing things more equally, instead of the lords owning everything and controlling our lives."

"Barbaric," Sam said.

"But there are bright sides to it," she said. "Sailing in our ship, for example. A good crew can feel like family, and as we endure together the bonds can draw us close. My real family might be systems away from here, but my fellow crewmembers are always with me."

"Yes," Bella said, moving to walk alongside her. "We have enjoyed sensing the companionship of your Human crew. It's so strange to see nonfamily members surviving for so long together."

"But Theropods crew ships, too."

"Only in family units," Sam said, moving to flank her other side. "Nonfamily crews can't last more than a few months before fighting breaks out. We learned that many generations ago."

"I wonder how the Theropod pirates survive?"

"Treachery and constant movement, I suspect."

Amelia glanced at the pair of reptiles lowered in their walking stances on either side of her. Their powerful legs moved with feline grace, their long tails out to balance their bodies leaning forward. Both had raised their heads to see better through the crowds. Every movement was quick and precise, almost bird-like.

"Our two peoples appear very different," she said finally, "but in our hearts I think we are much the same. We love, we fear, we fight for what's important. And mostly, we just want to be left in peace."

Sam barked in appreciation. "We have enjoyed sailing with you, and your crew family."

"Really?" Amelia was genuinely pleased to hear that.

"So long as we're together," Bella said, "any adventure is a good adventure."

"I wish you could stay," Amelia admitted. "Any idea what your next move is?"

"We will look for opportunities here on Morassia— another restaurant or café that caters to Humans."

"If there's a good location available we'll start our own," Sam added, "but there's usually somebody looking to sell. We've turned around a failing café more than once."

"I believe it," Amelia said. "The crew certainly love your cooking. And I still feel I owe you everything, for how you helped me rescue Liam."

"The protection of a mate is the highest service," Sam said. "We were honored to do so."

"And look," Bella said, nosing her head forward to indicate a familiar group of Humans moving slowly through the crowds ahead of them, "there is your mate now."

Amelia grinned as she saw Liam, his tall, lean form slipping through the crowds as he followed Commander Riverton. Swift and Sky were close behind. All of them were in nondescript civilian clothing, and at a glance would have completely blended into the crowd, but Amelia could always recognize Liam's gait, his stance, his handsome features.

"I think they're moving toward our quarry," she said, suddenly even more interested as she pressed forward to close the distance. "Let's watch."

LIAM KEPT HIS HANDS CLOSE AS THEY MOVED through the bustling crowd of Humans and Theropods. He'd never seen so many brutes in one place, but they were scattered and self-absorbed. Instinct made him immediately wary of their alien, predatory bodies, but experience told him that there was nothing to worry about. Theropods never acted in groups larger than half a dozen and were more likely to turn on each other in such close confines than on a Human.

He knew he should be more worried about the Humans around him, but the heat robbed everyone of their vigor, and the fellow members of his species either slouched along or hunkered at their tables, their eyes down. Everyone was just enduring until the relative cool of winter reached this side of the planet in another month or more.

A familiar form caught his eye, and for a moment he fixed on Amelia, no doubt returning from her stores run. The two Theropods were still with her, hard to recognize in their new clothes. She glanced at him with a little smile. He gave her a wink before turning to follow Riverton through the crowd.

Swift and Sky were close behind him, in case bodyguards suddenly became necessary. Butcher and Brown were on duty in the ship. With all the unregistered vessels in orbit Liam would have felt more comfortable if Templegrey was free to join them, but Riverton was still insistent that she remain under house arrest. His urgent, quiet words that morning had seemingly fallen on deaf ears.

As he followed the captain past a line of potted, broad-leaved plants and into the welcoming cool of a covered stone portico, however, he remembered that Riverton had much more pressing matters on her mind.

The patio was popular, but the tables were widely spread to offer ease of movement for Theropods and provide a modicum of privacy for each group. The relief from the heat was welcome but did nothing to ease his mood as he spotted the table toward which Riverton approached. Lounging in a chair with a water pipe in hand, Captain Lord Silverhawk lifted his drink to his lips before gesturing languidly.

"Sophia," he called, "what a pleasant surprise."

He was dressed in a white shirt and trousers, his black boots gleaming with polish as he crossed one leg over the other. His gold coat was unbuttoned and the rapier on his belt hung loosely. His eyes rested on Riverton for a long moment, shifting to Liam and then to Swift and Sky behind him. He made no effort to rise but indicated the two empty chairs at his table.

The table beyond him was occupied by what could only be bodyguards, Liam assessed. A pair of grim-faced, clean-cut Humans who decidedly ignored their drinks as their eyes scanned Liam and his group. Liam gestured behind his back for Swift and Sky to take the empty table on the near side of Silverhawk, then he sat down next to Riverton. His back brushed up against the potted plants, giving him an easy line of sight to anywhere within the patio.

A Theropod waiter appeared immediately, providing

fresh glasses and another jug of iced water. He paused for a moment, waiting, but when neither Riverton nor Liam spoke he took the hint and retreated.

"I confess I didn't expect you to show your face in person," Silverhawk mused.

"I was surprised indeed when I saw *Arrow* in port," Riverton replied smoothly. "Thank you for meeting with me."

"It's always a pleasure to meet with another civilized person," he said, offering a derisive gesture at their surroundings. "But what are the chances of us both being here on Morassia at the same time?"

"We seem to be meeting by chance quite a lot lately," Riverton replied. "One has to wonder."

"I suppose we're both drawing on the same information. I'm just able to act more swiftly and more effectively." He took a long puff on his water pipe. "It would explain why His Imperial Majesty granted me a letter to complete the work that you can't."

Riverton folded her hands on the table, offering a courtly smile. "Let us speak plainly."

He returned the smile, gesturing indulgently. "As you wish."

"My ship is doing real work for His Majesty, which takes time and effort. Your attacks on our targets are making my job more difficult."

"Why would I care about that?" His eyebrows furrowed. "Your difficulties are not my problem."

"They are when they become the Emperor's problem."

"And how in the stars could that be the case?"

"We have a mission to accomplish, for the safety of the Empire."

"Oh, Sophia, don't overdramatize." Silverhawk placed his hand over hers, leaning in like he was sharing a secret. "Hunting down a band of brigands is hardly about 'the safety of the Empire.' You and I both have free rein to circumvent the tiresome rules of engagement the Navy suffers under, to send a message to random criminals, and to each take home a hoard of gold. It's great fun. Or at least, it is for me. Perhaps not so much for you now that you have real competition."

To her extreme credit, Liam thought, Riverton left her hands folded under Silverhawk's. Her luminous eyes were afire, but her voice remained calm.

"Hunting pirates is a means to an end," she said. "We need to find information on the larger threat—"

"Let me explain something to you," Silverhawk interrupted. "There are always threats to the Empire, be it pirates, or bugs, or these filthy savages we let into our borders." He gestured toward a pair of Theropods who were just sitting down on stools over his shoulder. "None of them really threaten us—they're just nuisances. But they give us convenient excuses to go to war, to conquer new worlds, and"—he squeezed her hands—"to profit handsomely while doing it."

The two brutes beyond Silverhawk, Liam realized, were Bella and Sam. He scanned the patio and saw Amelia grabbing a tray of waters from the bar. She came over and sat down with them, her back to Liam's table but clearly aware of her surroundings. Silverhawk's two bodyguards seemed unconcerned, their gazes moving between their employer and Swift and Sky at the table beyond.

"I think your assessment of the situation may be inaccurate," Riverton said slowly. "There is more to this threat than usual."

"You mean Dark Star?" Silverhawk scoffed. "A convenient bogeyman to frighten children with? Trust me, Sophia, there is no such man."

"I would like to believe you. I'm just not sure I can trust you."

"Trust is for fools," he said, rolling his eyes. "But if there was really a person called Dark Star—an actual, flesh and blood person—I would know about it."

"And why is that?" she asked carefully.

"Because I know things you don't." He gave her hands a final squeeze and sat back. "You're wasting your time."

"Then let me carry on with my fool's errand," Riverton said. "You can prey on whatever criminals you like—as you say, there's a galaxy full—but leave me to hunt those few ships that interest me. What is it to you if I waste my time chasing ghosts?"

Silverhawk took another puff from his water pipe.

"A clever attempt, but no. You see, I've figured out that you have a knack for finding the best targets—except for that last one, don't waste my time again—and I can't have you winding up wealthier than me."

"Why did you destroy that last one?" Riverton asked suddenly. "If it was of no value, why not just leave it be?"

"Because it might have had some value to you," he sighed. "And I can't allow you to have any advantage."

She sat back, folding her arms as she stared at him with narrowed eyes.

"This is all just a game to you, isn't it?"

"That's your problem, Sophia," he sighed. "You don't realize that *everything* is a game. It doesn't matter where we get our orders from, or who happens to be pulling the strings. Everyone is playing the game. And I intend to win."

He nodded to one of his bodyguards, who promptly rose and strode out of the café. Silverhawk sipped at his drink, then seemed to notice Liam for the first time.

"You really did choose poorly, Blackwood."

"How's that, sir?"

"Had you stuck with me, you'd be on your way to riches and a reputation in the Imperial court."

The idea of spending even one more day in this man's service made Liam's fists tighten. But taking his cue from Riverton's unshakable serenity, he kept his voice calm.

"I go where I'm ordered, sir."

"You should have tried harder to 'arrange' your orders, then." He rested his chin on his fist. "You're actually quite useful. Why don't you join my ship now, while you have the chance?"

The question, posed so casually, caught Liam short. He couldn't help but glance at Riverton, whose expression had darkened.

"My executive officer is not available," she said.

"I think I'd rather let him choose. What say you, Blackwood? I could use a competent second to keep that rabble of sailors in line."

"Why in the Abyss would I do that, sir?"

"Because the game is over, and Sophia has lost. That man I just sent out"—he gestured airily—"is going to report to a local merchant whom we all know works with the pirates. He's going to tell them that the ship in port known as *Soaring Swan*—yes, Sophia, I figured out your little ruse—is in fact the Navy ship *Daring,* also known as the merchant ship *Sophia's Fancy.* I suspect you have about an hour until the local hooligans attack your tub of a ship. With your command team ashore, and no doubt some of your crew on liberty, I think they'll make short work of her."

Liam was on his feet with Riverton. Around him he heard the chairs push back for Swift, Sky, and Silverhawk's remaining bodyguard.

Silverhawk, still seated, reached for his water pipe again. "That ship will be destroyed, and you two, and your two goons at the next table, will be stranded—and marked. If you want to get off this planet alive, I suggest you reconsider my offer."

A stunned silence hung over the table, but no one moved. Liam's mind raced to think of a way to get a message to Brown aboard *Daring,* but he waited for Riverton to act.

"You can't do this," Riverton stated firmly. "If one of His Majesty's sailing ships is destroyed because of your treachery, you'll hang for treason."

"Oh, Sophia," he said, rising lazily to his full height. "I see your notions of power are as quaint as Blackwood's."

"I will personally see you hang," she said, stepping forward.

"Oh, will you?" His unconcern shifted into scorn. "The second child of a middling, outer-Hub house? A mere commander in the Navy? You are less than me in every way. No court in the Empire would support you."

Liam motioned sharply to Swift and Sky, who rounded their table and closed in.

"I will arrest you here and now," Riverton said. "And take command of your ship to deliver you to justice. Unless you call off this insane betrayal."

Silverhawk stepped back, his gaze sweeping imperiously over the *Daring* crew. Behind him, Liam saw, Amelia sat motionless, leaned in close to where Bella and Sam had their necks forward, translators resting on the table by their heads.

"You will do no such thing," Silverhawk stated, holding up a hand to halt Swift and Sky. "You have no authority over me, Commander Lady Riverton. And if any man or woman under your command were to harm me, it would be on your head."

He turned to face the patio at large.

"I am Captain Lord Silverhawk," he declared for everyone to hear, "representative of the Imperial court on Morassia. I am here on official business for His Majesty, and I will not be waylaid."

In the sudden quiet, Liam heard nothing but a low

growl from a Theropod. No one in the café moved. As Silverhawk surveyed the room, most patrons quickly looked away.

Liam frowned, wanting to shout his frustration. Silverhawk had called Riverton's bluff with such easy disdain there was no point in even trying to threaten him. By the rules of the Navy he was the senior officer, and by the rules of the Imperial court he was the ranking noble. Riverton had no authority to stop him, and if any of the *Daring* crew acted now, there were dozens of witnesses who would report an assault on a high lord.

Damn the rules, he cursed inwardly. Damn the whole system!

They had no choice but to let him go and try to save *Daring*.

WHY WASN'T LIAM DOING SOMETHING? AMELIA kept her head low, Sam's and Bella's noses in close as they listened to her. Why didn't he just smack that snob right in the face? Damn the nobles and their stupid rules.

"I don't understand," Sam said to her, his translator turned down to a whisper. "Why is your captain not stopping this lord?"

"The rules of our society," Amelia muttered, hearing Silverhawk step past her chair and call for his bodyguard. "He outranks even our captain, so no one's willing to risk fighting him."

"Is he that dangerous?"

"Not personally, but any man or woman from *Daring*'s crew who attacks him will be executed, according to the laws of our society."

Bella hissed in disgust.

Amelia sat back, keeping her eyes down but watching as Silverhawk took his feathered hat from his bodyguard and donned it with a flourish.

"And what is he doing now?" Bella asked.

"He's given the order to destroy our ship." She stayed motionless, even as her entire body tensed. "And everyone on board."

The Theropods lifted their heads, leaving the translators on the table. Their vertically slit eyes locked for a long moment, then as one they rose from their stools. Amelia made to speak, but words escaped her as the Theropods padded away, rounding a table before heading for the exit. She watched as their lean forms slipped out into the crowd and disappeared.

They probably had the right idea, she decided, making their break before they became too associated with *Daring*. She couldn't blame them.

But they could have at least said goodbye.

She turned in her chair. Liam and the others were still standing, powerless to act as Silverhawk leisurely folded his gloves over his belt.

"I suggest you disappear, Sophia," he said. "When I return to *Arrow* I'm going to broadcast your faces so the pirates can hunt you down personally."

"Why?" Riverton asked breathlessly.

"It seems you've both made some powerful enemies, I'm afraid. And they pay well for information on you."

"Who pays for information on us?"

"I don't care," he said with a distracted shrug.

Riverton stood in stoic silence. Liam fumed behind her. Swift and Sky both looked ready to pounce, but they wouldn't act without Riverton's order. Amelia fought to stay seated, realizing she hadn't yet been identified and hoping that might bring some advantage. She silently begged Riverton to give the order to take that fop down, but she knew that Silverhawk's words were true. If any man or woman under Riverton's command touched Silverhawk, the captain herself would hang.

With a courtly bow, Silverhawk turned and strode out through the entrance, bodyguard in tow. Beyond the crowds bustled, but Silverhawk suddenly stopped, his feathered hat clearly visible in the sunshine. Amelia heard his indignant shout, and in response a heavy growl. She was on her feet, moving toward the patio entrance. She knew that growl.

Bella was standing in front of Silverhawk, her body low and teeth bared. Anything she might be saying was lost in translation, and Silverhawk's words were equally ineffective. The noble held his ground warily, gesturing his bodyguard forward. The man reached for his sword.

Along the line of potted plants in the other direction, Amelia caught sudden, swift movement. She jerked back as Sam's charge went airborne, his body launching into attack. Both feet slammed into Silverhawk's back. The Human crumpled under the force, collapsing forward into his bodyguard. Both men went down to the pavement. Sam landed on Silverhawk's back, his head lashing down. Bella leaped on the bodyguard. Her foot stomped his head while the other pinned his sword arm. Sam's head snapped out, and Amelia heard a sickening crack. Bella's foot stomped again, and Amelia noticed the first of the blood seeping across the ground.

Liam rushed to her side. He surveyed the carnage for a moment, glancing at her and then back. His eyes narrowed in cunning as he shifted his expression into one of overdramatic horror.

"No!" he shouted. "Stop those brutes!"

Sam and Bella looked up, both of them roaring. Then they turned and ran, the shocked crowd parting before them.

"Check Lord Silverhawk," Liam shouted again. His voice was very loud, Amelia thought.

She obeyed his order, though, and raced forward to inspect the mangled bodies. The bodyguard's head was half-crushed and she averted her eyes from the mess. Silverhawk lay sprawled on his stomach, his feather hat still on his head. She lifted the brim aside and smelled the familiar reek of blood. His white shirt was soaked red from the gash across his throat. No, more than a gash, she realized. An entire chunk of his neck was missing. Or displaced, she saw a moment later, spotting a pulped, bloody mass of flesh on the ground, spitting distance away.

Liam crouched next to her, patting down Silver-hawk's shirt and reaching into his coat pockets. Folded parchments slipped into Liam's own pockets.

She looked up, where Riverton loomed over her.

"He's dead," Amelia said simply, not sure at all what emotions were flooding through her.

"We must find those brutes!" Riverton declared. "And avenge Lord Silverhawk!"

Liam grabbed her arm and pulled her up into a run. Riverton, Swift, and Sky were close behind. She sprinted along with him, the crowd parting as Liam drew his sword and shouted for them to make way. Was he seriously trying to hunt down Bella and Sam to avenge Silverhawk?

The furious pace left no time to question, though, and Amelia was gasping for breath when they finally paused at the edge of the square. Liam sheathed his sword, making a show of looking wildly in every direction. Then he shouted and started running for the nearby boat jetties. Liam slowed to a stride as they moved out along the wooden platform, searching for *Daring*'s two boats.

"What are we doing?" she finally managed to ask.

"We're heading to orbit," Liam said, spotting Master Rating Faith and signaling for the boat coxn to prepare for departure. "We have to get back to *Daring* before the pirates find her."

"Right."

"But you," he said, slowing to a halt as Swift and Sky climbed aboard, "are taking the other boat. And you're going to wait up to thirty minutes to see if any passengers arrive."

"What passengers?" Amelia demanded. *Daring*'s second boat was moored alongside this one, Able Rating Hunter looking on curiously.

Liam handed Amelia the two abandoned translators. Riverton appeared at his side, a gleam in her eye.

"You make the most useful friends, Amelia," she said.

Amelia took the translators, her mind whirling over the last few frantic minutes.

"You're not mad at them?" she finally asked.

"I'd have kissed them both on the spot," she retorted. "But with all those witnesses we had to show our support for the noble Lord Silverhawk."

"Officially," Liam added, patting the boat's hull, "we're setting off on a chase. Too bad we'll never find those anonymous brutes."

"You clever bastard," she breathed.

"We'll celebrate later," he said, his face hardening. "Right now we have to save our ship. See you in orbit."

Riverton leaped aboard and, with a wink, Liam followed. The boat pulled away from the jetty, rising smoothly into the air.

Amelia walked down to the next boat, where Hunter looked more confused than concerned.

"Everything okay, PO?" he asked.

"Yes and no," she replied. "We're waiting to see if our loyal Theropods join us. There was a bit of excitement and we got separated."

"Where are the others going in such a rush?" he asked, glancing up at the boat, which was already disappearing into the deep blue sky.

"Back to the ship. And things might be a little dicey when we get there."

"Well, it beats boredom," he said with a laugh.

"Set the hourglass for thirty minutes," she said.

They waited in the sweltering heat for twenty long minutes. A pair of sailors standing idly by their boat, they drew no attention from the few passersby. All the violence of the square seemed a world away, and in the chaos of the mixed Human-Theropod society of Morassia, Amelia suspected that attacks like that were at least a weekly occurrence. No doubt word was already spreading that a high lord had been murdered, but no Theropod would care, and no Human would be able to tell one brute from another. And everyone would say how the loyal officers of *Daring* had leaped to their lord's defense. Too bad, she thought, allowing herself a cruel smile, that it had all been in vain.

She would gladly have waited an entire day to give her friends the chance to join them, but she knew that *Daring* would be waiting for them in orbit, possibly under fire, and as the boat's hourglass slid toward empty, Amelia strained her vision to make out the heat-blurred shapes emerging from the town. Every reptilian form appearing along the pier front made her heart jump, but she spotted no familiar pair of Theropods. Theirs was an anarchic race, she knew, and perhaps that final act was their way of saying goodbye. One last battle to protect their friends before disappearing forever.

"PO," Hunter said, nudging her, "it's time to go."

She sighed, then nodded. He climbed aboard and sat himself down at the controls. She untied the final rope and looped it through the eye, holding the loose end. She gripped the gunnel to pull herself on board, and then took one final look down the jetty.

Two Theropods had separated from the crowd ashore and were padding along the wooden slats. She stepped forward, examining their gaits. Was it . . . ? They were both wearing porter uniforms, she suddenly realized, her heart sinking. No doubt locals summoned to offload a boat. She reached for the gunnel again.

The Theropods growled and hissed in their own language, but Amelia paid them no mind as she pulled herself into the boat. Then she heard a distinctive sound amid the growling.

"*Arr-meh-ley-arr . . .*"

She spun, staring at the two Theropods who had paused on the jetty before her. They were in different clothes, but as she examined their heads she recognized Sam's unique ridges and Bella's long, smooth nose. They stared at her, unmoving.

She couldn't suppress the grin that exploded across her features, finally remembering to cover her teeth before gesturing them to board. Bella leaped over the gunnel and Sam was a step behind. Amelia handed them their translators, wanting nothing more than to hug them both.

"Thank you for waiting," Bella said as Amelia released the line and Hunter started to back the boat out of its berth.

"You took long enough!" Amelia retorted.

"We needed to disappear after the attack," Sam said. "And then find new clothes so that the Humans wouldn't recognize us."

They swayed in unison as the boat turned and lifted. Amelia strapped herself in and the Theropods followed suit. They all stared at each other for a long moment.

"Do you realize what you did?" she asked finally.

"Yes," Sam replied. "We did something that you wanted to do but could not."

"We are not bound by your laws," Bella added.

Amelia watched them both. They were calm, but focused.

"My Imperial masters may not see it that way," she warned. "They have a habit of applying their laws when and how they see fit."

"We know that Humans are contradictory," Bella said.

"You got that right," Amelia frowned. "Thank you for doing what my colleagues and I couldn't—no, *wouldn't* do. It needed to be done, no matter what our stupid rules of nobility say."

Sam barked. "You would make a good Theropod, Amelia."

She scoffed, appreciating the comment but suddenly filled with an impotent rage. What a ridiculous system the Humans lived under. Couldn't Liam see it?

Yes he could, she realized sadly. But he was too much a part of it to really break free.

"You once asked me why I rescued Liam," she said. "Now I ask you: Why did you do this?"

Their heads cocked, and she could see their side-mounted eyes meeting.

"Because you and your crew are like family to us," Sam said. "We hope that we are like family to you."

Amelia's eyes filled with tears and she blinked them away.

"Are you angry with us?" Bella asked.

"No." She reached out, then froze her hand. "Do you trust me?"

"Yes."

She moved her hand forward to rest against Bella's warm, scaly jaw. "This is from the captain, but it is also from my heart."

She leaned forward and kissed Bella's nose. Then she rested her fingers against Sam's jaw and kissed him between the ridges.

"You have done us another amazing service," she said. "Welcome to the family."

"Uh-oh, PO," Hunter said suddenly from the helm. "Looks like trouble ahead."

Amelia looked up through the transparent top of the boat, through the darkening sky. Dead ahead she could make out the distant mass of the orbital anchorage. And then, just to starboard, she saw the flashes of cannon fire.

CHAPTER 12

LIAM WATCHED AMELIA ON THE JETTY AS HIS BOAT lifted off. She strolled with apparent nonchalance over to Hunter and the other boat, glancing toward the port as she chatted with him. Liam smiled to himself. She was remarkable. His heart tightened at having to leave her behind, but as he turned his gaze skyward he wondered if she might actually be in the safer place.

"Hail *Soaring Swan*," Riverton ordered Master Rating Faith, "on one of the private channels."

The boat coxn manipulated his radio then sent the hail. Liam shuffled past Swift to grab the boat's only telescope, pointing it up toward the orbital anchorage.

The large, fixed anchorage was still difficult to make out through the deep blue sky, but he was able to discern the central hub and the dozen spars projecting out from it. Each spar had anchor points where ships could link up, and hours ago the place had been crowded with merchant ships. Based on the mass of smaller objects around the central hub, nothing seemed to have changed.

"*This is* Soaring Swan," the reply echoed through the boat. It was Brown's voice, Liam could tell through the static.

Liam reached for the radio, assuming that he'd continue the façade of their merchant cover. But Riverton took the radio from Faith.

"This is Swan Actual," she said. "Bring the ship to battle stations. Hostile forces have been alerted to our presence. I am inbound at best possible speed."

There was a long pause, and Liam could imagine Brown's impressive young mind racing as she processed the most unusual signal. It was correct Navy procedure for the captain of a ship to refer to themselves as "Actual" when they spoke on the radio, to distinguish themselves from just one of the officers, but this only applied when *Daring* was operating under her true identity. Never had they discussed the idea for a merchant disguise. But, Liam realized, none of them had ever anticipated a situation quite like this. The captain was improvising, and Liam could only hope that Brown was on the ball.

The sublieutenant didn't disappoint. The boat was rising swiftly now, and when her voice came across the radio it was free of static, and her words were punctuated by the beating of drums behind her.

"*This is* Soaring Swan, *understood. Request threat assessment.*"

"Uncertain," Riverton replied, "but plan for multiple hostiles. Get free to maneuver and arm all weapons. I say again: arm *all* weapons."

She was referring to *Daring*'s military armaments above and beyond the cannon, Liam knew. Those were never revealed except in a dire emergency. He glanced at the captain. Her expression was as calm as her tone of voice, but Brown's response revealed that the sublieutenant grasped the severity of the situation.

"*Yes, ma'am, arming all weapons.*" Her words rose and fell in volume, no doubt as Brown physically scrambled across her console to issue orders.

Liam looked around the boat. It carried the captain, the executive officer, the sailing officer, and the assaulter—and the quartermaster was still ashore. Almost the entire command team was not aboard the ship as it prepared for battle. Chief Butcher would serve admirably to get the crew to their positions, but he had no expertise as an officer of the watch. Sublieutenant Brown was alone, in command, and still required to do her regular job as officer of the watch.

"Ma'am," Liam said quietly, "we're still fifteen minutes away. Sublieutenant Brown is very capable, but I fear that this may be too much for her."

"She'll be fine," Riverton replied in a clipped tone. She took the telescope from him and scanned upward. "We'll be there soon."

Liam knew his captain well enough to recognize the moment to stop, but he pressed forward with what he knew needed to be said.

"There is someone aboard who could help her until we arrive, ma'am."

"Don't start with me again."

"But another qualified bridge officer would be invaluable right now."

"It's not an option, XO."

When she'd finished her visual assessment, he politely took the telescope back and scanned anew. *Daring* was already separated from the anchorage and thrusting clear, the first of her masts extending. He widened his search and spotted at least six ships already at full sail in the vicinity. And at least two of them were turning in the general direction of *Daring*.

"Ma'am," he persisted, "departing a berth is a full-ship evolution, which usually needs all of us on the bridge to accomplish." He gestured around the boat. "One sublieutenant is doing it on her own and may very well be under fire within minutes. She needs help."

"I am not," Riverton said, turning hard eyes to him, "putting a traitor on my bridge. Especially when we're under fire."

Every instinct of naval discipline and noble hierarchy told Liam to shut up and obey his captain. But if he'd learned anything from Amelia, it was to speak up when it mattered.

"She's not a traitor, ma'am," he said quietly. "You know as well as I do she was caught in a web of blackmail that she couldn't escape."

"Tread carefully, Mr. Blackwood."

Swift, Sky, and Faith all kept their gazes studiously

elsewhere. For a moment the only sound was the hiss of the boat's thrusters.

"Ma'am," Liam pressed, "she's desperate to redeem herself, and she has the ability to help Brown. We need her now."

"And what if she's working for Dark Star? Am I just handing my ship to the pirates by setting her free?"

"She was beholden to Silverhawk," he said, "not Dark Star. She'd have no reason to help the pirates."

Riverton's chin rose slightly in a courtly gesture of indignation, but her eyes remain locked on his.

"Subcommander Blackwood," she said, "I will hold you personally responsible if this goes sideways. Are you willing to bet your career on Templegrey's loyalty?"

The name had finally been spoken. The name that Riverton had been unwilling to utter since the revelation. And now everyone in the boat had heard that the captain considered Ava Templegrey a traitor. The chill of the upper atmosphere was seeping through the boat hull. Liam thought back to all the times he'd worked with Ava, from court intrigues to boarding battles to daily shipboard life, and he met his captain's eyes.

"I'd bet my life on it, ma'am."

"You just might be." Riverton grabbed the radio. "*Soaring Swan* this is Swan Actual. Where is Templegrey?"

The reply took several moments to come, and when it did it was a male voice.

"*Officer of the watch reports that the sublieutenant is still in her quarters.*"

Brown was so busy she couldn't even answer the radio herself, Liam thought. He watched Riverton's expression.

"This is Swan Actual," she said finally. "Sublieutenant Templegrey shall report to the bridge to assist Sublieutenant Brown."

"*Yes, ma'am.*"

Liam peered through the telescope again. *Daring* had three masts extended with the fourth in motion. Sheets were already billowing on top and bottom masts as she turned to head for open space. The sky around his boat was almost black as Faith guided them out of Morassia's thick atmosphere. Liam could see two ships steering toward *Daring,* and as he watched the starboard mast paused, then started to retract. Even as she maneuvered, Brown was preparing to fire a broadside.

"Come on, kid," he muttered. "You can do it."

Daring swung through a broad turn, keeping her starboard side toward the pair of approaching ships. Close enough to see with the naked eye, the first of the pair flashed at the bow as its leading cannon opened fire. Seconds later, the other ship joined in the attack.

The orbital zone lit up as a dazzling line of return fire erupted from *Daring*'s side. Tufts of smoke clouded the bow of the first attacker. More shots from the pirate bows peppered away at *Daring*'s hull, but moments later another full blast burst forth from her side. Chunks of outer hull visibly tore off the lead pirate ship. It began to turn, bringing its own broadside to bear, but *Daring* was already diving, closing the boat on ascent. Another broadside erupted from *Daring,* but instead of striking the pirate bow it tore through its sails. Brown had switched to chain shot, to slow her pursuers. Another broadside shredded the lead sails of the second pirate. *Daring* turned again, sails from three masts snapping in the chaotic solar winds of orbit, as she opened the distance from her pursers.

Faith signaled that the boat was on final approach, and Liam heard Templegrey's voice reply. She steadied *Daring* on a straight course for Faith to line up on, even as another blast of chain shot harried their foes. The boat swung to place its hull toward the ship, and Liam looked up at the deep green of Morassia far below them. On instinct he scanned for the other boat, desperately hoping to see it rising to meet them, but all he saw was another ship moving into view. It was a hulking brute, slow and heavy. It was purposefully moving to interpose itself between *Daring* and the planet, and as Liam watched a line of gun ports opened along its hull. He scanned it with the telescope. Not gun ports, he realized. Rockets.

That ship was lower in orbit to ensure a clear line of fire, and *Daring* was in the crosshairs. She needed to maneuver, to lessen her cross section, but she was holding course for the boat to link up. Liam gasped as the boat thumped against *Daring*'s hull, heard the hiss of pressurization even as the line of rockets unleashed from the pirate ship. The arrows of death fired across the open space, smoke trails behind them as they zeroed in on their target.

The first rocket exploded in flight as a dazzling beam slashed through it. Liam watched, frozen in his seat, as *Daring*'s self-defense weapons cut down the barrage. With Templegrey driving the ship, Brown was free to fight. And that clever officer had seen the threat and been ready for it.

"Sir," Faith shouted at him, "go!"

Liam realized that he was the only passenger still in the boat, and he hauled himself through the airlock. Scrambling to the deck, he caught sight of Riverton ascending the ladder to the bridge, Swift dropping down to sailing control, and Sky barking orders as she ran for the arms locker. Liam followed Riverton.

The deck shook as a pirate cannon broadside slammed against the hull, but Liam hung onto the ladder and continued to climb. He barely paused as he moved through the chaos of the gun deck, slipping past loaders as they brought up more chain shot. A rolling barrage forced him to hang on as the starboard guns fired again. Then he was up the ladder and onto the bridge.

"Repelled," Brown was shouting. "Beam cannons recharging. Maintaining chain shot broadsides to slow pursuers."

Riverton was climbing into her chair.

"Very good," she declared. "I have the ship. Maintain cannon fire and switch to round shot when out of chain shot range."

"Yes, ma'am," Brown said, crossing the bridge to confer with Chief Butcher and the weapons controllers. In full uniform, she moved with quick, precise movements and, except for the flush in her cheeks and a few stray wisps of hair, she appeared the paragon of the naval officer.

Liam strode up to the officer of the watch console. Templegrey stood at the station in her white pants, black boots, and untucked shirt, her golden hair cascading past her shoulders. With a pistol and cutlass strapped to her belt, she frankly could have been a pirate queen. But her face was set in determination as she plotted a course for lower orbit and called out commands to the helmsman and to sailing control.

"You're taking us down?" he queried.

"The winds are lighter in the planet's lee," she explained, barely looking up. "With their shredded sails the pirates will wallow if they try to pursue. And I assume we have another boat to collect?"

"We do," he said, clapping her on the shoulder. "Well done, officer of the watch."

He walked over to Riverton, quickly repeating Templegrey's plan to ensure they kept distance from their attackers. The captain nodded, glancing at the clock.

"That boat should be lifting off. We can hold in the shallows and exchange round fire until then." She looked up through the canopy toward the dazzling light of the Hub. "But we still have to get out of here, and I suspect there are more than three pirate ships gunning for us."

"There's no need to hide anymore," he said. "Silverhawk has already broadcast our identity and Ms. Brown's very effective light show revealed our true nature to anyone in visible range. We are HMSS *Daring* again, ma'am. We might as well act like it."

"Sublieutenant Brown," Riverton called across the bridge, "start a record of each of the pirate ships harassing us. I want their identities captured for transmission to the Fleet."

"Yes, ma'am."

Liam wasn't sure Riverton was following his line of thought. After so long playing their game of cloak and dagger, her old habits were dying hard. The deck rattled as another pirate broadside slammed into the hull.

"We have a full load of missiles, ma'am," he said quietly. "We could end this entire battle with three quick shots."

"And broadcast to the entire system that the Navy willfully destroys civilian ships," she retorted, "brazenly and in full view of both Human and Theropod witnesses in orbit and on the surface? No, XO, I don't wish to be known on Morassia as a mass murderer."

It was well-known that Navy ships had powerful weapons, but they were intended for use only against other warships—Sectoid warships, frankly—and Liam immediately understood her interpretation of public opinion. *Daring* was His Majesty's sailing ship, and no Emperor wanted to be known for killing private citizens in cold blood, pirates or not.

"We could argue that it was to avenge Lord Silverhawk," he offered.

"I'm not doing it, Mr. Blackwood."

He nodded, unable to muster further argument against her moral stance. But it was frustrating, he thought as he stepped away, to work for a diplomat.

He wandered over to Brown at weapons control, noting that the two smaller pirate ships were nearly out of cannon range, unable to maneuver in the planetary lee and holding off. The bigger ship, which had made the rocket attack against them, was still looming close. It only had a half dozen cannon, though, and its fire was more nuisance than anything. The beam weapons were recharged and ready in case the pirates launched another rocket attack.

"Bit of a stalemate, sir," Brown reported. "We can sustain this sort of barrage all day. I have all three targets locked for missile fire."

He noted the gleam in her eyes, guessing he'd had the same moments ago with Riverton. But he shook his head.

"Maintain your lock, but it's not our intention to use missiles. We're going to recover the other boat and get out of here."

"Yes, sir." If there was any disagreement within her, it was masked under a cool, loyal expression.

Liam walked back to the officer of the watch station, where Templegrey kept the ship steady on a course that maintained cannon arcs of fire on the large, nearby pirate ship. She was speaking on the radio as he approached.

"Captain, ma'am, officer of the watch," she called. "Second boat has departed her berth and is climbing."

"Very good," Riverton replied, not looking back. "Maintain course to recover and plot a heading to clear for open space, putting those pirates behind us."

Liam gave Templegrey a nod, then turned back to survey the scene. Morassia loomed huge to starboard and ahead, the big pirate ship was closing just abaft the beam. Sparks of cannon fire indicated its hostile intent, but he knew it was little threat at this range. Grabbing a telescope he peered down toward the planet. He could see the sprawl of the town they'd just left behind and the sparkle of movement as dozens of boats came and went from the port.

"Do you have tracking on our boat?" he asked over his shoulder.

"There's too much clutter," Templegrey replied. "But most traffic is staying close to the surface so I suspect we'll see them emerge soon."

Liam nodded, searching with his telescope again and ignoring the thumping of his heartbeat.

AMELIA PEERED THROUGH THE BOAT'S ONLY TELE-scope. She recognized *Daring*'s bulky form, free of the anchorage and maneuvering with three masts extended. The starboard mast was still retracted, and she knew that meant only one thing. As she watched, another ripple of fire blasted forth as her cannons loosed a broadside. Amelia swept her field of vision to the left, noting another, larger ship. It had only its top and bottom masts extended, suggesting it was firing from both sides. But something wasn't adding up.

"Hmm," she muttered.

"What is it?" Bella asked.

"It looks like *Daring* is under attack, but I'm not seeing a lot of fire from the pirate ship. Just a few random cannon shots—I'd have expected more of a punch from a ship so big."

"Perhaps your captain has already disabled it?"

"Perhaps . . ."

Amelia climbed aft in the boat to crouch next to Hunter at the controls. She handed him the telescope.

"Get a fix on *Daring*," she said. "And keep us clear of that big pirate ship seven points to the left."

Hunter took a quick look through the telescope.

"With only two masts it's not going to be able to keep up with *Daring*. We should be clear."

Amelia nodded, tapping her fingers against the bench. The sky was turning black as they rose into orbit, and the chill was setting in.

"Can we go any faster?" she asked suddenly.

"We're at full thruster," Hunter replied. "It would take time to rig the sails, and here in the shallows we wouldn't get much wind anyway. This is as fast as we go, PO."

She nodded, moving forward to the bow again. *Daring* was holding a steady course, it looked like, but the pirate ship seemed to be turning.

"THE NEAREST PIRATE IS TURNING TOWARD US," Brown reported.

Liam looked to starboard and concurred that the great bulk of the heavy merchantman was shifting to a bow aspect. The turn closed off most of her cannon arcs, and if she had any more rockets they would be mounted to fire from the beam. Was she trying to close *Daring*?

"Give her a full broadside," he ordered on impulse. "Let her know we're still dangerous."

Seconds later, the deck shook as all twelve of *Daring*'s starboard cannon opened fire. The impacts tufted against the big pirate's hull, but her turn continued. She settled into a course aimed aft of *Daring*. Was she trying to climb up to stronger winds? Only her top and bottom masts were extended. Both port and starboard were retracted, suggesting she was still ready to fight.

He heard Able Rating Hunter's voice on the radio, and Templegrey replied, giving him final course and speed for recovery. Looking planetward, Liam was just able to make out the dark shape of the boat climbing toward them. Amelia was on board, he knew. He wondered if the Theropods had shown up after all.

"Pirate ship preparing another rocket volley," Brown warned. "Beam cannons ready."

Liam looked at the pirate vessel, at her starboard bow aspect. The ship wasn't pointed at *Daring,* and he knew that rockets had to fly straight at their targets. But rocket ports were opening, revealing the weapons. They were a stupider cousin to *Daring*'s own missiles, unable to adjust in flight, but deadly enough when pointed in the right direction. And the pirates surely knew this, Liam realized. Why else would they have maneuvered such a brute of a vessel into lower orbit when they wanted a clear shot at *Daring*? He looked again at the pirate boat's aspect, then scanned forward to figure out their target.

"Oh no."

AMELIA LOWERED THE TELESCOPE WITH SHAKING hands. "Oh, by all the stars . . ."

Was the pirate ship going to fire its cannon at the boat? Amelia didn't know naval tactics well enough to know if they were in range, but she didn't want to find out.

"Alter course to open the distance to the pirates," she ordered.

Just as the boat hauled to starboard, there was a single flash from the pirate ship's midships and a plume of smoke that just seemed to grow larger. It was a strange cannon shot, Amelia thought. But as she watched, she spotted a silvery object racing toward them, leading the trail of smoke. No cannonball did that. It reminded her of when *Arrow* had fired a missile at *Red Sun* . . . Her eyes widened. She grabbed for Sam and Bella behind her.

"Get down!"

A rocket blazed past the canopy. The boat shuddered with the force of the passing.

"What was that?" Sam roared.

Amelia tore open the stores chest at her feet, pulling out the tightly packed emergency spacesuits within. She threw one to Hunter, then held up two more for the Theropods.

Bella took one in her clawed hand, turning the thick, folded package for inspection.

Amelia saw another rocket launch from the pirates, wincing at the blinding flash seconds later. The boat was still intact, she realized, and she scrambled to unfold and don her own emergency suit.

"Amelia," she heard Bella say quietly, "these will not fit us."

She turned, slipping her suit's sleeves over her arms. Sam and Bella hunkered behind her, their long, reptilian forms stretched out across the benches. The Human-shaped spacesuits wouldn't even fit their legs, let alone their tails.

Another rocket streaked past. The boat shook violently, and Amelia suddenly heard a faint, awful hiss. She scanned the hull, looking for a crack leaking air.

"There," Sam growled, stabbing his nose at a line of bolts along the starboard gunnel. "The seal is breaking."

Amelia grabbed a sealant pack and sprayed the whole area.

Sam leaned close, nostrils flaring. "It is still leaking."

Amelia looked up at the Theropods. Their breath was already becoming more shallow, and she could see a new paleness in their skin.

This was not the way any of them deserved to go down.

"Start randomly altering course," she screamed at Hunter. "But get us to *Daring*!"

THE SHIP'S BOAT WAS CLEARLY VISIBLE, ON A steady course to intercept *Daring*. The first rocket lanced forward, a bullet-straight trail of smoke behind it. It raced past the boat, so close that its smoke trail fluttered as the boat surged through it.

"Open fire on those rockets!" Liam commanded.

"But sir," Brown said, turning, "they're not aiming at us."

"They're targeting our boat!" he roared, striding forward. "Shoot them down!"

Another rocket launched. *Daring*'s forward self-defense battery opened fire, but the beam flashed above the leading edge of the smoke. A second shot corrected the aim, and the rocket exploded short of its target. Another rocket fired, and two attempts later it was sliced apart by the beams.

"We're not designed to hit crossing targets," Brown hissed at him. "I can't guarantee the boat's safety."

Three rockets fired together, and all four of *Daring*'s turrets slashed across the open space. One rocket went down. Then the second after two tries. The third finally exploded, close enough to the boat that Liam saw it rock.

"Those pirate bastards," Butcher growled. "That boat is no threat to them."

"Captain," Liam said, heart in his throat as he turned to face Riverton. "The pirates are firing upon an unarmed boat conducting innocent passage. That is a capital offense—overt Navy retaliation is now justified!"

Riverton glanced around at the busy orbital space lanes, then back at the boat desperately weaving toward them.

"Sublieutenant Brown," she commanded, "target the nearest pirate ship with missile, salvo size one."

"Weapon ready!" Brown replied immediately.

"Fire."

A dazzling burst of light charged forth from *Daring,* curving in flight to zero in on its target. The missile impacted two-thirds of the way down the pirate hull, tearing through the unarmored surface and exploding deep within the ship. The stern disintegrated in a rush of fire and escaping air, and the massive hull broke apart as it began to spin out of control.

"Get that boat docked," Liam snapped at Templegrey.

"They're hooking on now," she replied.

"Extend the starboard mast," Riverton ordered. "Execute your planned course to get us clear."

"Yes, ma'am." Templegrey's fingers danced over the console.

Liam wanted nothing more than to rush down to the boat airlock, but he knew his place was still on the bridge and he stayed put. The view outside slowly shifted as *Daring* heaved to port and began to climb for stronger winds. The space ahead looked clear of ships, and Brown reported that the other two pirates were not pursuing.

"It seems one missile sent message enough, XO," Riverton commented. "We'll be left alone to depart, and there were minimal casualties."

Liam nodded. His motivation no longer had any attachment to the Navy's or the Emperor's reputation.

Dark Star's people had fired on a defenseless boat. A boat carrying Amelia. They were going to pay.

IT WAS ANOTHER AGONIZING TWENTY MINUTES before *Daring* cleared orbit and Brown confirmed that there were no pursuers. Riverton gave the order to secure from battle stations, stepping down from her chair and approaching Liam, who stood restlessly next to Templegrey as she went through the process of standing down the ship and crew.

"Sublieutenant Templegrey," Riverton said, "you're out of dress."

The doctor glanced down at her untucked shirt flapping beneath the officer of the watch belt and brushed her long hair out of her face.

"I apologize, Captain," she said stiffly. "The summons from my cabin was very sudden, and I sensed that the need was urgent. I hadn't expected—"

Riverton raised a hand for silence. Her cold eyes bore into the young woman for another moment, then glanced at Liam. He wasn't sure if she was watching him for a reaction or wanted him to speak. He chose the latter.

"Sublieutenant Templegrey performed well," he said. "Her idea to head for the shallows made pursuit more difficult, and it reduced the exposure of our boat."

"Sublieutenant Brown," Riverton called, "take the watch, if you please."

Brown hurried over, confirming the ship's status with Templegrey before receiving the sword and pistol.

"Sublieutenant Templegrey," the captain continued, "get yourself sorted and report to my cabin in fifteen minutes. Subcommander Blackwood, you will attend."

"Yes, ma'am."

"But first," she said with a touch of warmth, "check on the recovered boat and its crew."

"Thank you, ma'am."

Relief flooded through him as he fled the bridge, sliding down the ladders to reach the boat airlocks. The passageways were filled with sailors securing equipment from the battle, but they all cleared a path for the executive officer. He knew he should slow down, take the odd moment to check on his crew, and project an image of steady command. But he just couldn't, not this time.

He descended the last ladder and jogged aft, hauling open the airtight door and stepping through into the boat area. Both Theropods were there, he noted, lowered into horizontal stances and their long necks down nearly at deck level as they watched intently through the airlock.

"Where's Amelia?" Liam shouted.

The Theropod heads snapped up as one.

"She is in the boat," Sam replied. "Trying to fix a broken seal."

"We must remain here," Bella added, "because we don't have spacesuits."

They both moved aside as Liam reached the airlock. He looked down through the open hatch.

"Petty Officer Virtue," he called.

"Yeah?" came a muffled reply.

"Come aboard, please."

"We're just finishing up this patch job."

"Hunter can do it, I'm sure."

Through the airlock he could see the shuffle of bodies in emergency suits, then Amelia's face appeared. She was frowning, but as her eyes met his, her expression lit up. She clambered up through the airlock and he helped her to her feet.

She glanced around at the passageway, empty but for them and the Theropods. "Boat recovered, sir. Some minor damage that we're just patching now."

He reached inside her helmet and gently placed a hand on the back of her head, leaning in to kiss her. She pressed her lips against his and wrapped an arm around him. When she finally pulled back, Liam actually blinked away tears.

"Very good," he managed to say.

She smiled up at him, watching him with that happy amusement that so often colored her features.

"We're all okay," she said finally.

"Yeah," he breathed, fighting down his own emotions. "I guess that one shook me a bit—pirates firing on an unarmed vessel."

"So if we'd been able to fire back"—she grinned—"you'd be okay with it?"

"I'd be better with it," he said with a laugh.

She kissed him again, then stepped back and extended her arms toward the Theropods.

"I'd like to take Sam and Bella to sickbay, to ensure there are no ill effects from the loss of oxygen."

"Of course." He bowed slightly to each of them. "Welcome aboard. You have our gratitude for your brave and unnecessary action. Again."

"We are building quite a list of places we can never go back to," Sam said.

Was that a joke? Liam wondered. He'd never heard of Theropod humor. There was obviously a lot they all still had to learn about these two remarkable brutes.

"You are always welcome here," he said.

"Thank you, my lord," Bella said.

Hunter pulled himself up through the airlock, knuckling his forehead to Liam.

"Boat's in good shape, sir," he said. "Ready for the next outing."

"Very good, Able Rating." Liam took a deep breath and cast an approving glance at them all. "Well done, all round. We've secured from battle stations, so you're free to return to your duties."

He turned forward and Amelia fell in step beside him. The Theropods padded along behind while Hunter secured the boat airlock.

"Get one of the medics to help you," he said. "I think the doctor will be busy for the next little while."

"Is she still confined to her cabin?"

"I don't think so."

He left them behind on Two Deck and continued up to the quarterdeck. Striding aft he immediately spotted

Templegrey, impeccably turned out in full dress uniform, pacing outside the captain's cabin.

She noticed his approach and stiffened to attention, saluting smartly. "XO, sir."

He returned the salute, despite his civilian attire, and offered her a smile.

"You did very well today," he said.

"Thank you, sir."

She stepped aside as he knocked on the captain's door. At Riverton's call he entered her cabin, shutting the door behind him.

The captain's civilian clothes had disappeared and she stood on the far side of the table in her own dress uniform. Glancing down at his shore outfit, Liam suddenly felt remarkably underdressed.

"I apologize, Captain," he said immediately. "I'll go and make myself presentable."

"Did I hear Templegrey outside?"

"Yes, ma'am. She's in appropriate attire."

"Then never mind your own uniform, XO. Let's get this over with."

He nodded, opening the door and gesturing Templegrey in. She stepped over the sill and moved to stand at attention. Liam shut the door and stood beside her. She saluted Riverton, but otherwise remained as still as a cadet on the parade square.

The captain gave her a long look up and down.

"Your appearance is once again befitting an officer in His Majesty's Navy."

There was a long silence. Liam watched Templegrey's lips shudder, desperate to speak but knowing her place. She kept her eyes straight ahead.

"I made some inquiries," Riverton continued. "Silverhawk did indeed foreclose on the Templegrey summer home, shortly after we last visited Windfall. But it wasn't enough to clear their debts. It seems house Silverhawk has been the banker for house Templegrey for several years, and recently issued a new loan at extortionate interest rates."

"Isn't that illegal, ma'am?" Liam asked.

"No, but highly unethical. As we suspected Silverhawk himself has amassed gambling debts and apparently took the role of the family's financial enforcer to pay them off. In this new role he has had considerable latitude to quietly make . . . ethically uncertain changes to a number of loans his family held. And he was pocketing the extra revenue. The Brightlakes were the first to be targeted, and now it seems the Templegreys are next."

Templegrey's cheeks were flushed, her mouth a tight line, but she remained motionless.

"So, this sublieutenant was telling us the truth," Riverton concluded. "She was being blackmailed by Silverhawk."

A soft sigh of relief sounded next to Liam.

"But that doesn't change the fact," Riverton snapped, "that she betrayed our trust and compromised our mission for the Emperor. An officer of questionable loyalty is a useless officer, and there is no room in my ship for any person who puts their own welfare above that of this crew."

She stepped around the table, towering over Templegrey.

"Is it time, Lady Ava, to end this amusing game of playing sailor and return to your courtly intrigues?"

"I have no wish to retire my commission, ma'am," Templegrey whispered, "nor do I consider this a game. Serving as an officer in His Majesty's Navy is the highest calling I aspire to, and I hope for a long and loyal career."

"So far, your career is neither of those things. Sub-commander Blackwood has often remarked privately to me that you are different from so many noble officers who are all show and no substance. I had some hope for you, but it seems that your intrigues take precedence over your duty."

"What else could I do?" Templegrey forced through clenched teeth. "My family was going to be ruined."

"You could have told us. You could have let us help you."

Templegrey blinked, her face a hard mask.

"We have two aliens on board," Riverton added, "who have demonstrated more loyalty than you."

Templegrey closed her eyes, fighting to keep her breath steady.

"I have no further excuse to offer for my actions," she said finally. "All I can do is swear my loyalty to you, Commander Riverton, and to this ship. And beg for your forgiveness."

Riverton's hand was so quick, the first Liam knew of it was the sound of it slapping across Templegrey's face.

"We will drop you in our next port, Lady Ava," she declared, "and you can find your way home."

The sublieutenant took the blow without reaction, lifting her chin again and staring forward.

"I swear my loyalty to you, Commander Riverton," she repeated. "And I beg your forgiveness."

The captain stepped back, a glimmer of surprise dancing across her features. She glanced questioningly at Liam.

It was never possible to read an aristocrat's true thoughts in one as well-trained as Templegrey. But Liam had spent enough time with her to recognize the fire of determination burning deep in her eyes. This was no game to her. She wanted to stay and was willing to endure whatever was forthcoming. If she really was a foppish noble, she would have taken the offer to leave.

"What good are such words," Riverton said dangerously, "from an officer proven to be a liar?"

"I can only ask," Templegrey said, "that you look at my entire record in your service. I've performed any duty you've given me, to the very best of my ability."

"And what if now I place you on cleaning duty in the galley and the crew's heads?"

"Then I will surrender my pride and do it willingly."

"And what if I assign you to the boarding party?"

"Then I will risk my life for you, Commander Riverton. And sacrifice it if necessary."

Riverton continued to stare down at her, but Liam could see the conflict churning in the captain's eyes. Foppish noble officers would never subject themselves to such indignity or danger, especially when a path to freedom had already been shoved at them. A fop would pack her things, leave the ship, and head home, convincing herself of the ridiculousness of the whole Navy.

But here Templegrey stood, willingly. And she really was a valuable officer, he knew.

Deep down, Riverton knew this as well as he did, he realized. She glanced at him.

He nodded his assent.

"Against my better judgment," Riverton said finally, "I accept your oath of loyalty. And I may one day even find it in my heart to forgive you."

Templegrey let out a short breath. She blinked several times.

"Subcommander Blackwood, amend the watch rotation to include Sublieutenant Templegrey. I want her on the bridge for the first watch. And schedule her for galley and heads cleaning stations."

"Yes, ma'am," he replied.

"You are restored to duty, Sublieutenant. But know this: if I detect any further disloyalty from you, I will consider it mutiny. And I will shoot you myself."

"Yes, ma'am," Templegrey whispered. "Thank you, ma'am."

"Dismissed."

Templegrey saluted and fled the cabin.

Liam didn't move for a long moment, afraid to do anything that might draw his captain's attention. But she hadn't forgotten him, and her icy glare moved to pin him to the bulkhead.

"We'd better be right about this."

"Yes, ma'am. We are."

"Then let's use our new freedom from that wretched Silverhawk," she said, rounding the table as she unbuttoned her coat. "We've got just over two weeks to decapitate this threat."

"Do you think maybe we just did?" Liam frowned thoughtfully. "Did Sam and Bella kill Dark Star?"

"I wish it were so," she sighed. "But no."

She motioned for him to sit down.

"Something else about Silverhawk's financial dealings came up," she said, "but I didn't feel the need to share it with our little ladyship. He's been receiving payment from an unknown source."

"Oh?"

"His gambling debts were apparently enormous. But right after the Brightlake seizure, fully half of them were forgiven."

"Perhaps he paid them off with his take from the foreclosure."

"No. I've tracked down every penny that he took from that estate. This debt was simply forgiven—written off by his creditor."

"Who is his creditor?"

"A gambling kingpin on Honoria, with tentacles stretching as far as Silica. And when Silverhawk foreclosed the Templegrey summer home, another small batch of his gambling debts were forgiven." She offered him a handwritten letter. "This was one of the papers you liberated from Silverhawk."

He read the letter, noting the clear instructions to forgive Silverhawk's debt if he carried out his foreclosure. At the bottom, where normally there would be a signature, was a stylized black cross.

"Silverhawk was clearly connected to our quarry," she concluded, "but he wasn't the mastermind."

"This writing looks familiar," he said thoughtfully.

"Yes, it's Dark Star's." Riverton gestured toward another pile of papers. "We've seen that mark before."

He'd already recognized the unique mark, but that wasn't what he was focusing on. He hadn't noticed the specifics of Dark Star's penmanship before, but in a letter this long he noticed a familiar pattern.

"Looks like Silverhawk was being blackmailed in turn." Liam tried to draw a connection. "Why would Dark Star be interested in this at all? Did the Brightlakes have gambling debts?"

"No. And nor do the Templegreys."

"But somebody clearly wants to punish them enough to blackmail a high lord into legalizing their dirty work."

"Do you know of any connections between the two families? Any business dealings?"

"Well, Ava did mention that her father's cousin, Lord Fairfield, married Brightlake's daughter, but they were both lost in that storm fifteen years ago."

He handed the letter back to Riverton. She examined it again.

"The more I look at this," she said, "I actually wonder at Dark Star's education."

"Oh?"

"The style of penmanship is remarkably similar to what I learned at school. I might inquire into the fates of my various classmates—see if there's anything odd."

So he wasn't the only one picking up on the handwriting. A sudden, stunning thought struck him and he burst to his feet, already heading for the door as he shot back, "Captain, I need to check something."

CHAPTER 13

AMELIA WATCHED AS SAM AND BELLA STEPPED FOR-
ward cautiously, their heads lifting up to peer through
the clear canopy of the bridge. It was the first time they'd
been allowed up here, and Templegrey watched them
warily from the officer of the watch station. The other
members of the bridge crew glanced back from their stations, but no one offered comment. The tone of the visit
was being set by Riverton's serene expression as she sat
in her chair, then turned to face her guests.

"So," Sam said finally, "this is Sectoid space."

"Doesn't look much different from Human space,"
Bella added.

"I know you find our notions of ownership puzzling,"
Riverton replied, "but I assure you there is no uncertainty
on the part of our Emperor or the Sectoid Queen. *Daring*
has crossed a line that no Human ship has ever crossed
peacefully before."

Sam's gaze scanned right to left across the field of stars. "Where is this line?"

"On our charts, in our minds, and"—she tapped her chest—"in our hearts."

The Theropods looked at each other. Bella cocked her head.

"We don't understand," she admitted, "but we accept it."

"Why are we here," Sam asked, "if it is such an offense to cross this line?"

"Because," Riverton said, turning forward and crossing one leg over the other, "we need to disappear. After our exposure at Morassia every agent of Dark Star knows this ship, and word will spread that we are a wanted crew. Every petty gang in the Halo will be looking for us, hoping for a reward from Dark Star."

"And by crossing this invisible line you disappear?"

"In a way. It will never occur to anyone to look for us here. By leaving Human space, we effectively don't exist anymore."

"In minds and hearts," Bella offered.

"Exactly."

The Theropods looked at each other again but said nothing. Amelia had thoroughly enjoyed the philosophical conversations of the past few weeks, as *Daring*'s guests had puzzled their way through Human customs and ideas. No doubt they'd learned a great deal in their years running the Cup of Plenty, but grand concepts like empire and sovereignty had probably not been too relevant on Windfall Station. That backwater, she realized, would have suited Theropods well. Just enough rules to avoid anarchy, but otherwise everyone was free to do as they wished. She often wondered how Sam and Bella were really adapting to the highly structured life aboard a Navy ship, or if they even realized just how organized things were around them.

"Quartermaster," Riverton said, looking over her shoulder, "would you go and find the XO, please?"

"Yes, ma'am," she replied as rehearsed. "May Sam and Bella stay on the bridge for a while?"

"Of course." The captain turned her gaze back to them, adopting a conversational pose. "Tell me about how you met."

Amelia heard Bella's bark as she started to regale the story of their first encounter, but the words disappeared as Amelia climbed down the ladder and departed. This whole visit was a ploy to keep the Theropods fully engaged and away from the senior mess, but at least the captain had the courtesy to make it a hosted visit to the bridge rather than a confinement to their quarters. She really was a diplomat, Amelia thought, when she wanted to be.

It was no coincidence that Templegrey had the watch, either. Not a word had been spoken among the officers and chiefs, but it was abundantly clear that Riverton didn't trust the doctor. The crew loved the fact that Dr. Templegrey had taken over some cleaning duties as part of her "health inspections" but no one in the senior mess was fooled into believing that this was anything other than an excruciating punishment. Amelia didn't know what Ava had done, but whatever it was had chastened her. Amelia found she missed the fun, flirty woman who had always brightened the senior mess—these days Templegrey said little and rarely socialized outside of meals. Liam was frustratingly tight-lipped about it, and Amelia wondered if it was some noble spat.

She was the last to arrive for the meeting in the senior mess, taking her seat at the table and examining the chart laid out between everyone. It showed their local section of the Halo, with a clear line weaving between systems designating the borders between Human, Sectoid, and Aquan space.

"Quartermaster, good," Liam greeted from the head of the table. "Let's get started. The captain's diplomatic contacts have given us this sanctuary in Sectoid space, but our presence here won't be tolerated for long. And every day we sit here is another day closer to Dark Star's forces moving on Honoria. We need to figure out where we're going next and get there fast: based on Aquan intelligence we have just over a week."

"I hope you want to head this way," Swift said, passing his hand over the chart in a general direction away from the Hub. "The winds are strong right now and from the reports we've received the outward blows are going to continue for the next few weeks."

Liam gestured toward a set of systems. "Good news, then, because Charlotte has finished chasing down the pirate shipments and we have two possible systems where we strongly suspect Dark Star could be personally based. And they're out here, near Aquan space: Morassia or Labyrinthia."

Brown leaned in and outlined their thinking, taking a few minutes to describe clues found in the hundreds of documents *Daring* had captured over the months. Pirate attacks were widespread throughout the Halo, but the smuggling activity that clearly funded the bulk of Dark Star's ambitions could be traced back to a local cluster of systems. Morassia seemed to be developing as a new pirate stronghold as Silica's influence waned after the destruction of the comet base, but their previous attempt to investigate had been cut short by Silverhawk's betrayal. And while Honoria was clearly the current focus for future attacks, most funding was from the gold smuggled out of Labyrinthia.

"From our position," Liam added, "we have the time to reach either Morassia or Labyrinthia before Dark Star moves in force, but not both—so we best choose wisely."

Amelia studied the chart, as if some navigational clue might leap out and reveal Dark Star's location. Around her the senior staff frowned blankly, but she could see a focused gleam in Liam's thoughtful gaze.

"Are we expecting a bunch of criminals," Butcher asked, "or a bunch of rebels?"

"We're not sure," Liam admitted. "But ultimately it doesn't matter. Our orders are specific: hunt down Dark Star and decapitate this organization."

"But it does matter," Amelia protested, noting all eyes turn to her. "If this is a criminal organization, then taking out Dark Star will just let another thug take over. If it's a revolution, then we might make Dark Star a martyr and create a bigger problem."

"This is something different from both of those scenarios," Liam insisted. He paused, and in the silence Amelia could tell he was choosing his words carefully. "It's too focused on the nobility to be common criminals, but it doesn't have the ringing propaganda of a local rebellion."

"You're right, sir," Sky said. "It doesn't matter, because we have our orders."

"But it helps to know what we're up against," Swift said, pointing at Morassia and Labyrinthia on the chart. "Do you think Dark Star has active control of these systems?"

"It's a shame we couldn't capture Silverhawk's ship," Butcher growled. "That traitor probably knew everything."

"Well we didn't," Liam snapped. "But we got our people out of there safely, and the Empire is rid of a useless twit."

Amelia started. Liam never spoke against his fellow nobility so openly. Something was clearly agitating him.

"What we're trying to find," he continued, studying the chart, "is a place called 'the boathouse.' It was mentioned specifically, in Dark Star's own hand, as a location to bring Captain Stonebridge when they captured him."

"Interesting that you were to be captured," Brown said, "and not killed like the other noble targets."

"Maybe we've done enough damage that *Sophia's Fancy* and her captain have earned an audience," Swift suggested.

"Sounds a bit like a petty emperor in the making," Sky scoffed. "Granting audiences."

"Didn't you say that Dark Star had excellent penmanship?" Butcher asked.

"Yes," Liam said, nodding slowly. "Clearly an educated hand."

"Could Dark Star be a noble, somehow gone rogue?"

"That would be impossible," Liam replied, although Amelia saw a flicker of doubt in his eyes. "The thing about noble titles is that they're hard to shake. The Empire keeps track of its nobles—we're not allowed to go rogue." He sighed. "And why would we? There's no benefit to giving up our titles. If we want to cause trouble we just do so within the system, like Silverhawk did."

Amelia caught his eye, giving him a wry smile. He was wedded to this system, but at least he could see its flaws.

"So someone educated," Sky said, "with an axe to grind with the nobility, operating for at least the past twelve years, and hiding out in some place called 'the boathouse.' Any ideas?"

Silence fell at the table again, all eyes on the chart.

"Where is Admiral Grandview's squadron?" Swift asked.

"Last we heard, here," Brown replied, indicating a rough area on the chart several days away.

"Close enough to reach Morassia or Labyrinthia, so that they can support us," Swift noted. "Let's hope we pick the right system."

Amelia was still watching Liam, and she caught the spark in his eyes just before he clamped it down with a noble mask. He leaned forward, tapping the chart.

"It's Labyrinthia," he declared. "That's where Dark Star is based."

Glances flashed around the table. Amelia watched Liam carefully, recognizing the façade of his calm, almost disinterested, expression.

"Why is that, sir?" Brown asked.

"That system is a maze of captured planets, asteroids, and dust clouds," he said smoothly. "It's the perfect place to hide. It has the regular smuggled ore shipments that we've seen are an excellent way to make money to fund the pirate activity. It's the most populated system in this corner of the Halo but it has almost no central authority and no noble holdings—so no one to cause trouble or get jealous as one person quietly takes control."

He looked around the table, inviting comment. Amelia knew there was something more in his mind but held her tongue.

"Makes sense to me," Swift said.

"It'll take us five days to get there," Brown added, checking her calculations, "with current winds."

Liam rose from his seat, decision made.

"I'll brief the captain."

THE TRANSIT THROUGH SECTOID SPACE WAS UN-
eventful, as *Daring* became a shadow in the darkness.
It was another four days before she altered course for
Human space again, and Amelia got the sense from the
officers that any pursuers were weeks away by now. A
lone signal had been sent to Rear Admiral Grandview
and his squadron of corvettes, but otherwise the ship
continued in silent sailing, keeping the distant Hub to
starboard as she tacked against the freshening winds.

As the wildlands of Labyrinthia approached, Amelia
found herself making any excuse to come to the bridge
and watch as the glowing clouds of dust grew larger
ahead. The ancient remains of a supernova cloud had
over the millennia been pushed by the solar winds into
a tangle of streams that sparkled as the charged energy from the Hub flowed through them. The former
giant sun had drawn millions of tiny objects into orbit
and the final explosion had scattered them throughout
the system. Labyrinthia was truly a maze of free-flying
objects, random orbits, asteroid clusters, and obscur-
ing dust clouds. A tiny white dwarf at the center held
the chaos loosely together, but beyond the few major
bodies nothing was stable. *Daring* navigated by sight
through the maelstrom, closing on the largest world.

Or remains of a world, Amelia realized as she
stepped up onto the bridge in her civilian clothes.
Against a backdrop of lightning that streaked down
one of the nearby dust clouds she laid eyes on their
destination.

"Wow," she managed, stepping up to Liam near the command chair.

"Makes it clear why mining is so lucrative here," he commented. "You don't even have to dig."

One half of the planet glistened in the dull starlight, its icy surface white with a myriad of dark cracks. The other half . . . was gone. Amelia stared in astonishment at the ragged edge of the world. Her mind kept trying to tell her that it was just the shadow of the night side, but the glowing dust clouds behind it revealed the violent truth. She was looking at a half planet, torn in two by unimaginable forces. The distant lights of civilization dotted the tortured surface of what had once been the planet's interior.

"I guess supernovas aren't gentle," she commented.

"This was one of the lucky ones," he replied. "At least part of it's still here."

"And apparently still home to many."

"Yes." Liam glanced at his own rugged clothing, then at Amelia's. "This first visit is going to be in and out. We make contact with the captain's Aquan friends, we arrange for stores, and maybe we take a quick look around. But nothing more."

"They're not my friends," Riverton said. "They were listed as reasonably trustworthy merchants through my diplomatic channels."

"Reassuring words, ma'am."

"All the more reason to stick to your plan. Have a look around and report back. When we go in, we're going with force. There's been no signal from Rear Admiral Grandview, so there's no telling how far away his squadron is. Until he arrives, we watch and wait."

"Yes, ma'am."

"You understand, XO?" she asked, actually reaching out to grip his sleeve. "Reconnaissance only. Get the information and get out of there."

"Yes, ma'am."

After the ambush on Windfall, Amelia well understood the captain's aversion to risk. She doubted any Aquan merchants would be as helpful as their Theropod friends had been.

"We're in boat range," Brown said from the officer of the watch station. "You're free to deploy at any time."

"We'll go now, ma'am," Liam said to Riverton, "and get clear of *Daring* before anyone notices her, just in case they're watching."

"Very well. Fair winds, XO."

"Following rays, Captain."

Amelia followed Liam down the ladders, heading forward to the boat airlock. Swift and Sky were waiting, both in rugged civilian attire that was bulky enough to hide an assortment of weapons. Amelia adjusted the pistol under her shoulder and grasped the dagger at her belt. She'd have felt better if she could have brought her spiked gauntlets, but today was all about blending in.

Faith and Hunter were both manning the single boat, and once everyone had climbed aboard they set off efficiently. *Daring* fell astern, all four masts still extended as her sails struggled in the scattered currents of Labyrinthia. Amelia cast her gaze across the vivid sky of dust clouds, watching the charges streak down them. There was scattered traffic around the planet as they approached, and no one seemed to take any notice of them. They were just another small craft headed for the surface.

As they descended, though, she realized that "surface" was a subjective term. The smooth ice sheets coating the crust of the world were deserted, and all the lights of civilization were dotted among the torn and shattered rocks that had once been the planet's interior. The settlements were nestled in the flat crevices between jagged pillars of rock. Amelia might have been tempted to call these pillars mountains for their size, but there was no sense or structure to any of them. These mountains hadn't been caused by volcanoes or plate tectonics but were the remnants of sheer destruction as a world was torn apart.

The boat dropped below the highest of the peaks, aiming for the lights of what *Daring*'s charts had reported as one of the largest settlements. All eyes watched the alien landscape rise around them, and Amelia could tell that even her seasoned companions had never seen anything like this before. The starlight disappeared as the ragged mountains towered ever higher above the boat, but it was finally replaced by a glow from below.

"We're into atmosphere," Faith reported.

"Really?" Amelia asked, watching the blackened, tortured cliffs around them.

"Gravity's still strong enough to hold an atmosphere," Liam said, "but on this side of the planet it pools in these valleys."

"So no climbing back to the ship, then?"

"Wouldn't recommend it," he said with a grin.

The sky around the boat brightened, but not in the usual blue of a healthy planet. It was a golden light, cast upward by the thousands of artificial lamps in the town below. It was barely enough to see by, and Faith steered the boat down to a long line of public docks with difficulty. Hunter jumped ashore and tied them fast, scanning the broad platform. Amelia followed Sky in stepping down to the dock and did her own survey. Boats of various vintages and conditions were tied up along both sides of the jetty. Some were unattended, others had crew loading or unloading stores. There were dozens of locals about, but none offered more than a passing glance to the newcomers. Other than the sparkling dust clouds high above and the ethereal golden light, this could have been any typical port in any system.

"Nothing unusual," Swift commented.

"I guess folks are just folks," Amelia agreed, "no matter where we go."

"Except these folks work for Dark Star," Sky muttered.

Amelia stiffened, suddenly reminded of the truth of Sky's words. *Daring* had been hunting down pirates for months, but this was the first time the mission had taken them into the lion's den. She looked anew at the sailors and stevedores bustling along the jetty. No one was neutral here. No one could be trusted.

"We shouldn't be more than thirty minutes," Liam said to Faith and Hunter. "Our contacts have an office less than a block from the end of the jetty."

He motioned for Amelia and the others to follow and strode off down the jetty. She slipped in at his side, hearing the soft footfalls of Swift and Sky behind. The entire town was eerily quiet, and she realized that there was no wind. No movement of the cool, heavy air. When atmosphere clung to pockets in the rock like this, she realized, there was nothing to get it moving. They were in a breathable oasis in a shattered wasteland. Her eyes drifted up to the maelstrom high above them, but it was a chilling sight. She forced herself to look ahead and focus on the environment around her.

The town rose up from the jetty front, stone buildings that teetered in an old-fashioned style reminiscent of some Hub worlds. The cobbled streets were uneven and in disrepair, but carts still trundled along in both directions. There were a few merchant stalls active, hawking a variety of basic household goods. A small pack of Theropods loped by, laden down with heavy sacks. The crowd suddenly parted with shouts and curses as a group of what looked like rolling coffins wedged their way forward before turning sharply toward the jetty. Amelia stepped aside with her companions, watching in fascination as the Aquans passed, the tail end of their coffins swishing back and forth to drive the rear wheels. Liam had told her about his previous meeting with these aliens, and Amelia paused in delight, marveling at how the Aquans had adapted their environment suits to allow them to mimic their own natural swimming movements.

"Come on, Amelia," Liam prompted, tugging her sleeve.

She followed along, still observing all the details around her. Old women paused in their chores to watch from upper windows. Dogs, cats, and children scampered among the alleys. The usual rumble of casual conversation and wheels rolling spoke of a normal working day. In so many ways this was just like her home on Passagia—just with no sun, and more aliens.

Liam paused in the overhang of a house and looked back at his companions.

"That's our place," he said, nodding to an office across the street. "Anything to cause alarm?"

Amelia noted that the door was unusually wide, probably for getting larger cargo through, but otherwise saw nothing remarkable in the three-story stone structure.

"It looks more solid than a lot of the other buildings," Swift remarked. "But it would have to be if the Aquans have created a full environment for themselves within."

"A what?" Amelia asked.

"A giant fishbowl, so they can take their suits off."

"Huh."

"There are at least three people watching us," Sky said. "Two Humans and a Theropod."

"From the building?" Liam asked.

"No. From an upper window half a block back, from the tavern window up ahead, and that brute supposedly selling potatoes."

"Do you sense a threat?"

"No . . . but we should keep moving so we don't start to look strange."

Loitering, Amelia could see, was not something people did on this street. Liam seemed to agree and he motioned them forward. They approached the office door and Amelia noticed the sign on the wall: simple black text on a white background, except the symbols were in four languages. The blocky letters were for Humans, the scratched runes for Theropods, and two others. The elaborate crosshatches she recognized from her visit to the Sectoid ship, and the flowing curves she assumed were the Aquan language.

"Looks like they cater to all comers," she said, pointing at the sign.

"Let's hope they don't take sides," Liam replied, before pushing the door open.

The room within was larger than the senior mess back in *Daring,* but with only two dim lanterns to fight back the shadows it felt much smaller. The stone walls were damp, and a trickle of water dripped from the single heavy door on the far side. Shelves no higher than Amelia's waist lined two walls, half-filled with an assortment of goods, and a low, round table stood in the center of the room. Behind that table was an Aquan, floating in its environment suit and staring up at them with huge eyes.

Liam stepped forward. "Good day to you. My ship has just arrived after a long voyage from Cornucopia and I would like to replenish. I understand your company can supply the finest water for Human consumption."

"Our water," the translator in the coffin announced, "is worthy of your Emperor. We just sent off a shipment to Honoria, but I believe we can provide enough for you."

Liam nodded. Amelia agreed that the correct code words had been exchanged. This was their contact. Swift had stepped a few paces clear, and Sky took station by the window.

"Thank you for meeting with us," Liam said. "My quartermaster has made up a list of stores we need—"

"There isn't much time," the Aquan interrupted. "The Human who rules this place has eyes everywhere."

"Is Dark Star here?" Liam asked. "Is this the boathouse?"

The Aquan fluttered around the table, moving close as the volume of the translator dropped. "It is at the northern end of this valley, on the highest central peak."

"Thank you. May we repay you by making use of your services?"

"We have little to offer, because that Human is cutting us out of the trade."

"We will put a stop to that."

"You must go." The Aquan started to roll backward.

Liam glanced at Amelia, then back at the Aquan. "What's wrong?"

"Sir," Sky called from the window, "there's a group approaching—Human and Theropod mix, with weapons."

"We're moving," Liam said, bursting into action as he crossed the damp floor, threw open the door, and stepped out into the street.

Amelia was right behind him, looking to her right at the gang approaching them. There were at least a dozen, and their faces lit up as soon as she and Liam appeared.

"I'm happy to run," she said, pushing him forward.

"No point," he said, drawing his saber and pistol.

She looked past him, toward the jetty, and saw another gang of thugs approaching, led by a woman in a silver breastplate, a black cross fashioned across it. As she moved forward she glanced left and right, black ringlets of hair falling past her ears. The street was blocked in both directions, but the alley running alongside the Aquan building looked clear.

"This way," Amelia said, stepping toward the alley.

"You three go," Liam hissed. "I'm the one they want."

"We're not leaving you," she shot back, edging toward the alley. Swift and Sky were next to her, weapons out.

"We know they won't hurt me," Liam said, his eyes flicking back and forth between the two approaching groups. "Because Dark Star wants me unharmed."

"Unless their orders have changed," Swift said. "We can still make it if we run."

"Get back to the ship," Liam insisted, "and tell the captain where the boathouse is. I'll wait for rescue."

"You can tell her yourself," Amelia said, edging closer to him as she drew her own pistol and blade.

"They'll just cut us off," Liam said, visibly angry. "I'll delay them while you three escape and get help."

"Like we'd ever do that," Swift said, lowering into a defensive stance.

"I am ordering you to escape," Liam growled, taking his eyes off the enemy long enough to pin Swift with his glare. "Lieutenant Swift, Chief Sky, and Petty Officer Virtue, withdraw and get help."

Amelia glanced at her two senior colleagues. Their steely expressions darkened, and they both started to back up.

"Yes, sir," Swift muttered.

"We'll come for you," Sky added.

They edged into the alley, still watching for an attack.

"You as well," Liam said, elbowing Amelia back.

"Not a chance," she said, moving to his side. Her own anger was flaring. Why did he have to be such a big, dumb hero?

"That is an order, Petty Officer." His eyes locked with hers, and she could see the desperation in his gaze. He was just trying to protect her, she knew. Well, who was going to protect him?

"I resign my position," she said, spitting on the ground. "And I stand with you."

"Insolent cur," he muttered, even as his eyes sparkled. Then over his shoulder he barked: "You two, get out of here!"

After another long, reluctant pause, Swift and Sky turned and ran.

Amelia felt Liam's arm brush against her shoulder as they moved to defend. The group of thugs ahead of her were well-armed, and she could see pistols being drawn. She raised her own directly at the lead Human.

"Get back," she warned. "I have enough rounds to drop every one of you."

"Captain Stonebridge," she heard a female voice call. The woman in the silver armor stepped forward. "Put away your weapons, before something happens that none of us want."

"I know you have orders not to harm me," he declared.

"Yes, but that doesn't extend to your crew," she replied, pointing a pistol at Amelia.

Amelia swung her own weapon to point right back. Liam's expression hardened.

"If you hurt her," he warned, "I will fight to the death. But if you promise to leave her unharmed, we will come willingly."

The woman holstered her pistol and lifted her hands to calm her two bands of thugs. She was tall and slim, her curly black hair hanging just past her collar. Large, dark, intelligent eyes shifted between Amelia and Liam.

"A perfect solution, Captain," she said. "We will have two guests, then."

Amelia watched the easy authority that this woman exercised. The thugs lowered their weapons at her gesture, and she stepped forward to take Liam's weapons. He handed them over, a curious look on his face. She held his gaze for a moment, and the hint of a smile tugged at her lips.

"Think hard, my lord," she said.

She turned to Amelia, extending her hands. Amelia surrendered the pistol and dagger. This was a terrible situation, she knew, yet she couldn't help but marvel at this woman.

"Are you Dark Star?" she asked.

"No," the woman replied with a soft laugh. "But when Lord Blackwood finally remembers my name, I'm sure he'll tell you what it is."

Her easy words almost glided right past Amelia. Then she realized that the woman had just used Liam's real title. Her eyes snapped over to him. He was staring intently at the woman, but Amelia could see no fear. His expression was calm, with possibly a spark of anticipation.

The woman stepped back, motioning forward two thugs with manacles.

"I'm sure you both understand," she said smoothly as Amelia felt her arms being wrenched back and cuffed. "But I don't want to take any chances that you'll do something foolish and damage yourselves. Dark Star wouldn't be pleased."

Amelia didn't resist as they were led away. She glanced up at Liam. His expression was clouded, but he noticed her gaze and gave her a wink.

"You know something," she whispered to him.

"I'm not sure," he whispered back. "But we're going to find out soon."

CHAPTER 14

BUNDLED INTO A SHUTTERED CARRIAGE, AMELIA and Liam couldn't see where they were being taken, but the length of the journey and the steady uphill climb gave them a good indication that they were headed for the boathouse. A pair of burly men crowded into the carriage with them, so conversation was impossible, but Amelia took strength from Liam's serenity. He truly seemed convinced that they would come to no harm.

Amelia had seen enough gangs and petty kingpins over the years to doubt his conviction, though. Just growing up in Passagia she'd always seen the criminal elements in the shadows, broken men and women who enjoyed the act of intimidation and reveled in delivering pain. From everything the *Daring* crew had seen of the pirates' activities, she didn't think Dark Star's people were any different. But, as the carriage bounced along the street, the two thugs sat in silence, idly watching their prisoners but offering no threats.

The carriage finally trundled to a halt. The door opened and the wooden steps were lowered. The man next to Amelia motioned for her to get out. She stood shakily, unbalanced by the manacles constricting her. A strong hand reached up and took her sleeve, guiding her down to the ground and leading her toward the towering black form of a rocky shard. The surface was surprisingly smooth, she thought as her eyes scanned upward, and she tried to imagine what natural forces could have carved it so when this planet was torn apart. Up beyond the tip of the shard she could see the flashing dust ribbons of Labyrinthia against a starry backdrop. A familiar-looking silhouette caught her eye, and she realized that there was a sailing ship docked right at the very top of the shard. Spaced at intervals down the entire vertical surface, short jetties extended from the rock and a variety of boats were tied up. The golden glow of the surface shined dully off nearly a dozen hulls. The light was muted here, but glancing back Amelia saw the town nestled below them in the valley. Liam was brought up and together they were led through a heavy door into the shard.

The guards closed in tight around them as they moved through warm corridors carved from the rock. Amelia tried to keep track of the lanterns as they passed on the walls, but eventually lost count through all the twists and turns. And stairs. She started counting how many stairs they climbed but gave up after three hundred.

The ache in her legs told her everything she needed to know—they were headed for the top. The steps finally ended in a long corridor, which itself ended at a set of double doors. They were opened by guards and Amelia followed her escort through.

Her first thought was that they'd stepped outside again, as the vista of the tortured valley spread out before her, with the stars and the charged clouds high above, but there was no change in air temperature or pressure. She was looking, she suddenly realized, through walls of pure glass that stretched up and over this enormous room. Beyond the glass was a wide wooden deck, narrowing into a jetty. And floating alongside was the sailing ship she'd seen below. Its hull was raked, with a bowsprit that reminded her of Silverhawk's *Arrow*. A fast cutter, then.

One of her guards suddenly motioned for her to stop, and another came up behind her to remove the manacles. She eased her arms forward, flexing her fingers and rubbing strained muscles. Liam was also freed, and the guards stepped away. There were a few other guards behind them, Amelia noticed, and at least one more silhouetted against the stunning glass walls. The woman who had commanded the capture team stepped into view again. She'd shed her breastplate and stood before them looking every inch the pirate, complete with a waist sash wrapped through her weapons belt. Beyond her the floor was tiled, with elegant rugs laid out to center the high-backed chairs and carved tables that could have come from any noble sitting room.

"So, Lord Blackwood," she queried, "do you remember my name?"

"I remember you from Windfall, and that they called you 'the Piper' . . . But that isn't quite right, is it?"

She folded her arms, eyeing him doubtfully.

Liam shifted his shoulders, rubbing his wrists absently. He gave her a long look.

"Piper Sunstone, isn't it?" he said finally.

"Ha!" came a new female voice. Amelia looked around. Was it the guard by the windows who had spoken? "I told you he was different. He always took notice of the common folk."

The accent was clearly aristocratic, though softened. Liam's eyes were suddenly alight, Amelia noticed.

Piper raised an eyebrow as she assessed Liam doubtfully. "I wonder if his memory would be so good if I was a man."

"Don't sulk, Piper."

"Very well," she sighed. "You win."

The figure at the windows turned and strolled toward them. It was a woman, Amelia noticed by the walk, of medium height and obviously very fit. Her black trousers and white silk shirt hugged her form, her hips unencumbered by weapons. But it was her hair that drew Amelia's attention—fiery red curls that cascaded down past her shoulders. Her features could have been carved from porcelain, high and noble and unblemished. Her green eyes passed almost unseeing over Amelia and fixed on Liam. Amelia tensed, ready to fight. But then she noticed that those eyes shined with something most unexpected. This woman looked at Liam with affection. Perhaps even love.

"Liam," she said softly, walking right up to him and reaching out slender fingers to caress his cheek.

He stared at her, struggling for words as he shook his head in wonder.

"Zara."

Her fingers slid gently up his cheek, and she leaned in to kiss him. A long, slow kiss that lingered in the silence of the room.

Amelia felt her jaw drop open. She was frozen on the spot, unable to look away as Liam's hands drifted up to grip this woman's waist as he kissed her.

When the kiss finally ended, they both seemed to remember that they weren't alone, and their gazes turned to her.

"Amelia," Liam said quietly, "allow me to introduce Dark Star. Her real name is Zara, once known as Lady Brightlake."

THIS IS NOT GOING TO GO WELL, LIAM THOUGHT TO himself as he looked into Amelia's eyes. Her face was expressionless, her mouth hanging open, but her eyes were burning with a primal fury. His hand was still on Zara's waist, he suddenly realized, and he pulled it away.

"This is Amelia Virtue," he said, stepping clear of Dark Star and putting himself at equal distance between the two women. He wanted to move fully to

Amelia, but frankly feared for his safety. "She is very dear to me."

"Always the gentleman," Zara said with an indulgent smile, "taking care of the beautiful young damsel. How many have there been, Liam?"

He could feel his heart thumping in his chest. It was singing anew at the sight of his first love, at his Zara. She was still alive, and now free. And more beautiful than ever, with a strength he'd never seen when they were young.

But even so, her comment was a smack across the face.

"Just one," he said firmly, moving closer to Amelia. "And I don't take care of Amelia. We take care of each other."

He risked a glance down at Amelia. She was staring at Zara.

Dark Star stared back with frightening confidence, but then her expression softened.

"I'll give you two a moment," she said. "When you're ready, please join me for refreshments."

She waved Piper and all the guards away, then strolled over to the sitting area, clasping her hands behind her back and gazing out at the chaotic view.

"Amelia . . ." Liam began.

"You *knew*!" She stabbed a finger into his chest. "That's why you wanted to be captured, alone!"

"I suspected," he admitted.

"So you decided to come and find out? Come and rekindle your old romance?"

"No," he said carefully. "I want to stop Dark Star. But we've been fighting her forces for months and not made any headway. I thought that maybe by talking to her in person I could succeed where the entire Empire has failed."

"Starting with a big, long kiss is a unique diplomatic tactic."

"I need her to trust me."

Amelia's anger blazed, but already he could see her intelligence shining through. And her faith in him. She took a deep, calming breath.

"Why didn't you tell me beforehand?"

He fought hard not to scoff. "What benefit would there have been? Do you think you would have taken it well if I'd explained how I was hoping to meet in person with my first love?"

She frowned, clearly not happy with her own conclusion to that question.

"But we're here now," he added. "And we have a mission to accomplish. We've done interrogations before, and this is no different. Except maybe I should be the nice guy this time."

She managed a tight smile. Her anger was clearly not dissipating, but she was fighting it down.

"What's the objective of this interrogation?" she asked.

"To learn as much about her plan as we can. And maybe to even convince her to stop going down this destructive path."

"Tall order."

"You up to the challenge, darling?"

"Against that flirty witch? Bring it on."

He glanced around. Dark Star and all of her minions were giving them an astonishing moment of privacy, alone in the middle of the room. Zara had seated herself and was pouring a cup of tea. Piper was off to the side of the towering windows, apparently gazing outward. The half dozen guards all loitered near the doors. He looked back at Amelia.

"So, are we good?"

She frowned, then punched him in the chest. It hurt.

"That's for not telling me beforehand."

"Sorry."

She reared back and slapped him across the face.

"And that's for enjoying that kiss so much." She leaned in, her eyes indicating their distant audience. "And maybe a bit for show."

"Thanks," he said, rubbing his stinging jaw. He gestured toward the seating area. "Shall we?"

She turned and began strolling toward the chairs. He caught up to her, suddenly remembering a similar incident in their past.

"When I saw you kissing another man," he muttered, "I hit him, not you."

"The day is still young," she whispered, her eyes on Dark Star.

Zara rose gracefully, offering a welcoming smile as she gestured for them to sit. Liam took the chair facing her, Amelia sitting down next to him. She poured them both some tea and sat back.

"I have to admire your cunning, Liam," she said. "You managed to disrupt my operations for months before I knew it was you."

"How did you figure it out?" he asked, genuinely curious.

"When my base in Silica was destroyed I took a new interest in what was going on there. My captains were screaming about a Sectoid invasion, but I knew the bugs were peripheral—they could never have gained the information on their own. It took a while, but everything seemed to point to one Julian Stonebridge. I'd never heard of a house Stonebridge so I told my network to start paying closer attention." She reached for a framed picture on the table next to her. "And then this came to me."

She placed the frame before him. It was the black-and-white image captured by the merchant on the Windfall promenade. A portrait of the noble Julian Stonebridge.

"But I have that image," Liam said, glancing at Amelia. She nodded in confirmation.

"One can make multiple copies," Zara replied, sitting back. "As soon as I saw that handsome face staring back at me . . . well, to be honest I was furious at first, but then I realized you were just doing your job. And doing it well enough that I needed to remove you from play."

"And here I am," he offered, looking around at the room.

"And I'm delighted to see you."

"What are you going to do with us?" Amelia demanded.

"For now, just keep you here as my guests."

"I find that hard to believe."

"Well, you don't really have a choice, do you, dear?"

"Don't patronize me, *dear*." Amelia started to rise from her chair.

Liam put a steadying hand on her thigh. She lowered back again.

"Zara," he said, leaning forward earnestly. "How is this even possible? How can you be here? You were killed in that storm."

"So the Empire believes," she said. "And frankly, at that time, I would have welcomed death. You have no idea, Liam, what kind of monster my *husband* was." She spat the word.

"I can only imagine," he said, his heart aching at the ancient pain that was billowing up. "I'm sorry I couldn't do anything to help you."

"And we both know you couldn't have," she said, leaning forward and taking his hand. Her eyes were surprisingly gentle, before the fire rose in them again. She leaned back. "We were prisoners in the system, forced to do what we hated, for the good of family. For the good of dynasty."

"There was no way to escape," he agreed.

"So I made a way," she said triumphantly. "I could never have left my husband and lived in peace. If I'd fled, I'd have only been hunted down and dragged back in disgrace. But if I was already dead, no one would ever look for me."

"And the storm that destroyed your ship?"

"Oh, there was a storm, but hiding within it was a little surprise I cooked up. Piper showed her true courage as my lady-in-waiting by taking my instructions and my money to a gang of pirates before we sailed. They attacked our ship during the storm, looted it, and then set charges to tear it apart. The storm did the rest."

"The passengers and crew?"

"I paid the pirates extra to torture my husband to death. The rest were left in the ship as it broke up around them."

The casual viciousness of her words was startling. But, he admitted, a part of him was drawn to it. She was no damsel in distress, and in her terrible actions she'd displayed courage he'd never been able to muster.

"And the pirates didn't turn on you?"

"I promised them more money once we got to Cornucopia. Piper and I broke into my husband's home and made off with enough loot to keep the pirates happy and get ourselves on a ship headed as far away as possible."

"To get lost in the maze," he mused, looking past her to the wild skies of Labyrinthia.

"Do you remember how we used to lose ourselves in the Brightlake maze?" she asked with a sweet smile. "It always took them hours to find us."

He remembered well many a stolen kiss among the perfectly trimmed hedges. In the end it had been the only place they could hide, and eventually her father had ordered the gardeners to cut through the hedges and transform the maze into an open, geometric garden.

"And then they banned us from the boathouse," he said wistfully. "I enjoyed those rows on the lake most of all."

"So I built my own boathouse," she said with a gesture taking in the entire shard. "Hidden within the maze. I guess I shouldn't be surprised that you found me."

"You left enough clues. For someone who knew what to look for."

"Are you going to tell her," Amelia interjected, "what happened to her family? And that lovely estate you're both reminiscing about?"

Her voice cut through the spell, and Liam wrenched his mind out of the flood of memories. It really was intoxicating, being face-to-face with a woman he'd known in nothing but dreams for fifteen years.

"What news of the Brightlakes?" Zara asked, expression hardening.

"They were foreclosed, only a few months past," Liam said. "The estate was seized and . . . and your father was murdered."

"When and how?" she asked, her eyes narrowing dangerously.

Liam glanced at Amelia, really not wanting to deliver the news.

"In front of all of us," Amelia declared, perhaps too viciously, "at a grand ball. He was stabbed through the heart with a sword by the man who took everything."

Zara sat like a statue for a long moment, staring at Amelia. When she spoke, it was just above a whisper.

"Did he suffer long?"

"No," Liam said quickly. "It was a killing blow."

She looked upward, apparently deep in thought.

"Too bad," she said finally. "I should have been more explicit in my instructions."

Liam caught an astonished glance from Amelia.

"You knew?" she managed.

"I orchestrated it," Zara said, sitting back again with her tea. "It's amazing how pliable even the highest lord is when he owes you more money than his entire family is worth."

"Silverhawk worked for you?" Amelia pressed.

"He didn't know it. He took orders from one of my people on Honoria. One of my gambling people who knew just how to entice that arrogant dandy into disaster. He was a tool, nothing more. But he was efficient in delivering revenge on Lord Brightlake."

"Zara . . . ," Liam breathed. "You ordered the death of your own father?"

She glared at him. "Do you think he deserved better, for what he did to me?"

Her anger washed over him, marshaling his long-simmering outrage: at Lord Brightlake, at the tradition of arranged marriages, at the chains of the whole system. A system that had sent him running to the Navy and had forced his beloved to fake her own death and flee into the outer reaches of society. He still remembered that sunny afternoon when he and Zara had been commanded to say goodbye. How they'd stood in the garden, unable to even touch each other as her parents stood watching them choke out words of polite fare-well. Tears had flowed freely down her cheeks as she'd curtsied to him, his own eyes flooded as he bowed. And then her father had ordered her to step away, practically dragging her back into the house. Lord Brightlake had ignored her sobs, assuming the strong, stony expression befitting the master of his house.

But those memories faded, replaced in his mind's eye with the image of a tired, broken old man, the bloody sword pulling free of his chest as he collapsed in a heap in his own home, humiliated in death in front of hundreds of witnesses.

"I don't know what to think," he said finally.

His anger was still there, he knew. It was always there, and at one level it had been steering his life for fifteen years. But it was a smoldering fire. Hers still burned white-hot, even after all this time. And that made her dangerous.

THIS WOMAN WAS DANGEROUS, AMELIA THOUGHT to herself. And possibly unhinged. But far too intelligent and charismatic to be called on it. Amelia sat back in her chair, looking around at the guards, who appeared so casual but whose gazes were all diligently observing. Piper in particular, she suspected, would have a pistol out and fired before anyone laid a hand on Dark Star. Liam's strategy of talks rather than confrontation made sense.

He was still leaning forward, gazing at his first love. And Dark Star was gazing back with equal rapture.

Amelia reminded herself firmly that Liam was just playing a role, as was she.

"Tell me," she said suddenly, interrupting their moment, "what's the reason for all this? I understand your desire to run away and live your life in secret, but why the elaborate web of criminal activity? You must know that this would eventually draw attention to yourself—doesn't that defeat the purpose of your escape?"

Dark Star's eyes—they really were a vivid green, Amelia had to admit—shifted away from Liam, and for a moment the woman seemed to be considering whether or not to even answer. But Amelia held her gaze fearlessly, and a glimmer of respect alighted in Dark Star's eyes.

"I can tell by your accent that you were born free of the noble yoke. So let me offer a counterquestion: Do you think our society is fair?"

Amelia crossed her arms, wondering how she could answer that question in the least rude way. Then she gave up and just answered.

"Of course not. You toffs sit at the top making all the rules and stealing everything while the rest of us eke out a living as best we can."

"Agreed," Dark Star said, refilling Amelia's teacup. "The common people are very restricted in what they can and cannot do. But we toffs have little freedom either—we live in cages designed by our own hands."

"They're pretty nice cages, from what I've seen. Care to trade?"

"Not at all. But I assure you . . . Amelia, was it? I assure you that you wouldn't care to trade either, after spending some time in a noble cage."

"I've been to your ancestral cage," she scoffed. "I could get used to it."

"It's beautiful, yes. And so expensive to maintain that my father was killed by his creditors. So expensive that he sold his only daughter into misery to prop it up for a few more years."

"You don't know what misery is," Amelia warned, thinking of the miserable, indentured workers she saw all around her hometown.

"Don't I?" Dark Star's expression hardened again. "Pretty clothes only cover wounds; they don't heal them."

Amelia bit down her initial response. Liam's world was as brutal as it was beautiful, she was slowly learning. Any system that gave a man like Silverhawk free rein was clearly broken. But, as she looked around at the wealth in this room, it was obvious Dark Star hadn't abandoned her lifestyle—she'd just rebuilt it.

"Nice tea," she said, hefting the delicate cup. "Guaranteed nobody back in my hometown will ever get to try it. Or drink from such fancy cups." She swallowed down the rich variety of curses rumbling up her throat, as her anger at the unfairness of the system threatened to boil over. "Something tells me you're not trying too hard to spread the wealth. This is no different from any lord or lady living high on the backs of the common folks."

"Yes," Dark Star said. "This is comfort. But it hasn't always been so for Piper and I—we spent years scratching an existence across the Halo. And in those years I learned firsthand the truth: our society is not fair to anyone. Not the nobles, and not the commoners. I could have escaped and lived a quiet life of sorts, but to what end? Simply to live? What would the point have been?"

"So you decided to do something about it?" Amelia snapped, venom dripping from her words.

"Exactly. I was free, I was anonymous, I had my dear friend Piper with me, and we had enough money to act."

"But that comes back to my question: You've rebuilt your comfortable lifestyle, but what else have you done? Building a criminal network doesn't make our society any more fair."

"That's just a means to an end," she said, waving her hand dismissively. "If you're going to overthrow an empire, you need money and people—preferably people who know how to fight. And over time, as word has spread about my activities, other like-minded individuals have been drawn to join me."

Amelia glanced at Liam. He was silent.

"You intend to overthrow the Empire?" Amelia asked.

"Yes," she said simply.

"What, by killing one noble at a time?"

"Of course not—I'm not a barbarian."

"We've seen enough noble ship captains tortured to death to think otherwise."

"Yes, that." She sighed, dropping her gaze for a moment. "I gained a certain notoriety for my vengeance against my husband, and some of my captains seem to think they're pleasing me by constantly repeating the act on others. I need to stamp that out."

"We figured your intent was to kill all the nobles."

"Personally, my intent goes no further than those who wronged us." She put her hand on Liam's. "The Brightlakes are gone. Once the Fairfields are wiped out, I'll be content."

"There are no Fairfields," Liam said. "Your husband was the last of his line."

"But lines never die out," Dark Star said. "They just change names. It's Templegrey now. It doesn't matter."

Amelia didn't know what to think. The Silverhawks of the galaxy could all rot, but the Templegreys?

"Not all the nobility are evil," she surprised herself by saying out loud. "Some of them are worth leaving alone."

"Agreed." Dark Star looked at Liam again. "I need skilled and courageous admirals to command my fleet and impose discipline on my captains. These random murders will not be acceptable when we take control."

"Take control of what?"

"Think of it, Amelia," she said, leaning back and gesturing grandly. "A new society, without social ranks, without restrictions based on class. A place where everyone is free to do what they want, live how they want"—she looked at Liam again—"and be with whom they want."

"I think that's a nice dream," Amelia allowed, "but how would it work in practice? We still need laws, and some kind of authority, otherwise we'd devolve into warring clans like the Theropods."

"I will provide that authority," Dark Star said with a kind smile, "and ensure that no one tries to reinstate the old ways. I will accept that burden, so that you and everyone else can be free."

"Wait—what? You'll be the ultimate authority?"

"I am the one with the vision, Amelia."

"So we just replace the Emperor with the Dark Star? I don't really see the progress."

Dark Star sipped her tea and nodded. "Oh, you think I'd just set up some kind of dictatorship? No, no, no . . . every world would elect its own rulers—temporary rulers, chosen from the people, to oversee the world for a period of time. And then new people would be chosen, to ensure that no one stayed in power for too long."

"Except for you."

"As I said, I am the one with the vision. No intelligent species has ever made this sort of communal rule work before. I would need to guide us in the early years to ensure the vision was implemented correctly."

"And then?"

"And then . . . I would retire, to a life of peace, and let our species continue on its way."

"Unless your children had other plans. I doubt the idea of hereditary power will be forgotten too quickly."

"An excellent point," Dark Star said, sitting back and crossing one leg over the other. "One that makes me the perfect person to oversee this transition. Thanks to my wretched husband, bearing children is impossible for me."

Her words were so smooth and so elegant that Amelia almost missed them. Dark Star sat in her chair, beautiful, powerful, intelligent, and dangerous. But suddenly Amelia's heart went out to her.

"I'm sorry," she said.

"Thank you."

Silence hung in the vast room, and Amelia felt no need to break it. Liam sat in his chair, staring down at his hands. Dark Star sipped at her tea and offered a sad smile.

"And I'm sorry," she said finally, "for any injustice you've suffered in your life. Liam and I endured a few, but I realize that we all carry our unique burdens. When the time comes, we'll build a new society together, free of the class system and its chokeholds."

"That sounds great, but I'm not really that impressed when I know you're only doing this to exact vengeance. That only leads to more death. I'm not interested in a reign of terror."

"I understand. And I admit that my original motivations were every bit as savage as you suggest. But my vengeance is strictly limited to those who hurt me. With help, I'll rein in my captains, because once the yoke of class has been lifted, we'll need freedom and peace most of all. I've been out here in the galaxy for a long time, and I've seen how the majority of our people live. I know the common life, Amelia. Better than you might think."

"Not better than I know it."

"Quite. And so you understand why there is a need to change things. To bring real power to the people and to bring the nobility to heel. This is what I've learned, all these years in the wilderness, and I now have the power to lead the change."

The idea sounded pretty good, Amelia had to admit. It was just too bad that it could never work if led by a person who was in reality nothing more than a gangster with an accent. Amelia knew the common people better than either of the nobles seated with her, and she knew they'd resist any change forced upon them. Even if it was for their own good.

"It's quite a vision," she said, "but people don't like change. It won't be as easy as you think."

"After fifteen years of winning hearts and minds, I think I could do it."

Her words weren't bravado, Amelia could see. They came from a sincerity built on experience. She could think of no retort, and simply nodded.

"Piper," Dark Star called, "please escort Amelia to her room."

Amelia sat bolt upright. "What? I'm not going anywhere."

"I would like to speak to Liam in private," Dark Star explained patiently. "You'll be very comfortable."

Piper was approaching, with a pair of guards looming behind her.

"In your new society," Amelia said quickly, "will people be ordered around like this?"

"You'll be fine," Dark Star said, an edge creeping into her voice.

"But I don't wish to leave this room," Amelia insisted. "Am I to be forced against my will? Is this what happens in your new society as soon as someone disagrees with you?"

Piper reached Amelia's side and took her arm. Amelia wrenched it free, staring at Dark Star.

"Don't make me return the favor," Piper said quietly, stepping back and placing a hand on her pistol.

Amelia glanced at the woman's shoulder, remembering the chaotic seconds at the Cup of Plenty, then back at her face. Piper's dark eyes were alight, and there was even the hint of a smile on her face.

Dark Star sighed. "Fine. You may stay in the room. But *I* wish to speak to Liam in private—do you intend to stop me from doing so?"

Amelia didn't want this tart anywhere near Liam, but she caught his gaze and saw the quick shake of his head. Reluctantly, she rose to her feet.

"Show Amelia the sights," Dark Star said, gesturing to the towering windows behind her.

Piper released the grip on her weapon, indicating for Amelia to join her. Amelia squeezed Liam's shoulder as she passed him, then strode toward the glass.

LIAM WATCHED AMELIA WALK AWAY, LISTENING TO the soft thump of her boots on the stone floor. She stopped by the windows, crossing her arms defiantly as Piper began speaking quietly to her.

"She is remarkable," Zara said. "I can see why you're drawn to her."

He tore his eyes from Amelia and focused on the woman sitting across from him. Her beauty was startling—she was like a painting that had hung on the wall for fifteen years and suddenly come to life. Liam searched her face. She'd aged well, but the happy innocence of their youth was long since banished. Her smile came as easily as ever, and her eyes still sparkled like starlight, but there was something beneath them, and he feared it was madness. The ordeal of her marriage could have broken her, but she'd endured, alive and free.

"Zara," he said quietly, "my darling."

She took his hand again. "I know, my love, it's so much to take in."

"You have such a vision for the future, and you've accomplished more than any person I've ever known."

"Thank you," she said.

"Why didn't you ever contact me?" he asked, feeling the sudden ache in his heart again.

"I wanted to, but there was too much risk of me being dragged back to my old life." She squeezed his hand. "I just couldn't trust anyone. Not even you."

"And now you've built an army."

"A loyal following," she countered. "The start of a new age for us all."

She really believed that, he realized. This wasn't just pretty speeches to motivate her pirates and thugs. Her assurances to Amelia aside, he could see that Zara's anger burned so hot that she intended to tear down their entire society. And, he considered, given her imminent attack on the Honoria treasury, she might actually gather the means to do it. This had to end, now.

He reached into his pocket and pulled out the wooden box he'd kept in his cabin.

"Your mother sent this to me after the Brightlake estate was ruined," he said. "She thought I might like to have it. She was right."

He opened the box. Zara gasped, her expression a sudden torrent of emotion. She reached in and took up the diamond broach, staring at it.

"I'd intended to give this to you," she whispered, "after you got my father's permission to marry me."

"I know."

"It was my favorite," she said, closing her eyes as she held it tightly. "My personal symbol."

"You were the shining star of the Brightlake family." He smiled. "And this was the missing piece of the puzzle. Dark Star."

"Oh, you are clever," she whispered, leaning closer. "No one else would know why I chose that name. But you found me."

"Here I am." He leaned in, close enough to breathe in her sweetness.

When she kissed him, he was unable to resist. It was sensual, fueled by an ache of longing, but when their lips finally parted he realized that the spark died as quickly as it lit. He wasn't a foolish young lord anymore, and she was no longer his love.

"Zara," he said, taking her hands in his. "Let's work together to bring your vision to life. Perhaps in a way that doesn't involve so much bloodshed."

"Do you think I haven't tried to create such a way?"

"From what you tell me," he said honestly, "no. It sounds like you've been building this plan from the start."

"I have," she admitted, "and originally it was for vengeance. But then, as my anger cooled, it became more for protection."

"Your anger has cooled?" He tried to ease the question with a smile.

"Yes," she replied, without the hint of a smile.

"Then why continue with violence?" he asked. "Hide in your anonymity and wealth, and inspire change in the people from here."

"The people won't be moved by words. I need to prove that I'm a woman of action for them to follow me."

He nodded, trying to grasp where her thoughts were coming from, in the hopes of directing them.

"But overthrowing the nobility would bring chaos."

"There is no other way," she said sadly.

"Surely, if we contemplate other paths—"

"Darling," she interrupted, "I've been doing this for fifteen years. Take that twit Silverhawk, for example. Even when faced with financial ruin, his inbred brain couldn't grasp what my people were trying to hint to him—that with all his influence he could effect change and be rewarded for it. All he cared about was his own power in the current system: he just couldn't conceive of something different." She squeezed his hand. "I do honestly believe that some of the minor lords in the Halo, like you, will be able to see my vision. But the Imperial court is too corrupt and myopic to cooperate. Wiping them away is the only path open to us. Trust me."

"My apologies," he said, retreating from that line of discussion. "Perhaps, then, just get your pirate captains to stop the murders. There's no need for that."

"It's been hard to direct them," she admitted. "And keeping them motivated is useful."

"But does it help your cause, or does it just normalize murder?"

She pursed her lips in thought, then shrugged. "Maybe I need your help in this."

"As your admiral?" he asked, feigning interest.

"As much more than that."

Her gaze was intense, and he couldn't help but look over at Amelia. She stood by the windows, her back turned but her head positioned to keep Liam in her peripheral.

"Zara," he laughed, nodding toward Amelia, "things are a little more complicated these days."

"I don't mind sharing you . . . for a while."

"I will see no harm come to her," he said firmly.

"Nor I," she said in sudden shock. "I have many important posts for a person of such caliber. But most of them," she added with a sly look, "are several systems away."

He gave her a conspiratorial smile, but his mind was already starting to race. If she wasn't willing to consider changing her overall strategy, it was time for him and Amelia to consider escaping.

CHAPTER 15

DINNER WAS A SURPRISING AFFAIR. AMELIA HAD expected either to be thrown in a cell, or perhaps forced to endure a private meal with just Dark Star and Liam as companions. But Piper led them all, including Dark Star and the guards, one floor down from Dark Star's observation room, along a broad hallway and into what could only be a large mess hall. Long tables were crowded with seated men and women helping themselves to a variety of dishes laid out in central pots and platters. The noise of friendly chatter didn't pause as Dark Star entered the room—no sudden standing to attention, no trumpets or other heraldry. A few people near the door looked up and offered friendly salutations, but it seemed the arrival of their high commander was of no special import to anyone.

A section of chairs had been reserved, though, and Amelia sat down between two of the guards, across from Piper. Liam and Dark Star sat at the end, just far enough away that she struggled to hear their conversation over the general din, but she watched their body language and saw nothing unusual in Liam's manner. He made eye contact with her on occasion but was clearly engaged fully with their host.

Piper stood slightly to lift the lid of the pot between them. She hefted a ladle of soup and regarded Amelia inquiringly. "Something to eat?"

The smells were delicious, and Amelia doubted a common pot would be poisoned, so she lifted her plate and received Piper's offering.

"Where you from?" the guard on her left asked her. He was about her age, with stubble masking his rough features. The darkness of his skin suggested he was from a Hub world.

"Passagia," she answered, seeing no reason to hide anything.

"Never been there . . . but I hear you have night sometimes."

"Sometimes, yeah."

"What's that like?"

His question seemed earnest, and Amelia noticed several people around her watching with genuinely curious expressions. Hub worlds had skies awash with light from all the nearby stars, and she knew that most Humans only saw blackness when they were in space. Night was something she'd just always understood, but between spoonfuls she tried to explain what it was actually like.

After a while, as people around her interjected with questions and comments, she realized that she could have been in any junior mess on any ship in the Imperial fleet. These people might be pirates, but they weren't much different from Flatrock, Hedge, or any of her crewmates.

Piper's refined voice and mannerisms set her slightly apart, and the admiration she enjoyed from her compatriots was obvious, but even she just joined in the conversation with a casual comfort. Her dark eyes watched Amelia carefully, but there was no obvious malice in their depths. She chatted politely, even at one point complimenting Amelia on the capture of Blade.

"Honestly, how did you take him down without killing him?" Piper gestured around at the table. "None of us have ever bested him with a blade."

"I didn't use a blade," Amelia said, surprising herself with a smug grin as she raised her fist. "I was wearing spiked gauntlets, and I slugged him in the face."

Piper's throaty laugh led the chorus of guffaws around them.

"Obviously he was expecting a more refined attack," she said. "My compliments on your improvisation."

"Enough years on the street taught me a thing or two about improvisation," Amelia said.

"No doubt," Piper said with a respectful nod. "And you're not a bad shot, either."

"Well, I wasn't aiming for your shoulder."

That got a reaction from the surrounding people, and Amelia sensed a sudden uptick in the interest directed her way. She tried to downplay it and assured her listeners both that Blade was alive and well the last time she saw him, and that she and Piper had just had a misunderstanding. Amelia didn't know whether to be mad at herself, but she found she actually liked the attention from these hardened professionals.

But what she definitely hated was that it was actually hard to hate Dark Star. Oh, she was flirting with Liam far too much, but despite her noble accent she lacked the usual pretensions Amelia always expected from a lady of privilege. She was surprisingly grounded, and she clearly held her former lady-in-waiting Piper in the highest respect.

The meal finally ended, and she and Liam were escorted down the corridor to a heavy, locked door. Beyond was a windowless room with two bunks and an alcove for ablutions. A single, wall-mounted lamp cast a dull glow in the small space.

"Apologies for the simple quarters," Piper said from the corridor. "Hopefully we can make arrangements for something more civilized in time."

The door shut with a heavy click, leaving Amelia alone with Liam.

"They trust us enough not to separate us," she said with some surprise.

Liam stepped forward, his strong hands gripping her waist as he leaned in and kissed her. The passion caught her by surprise, but after a moment she welcomed it, reveling in his closeness.

"I've wanted to do that for hours," he said when he finally drew back.

"Glad to hear it," she replied. "You're quite the charmer, as always. Almost had me convinced that you were Lady Zara's lover once more."

"All part of the training," he said, sitting down heavily on one of the bunks. "I'm just glad she didn't want to really rekindle that relationship this evening."

"Maybe she's kindly offering me this final chance to be with you," she said, sitting across from him, "before she expects you to take your new place."

"She is crazy," he breathed. "It breaks my heart to see her like this."

Amelia wasn't sure "crazy" was the right word to describe Dark Star.

"It's a shame she couldn't be redirected," she offered. "I don't like her current tactics, but even I can see her potential. She's intelligent, even visionary, and obviously has the ability to draw people to her cause."

"But her cause is madness," Liam said sadly. "It's delusional."

"Destroying noble houses and overthrowing the Emperor isn't really something I want to get behind," she agreed.

"That, but even her dream of what would come afterward."

"You mean her idea of independent systems and rule by the people?"

"Madness," he repeated. "The people don't know how to rule themselves. You said yourself it would never work."

Amelia frowned, thinking back over the conversation. "I said that people don't like change. But I'm not opposed to her idea in principle."

"But how would society function," he asked, "without a system of rules, and etiquette, and accepted behavior?"

"Just like it does in any town. We all more or less respect the law, and we sort out our differences."

"Through brawling, bullying, and petty thuggery?" he said, disdain coloring his expression.

"And how is that any worse than how you deal with things?" she demanded. "With your doublespeak, your rituals, and your treatment of human beings like chattel?"

"You know I'm opposed to that," he said, suddenly defensive. "I treat everyone with respect."

"You do," she conceded, "but you're an exception. And you're not that much of an exception."

His eyes flicked up to her questioningly.

"I didn't see you speak out when Lord Brightlake was murdered in cold blood."

"What could I have done, with twenty armed guards behind Silverhawk?"

It was a fair point, but it was also a deflection. She leaned forward, her hands on her knees, and stared into his eyes.

"There, perhaps nothing. But what about in the café

in Morassia? There were four of you and Silverhawk had only one bodyguard. Sky alone could have taken them both out. Yet none of you moved, not even after he'd declared his intention to destroy us all."

"We couldn't . . ."

"Why not?"

"Because he was a high lord! And if any of us were seen accosting or assaulting him, we would have hanged."

She sat back, folding her arms. "And you think that's okay? You think that's normal?"

"Yes."

"You think it's okay that a person can act with impunity, killing and stealing at whim, with no consequences solely because of their family name?"

"Well . . ." He raised his palms in frustration.

"At least Sam and Bella were able to see a solution," she said.

"Which the captain and I pounced on," he added, "and for which we are eternally grateful to them. They did something that we could never have done."

"Two intelligent, authoritative, and empowered Humans couldn't act, just because of a name. And you wonder what's wrong with the system."

"The current system is flawed, for certain," he conceded. "But it would need to be reformed from within. We can't just overthrow our entire society and expect a paradise to emerge from the ashes."

"True . . . but how will it ever be reformed if those in power see no need to reform it? Maybe the impetus needs to come from outside."

"If you think the people will be resistant to change," he warned, "just try and impose a new order on the nobility. They'd close ranks. And they have all the money and all the weapons. It would be ugly."

There was a defensiveness in him she wasn't used to seeing. Was he simply rattled because he'd rediscovered Zara Brightlake, or was there something else?

"Are you threatening me, my lord?"

"What? Of course not! Amelia, come on. I hope you know me well enough by now to understand that I don't believe in our system of nobility and would love to see it changed."

And yet, she realized as she watched him, *you are so much a part of it that you can't even imagine it being replaced.* The thought didn't fill her with much hope for her species.

"We can discuss philosophy when we're safely back in *Daring,*" he said. "Right now, we need to think about escape."

IT WAS HARD TO GAUGE THE PASSAGE OF TIME IN their cell, but as Amelia dozed next to him Liam focused his mind on an old song he remembered from childhood. It had a steady cadence, with a single long verse that simply repeated over and over, with the number of bricks in the wall going up by one each time. At his best guess it was probably by now the first hour of the morning watch.

It was with some surprise, then, that he heard the lock in the door snap open. He nudged Amelia, rising to his feet. The door opened a crack, and through the opening he heard the familiar clatter of people running and swords jingling. Piper's face appeared in the opening, her expression grim.

"Come with me, please," she ordered. "Both of you."

Liam glanced down at Amelia, who was quickly shaking off the cobwebs of sleep.

"Where are we going?" he asked.

"Do you really think I'm going to explain?" Piper snapped.

"Sounds like trouble," he offered, peering past her at the corridor beyond. There were two guards with her, and the sounds of many more nearby.

"Are you going to give *me* trouble?"

He glanced at Amelia. She shrugged.

"Lead on, then," he said to Piper.

She pushed the door open and motioned for them to follow. Liam tucked into her wake, feeling Amelia's fingers brushing loosely next to his own. The pair of burly guards fell in behind them. A trio of Theropods hustled past, swords strapped to their tails, eyes fixed on their mission. Up ahead, the doors to Dark Star's observation room were open. Piper led the way through, and immediately Liam was struck by a chill in the air.

The cavernous space looked much the same as before, except that now it was bursting with armed Humans and Theropods. One of the towering glass panels was open, and a steady stream of supplies was being loaded onto the sailing ship that was tied to the jetty. Armed pirates manned the edges of the deck, the sound of their musket fire punctuating the scene.

Zara strode up to intercept them before they'd traversed a quarter of the way across the room. She was dressed in a dark shirt and trousers with no weapons, her hair loose and cascading around her shoulders as she fastened a lightweight cloak with a broach. Her star broach, Liam noticed immediately.

"Thank you, Piper," she said, her tone clipped as she fell in alongside Liam and took his arm. Their pace toward the open glass didn't slow.

"What's going on, Zara?" he asked.

"It seems your friends have found you, darling." She sighed. "They're storming the gates at ground level."

They passed through the open glass wall, the chill damp of the atmosphere sending a shiver through him. The distant sounds of combat were a dull roar beneath the musket fire on both sides of the deck. He scanned the dark sky but saw only the lightning-streaked clouds of the nebula against a vivid backdrop of stars. Was Riverton launching a ground assault?

"Perhaps we can call a cease-fire," he said suddenly, drawing to a halt. "Let me talk to my people and prevent bloodshed."

"A noble idea," Zara clipped, "but no. I'm not so foolish as to let you link up with your people—you've proven yourself far too cunning."

He looked again at the stream of pirates loading supplies onto the ship.

"And so," he asked, "what are we doing?"

"We're departing," she said with a smile, gripping his arm and compelling him into motion again. "The boathouse is designed to withstand a direct assault like this, and I'm sure my loyal followers will make short work of your crew. But just in case, we're going on a short voyage."

"To where?" Amelia asked from behind them.

"It will all become clear in time."

The cargo line paused as people scrambled to clear a way for Zara. She led the way across the gangplank, and Piper gestured for Liam and Amelia to follow. As he stepped out onto the narrow platform he slowed, feigning uncertainty so that he could take a longer look down at the ground far below.

There were three covered carts in the courtyard, with flashes of gunfire erupting from each. A fourth machine was up against the shard's main doors, battering repeatedly as the pirates' withering fire chipped away at it. All the wagons displayed the stylized symbol of the house Grandview—a circular sun rising over two triangular mountains—and Liam guessed that the admiral's squadron had arrived. But there were no cannons on either side that Liam could see, and thus little hope of either breaking down the doors or smashing the wagons. It was a stalemate from the start.

He reached the ship's brow and stepped aboard, breathing in the warmer, drier air. The passageway was wide, and as the sounds of battle outside faded they were replaced by the familiar hubbub of a ship preparing to sail. Piper pushed from behind, moving him clear of the brow area as he followed Zara aft. Sailors pressed themselves against the bulkheads to make room as they all passed, and after climbing up a single ladder they emerged onto the bridge.

The canopy was long and raked, giving an excellent view of the stellar maelstrom above. A woman with an air of authority greeted Zara and gave an efficient report on the status of the vessel. Liam understood the terminology well and figured that the ship was only minutes from sailing. All around them the small bridge crew worked efficiently.

"Welcome aboard my personal ship, *Freedom,*" Zara said, turning. "She's built for speed, but I assure you we've been able to work in some comforts as well."

Although it was his first time aboard a cutter like this, he'd already recognized the familiar form.

"Does *Freedom* also sail under the name *Arrow*?" he asked.

"Sister ships. *Arrow*'s on her way home now, having been a tremendous asset in helping to find you."

"Are we going far?" Liam asked, glancing around casually as he searched for a chart.

"Allow me just a few more surprises, darling," she said with a wink, before turning back to discuss ship status with the woman Liam assumed was the master of the vessel.

He felt Amelia brush up beside him.

"This is not good," she muttered.

"Agreed," he said, continuing his casual scan of the bridge. The crew was all occupied, but Piper and two guards stood squarely between Liam and Amelia and the ladder down. If they didn't move now, however, the ship would depart the jetty and there would be no escape.

"You knock down Piper," he whispered, "and I'll get past the two guards."

"Ready . . . ," Amelia said, crouching in preparation. "Now!"

They burst into movement. Liam threw his shoulder into the first guard, knocking the big man back. Pushing off he swung his fist at the second guard, feeling the power of the impact as his entire body followed through on the blow. The thug toppled backward. Piper was staggering as Amelia straight-armed her in a full charge. The ladder was only steps away and Liam lunged for it.

Just as he reached the opening, a sailor's head appeared, followed by shoulders as the man hauled himself up the ladder. Liam barely saw the sailor's eyes widen in shock before he impacted the rising form. The sailor slammed backward as Amelia's momentum carried her into Liam a heartbeat later. The sailor collapsed against the hatch, his body sprawled painfully through the opening.

Completely blocking it.

Liam saw the first of the guards rising to his feet but he turned as he heard the awful sound of a sword being drawn. Rolling to his feet, he squared off bare-handed against Piper as she flicked her rapier through a series of short swings.

Amelia paused at the hatch for barely a second, assessing, then scrambled headfirst downward. Liam reared back and delivered a crushing back kick to the guard looming behind him, determined to buy Amelia the seconds she needed to escape. He staggered as the second guard landed across his shoulders, and he slipped out of the attempted headlock before snapping an elbow back into his attacker's face. There was no time for these goons: Piper was advancing and Amelia's legs were still in reach. Why wasn't she disappearing down the hatch? Liam stepped forward to cover her and just saw her reaching around the fallen sailor's body. Reaching for his belt.

The rapier slashed down but clanged against a heavy blade that swung up through the hatch. Amelia rolled, swinging her stolen cutlass again. Piper danced back, her eyes wide. One of the guards lurched for Amelia and she hacked through his knee as she rolled again. Blood sprayed across the deck as the man collapsed. Amelia leaped to her feet and advanced, her cutlass swings forcing Piper to give ground.

Liam looked back at the remaining guard. He was just pulling himself off the bulkhead in a daze. Liam unleashed another kick to his bowed head, then with a smooth motion pulled the guard's own sword free and ran him through. The cutlass was heavier than his own saber, and poorly balanced, but Liam had swung enough blades in his time to adjust quickly.

The drums of a general alarm suddenly boomed throughout the ship, and Liam saw the bridge crew drawing swords. He and Amelia moved to flank each other, staring back at half a dozen armed pirates. Piper's cool gaze moved between them, a growing anticipation in her eyes.

"Hold fast," Zara suddenly commanded. She stood alone at the center of the bridge, unarmed, her gaze sweeping across the scene. "Liam, this is absurd."

"Kidnapping calls for desperate measures," he replied, ready to counter the first movement from any pirate. "I think you're being quite ungracious, Zara."

"It isn't kidnapping," she said, "when it's for your own protection."

"My protection, or yours?"

"What's the difference?" She shrugged. "We are one, now."

Liam risked a long glance at her and saw the fire of affection in her eyes.

The entire bridge remained frozen in tableau, until the ladder thumped with the first pirate climbing up. Liam kicked the hatch door shut, clanging it down on the pirate's head. He crouched and quickly snapped on the dogs with his free hand, securing the hatch.

"We're free of the jetty," the ship's master reported.

"Make sail," Zara ordered calmly.

Several sailors moved to obey, but Piper and two sailors maintained their vigil. Liam lifted his own blade, watching as Zara stepped forward, her hands open.

"Liam," she said with a smile, "this is all quite unnecessary. We've departed this world and your crew is bashing themselves against my boathouse doors below. By the time they realize you're not there we will have disappeared into the maze."

Liam's eyes were instinctively drawn up to the canopy and the charged dust clouds beyond. It was a maelstrom of movement and light. Even if Lord Grandview saw this ship launch, he'd never be able to keep sight of it against that chaotic background.

"They're just trying to rescue Amelia and me," he said. "If you set us free then there need be no further trouble."

"I wish I could believe you. But I know that you and your forces have been hunting me for the better part of a year. While you may be glad to see me, darling, I doubt I'll receive such a warm welcome from your lieutenants."

She was ready for battle, he could see, but her eyes still shined with a strange kindness as she regarded him. As she shifted her gaze to Amelia, though, a new expression took hold.

"Please, Zara," he said quickly, stepping forward and lowering his sword. "This day isn't going the way I'd hoped."

"I don't blame you, Liam," she said, looking past him to the two dead guards slumped at the back of the bridge. "I know that you were just trying to protect Amelia. I'm sure your past failure to save me has haunted you."

Amelia tensed as Zara's gaze rested upon her. Liam doubted either woman would survive the other's presence for long.

"We were frightened," he said. "If you let Amelia go, I'll stay here with you."

Zara turned back to Liam, her perfect lips parting in a smile. "Such a gentleman, as always."

"There's no need for her to suffer. Just let her go and I'll gladly stay here with you."

Triumph flashed through Zara's eyes and she lifted her chin toward Amelia. Amelia dropped her gaze. Liam lowered his cutlass to the deck and took another step closer to Dark Star.

"Please, Zara. Let her go, for my sake."

She motioned for the two sailors behind her to sheathe their swords, then stepped forward to nestle against Liam. Her hand ran up his back and then down again to settle around his waist. He forced himself to relax, putting an arm around her shoulders.

"Heavy traffic, madame," the ship's master reported as the ship heeled to starboard, "we're trying to keep clear."

Liam looked past Zara, noticing another sailing ship looming large ahead. *Freedom* was altering to starboard to keep clear, but the other ship didn't seem to be reacting.

Zara paid no attention to the sailing situation, her eyes still resting on the hostile presence on her bridge. Liam followed her gaze. Amelia didn't move, her sword up and her eyes wary.

"Oh come, Amelia," Zara said, "there's no need for this. I hold no ill will against you. You're a fine adversary, and I would still welcome you as an ally."

Liam watched the flurry of emotions dancing across Amelia's face. She was many things, but she would never win at poker. He saw no jealously in her, but rather fear mixed with respect. And a healthy dose of uncertainty. But, finally, she lowered her cutlass.

Piper's rapier snapped out, past Amelia's clumsy parry, burying its tip in her chest.

"Piper, no!" Zara cried. Liam felt her entire body stiffen next to his.

The former lady-in-waiting recoiled into a perfect fencing pose, watching as Amelia clutched at her chest and fell to one knee.

"She would never have been trustworthy," Piper declared. "I live to protect you, Zara."

Liam tried to rush forward, but Zara clung to him. And Piper stepped in his way, rapier at the ready.

"Loyalty to Dark Star must be absolute," Piper said to him, "and so long as this woman lives you'll be conflicted. I will resolve that."

She turned to face Amelia, raising her sword in salute, pommel to her nose and blade high in the air. Then she slashed down.

Her blade struck metal as Amelia staggered sideways and blocked, launching to her feet and grabbing Piper's sword hand. The rapier clanged against the deck as it was forced down. Amelia brought up her own cutlass, but Piper wrapped a strong arm around her and drew her inside swinging range. For a moment the two women grappled, stumbling together as the deck heaved again.

"She's not changing course!" the ship's master shouted.

Liam nearly tripped as Zara pushed him back, away from the fight and the stray blades. As he steadied his footing he looked up through the canopy and saw that the other sailing ship was very close, covered in dust and bulky under external cargo bays. She was turning sharply now, but still closing fast. And her nearest mast was already retracted. As one, along her highest through-deck, cannon ports opened.

"Get down!" He grabbed Zara and hauled her into a crouch.

A flash of light outside was followed by a thunderous crash against the hull, then the groaning of outer hull plates as *Daring*'s grapples took hold.

Piper's rapier swept up off the deck, but Amelia's foot danced clear. Their balance shifted, forcing Piper back. The cutlass was still loose, but Amelia didn't have the room to swing it. Piper grabbed Amelia's upper arm and raked her boot down Amelia's shin. Amelia hissed in pain but stepped forward, keeping Piper off balance. Blood was soaking through Amelia's clothes and her face was pale, but she pushed forward again, wrenching her sword arm free.

Her hand was buried under the heavy metal guard of the cutlass, but her fist collided with Piper's face so hard that the metal dented. The swordswoman gasped in pain, staggering back but unable to escape as Amelia held her arm in an iron grip. The metal guard smashed against Piper's jaw again. Then a third time.

Liam fell forward to his hands and knees as the entire ship jerked to starboard under a deafening crash. He looked up and saw *Daring*'s top mast snapping against *Freedom*'s as the two ships collided.

Piper was still falling as Amelia's cutlass swung into her lean form, the heavy blade slicing through flesh and bone.

"No!" Zara screamed. She flailed forward helplessly on her hands and knees, then tumbled as the deck shook again.

The rapier fell from Piper's dead fingers, clattering on the deck next to Liam's hands. He grabbed it and looked up at his beloved.

Sweat soaked Amelia's hair and her eyes were dulling with pain against white skin, but she nodded to him and turned toward the pirate crew.

"Repel boarders!" the master ordered, and another rumble of drums sounded through the ship.

The pirates on the bridge clearly thought Amelia was the threat, and two of them charged toward her. She heaved up the rapier in desperate defense, stumbling backward. Zara was on the deck, sobbing as she held Piper in her arms. Liam leaped over her and stabbed the nearest pirate. The rapier blade was out and buried into the second pirate in a single motion.

These pirates had fired on Amelia in a defenseless boat, he reminded himself. Liam wrenched the rapier free again and hacked down the ship's master as she drew her own weapon. And their lieutenant had stabbed Amelia after she'd surrendered. He leaped forward, the blade swift and deadly as he struck down his foes. The rapier sang as it slashed through the close confines of the pirate bridge, blood spraying under its deadly advance. Finally he stopped, gasping for breath and looking back over the trail of bodies.

Amelia stared at him numbly from where she stood, the cutlass dropping from her fingers. He ran to her, catching her as she collapsed. Zara was just now rising to her feet where Piper lay dead. Her eyes were grim as she surveyed the carnage on her bridge. The sound of heavy fighting was clear on the deck below.

Zara watched Amelia sink to her knees, and she clenched her hands.

"I'm so sorry. I never wanted that to happen." She gestured at Piper's mangled form. "She always just wanted to protect me."

Liam eased Amelia into a sitting position against one of the consoles. She desperately needed medical attention, but he couldn't lower his guard against Zara. Keeping the rapier up, he reached for the general speaker system. He pushed every button on the panel and grabbed the microphone.

"This is Subcommander Blackwood," he said, hearing his voice echo through the speakers, "medical emergency on the bridge." He repeated the message two more times, hoping that someone from his boarding party heard it over the chaos below.

Something hard struck the hatch beyond Zara. She jerked away, and Liam edged closer. He could hear voices below, shouts and growls. They were not, he could tell by the cadence and style, *Daring*'s crew.

"You reminded them of your position." Zara sighed. "And they know I'm up here. They probably think I'm the wounded party. Which means they'll stop at nothing to get in."

The hatch heaved on one side as a huge impact knocked it free of the combing, and the dogs on the port side snapped free. Another impact shattered the dogs on the forward side. The hatch bent open a crack, and Liam saw a pirate face peer through. He stabbed the rapier through the opening, feeling the brush of flesh against the blade. He readied himself, knowing the next impact would blast the hatch open.

A new roar of voices sounded, as a cacophony of sword clashes echoed up from below. Liam held position, waiting for another strike against the hatch. He glanced at Zara in his peripheral.

She was watching Amelia closely. She made to move but Liam flicked the sword in warning.

"You need to help her," Zara said.

"I know, and help is on the way."

"You underestimate my people. It may be a while."

"And that makes you happy, I suppose?"

She looked up at him in shock. "Not at all."

Amelia moaned, her eyes fluttering as she fought to stay conscious.

"She's going to die," Zara said. "Let me help her."

"How can you help?"

She pointed at a medical kit on the bulkhead near her. "I can stanch the bleeding, at least."

"You think I'd let you near her?"

"What choice do you have?" Zara's expression was cool but tinted with concern.

Liam hesitated, knowing that he couldn't let down his guard.

"Do you really think I'm that much of a monster?" Zara asked.

He honestly didn't know what to think, and with battle adrenaline surging through him he barely trusted himself to speak.

"If I wanted her to die," Zara said finally, "I could just sit here and do nothing."

He glanced at the bent hatch, then back over at Amelia. She was still conscious, and he thought he saw her head bob in the slightest of nods.

"Help her," he said.

Zara scrambled up to grab the medical kit and crouched in front of Amelia. Liam moved with her, keeping within easy striking range as she pulled Amelia's jacket off and cut through her blood-soaked shirt. Zara's fingers moved with assured swiftness as she pressed a bandage against the short wound and wrapped it tightly in place.

"She needs blood," she said at one point, holding up a bag of plasma. "I can feed this into her if you'll permit me to inject her."

He nodded, his gaze flicking between the hatch and Zara's hands as she inserted the needle and started the feed. Then she rose to her feet, holding the plasma bag high enough to let gravity take effect.

Liam risked exposing himself long enough to reach down and check Amelia's pulse. It was weak, but steady. Her breathing was shallow but consistent, and her eyes still fluttered as she fought to stay awake.

"Hang in there, my love," he whispered to her, then rose to cover Zara again.

She wiped her bloody hands against her dark trousers and stared at him with a sad smile.

"I never imagined our reunion going quite like this, darling."

The sounds of battle below had faded, and with Amelia stable he allowed himself to relax slightly.

"At least you imagined it would happen," he replied. "I still feel like I'm talking to a ghost."

She nodded. There were new shouts from below, and Liam recognized Flatrock's rough baritone, followed by Sky's calm, sharp words. By her expression, Zara also realized who was coming.

"So," she sighed, "what happens now?"

"Your network is compromised with the information we'll no doubt capture today, and the Fleet will mobilize to break up your gathered forces and your crime rings. Your attack on Honoria will never happen. It's all over."

"But what happens to me?" Her gaze was intent and focused only on him.

"There will have to be justice," he said with a heavy heart. "You know that, Zara."

She exhaled sharply, fighting down emotion.

"Justice? You know what they'll do to me."

He did indeed. And his anger at the nobility came flooding back. Had they not made this woman suffer enough?

"That's why I tried to talk to you, why I hoped I might convince you to stop your attacks and just disappear."

"But you know why I can't!"

"No," he said with perfect honesty, "I don't. Take your freedom, yes. Even avenge yourself, yes. But topple the Empire?"

The question hung against the chaotic sounds of battle beneath them.

"You thought you could just waltz in and change my life path of fifteen years?" she asked, amazed. "You might not understand yet, but I've built something here. I've seen what the future for all humanity can be. And I can make it happen. You thought I'd just give it all up?"

"I didn't know what to think." He managed a smile. "But I can see your passion, and your drive. And I see now that you'll never stop."

Her expression darkened, but whether in anger or sadness he couldn't tell.

"This has to end," he said.

"Darling, please." She reached out for him, then withdrew her hand as he raised the sword. "Liam . . . please. Don't take me back. Please don't condemn me to that fate."

"I'm sorry, Zara," he said, feeling his heart tear.

She wiped away tears, keeping her eyes on him.

"I know you couldn't help me fifteen years ago, and I've never blamed you for what happened. You had no power then." She dared to reach toward him. "But you do now."

He couldn't form the words to answer her. At least, not the words she wanted to hear. She was a victim, and her terrifying rage at the system was justified, but she had more than paid back any wrongs done to her in fifteen years of violence and crime.

And more than that, Liam knew, he was a sworn servant of the crown. Noble title be damned, he was an officer in His Majesty's Navy, and his oath of loyalty had to outweigh any personal feelings he might have.

"I'm sorry, Zara," he said finally. "Truly sorry."

Her hand fell away. "Then kill me."

"Zara . . ."

"Death would be merciful compared to what you know awaits me back on Homeworld."

"I could never do that."

"You have that power, my darling. Right here and now."

He stared at her, his first love. The face that had filled a thousand dreams.

"I lost you once already," he said. "I could never . . ."

She flicked back her cloak, her hand resting for a long moment on the broach at her neck. Then she opened the top of her shirt, exposing the skin over her heart.

"Do it, Liam, before your people get here."

"Maybe the court will be merciful . . . ," he started to say, but their eyes met and the words died in their own absurdity.

"Please, Liam."

He raised the sword, turning it in his hand. She clasped her hands behind her back, taking a deep breath as she closed her eyes. He lifted the delicate blade.

And then lowered it again.

"Zara, I just can't."

Quick thumps indicated someone ascending the ladder to the bridge.

"XO, sir?" Sky was at the hatch, banging on it. "Are you there?"

"Here," Liam called. "With one casualty and one prisoner."

CHAPTER 16

AMELIA STRUGGLED THROUGH THE FOG, WANTING to shy away from the pain below her shoulder but knowing that it was her strongest link to consciousness. She could see Liam's boots on her left, and what she thought were Dark Star's on her right. They were talking, and she swam up toward those words. What Amelia really noticed was the fear in Dark Star's voice, and the sadness in Liam's. She listened to their tender exchange, feeling almost like an intruder in such an intimate moment.

A metallic bang shook her and she blinked open her eyes. The hatch of the pirate ship bridge was flung open and figures emerged onto the deck. But they were familiar figures, she realized, and moments later she saw Able Rating Song kneeling in front of her.

"PO, can you hear me?" he asked.

"Yes," she forced from her lips.

"You're gonna be okay," he said, already inspecting the bandage wrapped around her bare shoulder. He reached into his bag, and then she felt a prick in her arm. Something warm coursed through her, and suddenly the room started to clear. He nodded and gripped her good arm. With his help, she rose to her feet.

Liam still carried the rapier. Sky, Flatrock, and Hedge had weapons drawn, all eyes on Dark Star, who was now manacled.

Liam stepped into view, concern etched across his face. "Amelia, can you walk?"

She took a tentative step forward, then another. Whatever Song had shot her up with, it was working. "Yes."

"We have to move. The pirates are still loose and we have to get you and Zara back to *Daring*."

"Okay."

Sky pulled out a pistol and handed it to Amelia. "Can you handle this?"

She took the weapon, feeling the warm grip and balancing it in her good hand. She nodded.

With Sky in the lead, the team evacuated the pirate bridge. Amelia hustled along behind Song, listening to the steady jingle of armor and weapons along the wide passageway. There were distant shouts behind her and the crack of a bullet hitting the bulkhead, but she just kept moving. They turned to the left and stepped onto the familiar airlock tube. Seconds later she was aboard *Daring*.

But it was hardly a friendly homecoming. Sky motioned Amelia to clear into the passageway, next to where Flatrock and Hedge contained Dark Star at sword point. Faith and Hunter guarded the airlock, with Sam and Bella looming behind them, cutlasses strapped awkwardly to their tails, pistols in each hand.

"Swift and his team are still in the pirate ship," Sky briefed Liam. "There's heavy resistance. Do we press on or withdraw with the prisoner?"

Liam donned the breastplate offered to him and strapped on a standard belt with saber and pistols. He looked at Dark Star for a moment, then peered back through the airlock tube.

"I suspect they'll fight to the death to recover our prisoner. We need to get our people back and withdraw while we're ahead."

Amelia watched as Sky spoke in her radio, pausing as Swift responded.

"Swift's team is cut off," Sky reported. "One deck down, midships."

"Then let's cut a path open for them," Liam replied. He surveyed the assembled sailors. "Song, Flatrock, Faith: you're with the chief and me. Hunter, Bella, Sam: you guard this brow with your life. Hedge, you and Amelia get the prisoner down to the brig and locked up. Then get back up here to hold the brow."

Acknowledgments all around. Liam and his team charged through the airlock tunnel again. Amelia nodded to Hedge, who shoved Dark Star toward the ladder.

"Let's go, princess," she growled.

Amelia went down the ladder first, then kept her pistol trained on Dark Star as she struggled down in her manacles. Hedge followed, motioning them forward. They moved along the passageway, passing the boat airlocks, when suddenly there was a shout from above and pistol shots, followed by the clash of swords. Hedge swung back toward the ladder.

"The pirates are attacking!"

"Get up there and help," Amelia snapped. "I can watch the prisoner."

Hedge hesitated, staring at Amelia's wound.

"I've got this," Amelia said, holding the pistol. "But if we lose the brow we lose everything. Get up there!"

Hedge ran for the ladder, vaulting up the steep steps and screaming as she joined the fray.

Amelia relaxed her arm, but kept the pistol aimed squarely at the woman standing before her. Dark Star watched her calmly, then glanced back toward the ladder and the furious sounds of battle.

"Your people are devoted," Amelia said.

"As are yours."

They stared at each other for a long moment.

"There are lots of good people in the Empire," Amelia said finally. "You don't need to tear it all down."

"Sometimes a system is so rotten that there's no choice."

"But if you tear it down, there's nothing left to rebuild with. Better to cut out the rotten bits and build on the good." Amelia gestured around at the ship. "Like this crew. Brutish and uneducated, yes, but smart and loyal and capable of great things."

"I've spent fifteen years with the brutish and uneducated, Amelia. I know well their potential."

"But maybe you don't know the potential of the nobility." She shook her head. "I can't believe I'm saying this, but some of them are good, too."

"Liam is an exception, I think. And as he commands this ship he no doubt sets the tone for his officers."

"Liam isn't the captain." Amelia was strangely pleased at the surprise on Dark Star's face. "But our captain is an amazing woman who forged an alliance with the Sectoids, extended friendship to the Theropods, and even earned the respect of the Aquans."

Dark Star's eyebrow arched in interest.

"Many of the nobles are self-absorbed, idle, malicious toffs," Amelia added. "But not all of them."

Dark Star nodded, shifting her wrists against the manacles.

"Why are you even telling me this, Amelia? To gloat as you see my vision die?"

"No." Amelia kept the pistol steady, even as her thoughts raced. What was she trying to say? "I guess . . . I admire your vision, but I disagree with your methods. Building a criminal empire is worse than building an overt empire, and replacing the Emperor with yourself, no matter how noble your intentions, is no better."

"As I said, all a means to an end."

"The right end, but the wrong means. Surely there's another way to bring change."

"Not from within," Dark Star said sadly. "Those in power will never surrender it willingly. Do you think I haven't spent years trying to think of a better solution?"

"Maybe you need to keep thinking."

"What for?" Dark Star looked back at the ladder, and the sound of fighting. "Because unless my people break through—and you don't shoot me—my movement dies today. Liam said that my network will be exposed, and all my people hunted down."

"It's true. The Emperor will want no chance of one of your lieutenants just taking over. Even if you're rescued today, it's only a matter of time before you're hunted down again."

"And now," she said, shaking her head in defeat, "my true identity is known. Oh, what a spectacle it will be, the disgraced Lady Zara Brightlake paraded in chains before the Imperial court."

"But surely you could still make a difference, plead your case for change in the court?"

Her laugh was vicious. "You've never been to the Imperial court, have you? I won't even be allowed to speak. I'll be allowed to scream when they torture me, I suppose, but I don't intend to give them that satisfaction."

It was such a waste of a remarkable person, Amelia knew. A person with a vision and the proven means to rally people to her cause. But she could never escape her past. Even if she and Liam were to keep her noble heritage a secret, she was still a criminal overlord who was number one on the Emperor's execution table.

The sounds of battle eased, and Amelia could hear Hedge's taunts as her foes fled.

"Is there anything I can do to help you?" she asked, gesturing to her bandage. "As thanks for saving my life?"

"I'd be grateful if you just put a bullet in my head," Dark Star replied. "It would be a kindness."

Amelia didn't know if it was the medicine Song had pumped into her, but her mind was amazingly clear. And suddenly she could see a path out of this sadness. But she didn't dare. Unless . . .

"Do you still love Liam?" Amelia suddenly asked.

Dark Star's eyes flicked down to the pistol still pointed at her. But her expression became serene.

"Yes. But I know it's just a dream. And I think he knows it, too. You have nothing to fear from me."

"My fear is that Liam would end up on your next noble hit list. Spurned lover and all that."

"Stars, no!" she exclaimed. "I would never want that. He's one of the good ones, as you say."

"So if your people were to rescue you, Liam would be safe?"

"On . . ." She grasped for words. "On whatever is left that is sacred, I swear I would never harm Liam. Or you, Amelia. You're much too valuable a person, and I can see how much Liam loves you."

"Likewise," Amelia said. "But this isn't about him. This is about our people. And what you can do for our future."

Dark Star stared at her strangely. Amelia stepped forward.

"Lift your hands," she said, raising the pistol. "As best you can."

Dark Star winced as she lifted her manacled hands a few inches away from her back. Amelia placed the barrel of her gun next to the chain and fired.

The metal snapped, and Dark Star hissed a most unladylike curse as the bullet sliced across the edge of her buttock. A thin line of blood tricked along the gash in her trousers.

Amelia stepped back and gestured toward the boat airlock with her pistol.

"Do you know how to drive a boat, Zara?"

"Yes." Confusion furrowed her porcelain features.

"Then open that airlock and climb through. I can't guarantee you won't get blown up trying to escape, but I'll make sure you have a head start."

Zara took a slow step toward the airlock. Then, when she realized Amelia wasn't going to stop her, dashed for the hatch and began unwinding the lock. She glanced up once.

"Why are you doing this?"

"Because you have a vision, and you have the means within you to rally people behind you. But not as a pirate queen—come up with another way. Forget vengeance, forget revolution. Always remember: Who suffers most in a war? The common folk. Don't make us die for your vision. Win hearts and minds, build a movement, and be the change."

"I can do that," she said, with sudden fire in her eyes.

"I know."

"Come with me."

Amelia started, surprised mostly at just how tempted she was by the offer. But she smiled.

"No, I have too much here, and a life waiting for me back home. But you have a clean slate—again—and the freedom to act. Use it."

The airlock hatch popped open, and Zara eased her way through. She looked up one more time, locking eyes with Amelia.

"Thank you."

The airlock door slammed shut. Amelia waited until she saw the boat disengage from the hull, then fired her pistol twice at the bulkhead. Then she ran for the ladder, and the sounds of battle.

IF THERE WAS ONE THING DR. TEMPLEGREY WAS very good at, it was not fussing over her patients. But Amelia really didn't mind when a delicate hand suddenly reached out to steady her mug as she took it from Bella.

"Just be careful," Templegrey said with a smile, helping Amelia grip the mug. "Your muscles don't always react like you think they will after they've been punctured by a blade."

"I know," Amelia said, switching the mug to her other hand. "When does it stop aching?"

"Probably about a week," Templegrey said, leading the way over to the table. She pulled out the chair next to Brown and offered it to Amelia, who gratefully sat down.

The table was covered in charts and bundles of parchments, and Amelia just kept hold of her coffee for lack of space to set it down. Templegrey sat down across from her, between Sky and Butcher. Liam was in his usual seat at the head of the table, and Riverton sat at the opposite end. The captain's expression was as cold as ever, but Amelia was pretty sure she could see a spark of satisfaction in those dark eyes.

What gave Amelia the most satisfaction was that no one seemed to mind discussing sensitive information with a Theropod in the room. Bella stayed back along the forward bulkhead with the drinks, but the room just wasn't that big, and no attempt to hide the charts or speak in whispers was made. The gesture said more than any praise or medals could.

"I received an update from Rear Admiral Grand-view," Riverton said without preamble. "He's ordered three squadrons to the Iron Swarm and another to Silica. Word has come that the Emperor himself is mobilizing the other admirals to hunt down every last ship and outpost on the lists we captured. The criminal network of Dark Star is broken."

"Good news, ma'am," Chief Butcher replied. "But it's not going to wipe out crime in the Empire."

"No, but the threat to the Empire is vanquished."

Butcher nodded.

"Let's hope Dark Star died of her wounds," Brown interjected. "I'd hate to see her rally her forces."

"I was there," Amelia said quietly. "I'm sure Dark Star died before that boat crash-landed."

"You shouldn't have been left alone in your weakened state," the sublieutenant said sympathetically.

"It was my call to send Hedge back to the brow. Holding our own ship's defense was top priority." She'd heard Liam say similar things enough times to justify difficult orders in battle, and it appeared to work. Brown nodded solemnly.

"It was the right call," Sky added, looking at Amelia in approval. "We were stretched too thin already, and holding the brow is everything. If we'd lost that, our escape route was cut off."

"Petty Officer Virtue acted correctly," Riverton concluded. "And you say you wounded Dark Star as she fled?"

"I saw her blood from my shot," Amelia said carefully. "I'm certain that Dark Star is dead. We just don't have a body to parade before the Imperial court."

"Which is fine," Liam added.

Everyone seemed to believe her official story, of Dark Star attacking her and knocking her back before trying to flee. And of her heroically shooting the villain but unable to stop her escape with the boat. The trust within this crew was impressive, and Amelia had already buried the shame of her betrayal deep, deep down. Sometimes, there was an even higher calling than loyalty.

"We'll leave the mop up of Labyrinthia to Lord Grandview's people," Riverton said, "and head back to more civilized space for repair and replenishment. XO, would you care to command *Freedom* for the voyage home?"

Dark Star's beautiful ship was the largest piece of loot captured in the battle, and it was the only one unable to be stored in *Daring*'s holds. Amelia wasn't used to them keeping captured ships, but with *Daring*'s identity now compromised, and the war against Dark Star over, there was no reason to hide anymore. And *Freedom* needed a skeleton crew to bring her home.

"Thank you, ma'am," Liam replied, gesturing broadly at the table of charts and papers, "but I actually have a great deal of coordination to conduct with Admiral Grandview as we hunt down the remaining criminal elements. Might I recommend that Sublieutenant Brown have her first taste of command?"

Amelia glanced to her left, watching Brown's eyes widen in surprise. Beyond, Riverton's gaze moved toward the sublieutenant.

"Very well," the captain said, ignoring the grin of delight that broke out across Brown's face. Instead her eyes moved to the other side of the table. "And I think she should be assisted by Sublieutenant Templegrey. They've proven themselves to be a fine team."

Templegrey's courtly training wasn't quite good enough to hide her surprise, and she lowered her head in a slight bow. "Thank you, ma'am."

"Thank you, ma'am," Brown echoed.

"Well done, everyone," Riverton said, rising to her feet. Amelia scrambled with the others to rise. "I'm honored to serve with such an excellent and loyal crew."

Riverton's gaze swept around the table, passing Amelia just as the captain said "loyal." Amelia felt herself flush, but she remained still and silent. Dark Star was dead, she reminded herself, even if Zara still lived. And that was one secret not even Liam needed to know about.

CHAPTER 17

LIAM STARED AT THE NEW SHIP ON LORD GRAND-view's desk. Etched in crystal it stood proudly on its pedestal, all four masts extended and sails billowing in an impossibly perfect stern wind. A single line of cannon dotted the first deck, and blocky cargo holds extended beneath, along its stubby hull. As the sunlight streamed in through the office windows the ship seemed to glow, and Liam admitted to himself that it was a truly beautiful sight.

"I can't believe he actually had one made," Riverton commented at his side. "I really should just take it—it's my ship, after all."

The model of HMSS *Daring* now held pride of place in the elegant room, which was already crowded with trophies and memorabilia of Lord Grandview's prestigious career. Here on Liam's home planet of Passagia, the admiral was becoming a bit of a living legend.

"I understand Lord Grandview is to be honored by the Emperor himself," Liam said. "Perhaps even with a visit to Passagia."

"The Imperial court coming here?" Riverton gave him a look of sympathy. "I hope there's room on the planet."

"I don't intend to be here, ma'am. The admiral is welcome to the limelight."

"Good instincts, Mr. Blackwood." She glanced over her shoulder at the rising sound of voices approaching. "I think we should both disappear for a while."

Rear Admiral Grandview burst into the room, his entourage of officers pausing at the threshold.

"Ah!" he declared with a smile. "I see you've discovered the most recent addition to my crystal fleet."

"A beautiful likeness, sir," Riverton said mildly. She followed Grandview's gesture to take a seat, and Liam was only steps behind her.

"We're honestly still cataloguing the extent of the prize money," Grandview said, waving back vaguely toward his staff, "but I intend to have the first installment issued to your crew by the end of tomorrow."

"Thank you, sir. They've been patient but are eager."

"As are we all," he said with a sparkle in his eye. "The Emperor sends his personal gratitude to you, and he considers this mission complete. This strange threat to the Empire was most unsettling to His Majesty, and he is relieved to know that we have dealt with it. His only regret is not having Dark Star in person to make an example of."

"Such is the chaos of battle, sir," Liam said quickly. "We attempted capture but were forced to shoot her as she fled."

"Just knowing she's dead is good enough for His Majesty," Grandview replied. He eyed Liam thoughtfully. "I confess a personal curiosity, though. You met Dark Star in person, Liam. Who was she? What was she like?"

Liam stalled by making a show of thinking. He glanced at Riverton for guidance. The captain knew the full truth about Lady Zara Brightlake but he felt no need for this knowledge to go any farther.

"From what Subcommander Blackwood tells me," Riverton offered blandly, "she was nothing more than a common criminal."

"She was intelligent," he added, "and held her network together with an iron grip. But so do many kingpins of the underworld. She was ultimately just a common blaggard who had reached farther than most. No one of note, sir."

"Hmm. Let's hope our current sweep of that underworld discourages anyone else from attempting to imitate her."

"I agree wholeheartedly, sir."

"I hear that the Emperor is so grateful," Riverton interjected, "that he may be paying Passagia a visit to honor you, sir."

"Idle talk," Grandview said dismissively, although the renewed sparkle in his eyes suggested otherwise. "It would indeed be an honor, but also a great responsibility."

"I'm happy for your world, sir. But I may have returned to my own by then."

"And I'm sure you'll be taking your executive officer with you?"

"If he wishes to accompany me, and if His Majesty has new need of us."

Her reply hung in the office for a moment, and Liam felt a knot of tension growing in his gut. *Daring* had accomplished the mission she'd been charged with, and it was unclear if her letter of marque was still considered active. In all the excitement and work of cataloguing the latest prize, there had been little time to consider the future.

And, Liam suddenly realized, there was no small desire in his heart. *Daring* might be an old, dusty frigate with an unconventional layout, but she had a heart of oak. And Sophia Riverton might be an aloof, enigmatic noblewoman who lacked the common touch, but she was a commander he would follow to the Abyss and back. He didn't want this to end, and Grandview's silence was painful.

"That matter of Captain Silverhawk's interference," Grandview said finally, "was a damned nuisance. Had he not met that tragic, accidental end on Morassia, I fear he might have compromised this entire mission."

"I have no doubt of that, sir," Riverton replied coldly. "But my hands were tied. I had no authority to stop him."

"Quite." Grandview glanced toward the officers mingling at the door and leaned in, lowering his voice.

"And between us, incompetent fops being promoted beyond their ability might yet prove to be our defeat if ever the Sectoids turn on us, or the Theropods get organized. Did you know that once Silverhawk's estate was being sorted, it was discovered that he had huge gambling debts?"

"Really?" Riverton breathed incredulously.

"He was quite unsavory beneath all that finery, and his family is making great pains to distance themselves from his scheming. I understand the Imperial court is investigating some unusual financial pressure he was placing on other noble houses."

"Good to hear His Majesty has no time for such skullduggery," Liam added.

"If only we could convince His Majesty to clean up the Navy." Grandview shook his head. "At least promotion to the admiralty is truly based on merit, even in the Hub. But there are too many idiot captains on half pay causing trouble, and they can get in the way of real operations."

"I agree, sir."

Grandview suddenly stood, snapping his fingers toward the doorway. As Liam rose to his feet next to Riverton, he saw an officer enter with three scrolls. Grandview took them, and Liam noted the Imperial seal on them.

"The Emperor has a new mission for *Daring,* and he would like her current command team to undertake it. But he is most annoyed at the interference you've encountered, and he accepted my suggestion to ensure that this doesn't happen again." He handed one of the scrolls to Riverton. "Congratulations, Captain Riverton."

She took the rolled paper in silence.

"And such an important ship as *Daring* requires an equally senior executive officer," Grandview continued, handing the second scroll to Liam. "Congratulations, Commander Blackwood."

Liam felt the crisp parchment in his hand. He cracked the wax seal and unrolled the paper, reading the elegant script held therein. It was indeed a promotion to the rank of commander, with all the rights, privileges, and responsibilities bestowed. It was addressed to Liam personally, and it was signed by the Emperor's own hand.

"Sir," he managed to say, "I'm honored."

"Thank you, sir," Riverton echoed.

Grandview held up the third scroll and invited them both to sit once again. He handed it to Riverton.

"This is a new kind of mission," he said as Riverton unraveled the orders. "One that will require all of your skills. It is quite unlike anything our Navy has undertaken before, but I'm confident that I have the right officers seated before me."

Riverton read the mission, tilting it so that Liam could see the three short paragraphs. It was hard to grasp the depth of meaning buried beneath the simple words, and as he looked at Riverton he saw her eyes alight.

"*Daring* will need to be refitted," Grandview said, "and you'll want to consider taking on a bit more crew.

I can make some recommendations if you wish to hear them. But His Majesty will expect *Daring* to depart within three months of today."

Riverton turned her head slowly to Liam. There was a question in her gaze, but also a knowing smile. He returned the smile, and nodded.

She stood up and extended her hand to Grandview.

"Lord Grandview, my executive officer and I accept this commission."

ACKNOWLEDGMENTS

This was a fun book to write, but it was even more so because of my editor, Vedika Khanna, and her enthusiastic support. I've lost count of how many times she would make a suggestion and I'd scramble to jot it down, thinking, "Oh, that's gold!"

Books take time to write, and the time spent on this book was made much more enjoyable by the members of the Boyz Club, who were routinely shouting "Huzzah!" even before it was cool.

Finally, to my beloved Emma: you are a rock star. Thank you for everything.